THREE HOURS

THREE HOURS

Roslund and Hellström

Translated from the Swedish by Elizabeth Clark Wessel

Quercus

Quercus

New York • London

Copyright © 2018 by Anders Roslund
English translation copyright © 2019 by Elizabeth Clark Wessel
First published in the United States by Quercus in 2019
First published in Sweden in 2018 by Piratförlaget under the title *Tre timmar*

ISBN 978-1-68144-338-6

A catalogue record for this book is available from the Library of Congress

Distributed in the United States and Canada by
Hachette Book Group
1290 Avenue of the Americas
New York, NY 10104

Manufactured in the United States

2 4 6 8 10 9 7 5 3 1

www.quercus.com

In memory of
Börge Hellström,
my dear colleague and friend.

PART ONE

THE MAN LYING NEXT to me died two days ago. If I reach for him, stretch my hand as far as I can to the left, and touch his cheek, it's as cold and still as what I think death might be from the inside.

The man lying on my right has been dead even longer. Almost from the start of our journey. One of the first, the oldest, who are always weakest. And the one below me, *just* below me in the second highest layer, had been breathing slowly and deeply until just a few hours ago, then that rhythm, which reminded me of the rocking of the ocean, ceased.

So quiet.

Other than a scratching sound on the far wall, as if something sharp were being dragged across a metal surface.

I want to shout, beg.

But I can't spare the oxygen.

I still have hope – maybe I'm not the only one who hasn't given up.

SO BEAUTIFUL.

A white boat, typical of the archipelago, puffing smoke as it glided through the gentle waters of the Baltic Sea. Seagulls and terns trailing behind it, diving now and then into its foaming wake and flying off with their catch floundering in their beaks. This – a June morning with the sun warming his slightly wrinkled face – life didn't get much better than this.

Ewert Grens was sitting on the same stone he sat on every Saturday morning.

A high and flat piece that time had carved and placed just right, which fitted a tall man, who was getting just a little older, perfectly.

His own seat close to the nursing home and what used to be her window. The one she stared out of day after day for almost thirty years at a life she couldn't take part in. Their shared life. Now someone else was living in her room, and he didn't even know who.

'Superintendent Grens.'

He jumped slightly. That voice? The past.

'One moment, Superintendent, I'll come to you.'

Her name was Susann, and long ago she'd been the carer who looked after Anni. Later she became a doctor and a geriatric specialist. Now she was exiting the hospital's new entrance, approaching him with long and energetic strides, until she stopped in front of him, obscuring his view.

'The last time we talked you'd been sitting outside her window for twelve Saturday mornings in a row. I decided to let you be. But it's been . . . could it be four years? And you're still sitting here.'

'I've stood up now and then.'

'Do you remember what I told you last time? That you were hurting yourself. That you were making time for your grief, living for it, rather than with it. *What you're frightened of has already happened.*'

4

'I remember. Every word.'

'You don't seem to care.'

Ewert Grens did what he always did – glanced towards the window of a room where the lights were on. Anni would never have been awake this early. She liked to sleep late.

'I know she's not here any more.'

'What I said, Superintendent, was that I didn't want to see you here again.'

He stood up from his stone chair.

'And I know you meant well when you said that.'

And smiled.

'But I'll keep sitting here. Every Saturday at dawn for the next four years.'

He left the young woman, who was so much wiser than he ever had been or would be, headed to his car, which stood alone in the small visitors' parking lot, and turned just before opening his door.

'Because it's the only thing that keeps me sane.'

He shouted to her.

'Do you understand?'

She looked at him, one hand on the steps that led up to the main entrance of the hospital, seemingly considering what to say. Then after a slight, but unmistakable, nod, she went back inside.

Grens drove across a still sleepy Lidingö, an island close to Stockholm, and reached the bridge where he always pulled over for one last long look at those glittering waters. He'd just lowered his window and been met by a lazy gust of wind when a call crackled out of the two-way radio on his dashboard.

'Ewert?'

Wilson, his boss, who should know better than to disturb him right now.

'Ewert, hello?'

He let him shout. This was a private moment.

'Ewert, I tried to call you, but your phone is off. If you hear this, contact me. We just received an emergency call that I think you should check out.'

To the right of the radio stood a tape deck: one he'd spent weeks looking for after its predecessor had decided to play its final note. The market wasn't exactly flooded with tape decks these days; some shop assistants weren't even sure what they were. A scrap dealer just outside Strängnäs was his salvation. Two songs. That was how long he planned to sit here. That was how long he always sat here. Emergency or no.

The tears I cried for you could fill an ocean

Siw Malmkvist. A mixed tape of her repertoire. First her Swedish version of 'Everybody's Somebody's Fool', his all-time favourite, then 'Today's Teardrops', a forgotten gem.

dry your eyes, little girl, dry your eyes, and we're gonna see skies of blue

Her beautiful voice, singing in the sixties, calmed him, and the lyrics too, which the people in his life laughed at, but didn't listen to, the nonsensical rhymes he no longer heard, just leaned on.

'Ewert? Pick up . . .'

The radio again, Wilson again.

'. . . dammit!'

Siw Malmkvist was done singing. His break on the bridge, and his morning on the stone in what had once been Anni's world had all given him the strength to make it through another day, another week.

So he picked up.

'Grens here.'

'Ewert, where the hell have you—'

'Like I said, Grens here.'

Erik Wilson fell silent, Grens could hear him clearing his throat, as if trying to collect himself, to change his tone.

'Ewert, I want you to head to Söder Hospital immediately. No need to stop by the station. Just go straight to their morgue.'

Grens had left Lidingö Bridge and was now driving on the Northern Link, it was much easier to circle around the inner city than to drive through it.

'Morgue?'

'The mortuary technician found a corpse there about half an hour ago. A dead male.'

'Sounds reasonable enough. That's why they're there. Death, I mean. Was that all?'

'She has one dead man too many.'

'No riddles, Wilson.'

'One corpse too many.'

'Still not following.'

'When the mortuary technician arrived shortly after six this morning and made her first visit to cold storage she had a feeling like something was off. On her second visit this feeling continued to grow, so she counted the corpses. There were seventeen in cold storage when she went home yesterday. Five more had died in the hospital in the interim. There should have been twenty-two bodies.'

'And?'

'Twenty-three. Twenty-three bodies, no matter how many times she counts them.'

Detective Superintendent Grens pulled his car into the access lane, sped up.

'One of those bodies shouldn't be there, Ewert. There's a corpse with no paper trail, no registration. A dead man with no identification, no history. He doesn't exist.'

ONE MORE BREATH.

If I inhale slowly, keep it in as long as I can, then let it out bit by bit, it might last longer.

I estimate we've been lying like this for three, four, maybe even five days. I can't say for sure. Everything around me is blackness, the little hole where they looked in on us at the beginning has disappeared, and seconds have turned to hours have turned to days – morning, night, the darkness is the same.

It's been a long time since I've sensed any movement.

The last time was surely when the container we lie in was lifted up, for a moment it seemed to float in the air, hanging there, swinging back and forth, then it fell to the ground with a heavy thud, damped by the layers of bodies beneath me.

An enormous coffin being thrown into its final resting place, that's what it felt like.

SÖDER HOSPITAL'S ACCIDENT AND emergency had patients all along its walls, every chair occupied, and also stretchers with the injured who couldn't fit into the already packed exam rooms. It was that kind of morning. A few shootings and assaults and a pile-up on the South Link. Ewert Grens should have entered through the main entrance, but he parked by the ambulances near the unloading ramp purely out of habit. He'd used one of these operating rooms as a temporary command centre the last time there was an emergency inside the morgue – when a trafficked and desperate prostitute had rigged the whole place with explosives and taken a doctor and his medical students hostage. He hurried through the same corridors, but with a different feeling. Back then, death was an immediate threat. Today, death had arrived already, deposited itself here.

One corpse too many.

One dead man too many.

'Good morning.'

The mortuary technician, a woman in her fifties, was waiting for him outside the heavy steel door of the morgue, as promised. Her whole presence radiated a kind of grounded curiosity. Her mouth was curved in a soft smile. Grens didn't understand how a person who spent her time carving up dead people could be so full of life.

'Laura – I was the one who called this in.'

A white lab coat, a plastic apron like an extra layer of skin, a mask dangling around her neck, and, after pulling off a pair of plastic gloves, a hand stretched out in greeting.

'Don't worry, I'm still fairly clean, today's first post-mortem will have to wait.'

Grens took her hand, and then she waved for him to follow her into a narrow passageway, passing the office and the archive, and then into the main mortuary area.

'Just a regular morning. A cup of coffee – or a couple of cups if I'm being honest – while I went through the paperwork, then I started to prepare my new patients for transfer to their storage compartments. Patients, I call them that. Corpse or body, it just doesn't sound right.'

She opened the door to the much larger space behind the mortuary hall. Cold storage. Glaring overhead lights and a temperature of eight degrees according to the thermometer above the work counters. The storage racks she was referring to were stainless steel, and each one had twelve compartments, divided into three rows, and wheels that made it easy to roll them over to the white-tiled walls.

'Three older men, one young woman, and one six-year-old child. Those were my new patients, according to the referrals. I lifted them over one at a time. There's a machine we use, sort of a small crane, so we don't strain our backs.'

An odd scent.

It had become more noticeable since leaving the mortuary area.

Meat. That's what it smelled like.

'A completely normal morning – until then. When I started moving them over, I realised . . . I had too many. Patients, that is.'

The steel rack closest to them had eight occupied compartments and four empty. Motionless bodies wrapped in white sheets, each with a small red name tag attached to the middle.

'I counted them three times. But no matter what, when I compared my notes to the computer, they didn't match up. There was always one too many. So I pulled them all out like this, and checked their name tags, then their faces, then – when it became necessary – their identifying characteristics.'

She smiled again, and a smile in that environment, under those circumstances, should have seemed morbid or even insane. But not her smile. Ewert Grens was standing next to a person who tried to convey calm, who realised a guest here rarely felt comfortable; and she succeeded. Her smile was warm and sincere and made him relax. He was used to visiting morgues – a detective in a big city has to be – and usually he masked his discomfort by touching things, like grabbing hold of a foot, while saying something funny or sarcastic. There was no need today. She pulled out a drawer from the steel chamber, the one at the bottom far right, which held a white bundle the size of a man, and he followed her lead by staying calm.

'This is where we keep the patients who have yet to be autopsied. I was preparing to remove their organs, so the pathologists could find cause of death.

'Here. This is the patient who isn't my patient. This is the body that didn't add up.'

She pulled the white sheet aside. And there he lay. Dark skin with a change in the pigmentation on the throat that was visible despite the lack of movement or life. Short hair and fairly skinny, around thirty. Or so Grens guessed. Death plays tricks with age.

'Naked, just like the others. Wrapped in a white sheet, just like the others. Even a red name tag with something unreadable on it has been attached. But there's no trace of him in our records. No registration. And he wasn't on this rack last night. I didn't do a count before I left, but I'm sure of it. This is my job. I care about these patients too much. I treat these patients with the same care as the nurses and doctors upstairs treat the living.'

The mortuary technician, Laura, gently laid her hand on Ewert Grens's arm. Perhaps to emphasise how important this was to her. Perhaps worrying about not understanding what she was actually seeing. Or maybe this too was how she made her visitors feel calm. Whatever the reason, Grens let her keep it there, despite the fact that he usually avoided such contact.

Just the two of them, in a room that belonged to the dead. And it almost felt good.

'Has this ever happened before?'

'What do you mean?'

'An unidentified body?'

'Never.'

He leaned over the unseeing face, carefully pulled back the sheet, exposing a naked body.

Undamaged. On the surface.

An apparently healthy person with no external signs of violence.

Ewert Grens's eyes scanned a room that felt as cold as it looked.

Who are you?

Why did you die?

And how the hell did you end up here?

I CALLED HER NAME.

Alyson. *Alyson.*

I know we're not allowed to talk. They told us that. But over the last day the sound of breathing has stopped, even the metallic scrape has fallen silent, and as stink turned to the stench of decay, I just had to.

Alyson.

She didn't answer.

So I shouted again, for anyone at all, and my voice drowned in that tight space. No reply.

Maybe they don't dare.

Or maybe I'm alone now, though we were once so many. Maybe I'm the last one alive.

WHAT A STRANGE MORNING.

It had started out so fine, on his rock outside Anni's old window, and ended with him following an unknown dead man from one morgue to another. This morning's emergency call was now an official investigation, which would continue at Forensic Medicine in Solna.

An hour later, Ewert Grens was standing near a bright lamp, which shone directly onto a gleaming metal gurney and the body of a still nameless young man.

'Widespread livor mortis. Full onset of rigor mortis. But the pupillary constrictor clearly reacts to light. And here, Ewert . . .'

Ludvig Errfors – the coroner who was one of the few colleagues Grens had come to rely on over the years – thrust a needle into the eye, through the pupil, filled the syringe and emptied the contents into a test tube.

'. . . when I measure the potassium content of the vitreous humour, I can see it's gone up. I'd say . . . just over a day. Twenty-five, maybe thirty hours. That's when he filled his lungs for the last time.'

Grens felt calmness be replaced by restlessness and agitation.

'*When* he died doesn't tell me shit about who he is.'

'The whites of both his eyes and the inside of his eyelids reveal small haemorrhages.'

'And?'

'He suffocated, Ewert.'

'*How* he died still doesn't tell me shit about who he is.'

Then the agitation and restlessness turned to the anger that always lay in wait, and he left the gurney and the bright light and began pacing back and forth across a room that smelled even more like meat than the last one. He slammed his fist on a trolley cart that was as gleaming as everything else, and a metallic sound echoed round and round.

'Dammit, Errfors – give me something that can help me identify him! Where is he from? Who is he?'

The medical examiner was still bent over the lifeless face, as unconcerned as he had been before, neither surprised nor afraid. They'd examined a couple of hundred bodies together and he knew that the detective's fear of his own death turned into aggression in here: a not uncommon reaction, two sides of the same emotion.

'Africa.'

'Africa is quite big.'

'Far west, Ewert, and far north. But not on the coast of the Atlantic or the Mediterranean.'

The agitated detective started to raise his hand for a second blow – this time his target was a stack of plastic aprons – but froze as Errfors prised open the dead man's mouth and pointed towards a row of white teeth in the upper jaw.

'Do you see? Those spots on the enamel? Fluorosis. He grew up in an area where the groundwater contained extremely high levels of fluoride.'

Grens got closer. White dots on white teeth. Large ones. Everywhere.

'Fluoride which in principle is good for teeth, builds up – eventually damages the enamel.'

'High levels of fluoride can be found everywhere.'

'Not *that* high. And if we look at the rest then we have . . .'

The medical examiner tapped each tooth lightly with a metal instrument.

'. . . strong, healthy teeth. Until you get here.'

Two canines. Which were far from white.

'We usually say that they've been "burned to the ground". So badly decayed that they're beyond saving. If he'd gone to a dentist, they would have had to pull them out. But he hasn't been to a dentist. Ever.'

He pushed the jaws back together again, which also seemed to require all his might.

'I've seen it in several autopsies of people who grew up in Africa. Amazing teeth despite non-existent dental care. And at the same time, serious damage to a few of them. That, in combination with the fluorosis – the white spots on the enamel – and, of course, his appearance, point to West Africa, or perhaps Central Africa.'

Ewert Grens stood beside the medical examiner longer than might have been justified while the body was slowly dismantled. There wasn't much more information to be found here now. He had probable cause – suffocation. Probable time – twenty-five hours ago. And probable origin – West Africa. But it was difficult to leave the dead man's face. In other investigations he'd sometimes felt the deceased staring back at him. But that wasn't the case now. No, now what he felt was a kind of responsibility to the young man who'd been hidden in a morgue under a false name. And while he lingered on that face, which couldn't answer the question of who it belonged to or how it came to be here, Grens realised something. There's a price to be paid for taking a person's life, but there isn't much risk in taking their death. It shouldn't be like that. It was his responsibility to give this young man his death back.

The Institute of Forensic Medicine lay only a few kilometres from the Northern Cemetery, and on his way back to the inner city and the police station, Grens made a stop at the place he used to hate with all his heart.

Frightened of what had already happened.

This was where he wouldn't dare to go. But did so now. To the grave that was one of thirty thousand, located in something called Block 19B, and bearing the number 603. A simple white cross and a brass plate with her name engraved on it. Anni Grens. He cleared away the leaves, watered the rosebush and the heather and the two plants that bloomed in dense bunches and that were called Life-Everlasting in Swedish. He sat on a park bench staring at the grass, his thoughts on that face on the cold mortuary table. Was someone missing that young man the way Grens missed his wife? And did that young man have someone to miss him as Anni would have missed her husband?

The unexpectedly heavy traffic of the early morning had slackened, and it took just a few minutes to drive from the cemetery to Kungsholmen, where Grens found a parking spot just outside the Kronoberg police station.

His first stop in the investigative department corridor was at the vending machine and button 38 – coffee, black, two cups. He downed one of them immediately, refilled it, and went on to his next destination, Mariana Hermansson's doorway.

'Good morning.'

He rarely stepped inside. That's just how it was. The much younger woman – who he was proud to have hired, who he sometimes considered the daughter he'd never had, though she didn't know it – had built her own barrier of integrity, and it stood at her door.

'There are no matches for his description on the Swedish Wanted List, Ewert. I also checked with Copenhagen, Helsinki and Oslo. No success.'

He'd called them both on his way from the hospital to the medical examiner – Mariana was already at work, a stack of twenty cases or more in front of her, and Sven had just left the breakfast table and his wife Anita and son Jonas.

It was to his doorway that Grens headed next.

'Sven?'

The only colleagues he could stand. The only colleagues who could stand him.

'I dropped by C-House and Interpol on my way here, Ewert, like you asked me to.'

'And?'

'Nothing. No dental or fingerprints. He's not wanted by any police authorities in the world.'

Next, three doors down to his own office, where he set both mugs on the rickety coffee table next to a corduroy sofa that had once been dark brown and striped. A tape deck stood on the shelf between the binders of completed investigations and the books about police ethics, which kept on arriving even though he never read them. He had just put on Siw Malmkvist's 'Tweedle Dee' and sat down on the sofa, which was much too soft for his heavy body, when a face appeared at his door. One as wrinkled as Grens's own. Nils Krantz, the forensic technician, who'd worked here as long as Grens.

'Do you have a minute, Ewert?'

'Not yet.'

'Two minutes and . . .?'

'Two minutes and forty-five seconds.'

Krantz left the doorway and sat down in the visitor's chair on the other side of the coffee table. Waiting. The amount of time it would take for Siw Malmkvist to finish her song. He'd argued with the detective in the past about how ludicrous it was to delay urgent police business until an old song faded out, but he'd learned to let it be. It saved time in the long run.

Tweedle-deedeli-dee.

Ewert Grens stretched out on the sofa, then turned to his visitor.

'Her very first recording. Ever. Did you know that?'

'I want you to sit up, Ewert. It's easier to read.'

The forensic technician had entered the room with a piece of paper in his hand.

Now he put it on the coffee table, pushed it over to Grens.

'I made my first inspection of the body at Forensic Medicine. Trying to speed things up. You'll get the DNA test at earliest tonight, more likely tomorrow. But I saw something. Something that didn't add up.'

Krantz pulled his reading glasses from his chest pocket and handed them to Grens.

'There. Fifth line. I found obvious, even extensive traces of the same substance in several places. In the dead man's hair. On the skin of his face. On his hands. His back and his shins. That is to say, surfaces that would not have been covered by the clothes he was wearing at time of death, before someone undressed him and wrapped him up.'

The forensic technician's index finger was a little crooked, but it was possible to follow all the way to a word underlined in black marker.

Ammonium phosphate.

Grens shrugged.

'What does that mean?'

'Powder extinguisher.'

'Powder . . . extinguisher?'

'Ammonium phosphate is the most effective ingredient – and one of the most common – in extinguishers. It puts out fires by cooling them.'

'Now I'm even more lost. Fires? Burned bodies usually look a lot worse than that.'

The forensic technician held out his hand, waited until Grens took off the reading glasses and handed them back.

'That's what doesn't make sense – his body doesn't show the slightest signs of being in the vicinity of a fire.'

Then Krantz hurried off to the next investigation, like always, like they all were, and Ewert Grens lay back on his corduroy sofa and listened to music from another era. Listened and thought. About morgues – and how they'd been a part of his life since his very first murder case as a newly commissioned police officer. But still he'd never investigated a body that shouldn't be there.

A body that made its way there apparently on its own.

Who had no name or story.

Who seemed to be nobody at all.

ALYSON.

I remember that she whispered.

We hadn't gone very far, most of us were still alive, her cautious voice found its way through the darkness between breaths, searching for me, and I whispered back.

Alyson.

I received no reply.

I still haven't.

'EWERT GRENS?'

'Who's this?'

'Is this *Detective Superintendent* Ewert Grens?'

'Depends on who's calling.'

Grens had been lying down when he answered. A quarter to five. He looked out the window at the dawn light.

'What's this about? Who is this?'

'Laura. I was the one who . . .'

'I know who Laura is.'

He sat up in the shapeless corduroy sofa. He'd slept over, something his young colleagues liked to call the cliché. They didn't have a fucking clue. Ewert Grens could *never* be accused of being a cliché for sleeping in his office when an investigation forced him to stay late – he'd invented that move! It was everyone else who'd plagiarised it, they were the clichés. An original can never be a cliché.

'I know who you are. I remember you smiled.'

'What?'

'You . . . yes, you smiled. A nice smile, too. The kind that made me forget I was surrounded by bodies about to be dissected.'

'In that case would you consider coming here right now? Despite the early hour.'

'Here?'

'To the morgue. It's happened again. I have one dead patient too many.'

Driving through Stockholm as church bells rang out five o'clock could be an unbelievably beautiful experience. And it was that kind of morning. Grens enjoyed the view from Väster Bridge, didn't need to slow down once on Hornsgatan or Ringvägen, and even Söder Hospital – which frankly was no great work of art or architecture –

seemed inviting with the morning sun turning its upper floors gold. He parked next to the ambulances near the A&E entrance like last time, hurried through the same tired corridors, though now no injured patients lined the walls. It had been a quiet night.

Laura stood waiting for him outside the heavy door to the morgue. The same warm smile made him straighten up, put a spring in his step. He knew now that her smile wasn't calculated, or pasted on.

'You started early today.'

'I couldn't sleep. And at first I thought it was because I knew I had a big day ahead of me, that I'd need to prep and open a couple more patients than usual. There were delays yesterday – the extra body and your visit and all the questions from the hospital management.'

She nodded at him, asked him to follow her, and they walked through the narrow passage that led to the mortuary and the cold storage.

'But that *wasn't* why. It was . . . well, a feeling.'

'A feeling?'

'Yes, I don't really know. I can't really explain it, but somehow I just knew it was going to happen again.'

Laura was no longer smiling.

'Or rather, Superintendent, it had *already* happened again.'

She continued to the same steel rack the young man had been hiding inside, places for twelve bodies in twelve equal-sized drawers.

'I counted – those who lie in here, and those in the other rack. Even though I almost didn't need to.'

She pulled out one of the metal drawers at the far left, in the middle row.

'I just knew there would be an extra body.'

Wrapped in a sheet, just like the young man, and just like the others.

A red name tag fastened near the middle of the body, scribbled on as indecipherably as yesterday morning.

'And here is how she looks.'

Still eight degrees.

The thermometer was just hanging there and Grens couldn't stop himself from reading it.

'She hasn't been referred here either. Not by me or any of my colleagues at the hospital. But she's lying here as if . . . as if someone wanted her properly cared for – do you know what I mean? She also has no name or background. And she's painfully young. Even though death has taken her colour, her presence – it's still possible to see how beautiful she was.'

Ewert Grens looked at the naked body, exposed as the mortuary technician loosened and pulled down the sheet. They belonged together. The young woman in front of him now and the young man in front of him yesterday. Skin colour, hair colour, facial shape. Both completely undamaged on the outside. Both deprived of their lives as well as their death.

Someone got rid of you, too.

Somebody has dragged or carried you through the steel door, past the office and archive room and post-mortem room to put you here in cold storage.

Somebody took a sheet from that pile over there, wrapped you up, grabbed a tag from the plastic box on the wall and attached it to you without writing down your name.

Somebody hid you here where you belong, with a strange kind of thoughtfulness, made the effort to see you treated as you should be – and at the same time threw you away like you were nothing more than a piece of trash, hoping you'd disappear for ever.

'Laura – I want you to write down the names of anyone who might have a key here.'

'You got that yesterday.'

'Yes. And I want a new one today that's even longer. And then my two closest colleagues and I will interview everyone on that list. Even if we've already done so. And after you've given me that list I want to sit down with you in your office, and I want you to tell me again what your day is like, and how you make an incision from ear to ear and how you uncover the ribs, and how you drink your coffee, and what happens when it's delivered here, and how often you take a call and how sound moves in different rooms. Every detail that you think might be unnecessary, or mundane, or uninteresting. Because in twenty years of this work you have never seen anything like this, and in forty years of investigating murders I've never seen anything like this either, so we're going to need to ask questions and think in way we've never done before. If we're going to help a young man and a young woman get their deaths back.'

Laura covered the lifeless body and pushed it back into the rectangular steel compartment where it would be stored until – just like the body yesterday – it formally became part of an investigation and therefore had to be moved, examined, and treated as evidence.

Grens remained standing where he was for the time being, close, trying to catch the mortuary technician's eyes.

Waiting it out.

And when she turned around, he saw her smile was gone – the unexplainable had become so much larger.

I DON'T WANT TO.

But taking in each breath slowly, releasing it a little bit at a time is no longer enough.

The air has run out. The oxygen is gone.

I didn't know I'd be so afraid. That the closer I got to it, the more I'd feel that way. It no longer helps to reach out my left hand towards the cheek with no life in it, or my right hand to the man who died at the beginning, squeeze his stiff fingers.

I don't want to die.

I don't want to know if death is just as cold and still from inside.

IT WAS A BIT chilly on his feet.

Ewert Grens sat on the balcony of his penthouse apartment looking out over Sveavägen. Midnight, but still not completely dark, early summer in the far north made the hours kinder. He'd come out here barefoot with a glass of water, looking for some fresh air, and stayed, sank down into a wooden folding chair.

He spent more of his nights at home, no longer afraid that lying down in bed meant falling into a black hole. But tonight it was impossible to sleep. Just like the mortuary technician Laura, he had a feeling he couldn't quite explain. Her feeling had led her to a dead body. His own feeling was about entrances. Exits. How could somebody get a corpse into the morgue without anyone noticing? And how the hell did they do it again?

He, Sven and Mariana had watched all of the hospital's surveillance footage. The closest camera was placed in the corridor that led to the steel door. Not a single sequence, not even one frame of film in any of the videos, showed a person transporting an unidentified corpse. They divided up Laura's new list of key holders – medical examiners, orderlies, cleaners, coffee machine technicians, handymen, security guards – and interviewed each one. No one had any obvious motive. They all had an alibi.

He stretched out over the balcony railing. A younger couple was walking together far below, their arms intertwined in that special way of people in love.

Back in his day. Back in Anni's day.

Their day.

Late in the afternoon – following the lack of success with the surveillance cameras and equally futile interrogations – Errfor's postmortem was delivered by hand.

```
The patient exhibits multiple subcutaneous haematomas
on the knuckles, elbows and knees, while the whites
of the eyes and inside of the eyelids present small
petechial bleeding.
```

The woman with no name or history had struggled – beating against something or possibly being beaten by someone – just like the nameless man.

```
Estimated time of death, taking into consideration body
temperature and rigor mortis, approximately thirty-
six hours before post-mortem.
```

And then suffocated, just like the man.

```
Examination of the oral cavity revealed a large amount
of coagulated blood, and a plum-sized fragment near
the front part of the tongue. The edges of the tongue
show irregularities, such as dental imprints. Together
these findings suggest the patient died by asphyxiation
and with increasing panic struggled for air.
```

Ewert Grens took a deep breath of the air he took for granted. Panic.

Her anxiety had driven her to bite off part of her own tongue. Her last moments had revolved around only one thing – taking one more breath.

He unconsciously repeated that deep breath, held the city air for a long time inside his lungs, as if trying in some small way to comprehend what she went through. While he was still holding his breath, a long row of cyclists whizzed by down on the street below, then two shiny and expensive black cars drove by way too fast, in what seemed to be a pissing contest between stupid men, and then the street was just empty for a moment – few scenes are as forlorn as a big city that's fallen suddenly silent.

Nils Krantz's report was also almost a copy of yesterday's. The forensic technician had sent both blood and saliva to the National Forensic Laboratory for DNA analysis. He'd analysed dental impressions and fingerprints and found no matches, not in the Swedish nor international police registries. And – these last lines are what sent Ewert Grens onto the balcony barefoot – he once again found extensive traces of ammonium phosphate in the dead woman's hair and on her skin. The main ingredient in the flame retardant used to fight fires by cooling them down.

Even though she too was never in the vicinity of a fire.

You died less than a day before him.

You died for the same reason, lack of oxygen.

You died in the same place, with the same panic.

Ewert Grens couldn't stand still any more. He started pacing in a tight circle on the balcony, round and round. Anxiety. Restlessness. But also something else was making itself felt, intruding, something about an entrance, an exit. Something about how no unaccounted corpse was seen being pushed down the hall. After that first call and that first body, he'd recognised something. Without knowing quite what.

Maybe he knew now.

In that case this knowledge was many years old, and it had once led him to a dead woman.

He needed to call someone who'd lost her smile.

'Did I wake you?'

The mortuary technician had been asleep, he could hear it clearly in her voice when she answered.

'You're allowed. Since I called you before five this morning.'

'Are you far from work right now?'

'Not particularly. At this time of day I could drive there in fifteen minutes.'

'Then please do. I need you to look around one more time.'

Laura didn't ask why, just said *see you there* in a voice that was already a little more awake, and then hung up.

A person like him. He liked that a lot.

The second phone call went to the dog unit, the third and fourth to Sven and Mariana. Both were used to him calling at all hours, requesting their presence somewhere, often at the very moment after they'd gone to bed.

In a few minutes he too was on his way to Söder Hospital. But he stopped first at the police station, and the archive – where old cases were stacked floor to ceiling. It was near the back of the basement, as dark and deserted as the rest of the station. He needed a map. One that once revealed to him another world, during another investigation.

He'd had it backwards.

He'd assumed this transport had gone through one of the hospital's entrances, had continued down those endless halls and through the heavy steel door that was the border to the morgue.

But the bodies had come from somewhere else.

Somewhere inside.

SÖDER HOSPITAL'S MORGUE WAS the largest and best run facility of its type that Grens had ever visited. In his four decades as a police officer, investigations had led him to cold storage facilities all over Sweden: most were reminiscent of wardrobes, with space for just a few tightly packed bodies, others were overcrowded, with miserable hygiene, sites of rampant putrefaction. But here, with Sven and Mariana on one side and Laura on the other, he surveyed metre after metre of clinically clean floors, walls and ceilings. At one end there was something that resembled an industrial kitchen, decked out in stainless steel and white tiles, and at the other end there stood a few bleak rooms bathed in harsh fluorescent light. But not in the first section with its twenty-four stainless steel stations for what Laura called her patients, nor in the other section with its thirty-six square compartments for the lifeless to rest in, nor in the almost circular area with its brown wooden boxes where organs were stored, was he able to find what he was looking for.

Nor in the PM room where the actual work was performed.

Not in the visitors' room where the dead met their relatives for the last time.

Not in the cleaning cupboard, nor the archive room, nor the break room, nor the locker room, nor office.

But finally he found it in that tight and dim passage that connected the cold storage to the PM room. It was exactly what he was looking for, and it changed everything. The passage was an area you would usually pass right by, a wedged-in washroom with a sink, where the body was cleaned beforehand and the larger tools were cleaned afterwards, and a dishwasher for the blades and smaller tools. All the way in, behind the autoclave, which looked just like the giant pressure cooker and steriliser it actually was, there stood something that resembled a door. It was exactly the same colour as the rest of the walls. And it wasn't until you got very close to it that its edges became clear, not until Grens knocked on it that the dull sound of heavy iron echoed around him.

'What's this?'

Grens turned to Laura, who was at the sink trying to turn off a dripping tap.

'A bomb shelter.'

'A bomb shelter? In a morgue? In the case the dead need a place to hide in an air raid?'

The mortuary technician looked at the door, looked at Grens.

And shrugged.

'I've always assumed it was the door to a bomb shelter. That's what they usually look like. But I've never been inside. I've never, in all these years, even seen it open.'

Ewert Grens could feel his cheeks and neck turning red. That's usually what happened when his heart started to race.

When an investigation took a turn and, suddenly, he knew exactly where it was headed.

THE COARSE IRON DOOR was fitted with two separate locks. Despite a long search the security guards on night duty only found the keys for one – the top lock. But instead of getting angry, shouting or banging on things, Ewert Grens surprised everyone with a calm, satisfied smile.

'Good.'

'Good, Ewert?'

Sven Sundkvist had worked long enough with this large and erratic detective to know all his ways of dealing with disappointment.

Calm contentment was not one of them.

'Don't you remember, Sven? That's how this kind of door works. Only the national defence and rescue service have access to the second key. This confirms it *is* such a door. So soon we'll solve our first mystery – how these bodies got here in the first place.'

At the same time, Mariana Hermansson had made a quick decision. All of the city's locksmiths were already occupied or too far away, so she had woken up one of the force's bomb technicians, someone who usually worked on keeping explosives *from* detonating. But now they'd do the reverse – set off the perfect explosion.

And it was a beauty. If you can say that about an explosion. The doorframe came loose from the wall as if it were cardboard sliced by a box cutter, without dust or splinters, and fell backwards, outwards, away.

In its place stood a square hole.

They all stared into a darkness.

And smelled a scent like damp clothes and burnt leaves.

A TUNNEL.

That's what they stepped into.

The path someone had most likely taken in order to dump dead bodies.

This was how Stockholm used to be built. Public buildings were connected to each other through similar doors. Entrances, exits to the capital's system of tunnels. Kilometre after kilometre of concrete pipes big enough for people to move through, some by walking, some by crawling. Various kinds of tunnels, and all of them interlinked. The sewers were joined to the military system, which in turn was linked to the electrical and telecommunication and district heating systems. Each respective owner had a map of their part, but only the few outsiders who lived in these tunnels themselves – criminals, the mentally weak, or those on the run – had any knowledge of how they were connected. A Stockholm as large as the one above it. A single system, for example the sewers – one of the maps Grens picked up from the police archives – might contain up to a hundred miles of tunnels.

'*Someone* hired a guide, one of those self-appointed damn guides who reign supreme down here. *Someone* went down into one of the hundreds of entrances to the system. *Someone* climbed into a manhole or walked into a subway tunnel or stepped through a door in a public building or . . .'

Ewert Grens turned to Mariana.

'. . . by the way, where are those dogs? What happened to them?'

'Three minutes. Then they're here.'

Mariana Hermansson turned to the mortuary technician who had been silent thus far. A person who was used to spending most of her time alone with the dead. But who wasn't nearly as accustomed to watching the walls of her workplace being blown open.

'Laura, that's your name, right?'

The mortuary technician nodded and showed at least a hint of that warm, sincere smile.

'Yes. Laura.'

'I see what you're thinking. But it's not going to be a problem. These are specially trained dogs. With specially trained handlers. They will *not* be bothered by the dead.'

'The patients.'

'Excuse me?'

'That's what I call them. And I treat them that way too.'

Mariana examined the woman who she was coming to admire on a professional level, someone able to do the worst kind of work.

'Laura, the dogs won't interfere with your patients. I promise you. They're right outside, in the hospital corridor, sniffing the sheets the young man and young woman were wrapped in, and some clippings of their hair, and some of the ammonium phosphate found on their skin.'

And Mariana was right.

That powerful and eager German shepherd, all black and almost shining, and the Belgian shepherd, brownish with grey spots, passed through the mortuary and the organ storage area without even glancing around. They were on the scent already, their long lead lines rolled up. Completely focused on their handlers' next orders.

And soon they were at the opening of the wall, the entrance to the two and a half metre wide tunnel, identifying the odours with a whine and a wag of their tails.

Ewert Grens had been right.

The person who brought these bodies here came through that door.

WARM, DAMP.

Eighteen degrees Celsius year round.

Far below the streets of Stockholm. Where people walked by out-door cafés and beggars, and cars and buses jostled and fumed at red lights.

Ewert Grens was doing his best to ignore that he was sixty-four and not exactly in the best shape any more. He could still stand as they made their way through the first two tunnels of the drainage system. His eyes didn't smart as much from the contrast of the compact darkness and the roving shine of the flashlights. And the monotone barking of the dogs reminded him that no matter how difficult it was to hunch more and more with each tunnel, no matter how terrible the smell, no matter how creepy the sound of blind rats fleeing in the concrete pipe around them, they had to keep going, keep going.

'How you doing, Superintendent?'

One of the handlers had noticed his ever more ragged breathing, maybe even caught on to the attack of coughing he'd done his best to hide.

'Worry about yourself.'

'Maybe we should slow down a bit. Even though the dogs are pulling hard.'

'If we're changing pace we should go faster – I wanna get to the bastards who are throwing away corpses.'

The dogs' lead lines were stretched to their full length, their sensitive noses glued to the trail, while the tunnels gradually got tighter and narrower. When they signalled for the first time that the trail had completely changed direction, that they would have to enter an adjoining tunnel, there was a moment of deliberation. The keys you needed to move between these tunnel systems were in the hands of only a few individuals – people who for whatever reason had chosen to live their lives underground, found a connection to the underworld to avoid living in the society above.

And Grens was sure they were the ones who'd been hired to assist in dumping those bodies. They could crawl out of their holes into whatever building they wanted, whenever they wanted to.

Which is why he'd also ordered the bomb technician to accompany this group on their search.

So he could blow open doors that linked the sewer system to the military system as cleverly as he had in the morgue – to turn tunnel walls into entrances.

The connecting tunnel had lower ceilings and stank more than most. But, once they got through, the dogs barked just as eagerly and energetically and pulled just as hard on their harnesses, urging everyone forward. Grens's clothes were too heavy, and sweat poured from his hairline down, while his hip and knee ached in a way that would usually make him stop. Each breath felt like small knives in his chest, as if air was not enough.

But no, I won't give up.

The scent, you bastard.

The dogs are on it, I'm on it.

This is where you carried the dead. And we're getting closer.

Now and then as they passed by tunnel walls with small alcoves, images of a previous visit flashed before his eyes – an investigation several years ago that led him to a cavity that formed a room, a home, where a fourteen-year-old girl lived under the street. Four shipping pallets stacked on top of each other, which she'd used as a table, covering it with a red and white tablecloth, which she'd placed just so, straight as tablecloths are supposed to be when you're trying to make it nice. Back then Grens and Sven had found people living in virtually every single tunnel. It wasn't like that now. The entrances to this system were more heavily guarded these days. The authorities had tried to shut down and retake control of a world no one else really cared about.

Grens turned around, trying to catch Sven's eyes – Sven who walked much more effortlessly, didn't sweat, his breathing barely audible.

And with just one look passed between them, not a word – they both remembered.

The holes that had become homes, the smells that got so deep into the fabric of your clothes that they could never be washed out, the darkness that had been so different back when it protected rather than intimidated. Images neither of them were able to let go of. And it made things easier that the policemen familiar with this world were the same ones moving through it now in search of a murderer.

At the command of the barking dogs, they blew doors at two more connecting tunnels. The first led to the heating system, the second back to the sewers. After an hour they reached the centre of the city, passing beneath St Clara church according to the utilities map Grens sometimes held up in front of his flashlight. Half an hour later they chose, with the help of the dogs, a passageway leading north-east at the big intersection under Östermalmstorg. Another half hour after that they crossed under Valhallavägen, under asphalt and cars, headed in the direction of Gärdet.

'Superintendent?'

The handler who belonged to the shiny, black German shepherd – who had worried earlier whether or not Grens could manage the low ceilings – had stopped temporarily and indicated with the lead line that his dog should too.

'Yes?'

'This could take a while. The dogs have had a strong scent the whole time.'

'And?'

'Maybe you'd like to take a break, Superintendent.'

'And maybe you'd like to mind your own business.'

'Superintendent . . .'

'Drop the titles.'

'Your . . . your breathing is heavy and ragged. It doesn't sound good at all.'

'First of all, it's no concern of yours how I breathe. That's my problem. And secondly, if we continue in the same direction, if this tunnel lasts, we don't have far to go. According to my map, we're headed to Värta Harbour. We'll hit the sea.'

Grens couldn't be entirely sure of it – it was difficult to tell when your whole body shook and ached and roared from inside – but it felt like – despite his protests, they moved a little slower after that. And when, in that eternal darkness, he stumbled on a pipe, and Mariana and Sven competed to help him up, while telling him he had to rest *now*, it was as if that were a signal to move even more slowly.

Then the dog at the front just stopped. And the next dog stopped.

And both barked more loudly than before, chewing and pulling at their harnesses.

'Here.'

The handler put his hand on a round metal bar screwed into the tunnel wall, and leaned against it. Below it was a similar one, and below that the same, a regularly spaced column at thirty centimetre intervals down to the floor of the tunnel.

'The dogs don't make mistakes, Superintendent. This is the entrance we're looking for.'

The round metal rods also continued upwards. Step by step something to hold onto, to climb up. Grens knew what awaited them up there. A regular manhole, a cast-iron cap that looked like a round stain in the middle of the asphalt of a regular street.

He didn't think further than that.

Until a hand grabbed his shoulder and tried to push him aside.

'I'm going first. You wait here.'

Mariana had a firm grip on his jacket.

'You hear that, Ewert? *I'm* climbing up. *I'm* opening that cover and figuring out where we are. And *if* we're correct, if I judge that we're in the right place, and we all need to go up, only then will you be climbing.'

'You don't give me orders, Mariana, I give you orders.'

She didn't let go, instead her grip on his jacket was getting firmer.

'Ewert – I'll say what you usually say: mind your own damn business. Have you seen how you look? Have you heard how you sound? You stay here. And you come up only if I signal to you.'

Then she left. Towards those metal rods, onto those metal rods, up one step at a time.

And if she'd turned around, she would have seen her boss smiling just a little proudly.

The first thing she noticed was the air. With every metre it became less damp and easier to breathe. Gradually, the smells she'd almost got used to changed too, less mould and faeces and more car exhaust. The space she was slowly climbing up inside was circular and so narrow that she scraped her elbows and knees against the wall as she moved from one metal step to another.

She counted. Forty-five of them. Since the distance between the rods was constant she must have climbed fourteen, maybe fifteen metres. She stopped short and looked up. A weak strip of light in the otherwise complete darkness. So she was headed upwards to a street – only streetlights in the middle of the night shine like that.

With just a few steps left she hit her head on something. A plastic bag. It dangled in the air in front of her, tied to a string. She felt it, squeezed it, and understood what it was once she managed to fish out her flashlight with small, tightly circumscribed movements. Rat poison. Attached to a grille mounted just below the manhole. She pushed it aside and searched the cold iron rails for the huge padlock that should be sitting there.

It had been removed.

An entryway that could be used by anyone.

They *were* in the right place.

She lowered the grille against the wall and made sure it was hanging securely on its hinges, climbed two more steps up, and listened with the top of her head pressed lightly against the cap.

A car was approaching. It passed over her, disappeared.

She breathed in, out.

The cast-iron cover was heavy, she knew it would be, but hadn't realised exactly *how* heavy. She was able to maintain her balance by pushing her back against the wall. She raised her arms above her head, jammed her feet firmly against the metal steps, and with all the might she could muster, still she only succeeded in moving the lid just a few centimetres to the side.

She pushed again.

Again.

Again.

Widened the opening a little more each time.

And when the cap only covered about half of the hole, she squeezed her head, her upper body, her lower body, out into fresh air and another kind of darkness.

EWERT GRENS LAY STRETCHED out on the pavement, just a couple of steps from the intersection of Tegeluddsvägen and Öregrundsgatan. Mariana – after he followed her up from one world into another – had taken his hand, pulled him over the edge of the manhole, and refused to let go. His breathing had been jerky and irregular, his face fluctuating between flaming red and fugitive white, and he couldn't speak. Slowly, as Sven and the bomb technician and the two handlers – who brought their dogs up using ropes – joined them, Grens regained some of his colour and alertness.

'Let's go on.'

He said this as he stood up, took a few steps, stumbled, almost fell, but recovered the balance.

'Superintend— or Grens . . . Grens, you might want to rest a couple of minutes and . . .'

'Tell your dogs to seek. Until we find where those bodies came from.'

'Are you sure . . .'

'Now.'

The two dogs pulled on their lead lines like before.

Towards the chain-link fence along Tegeluddsvägen and through a large, cut-out hole they found in the middle of it.

Into an industrial area, near an empty loading dock.

Across three parallel railroad tracks that formed the symbolic border to Värta Harbour.

'Two hundred and twenty million olfactory receptors.'

'What?'

Ewert Grens looked at the handler, who looked about as excited and eager as Grens probably did.

They were close, and they both knew it.

'In a dog's nose, Superintendent. Human beings have only five million. So it doesn't matter to the dogs that there's so much more to smell up here than inside the tunnel. They won't drop the scent until we're there.'

A port area that was busy during the day – the gateway to Finland, Estonia, Poland – and on a summer night was dead quiet. They were approaching the older dock, and the ships anchored there waiting for the morning's passengers or for the stacks of orange and white and blue crates that contained goods headed for the next harbour.

'Ewert? Where the hell . . .'

Sven didn't swear often. And never because he was upset.

'. . . are we headed?'

Only if he was worried in a way that couldn't be pushed aside.

'Ewert? You listening? I've got a bad feeling about this.'

Grens slowed down a bit, nodding to Sven to do the same.

'I know. I feel the same. Something is wrong. The bodies, the trail, this area – I'm not sure I want to know where the dogs will stop.'

And at that moment they did stop.

A bit ahead of them in the darkness, illuminated only by the tired streetlights.

And the feeling of not wanting to know only increased as Grens approached.

The outside had once been green. But now was mostly rust.

The two dogs had stopped in front of one of the harbour's many empty shipping containers.

'In there.'

The dog handler nodded towards the container, knocked his hand on the metal.

'Our final destination. From the way the dogs are barking, they've found large amounts of at least one of the scents we've been tracking.'

A MILLION CONTAINERS PASS through Sweden's ports every year. This didn't look like the others, neither outside nor in.

Every valve, crack, every small opening had been covered over by grey tape to keep out sound and odour. The door had been locked with a total of four padlocks. And when a dockworker with an oxy-fuel torch cut open a section of the surface with smooth and sharp edges on the side of the container, Ewert Grens took a step back and turned around.

So he wouldn't have to see.

DEATH'S SCENT IS SWEET.

When it's fresh.

As the hours tick by that scent turns to a smell. As days become nights, smell becomes stench.

And that was what struck Ewert Grens. The stench of putrefaction.

As he cautiously approached the square cut out on one side of the container, he couldn't make any sense of what he saw. The contents were covered with a thick layer of now solidified foam.

Soon he discovered a hole in that hard skin.

That's where the stench was coming from.

And when he bent into the hole to see better, he met a pair of eyes. Staring. That's what they were doing. A stare that didn't blink once.

Next to those lifeless eyes lay a pile of clothes, and behind them, when he stretched even further in, another pair of lifeless eyes awaited him.

And another.

And another.

'Sven? Mariana?'

He moved aside, let them pass by, get closer.

'I . . .'

It was difficult to speak with that stench pressing its way into every inhalation.

'. . . I don't know . . .'

Or maybe it wasn't the stench at all. Maybe it was the impossibility of describing the worst thing he'd ever seen.

'. . . but it looks like a . . .'

The only words he could think of.

So that's what it would be.

'. . . a mass grave.'

Then he said no more. Just sat down on the asphalt and let the night's silence become his own. Nor did Sven or Mariana speak. They all understood. The most heinous crime of our modern times. Taking a human being's savings, locking them up and transporting them, not caring if they live or die. Because that's what they are, just money. Just sacks of potatoes. Just goods to make a profit on, like anything else.

Ten minutes. Maybe longer.

Until he could speak again.

'Sven?'

Sven Sundkvist was wandering aimlessly, circling around the container, his boss, and his sanity.

'Yes?'

'I'm thinking about those clothes, Sven, the ones inside the hole. It's like someone broke through that solid foam, took out a couple of the dead, undressed them. I'm thinking about those two bodies too many in the morgue and that pile of clothes. It's too big for just two. I want you to look at the map I brought. Check which hospitals in Stockholm have connections to the tunnel system. And then check which of those have active morgues. Then call and wake up whoever manages those morgues. And then give me the phone.'

He got up and took a few steps closer to the container.

A long life on the force spent investigating serious crimes meant a long line of murder cases. Two hundred and thirty-two. He'd investigated every kind, every quantity – single, double, triple murders. In one case four people had been executed: they lay lined up on their sides, shot in the back of the neck. One case had involved the stabbings of six women, attacked from behind, all naked. But not one, not one day that started in his office on his corduroy sofa, had ever ended like this.

How many were in there?

Thirty?

Fifty?

Seventy-five?

'I've seen this once before, Ewert.'

Mariana was now beside him, having approached him slowly.

'Or, not *this*, not so many, not like this. But a dead person trapped under the foam of a fire extinguisher. That time, the perpetrator had panicked, wanted to get rid of the smell, and it worked. It was his wife, dead almost two weeks when we found her, and she didn't smell. She'd been mummified by the flame retardant. Maybe that's why. Maybe that's what the perp was after. Hide the smell until they could get rid of the bodies.'

They were at the container again.

Every time they looked inside, they saw more.

The image was so alien that impressions came in bit by bit, as the truth slowly revealed itself.

People.

All dead.

Stacked on top of each other from wall to wall.

'I don't get it.'

'What's that, Ewert?'

'Why choose such a complicated way of disposing of the bodies? We usually find bodies floating in the Baltic Sea and Lake Mälaren. In the boots of abandoned cars. Buried in the woods or thrown out in a ditch. Right, Hermansson? So why go to so much damn effort, dragging those bodies around underground in order to get them into the system – after killing them? It's a strange kind of respect. Doesn't seem like the kind of thing your run-of-the-mill criminal would do.'

Mariana Hermansson had no answer to that. So they just stood there next to each other, staring at a mass grave. Until Sven came over and tapped his boss lightly on the shoulder.

'Ewert – I've looked into it as much as I can. In Stockholm County the deceased are taken to five hospitals with certified morgues. Besides Söder Hospital only one is geographically placed along the tunnel system and *might* have a door to it.'

'Yes?'

'St Göran's Hospital. On Kungsholmen. Not far from the police station.'

'Call them. Wake up the morgue manager.'

'She's already awake.'

Sven had a phone in his hand, and he was covering the speaker.

'She's waiting to talk to you.'

Now he handed it to Grens, who turned away from the container, away from the stench, while he spoke.

'Yes, good morning, my name is Ewert Grens, and I'm a detective superintendent with the City Police and—'

'More like good night.'

'Excuse me?'

'It's more good night than good morning. I was fast asleep when you called.'

'If you say so.'

'I'm sorry. I'm just so tired. Let's start again. Maria Eriksson, medical director for the morgue and mortuary department at St Göran's Hospital. And I'm almost awake.'

Her voice was friendlier now, but so quiet it was difficult to catch.

'I'm trying not to wake up my husband and kids. If you're wondering why I'm whispering.'

'At the morgue. Your corpses. I want you to go and count them right away.'

The director, whose name was Maria, cleared her throat. It was clear that she was walking somewhere, you could hear her footsteps.

'Now I guess it's my turn to say excuse me . . . Count them?'

'Yes. You need to check to see if the number of bodies corresponds to the number in your registry. And I need to know immediately.'

She spoke more loudly now, had left her sleeping family.

'Count them? Why? Do you think one . . . got up and walked away?'

'On the contrary.'

'On the contrary?'

'I think one might have walked in.'

As she awoke, she started to understand more of what this was about. She got dressed while still talking to Grens, then headed for the hospital just a five-minute bike ride from her home. Grens did like before, sank down onto the asphalt far enough away from the container to be able to breathe through his nose.

'Can you talk, Ewert?'

He looked up, and Mariana seemed to consider sitting down beside him for a moment, but chose to refrain.

'There are no surveillance cameras.'

'What?'

'This whole area, Ewert, has no camera coverage. According to a county administrator, no one has applied for a permit for this area. Which sounds reasonable – why would you need surveillance for *empty* containers, too heavy to move without a crane?'

Ewert Grens leaned back as much as possible, stretching his back, his shoulders – it had been one hell of a day. And one hell of a night. If he looked past Mariana, past the container, past the dock where a ship was preparing to depart – if he let his eyes float above the water, they soon came to Lidingö Bridge, where he'd stood just one morning before on his way home from his stone next to the nursing home.

'Mariana – I want you to find out what harbour and what boat this container comes from.'

'I will. But . . .'

'And who owns it.'

'. . . I'm convinced that's useless information.'

So calm, so happy, the complete opposite of what he felt now.

Looking out from the bridge in the dawn light, at the stillness of it all, had given him strength.

This, a mass grave abandoned by profiteers who were probably recruiting new desperate people right now, people willing to pay whatever they had and risk their lives – it drained all of his strength.

'Goddammit – I want to know *where* someone loaded up people and covered up all the breathing holes!'

'I do too, Ewert. But every day thousands of containers are shipped across the Baltic Sea, full of cargo in one direction, yet empty and unlocked on their way back. To and from Finland, Russia, Estonia, Latvia, Lithuania, Poland and probably some other countries, too. Anyone, with the right contacts, could fill them with . . . any kind of goods.'

The asphalt.

It was very hard.

He stood up and wandered over to a reddish container that lay right behind the open one, and knocked on its metal walls. A hollow sound echoed inside. Empty – just like it should be. The container to the right of that one was light blue and rang with the same, empty, echo. The next was green, the one after that was mostly rust. He continued to wander around, knocking on containers, while he waited for the team of forensic technicians and medical examiners; waiting for them to wake up, waiting for this terrible night to be over, and for a time when he could finally understand what had happened.

'Ewert?'

He jumped. Sven had sneaked up behind him, or maybe Grens himself was just too far away, too surrounded by death.

'The morgue manager. At St Göran. She's called back.'

Grens took Sven's phone, like before.

'Yes?'

'Superintendent – you were right.'

The medical director's voice was firmer now, she was no longer newly awake or whispering.

'I counted the bodies in our cold storage room. And compared it to the number in the registry. Three. There are three bodies too many here.'

THE SUN SLOWLY ROSE over Stockholm and Värta Harbour. A beautiful, crisp, soft light.

It made the image in front of him even more surreal.

Like a painting. Like an arranged scene.

The most bizarre tableau he'd ever seen.

Ewert Grens took a step back, struggling to make the surreal feel real again. Behind it, far away, a ferry was slowly approaching, inbound from one of the Baltic countries. All the carefree people on board would soon drink their morning coffee and stand in line for a last chance to buy duty-free Toblerone and Chivas Regal. A little closer, but still in the background, the harbour was beginning to wake up. Trucks were idling, loading cranes were creaking, seagulls were squawking. In the foreground, near to where Grens stood now, blue and white plastic tape marked this area off as a crime scene: a wide circle that fluttered and whistled in the breeze.

But it was what was at the centre of the composition that made it so bizarre.

Seventy-three bundles.

Placed on the asphalt in symmetrical rows.

Sixty-eight lifeless people, and five piles of clothes that had also belonged to people who held hopes.

One by one the bodies had been freed from the hardened blanket of fire-retardant foam, carried out, and laid on the ground. In order to get some sort of overview, some order in the chaos. The five piles of clothes were all complete, shirts and jackets and pants and shoes and socks – four seemed to be men's garments, the fifth appearing to belong to a woman. It hadn't been confirmed yet, but Grens was sure, as were Sven and Mariana – those five sets of clothes corresponded to the five bodies that had been hidden in the morgues of St Göran and Söder Hospitals.

It happened so suddenly.

A man who thought he could no longer feel.

Ewert Grens wept.

A sorrow from deep within, expressed in silent tears. What a shitty world we live in. Seventy-three human beings. He walked along the rows, met their empty eyes. One whole family, a man and a woman and their three children. They'd been lying in the same corner of the container, wearing clothes sewn from the same fabric. In another row, a middle-aged couple still holding each other's hands, even after death, the forensic technicians had had to prise their grip apart.

After a while he didn't even bother to wipe away the tears with his jacket. He couldn't believe anything could be more absurd.

Until it was.

A phone started to ring.

And everyone looked around.

Loud, insistent rings coming from the wrong place. Not from where Grens or Sven or Mariana or the forensic technicians or the medical examiners or the patrol cars stood. A ringing that stopped and then started again somewhere in the row of bodies and clothes at the far left, the ones they hadn't yet had time to investigate.

He lifted up the police tape and ducked underneath, rushed over to the forensic technicians' black van and to the box of plastic gloves that always hung on the inside of the back door. He pulled them on, both hands, and continued back across the surreal scene.

Climbing over bodies to make it in time.

The sound seemed to come from one of the clothing piles.

A baggy jacket, wrinkled trousers, worn shoes that had once been dark brown.

Clothing whose size matched the man they discovered first, the man wrapped in a sheet and left among the registered patients, and who, along with the woman found the following day, led them here.

Ewert Grens hunched down next to the ringing.

The thick, lined jacket.

That's where it came from.

He stuck down his hand into the spacious outer pockets. Empty.

But the ringing continued; he could feel it vibrating from the jacket, near shoulder height.

The fabric.

Inside the fabric.

In the place where a shoulder pad usually sat, a flat, hard square phone had been stuffed inside instead. It had been sewn into the fabric. His plastic-encased and eager fingers grabbed hold of the seam, tore it open, dug out what lay inside.

A satellite phone, considerably smaller and more advanced than those he'd seen at the police station.

And it stopped vibrating and ringing just as he was about to press the answer button.

IT WASN'T OFTEN EWERT Grens rolled down his window and put the magnetic rotating blue light on the roof of his car. And even more rare for him to turn on the blaring, monotonous wail of his siren. He did so now. The hard light and sound were his companions on his drive through the inner city, and he made his way to Bergsgatan in just a few minutes. He carried the small plastic bag through the corridors of the police station, up the stairway to the forensic lab.

Fingerprints.

It was, and would always be, the evidence Grens preferred.

Not because he was too damn old. Not because they'd been doing it that way since he'd first set foot inside this police station – a gram of powder and a small brush still the most common method of securing a print. It was about confidence. Fingerprints were as unique and much safer than DNA. A strand of hair or slice of nail could be brought to the scene of a crime by almost anyone. A fingerprint, on the other hand, had to be placed there personally.

'Is this urgent, Superintendent?'

'Very.'

The forensic technician was, in comparison to Grens, a very young man, around the same age as Hermansson. He now took the plastic bag containing two small strips with fingerprints brushed from the satellite phone.

From the hands that had once held it.

'If you'll just take a seat, Superintendent.'

'I'd prefer to watch your screen while you work.'

'This takes a while. And with all due respect, Superintendent, you don't exactly look fresh. A long night?'

Grens stayed where he was, about an arm's length from the neck he was breathing on. And the forensic technician was wise enough to let him. He realised the presence of the detective superintendent was unnecessary to the task, but though he had no idea what it felt like to see dozens of the dead lined up on just a bit of asphalt, the technician knew he couldn't ask Grens to just sit passively in a visitor's seat after that.

'I'm scanning-in both fingerprints.'

If he talked to him, explained what was happening on the computer screen – maybe the anxiety in the room could be at least slightly mitigated.

'Here, Superintendent. I see the *Galton details*.'

He pointed to the screen, and at the first fingerprint that filled it.

'And this – these are *independent ridges*. And there, those are the black *papillary ridges*. And here you see what we call *forking ridges*. No? Maybe if I enlarge them a bit more?'

He zoomed and marked each finding with a red dot.

'They say at least eight details are needed for a match. That's not enough for me. I want at least ten, Superintendent, to declare we have the grounds for a possible match.'

The dots were connected to each other by red lines, creating a pattern unique to only one human being. When the number of dots reached twelve, the pattern might be mistaken for a spider web, and the forensic engineer was satisfied, and loaded the fingerprint banks he'd use for comparison.

'We have a match, Superintendent.'

He'd gone no further than the first file – fingerprints related to ongoing investigations.

'How sure?'

'One hundred per cent.'

'And . . .?'

'One John Doe. Unknown male. Posted just thirty-eight hours ago. A body found in . . . what's that say . . . they must have entered it wrong – the cold storage at Söder Hospital's morgue?'

Ewert Grens had unconsciously leaned in closer to the screen, almost into the picture.

'That's correct.'

'Damn carelessness, I'm going to—'

'I mean that the information is correct – he was found there. Name-less. And that makes the *other* fingerprint much more interesting.'

At Värta Harbour Grens had crawled into the technicians' bus and, as usual, watched the forensic technician carefully dust the satellite phone with carbon powder as the fingerprints slowly emerged. It was well-executed work, and the quality of each line was close to perfect.

Point by point, a complete pattern emerged. A human being.

'You see that, Superintendent? I'm finding more than enough details. Ten or even eight would have been enough. Now I have four-teen. If he's – it's a he, the size of the finger indicates that – in any of the databases we have access to, we'll be able to make a hundred per cent match.'

It went almost as fast this time.

As soon as the forensic engineer activated the so-called A-file, more than one hundred thousand fingerprints from suspects in various criminal investigations, the computer screen flashed an angry red in the bottom column. He placed his cursor over the fingerprint that appeared there and clicked twice.

A name. A social security number. An address.

But just as Grens was reaching for his reading glasses to make sense of the unnecessarily small text, the screen blinked off.

'What . . . happened?'

The young man had deliberately turned it off.

'What are you up to? We have a match!'

'Yes. And I read it. But I'm not sure you should, Superintendent.'

'Turn it on again.'

'Because that name, the man who held that phone, belongs to a person I think you might care about.'

'I've never before had to . . . dammit, I'm investigating mass murder! I don't care about people who think they have the right to end another person's life. Never have, never will. So turn on . . .'

'You hear things. Unofficially. And I clearly remember how you—'

'. . . goddammit!'

The young man had chosen well. Grens understood that some-where, even in the midst of his anger. So he didn't scream again. Just took slow, deep breaths, as he'd learned to do when what was inside him risked coming out too fast and too loud. The power button was in the corner to the right, the forensic engineer pushed it to the side, and they had to wait a few seconds for the screen to light up again.

Still unnecessarily small text. But it could be made out.

If Grens leaned even closer.

Hoffmann Koslow, Piet

And still it didn't help. Even though he continued to breathe deeply and slowly.

'You . . .?'

He screamed, anyhow.

'You!'

'That's what I was trying to tell you, Superintendent, that . . . I'm one of the few who knows. First, about how they manipulated you to give the command to kill him – and we all walked around thinking you *had* killed him. And then last year—'

'Do yourself a favour and shut up.'

'—Superintendent, you have to understand *I* was the one who took his fingerprints after you'd gone to see him, far away. When you saved his life, his whole family. I'm truly sorry for your sake, I get it – seeing his name in connection to a murder investigation like this when you were the one—'

'Now you better keep that mouth shut before I . . .'

It was in another life that Grens used to punch people. And he had no wish to start that again with a young colleague who didn't know any better.

So he rushed out of the room, out into the corridor that was just as ugly and dusty as all the other fucking corridors, hurried down it, out through the building, which despite four decades spent there he'd never truly felt at home in.

You?

I don't understand.

You – mixed up in mass murder?

Thank you, Superintendent. For everything.

I picked you up at the prison gate. I drove you home. We said goodbye, for ever.

Take care of them, Hoffmann.

I left you with your family.

Don't do anything to expose them, or you, to danger any more, Hoffmann.

I believed you when you stood outside your house, with Zofia and the boys waiting at the kitchen table, when you looked into my eyes and said you'd decided to live another kind of life.

Every day, Hoffmann. The lawful, boring everyday, one day at a time. We'll never meet again. Right?

Those ugly fucking corridors eventually came to end. And he slammed open that ugly fucking door, and exited onto Bergsgatan, and continued out of the ugly fucking police station towards the ugly fucking car parked outside.

But he knew.

A fingerprint never lied. A fingerprint on a satellite phone in a container could not have been planted, it had to get there personally.

Papillary lines, forking ridges, divisions and spaces, they formed a pattern that existed before birth and remained after death.

A unique pattern, which could only belong to one person.

PART TWO

THE ROAD WASN'T REALLY a road. But during the hunger season this dry, riverbed was transformed into a route for caravans of vehicles crossing the Sahara Desert. A crooked, uneven stretch those last miles east of Filingué, until you reached the refugee camp, where thousands of tents were the only shelter against a relentless sun beating its warmth onto bare skin. A river that once carried water and used to guide a very different kind of caravan, people on camels making their way from West Africa to the Mediterranean.

Piet Hoffmann stared out through the windscreen of the car at the endless sand, trying not to lose himself in the bleary haze that always floated just above the ground, as if the heat itself were alive. He missed home. Missed Zofia and Hugo and Rasmus and his house in southern Stockholm. Tomorrow night. Then they'd meet again. He'd open the rusty gate to his garden, hear their voices just a few steps from the front door, hold them, squeeze them until they told him to stop. It was always harder the closer he got, when he allowed himself to let go.

But at least he'd be talking to them in five minutes. The day's most important moment, during those clattering, babbling, sticky breakfasts they ate together in the Hoffmann kitchen.

The sun was halfway across a bright blue sky, as beautiful as it was cloudless. They'd been travelling for almost a day since yesterday's morning pickup in Burkina Faso, where goods were lifted onto the trucks. At some point in the afternoon they'd crossed the border to Niger, and all through the evening and night they made their way northward, eastward, towards the desert and the famine.

Thirty-three degrees. Almost no wind. Just a slightest breeze from the west. Only the tyres of their vehicle released any sand.

Always read the room – no matter how big the room was.

Always be prepared.

Piet Hoffmann glanced over at the man sitting in the passenger seat. He hadn't had time to get to know him. Brand new. Frank, something or other. From Denmark. Tall, muscular, young. So different from the much older man who'd previously sat there – Rick from Nottingham, who'd planned to retire in a few years after working long and hard for a South African security firm that gave him, and everyone else in this modern version of the French Foreign Legion, one thousand dollars a day to protect the transports the UN's soldiers weren't allowed to – making sure that food arrived. And Rick did go home last week. But not to retire. His wife was sick. Rick had risked his life every day – and the person he loved ended up with cancer.

Quarter to eight. To the second.

Hoffmann pulled a satellite phone out of his vest pocket and dialled one of the few saved numbers, waited for it to connect.

He was in the lead position in a small caravan of five vehicles. The position that always took the first hit in an attack. With Rick at his side he'd been able to relax every morning during his call, concentrating on the voices on the other end, which were everything to him. Rick himself used to make a call in the evening, he and his wife had their own ritual, then Hoffmann would be extra observant for a few minutes, doing the work of two. He'd trusted Rick – a damn fine spotter. The lookout who sits in the passenger seat isn't there to read the surroundings, they're there to read *aberrations* in their surroundings. Bombs that might be buried in the road in front of them, or a little cloud of gravel and dust that indicated pirates rather than wind, or a rock on the horizon that formed the perfect place to lie in wait. Aberrations that someone like Rick, who knew this route and these surroundings well, found easy to detect, but that the Dane, Frank Something-or-other, would have a hard time seeing – even though he came here directly from a tough unit in Afghanistan, even though he smelled like alcohol in the mornings like everyone out here who came to kill sadness, meaninglessness, emptiness and were ready to risk it all.

'Daddy!'

Rasmus. He almost always answered, throwing himself at Zofia's phone and balancing it on the kitchen table between the yogurt, cheese, jam and toast. Piet could almost smell it all from a continent away.

'Morning, buddy. What are you eating today?'

'Sandwich. With just a tiny bit of melted butter on it.'

Hoffmann could see that toast in front of him. And it was drowning.

'Just a *tiny bit* of butter, Rasmus?'

'OK, maybe a lot.'

A spoon clattering on a plate, that's what he heard. Zofia, who was probably sitting opposite their youngest son, started her days with a bowl of oatmeal.

'And what are you eating, Papa?'

'I . . . haven't eaten my breakfast yet. We're driving right now, have been for a while, but I did just drink a cup of coffee.'

Rasmus didn't reply right away. He was chewing on too big a piece of toast, you could hear it clearly. Piet Hoffmann took the opportunity to roll down the window and replace the warm air inside the car with the equally warm air lurking outside. His standard equipment – a bulletproof vest, a gun strapped to one shoulder, and a knife strapped to the other – had become like an extra layer of skin since his time in South America, but on days like this, when sweat pooled on his chest, he became aware of them again. A quick glance back at the three UN trucks, loaded with rice and sorghum in fifty kilo sacks and corn oil in two litre bottles, and at the escort car at the back. Everything seemed quiet. A smaller transport than usual on their way to people with nothing to eat at all – they usually worked in groups of sixteen or eight men, today they were only four. Piet and Danish Frank in the front car, and at the back two trigger-happy and fearless South Africans who'd been doing private security for a long time.

'Rasmus, you still there?'

'Chewing, Papa.'

'Can I talk to your big brother now? Is that OK?'

'OK.'

'Are you there, Hugo?'

Hugo. Their oldest, growing so fast right now. Hoffmann was already there in his heart and mind, arriving at home to their kitchen, crouching down like he always did after a trip to ask Hugo if anything happened while he was gone. Hugo always answered, as children do, that nothing had. That's when Piet would grab his son's slim shoulders and say, *Yes it has, you've grown.* And then he'd push him over to the doorframe and draw a new line above the old one. Say, *Look, Hugo, two centimetres have happened.*

'Hugo? Are you there? You're not answering.'

Because it was true. So much happens in three months spent apart, and sometimes, if only for a moment, he felt like they were strangers. He looked into Hugo's face and didn't really recognise it. As if his son had become someone else. Which he was. And shame washed over him. He didn't recognise his own child – or maybe his child didn't recognise him.

'Hugo?'

'I'm here.'

A glass was placed on the table loudly enough to be heard. And now the refrigerator was opened. And the tap at the kitchen sink started running.

'Hey, Hugo – how's my oldest bud doing?'

'Good.'

Abrupt. Hugo had been like this for a while. Zofia talked about it, worried about it.

'What's good? Tell me, Hugo.'

'School.'

'OK. What's good at school then?'

Hesitation. Piet knew, but couldn't hear it. Still he knew. How Hugo sat there turning over the words he didn't want to let go of.

Then Zofia cleared her throat, whispered loudly, as much at the telephone as at their eldest son.

'Why don't you tell Dad about the A you got on your English test?'

More hesitation. And then he at least let out one word.

'English.'

'English, Hugo? Yeah? What about it?'

'That's going well.'

The road, or the riverbed, was bumpier here, rockier, and Hoffmann slowed down. Up ahead and to the west there was a small rock massif, the perfect spot for an ambush. He scanned those stone walls for anything that didn't fit.

'That's great. About the English. And do you know what else I think is great, Hugo?'

'No.'

'Tomorrow I'm going home. And then I'll get to see my boys and give them a kiss.'

The car passed by the rock massif and still there was nothing that didn't belong.

'Hugo, can I talk to your mum for a bit?'

Piet Hoffmann should, but couldn't, relax. There was something off. His job was to look straight ahead, concentrate on steering and guide the car through those final difficult miles to the refugee camp, and Frank was supposed to be the lookout. Still, he continued glancing towards the rocks in the rear-view mirror.

'Piet – I'm here.'

'Good morning, my love. Having a good day?'

'Just a regular day. And I like regular days.'

'And I like my wife who likes regular days. Tomorrow then . . .'

He interrupted himself. Couldn't be sure. However, there seemed to be some movement on the rust-coloured cliff. As if a human, or maybe even two, were on the move.

'Zo, wait, I—'

Then they came. The gunshots. An automatic weapon. From up on the cliff. A Kalashnikov.

'Zo, I have to hang up, I'll call back.'

He always kept his sniper rifle on two hooks behind the driver's seat. Now he fleetingly put a hand on the barrel, making sure it was ready, then grabbed his two-way radio and called up the three truck drivers and Lenny and Michael in the back car.

'Keep rolling! And speed up!'

More shots. In the rear-view mirror, the bombardment became visual as flames exploded out of the gun. From the same Kalashnikov. But not aimed at the lead car, which was always attacked first.

They also weren't shooting at the food, the trucks that were the real target.

Their target was the last car. And they emphatically missed it. Not even the newbies who occasionally cropped up in these local criminal networks were this bad.

It didn't make sense.

Nor was the site correct – the attack should have been initiated from the front, towards the east where the sun was brightest and prevented a full view.

That's when he saw it.

In the middle of the glowing sun. Just over three hundred metres away. Something shining. A metal surface reflecting.

Piet Hoffmann peered into the light. It was the direction Frank, who was looking back at the rock massif, was supposed to be monitoring.

Towards what could be the outline of a small truck.

'*Everybody stop . . .*'

This time he shouted it.

He knew if you added blinking metal to what you usually find on the beds of stationary trucks around here, the sum was exactly what the attack from behind was supposed to distract them from.

'*. . . now!*'

He hit the brakes with all his might, and the tyres tore up the dried riverbed as both the car he was driving and those behind him stopped short. Simultaneously, four, maybe five metres in front of him a high-explosive shell went off. A cluster bomb with eight hundred steel balls inside it, that lodged in a sand embankment instead of spreading death.

A grenade rifle. Fired from the site where he'd seen the reflection. The South Africans in the back loaded an antitank rifle in six seconds. There weren't many out here capable of that. The ones he usually ran across could do it in ten, maybe twelve seconds in a best-case scenario.

That's all the time he'd bought them.

The amount of time they had to knock out the grenade shooter before they could reload.

He grabbed the sniper rifle hanging behind the driver's seat, jumped out of the car, put the rifle on the bonnet of the car. And all these thoughts ran through his head when he saw through his rifle scope that the grenade shooter was aiming at him.

Did Zofia know?

Did the boys hear?

If he takes the shot before me – was that last time I'll ever hear their voices? Or they'll hear mine?

Next to the shooter stood the reloader who had just picked up a new high-explosive shell and pushed it into the grenade shooter. He was about to give the shooter a tap on his shoulder, the signal to fire, when Piet Hoffmann took his shot. At the upper portion of the shooter's forehead. The loader seemed confused as his colleague's face hit his shoes, and he turned in the direction the shot had come from. At that moment Hoffmann was able to see him clearly – *and recognised him*. Without knowing why, or where from. If he'd met him as friend or enemy. And Hoffmann hesitated. Let his forefinger rest against the trigger. Until the loader bent down and picked up his colleague's grenade launcher to take the shot himself. Until Hoffmann, for the first time in a long time, had to think *You or me. And I care more about me than about you, so I choose me.* And took his second shot. Right at the loader's left temple.

The silence that followed was always the same. Death had arrived and hadn't yet decided if she'd stay.

Piet Hoffmann grabbed his two-way radio again, called out.

'*Koslow here – Lenny and Michael, the fake attack, how's it look?*'

'*The shooters on the cliff are gone. We're sure of it.*'

'*And I'm sure the shooter and loader to the east were alone. Let's wait five minutes. If the situation stays the same, you stay here with the convoy and keep an eye on the rocks, and Frank and I will go pump those corpses for information.*'

They listened to breeze, months of drought, ruthless starvation. And started driving towards the place where the assault had come from.

Hoffmann looked at Frank. Who was bleeding from his forehead.

'How's it going?'

'You hit the brakes.'

'Sorry.'

'No, no, thank you, my friend! You saved my life. Our lives! We'd all be face down on that fucking riverbed if you hadn't done *my* job!'

Calm. That was how Piet Hoffmann felt. Always did after something like this. Not worry, fear, anxiety – just a calm that seldom filled his chest. Even the face of the young Dane sitting next to him had changed. Not because of the blood that would soon dry in this heat, nor his broken sunglasses, which had exposed one of his eyes – there was a new energy inside him, he was no longer empty. He was the type most alive when he's risking death, who probably thought his day couldn't have started better. An attack, a fight for your life, replacing alcohol with adrenalin.

'You were on the phone when they started shooting?'

'Yes.'

'You have kids, Koslow?'

'Two boys.'

'And a wife?'

'Mhhhm.'

'And tomorrow – you head home?'

'Yes. Tonight Niamey and the hotel. Tomorrow the airport and Sweden and my family. Two weeks. My return to life.'

The grenade shooter's position lay beyond the road. Loose sand and stones made it hard to reach.

'What about you? Home to Denmark?'

'Denmark?'

'Yeah, home. Before that beautiful energy I see on your face runs out.'

'I don't have a home. Or I guess I don't have one *home*. I'll use this energy in Zarzis. At a dive bar on North Africa's most beautiful beach. That's *my* return to life. You wanna come along, Koslow? Two weeks in Tunisia. You and me, sleeping all day, drinking and dancing all night.'

Piet Hoffmann stopped behind the truck that could have meant their deaths. Frank almost threw himself out of the car, his weapon raised as he approached the back of the truck. Even though there was no one there. Piet knew that – he never would have brought them up here if he wasn't sure. But he let the adrenalin-junkie go ahead and studied him at the same time – who the fuck vouched for you? Who thought you were worth a thousand dollars a day and had the skill set to do this job? Whose reference claimed you were mentally stable, able to handle several weeks in the middle of nowhere, wouldn't go berserk or flip out, and could hit your target?

'Safe!'

Piet Hoffmann smiled at Frank, informing him of what he already knew.

'Good.'

Then he went over to the truck, counted the large grenade shots which weighed three and a half kilos each and lay in the centre of the truck bed. Eight. They must have had ten.

'They weren't after the food.'

'No? Food's what we've got.'

'They were going to eliminate security, then they were planning to hit the food. Not to eat it, or resale it, they wanted to destroy it. Create more refugees.'

The Dane didn't look particularly convinced as he turned towards the grenade shots, stretching out a hand to touch them, then changing his mind.

'That's how it works around here, Frank. Sure, sometimes they *are* after the food. Sometimes to eat it. Sometimes to sell it. But almost every assault lately has had this goal – destroying the food to increase the number of refugees. The more refugees there are the more money they make. We're at the meeting point for refugees headed north through Africa – nine out of ten pass through Niger on their way to Libya and the boats to Europe.'

One body, the shooter, had fallen halfway down from the truck bed and the other, the loader, lay face down in the sand. Both in their thirties. Not from around here. North Africans.

'Koslow?'

Frank was leaning over the dead shooter, as if about to speak to him.

'I mean it – you saved my life. I owe you one. At any time, Koslow, anywhere.'

Piet Hoffmann also studied the shooter whose insides now covered most of the grenade launcher. But he wasn't the one who interested him. The loader. That face he recognised. Hoffmann approached the unmoving body, lying on its stomach in the sand, grabbed the shoulder, turned it over.

The face *was* familiar. Even though it was partially destroyed. It hadn't even been that long since Hoffmann had seen it.

But it was only when he saw the ear of the dead man that he was sure who he was.

Just half an ear, the top was gone. The kind of ear that wouldn't hold up sunglasses. That's what he'd thought when they met three weeks earlier. In a harbour that smelled more of human shit and sweat than fish and tar.

'Koslow, I mean it. This will never happen again. You'll never need to do my job again. Anything. Whenever.'

'Well, start by gathering all the maps and GPS and phones and any other information you can find, so we can send it on to headquarters. I have to finish my call.'

Piet Hoffmann took a few steps away in the sand. The sun and heat danced around him, but he didn't notice them. He was about to talk to the only people who mattered.

'Piet?'

Zofia picked up on the first ring. As if she'd been waiting with the phone in her hand.

'What happened?'

And she whispered so the two boys wouldn't hear.

'Nothing.'

'I could hear something happening.'

'Just a roadblock.'

Hoffmann turned away, while Frank walked around, plucking at the two bodies, going through their clothes, searching the whole area.

'A roadblock?'

'Yes. Something was blocking the road. But not any more.'

He recognised that silence. When she was seeing straight through him. When she knew.

'Piet, now's not a good time, we're in the hallway about to head to school.'

'Do I have time to say hello to them?'

'Of course.'

'Can I talk to Hugo first – it didn't feel like we were finished?'

This silence on the other end was different. As was her tone.

'He . . . left already. Always in a hurry to get to school. But Rasmus is here.'

The phone crackled as she handed it over. The seven-year-old tried his best to get a good grip on it.

'Hi again, Dad.'

'Hi, little buddy.'

'We have to go now. Otherwise, we'll be late. See you tomorrow, Papa. For real. No phone.'

Then his son hung up.

And there was only the electronic silence.

Which was worse than all the others.

PART THREE

SOME MORNINGS IT WAS hard not to cry. Not because she didn't want to – it was the good kind of crying. It came from joy and relief, made your body lighter – soft, roaring, still and jittery at the same time. It was more because it shouldn't become a habit. Or rather, feeling this way should become a habit. Allowing yourself to realise that of course you could wake up in your own house, being able to call your children by their real names without being afraid.

Zofia readjusted a flowerpot in the kitchen window, so she could watch Hugo and Rasmus in their backpacks walking away down their residential street. Every morning. Being able to meet their eyes when they asked questions, to open the door and watch them walk away without the bodyguards Piet insisted on for so long, to know that they were going to school with other children, and there was no reason to hide.

Years of being on the run loosened their grip on you slowly, piece by tiny piece.

Not until she'd returned home, had time to adjust, had she really started to understand the hell they'd been living in.

It'd been so much easier for the boys. At least for Rasmus. He'd adapted to his new life as easily as he'd accepted the old one. He crawled through the hole in the hedge to the neighbouring house. And he still ran just as boisterously up their stairs, his whole foot landing on every step, and always forgot to turn off the light when he left a room. Maybe it's easier when you're younger. Hugo, on the other hand, wavered from time to time, his eyes still filling with the same sadness as the morning they'd first left their world in Sweden behind. He needed routines. He was thoughtful, and worried more than a child should. He'd never fully adjusted to South America, and hadn't yet made peace with this new version of his old life. As if he weren't quite sure if he'd have to give it all up again.

Soon she'd walk the same way as the boys, towards the same school, where she taught French, and Spanish – the language she'd mastered in Cali and Colombia. Sometimes in her classroom she found herself unconsciously doing what she was doing right now – staring out the window, following the movements of her two boys. They seemed happy, secure, even Hugo. And they had friends! Two siblings with only each other for so many years, way ahead in their school subjects because of years of private tutoring, were far behind when it came to social skills after years of isolation.

They played in the schoolyard. Rough and tumble. Running after balls. Or they just stood in some corner hanging out with a group of other children, as if they *were* like other children.

Now it came back again, the joy, the relief, she trembled as it rushed from her gut to her chest and lodged itself there. They were living the life she'd dreamed of for so long, the one she'd imagined day after day in order to keep going, dreams she escaped into even as being on the run pushed them further away. Her youngest son had already adapted and her eldest would eventually, he just needed more time.

They'd just finished their call with Piet, while eating breakfast, same time as always. A routine that made it easier to get the boys going in the morning. She would set the table, place the handset between the cheese and the bread, on speakerphone. But their conversation was interrupted this time, something happened to him. She was sure she'd heard a gunshot just before he hung up. A quick look at the boys – still drinking orange juice and layering their toast with too many slices of cheese – they didn't understand what she did. Danger. A while later, after the boys were done eating, had brushed their teeth, and were standing in the hallway about to leave, Piet called again and assured her everything was fine. And she was grateful her husband never wanted sympathy for its own sake, that he always first and foremost protected their children from worry, from another reality. But the conversation had nevertheless been different. Hugo – while Rasmus lingered inside – had taken off, opened and closed the front door and sat down on the outside steps waiting. The first time he'd missed the family's morning conversation, moments that – if you closed your eyes – could almost be an ordinary breakfast at a kitchen table with a dad and a mum and their two boys all together.

Always protect the children.

Piet, who, after years of lying, had finally promised to always tell the truth, share it with her, no matter how unpleasant it was. That's how they survived South America and the cocaine business, the violence, the killing he'd become a part of. That was how they were able to live with each other, the reason they'd stayed in something resembling a family. And what he was doing now, away for long periods of time then home for a couple of weeks, she'd got used to it, it was everyday life, making a living. Back and forth to Africa as an employee for a private security firm commissioned by the UN. He was doing good work for maybe the first time in his life. And making a huge amount of money that would last them for years.

She couldn't see the boys any more. At the big house at the end of the street where an angry bulldog barked at every passer-by while running along the fence, that's where she always lost sight of her beautiful sons.

She moved the flowerpot back, straightened the curtains, and was just turning around to head to the hall, when the scene changed.

A car she recognised without remembering why.

A driver driving too fast, too carelessly to be a neighbour. And their destination was obvious – straight into the cul-de-sac and right up to her gate and driveway.

She stayed at the window while the driver opened his door and climbed out. And immediately wished she hadn't.

Him?

Detective Superintendent Ewert Grens?

She felt a little ashamed, she liked him, even though he'd once sentenced her husband to death, but he'd also travelled to Bogotá and Washington and saved her husband's life of his own accord. Helped her whole family. An older man who under his craggy surface was warm and lonely, someone even the boys when they stood at the airport, heading home for ever, dared to meet.

Hello. My name is Ewert. Uncle Ewert. And are you . . . Rasmus?

I'm Sebastian.

She recalled how the detective superintendent had hunched down on one aching leg, winked, and whispered.

I know you're real name is Rasmus. A fine name. And after we've landed in Sweden, you'll be Rasmus again.

And how Rasmus glanced at his father, until Piet nodded, and also whispered to him.

Uncle Ewert . . . he knows.

And how the six-year-old's face had slowly softened.

Rasmus. For real.

That's why she was ashamed. She should feel gratitude, want to invite him in. But they were never supposed to see each other again. That was what they'd decided. The fact that he was walking up to their front door, ringing their doorbell, meant something was wrong. Something that had to do with Piet, it always did.

She stood for a long time with her fingers on the door handle without pushing down. It was becoming embarrassing, he was a detective superintendent, of course he'd noted the sound of her steps, seen her shadow on the wall through the window, perhaps even picked up on her troubled breathing.

'Hello.'

He smiled, not much, but as well as he could. Perhaps he was as uncomfortable as her, wanted to be standing across from her as much as she did.

'Ewert? What . . .'

'Can I come in?'

She nodded, stepped aside, let him pass.

'I'm sorry, I should offer you something, a cup of coffee at least – but I don't have time, my first class starts soon.'

'No coffee. But a glass of cold water here in the hall would be good, it's been a long night.'

Like him, she smiled weakly, then hurried, still ashamed, into the kitchen, let the water flow until it was ice cold and filled the biggest glass she could find.

'Tap water. The best in all of Enskede.'

She handed him the glass – the time it would take for him to drink up was the time she had to think.

What was he doing here?

What had happened?

Why aren't you saying anything? Can't you tell this is terrifying me? 'Zofia, I . . .'

'That's my name. For real.'

They both gave a short laugh, remembering when she lived under a false name – that's how she'd answered him then. Because Piet had decided to trust the Swedish policeman, she did too.

Then the laughter ended.

They had to look at each other.

To continue pretending he had no reason for being here was starting to seem ridiculous.

'Zofia, I think I—'

'We weren't supposed to meet.'

'—need your—'

'So you're not supposed to be here.'

'—help.'

It was a big glass, held half a litre. He turned it upside down and shook it, as if to prove it was empty. She was sure now, he *was* as uncomfortable and nervous as her.

'A couple of hours walking in a . . . well, quite dirty environment, and just as long around a stench that . . . could I have another glass?'

She filled it again, cold and up to the edge, waited while he drank, and the chasm between them grew.

'I can't take it any more, Ewert – why? Why are you here? I don't want to, I . . . we're done with each other, once and for all, this can't be a private matter, so it has to be for the police – speak to me! What do you want?'

She never screamed. Piet screamed, the kids too, both in Polish and Spanish, but not her.

She did so now.

'Answer me!'

It wasn't his fault, she realised that, he wasn't here by choice. But it didn't matter. It was Ewert Grens who placed himself in front of her, and it was he who received the full blast of a despair she thought she'd felt for the last time.

'Why, Ewert?'

There was a stool next to the shoe shelf, she pushed away the bag lying on it and sank down, there wasn't much more to do when your legs refused to carry you.

'Piet.'

He could barely look at her when he spoke, thought he might know how she felt.

'I have to get hold of him, Zofia. Talk to him.'

'About what?'

'About something only he can answer.'

'I don't understand . . . what's happened?'

'I don't know. Yet.'

He stifled an impulse to pat her cheek, try to comfort her. An older man shouldn't bother a younger woman, just like a police officer shouldn't investigate the truth while protecting the people involved.

'But if you just tell me where to find him, then maybe I can figure this out.'

IT WAS STILL MORNING in Stockholm. Not that Ewert Grens noticed. Time no longer seemed relevant in a world where people were abandoned to die in a shitty container like so much trash. Time of day didn't matter until he finally found his way out of the maze of the small streets surrounding the Hoffmanns' home, and saw the highway that led back to the city was nothing but idling and unmoving vehicles. At this hour putting on his blue light and siren to gain a few minutes of breakfast at the police station was out of the question. So he too became one of many headed to work, trapped inside a metal shell, insulated by his own thoughts. And it was unexpectedly pleasant. This imposed stillness. A place where rage and worry could roam around freely, and when he was tired of them, all he had to do was roll down the window and let them go.

Africa? Niger? That was what she'd said.

If he'd been only vaguely aware of where Colombia was last year before heading off on a moment's notice with his old suitcase in hand, Niger was an even blanker spot on his mental map.

Piet Hoffmann was improving his grasp of geography once again.

'Ewert?'

He'd called Sven, who picked up after a single ring.

'Ewert, is everything . . .'

Now the voice of his closest colleague floated out of the loudspeaker in the ceiling and hung around him in the car.

'. . . OK?'

'I don't honestly know.'

'You disappeared. With the ringing phone. And the fingerprints Krantz lifted off of it. How . . .'

'Niamey, Sven.'

'Excuse me?'

81

'The capital of Niger. In West Africa. That's what it's called.'

'OK?'

'Apparently there's a flight that leaves from Arlanda every afternoon. Ten-hour trip with a layover in Paris. I've decided to pull out of this traffic jam, circumvent the whole city, and head north. For the international terminal. I want you to book me on that flight and pay privately, for now – I'll pay you back later.'

The speaker in the ceiling didn't crackle as electronics sometimes do, didn't buzz, didn't swallow any words or sounds. The reception was perfect. So Grens was able to hear during Sven's long pause that he was still in the harbour, still near the container and the rows of bodies laid out on asphalt like pieces in a board game. The wind was blowing, gulls cried out, the massive lifting cranes screeched, and the enormous engines of ships were starting to run.

'West Africa, Ewert?'

'I can't explain more than that. Yet. In a day, maybe two, when I've tracked down the only person who could be a match. When I figure out how it got there, and why. Last time I met him I was convinced it was for the last time.'

That long pause again. Ewert Grens could picture Sven running his hand through his hair as he always did when he was thinking. He probably had his back to the container and the bodies – Sven who dreaded death, who always asked to skip the trips to the medical examiner and was grateful every time he was sent off to investigate anything besides the body of a human being who had taken their last breath. You learn these things about your closest colleagues. Peculiarities. And if you respect them, you receive respect and loyalty in return.

'Very well, Ewert. I know you won't tell me more no matter how hard I push. So I'll book your ticket and send a car with your passport and vaccination certificate. And I expect a detailed answer the next time we meet.'

An answer?

Grens hadn't really thought that far. He'd planned to go and meet someone who could give the right answer. But what about the wrong answer? What if Hoffmann *was* somehow involved in human trafficking? Then not only would Grens have to investigate, he'd have to return to a house in Enskede and give the wrong answer to a woman who never wanted to see him again.

'While I'm gone, Sven.'

'Yes?'

'I want you to . . .'

He trailed off. He'd been about to ask Sven to check on Zofia Hoffmann, make sure his own visit hadn't disturbed her more than was necessary. But another police officer knocking on her door would be no help. On the contrary, it would just reopen old wounds.

'. . . remind Hermansson to turn the company that owns that container upside down? I don't care if she thinks it's useless. And while she's at that, you start searching those tunnels for the so-called guide who lives down there. Find him no matter what hole he's crawled into. The one who somehow procured a set of keys to all the public buildings that nobody but national defence and the rescue service should have. Those keys represent all his years spent underground and all his years yet to come. Those keys mean power, dignity, they're a requirement for continuing to live separate from everyone else. And only he knows who hired him. Who he took to the manhole cover, and who he opened up doors for. Who dragged around the dead in order to get rid of them.'

There was a lot of honking when Grens pulled out of the line of cars and started driving in the narrow access lane at the side of the highway. After a couple of hundred metres, he got tired of the honking and put the rotating blue light on top of his car, as he did earlier this morning, and turned on the siren. Once, years ago, when still a very young man, he'd flown to Paris to get married. Now he was headed much further south. To a city he'd never heard of before. To find the answers he needed, even if they were the wrong ones.

THE SUN HAD FINALLY decided to set at the Diori Hamani International Airport. The broiling, glowing, globe-shaped fireball left the sky quickly and in the company of an Air France airplane.

Sand. Steppes. Dry grass.

The last image Ewert Grens caught from his seat near the window as the wheels bumped hard against the runway and the whole heavy body of the aircraft heaved, bouncing back as the outer layer of the tyre's rubber was sheared off, and then the plane heaved in the other direction, bouncing a third time, until it found the right course for a reasonably safe landing and headed toward the unremarkable terminal building.

The detective superintendent stayed in his seat long after being welcomed to Niger's capital city. His breathing purposely slow – in out in out, in order to stay calm – clashed with the voice blaring over the loudspeakers and into every row – the flight attendant's mechanically recited information about the local time and a temperature that hovered between thirty-four and thirty-five degrees Celsius, with a low of twenty-seven during the night.

Another world.

His first thought on the continent of Africa.

And Grens realised he almost liked not knowing where the next step would lead, something he used to fear and avoid. He had been completely dependent on his routines for so long, and maybe still was to some extent – a crutch that kept him from falling apart. Not that long ago something like this – getting out of bed in Stockholm with no clue that in just thirty-six hours he'd be picking up a rush visa from over a counter and stepping straight into a wall of heat in a completely unfamiliar place – would have made him long for his sixties music and his corduroy sofa in the police station.

He might be close to retirement, but he was still a work in progress.
'Shall we split it?'

There was only one taxi parked outside the terminal building
entrance. Ewert Grens looked at the man who'd already opened the
door to the passenger seat and, in a very proper Swedish accent, offered
him the back seat. Fifty-five, Grens's height, but slimmer and with eyes
the same colour as his hair – Grens had never seen such grey irises.

'I was in the row behind you on both the flight from Arlanda and
Charles de Gaulle. We're lucky to be travelling with just our carry-ons
– we'll be checking in to the hotel in Niamey, while everyone else is
still waiting on their luggage.'

Cosmopolitan.

In all the ways Ewert Grens was not. Those things show. The slim
man moved, spoke, even dressed in that way – the lightweight and
light-coloured suit of someone who's lived in this climate before,
unlike his own dark and far too thick and already sweaty suit.

'Thank you. I'm headed to a place called . . .'

Grens pulled a piece of paper from the inner pocket of his jacket.

'. . . Hotel Gaweye. And it's located, let's see here . . . Near the
Kennedy Bridge, I think, and the Niger River. At least according to
my co-worker Sven, who's usually good at most things, other than
making his handwriting legible.'

'Then we have the same destination. Best rooms in town – I always
stay there.'

The temperature inside the car made the outside air seem cool.
A corrosive, blazing heat that wrapped around him. It was unlike
anything Grens had ever experienced.

'You get used to it.'

The cosmopolitan in the front seat had turned around and got a
look at Grens's shiny, red face.

'It may sound strange, but your body adjusts after a couple of days.'

'I'll be home by then. In twenty-four hours I'll have taken care of
what I need to do.'

The car started to roll, but not very fast. It was as if it too were
trying to save whatever energy the heat didn't devour, or as if the driver

wanted to stretch out the nine kilometres that separated the airport from the heart of the capital.

'Business?'

The driver spoke in English. He was broad-shouldered with powerful hands, but steered his passengers with gentle and careful movements through Niamey's south-eastern suburbs, down a road called the Route Nationale 1. And he smiled just as gently, after his question, and looked back and forth between the cosmopolitan in the front and Ewert Grens in the back, waiting for the conversation to continue.

'Yes. Business.'

They both answered at the same time, also in English, and now the two passengers smiled. At each other. And the cosmopolitan stretched out his hand.

'Thor Dixon. I work at the Ministry for Foreign Affairs. And my *business* is arranging meetings between UN representatives, relief organisations and local government representatives. In order to discuss how we, Sweden, can offer the most effective help here.'

'Ewert Grens. Detective Superintendent at City Police in Stockholm, here to investigate a mass murder. Refugees suffocated in a container.'

Neither of them were smiling any more.

The government representative's face was furrowed but in an elegant way, the way some people age, wisdom you only gain from a long life of experiences. Grens's own wrinkles were anything but elegant, and they mostly made him look tired and old.

But now they both wore the same expression.

Anger and sadness.

As did the government representative's voice.

'I saw it in the headlines before I boarded at Arlanda. And, well, I didn't really know what to think. So it's true? And the trail leads . . . here?'

Grens had also seen the big headlines in the press, each with only the sparsest information below them. He'd bought one of each of the papers and quickly scanned through the blurry night shots of Värta Harbour, all taken from a distance and blown up by many magnitudes, flanked by a few quotes in bold from a police source saying the refugees might have been killed by some kind of chemical powder.

'The number was right, at least.'

'Number?'

'Seventy-three people struggled for their last breath.'

On both sides of the road mosques and minarets glittered in the sunset, and small clumps of people stood around talking. Apparently they had all the time on their hands that Grens didn't.

'Confined refugees. Also, a type of business, Superintendent. And their journey usually begins here – you're in one of the biggest growth zones for refugees.'

The government representative had turned around completely, his grey eyes serious.

'It's a business worth hundreds of billions – sneaking poor people into rich countries. People dreaming of a better life. The new kind of tourism – *come with us to the land of opportunity.*'

The buildings and traffic were getting tighter, and the number of pedestrians was increasing as they neared Niamey. The long trains of women carrying sacks on their heads through the evening darkness, young men with overloaded wheelbarrows, girls on large men's bicycles, badly parked trucks groaning under piles of boxes, vehicles that occasionally slipped into the wrong lane. And somehow the driver succeeded in making his way forward calmly, never stepping on the brakes or rolling down his window to shout.

'In just the last few months, Superintendent, over fifty thousand refugees have passed through Agadez, a town a bit further inland, the gateway to the desert, which leads to the Mediterranean and Europe. Four days over sand dunes and rocky land to get to Libya. A sixteen hundred kilometre journey. They're fleeing terrorist attacks and militant Islamists, but above all they're fleeing starvation. Niger is Africa's poorest country. Every third inhabitant is hungry. They even call it the hunger season, and it lasts until August. In many places there's nothing but dry leaves on the trees and wild berries to eat.'

Bumpy asphalt gave way to gravel roads, even though they were on a well-trafficked road, and then turned back to asphalt again when they neared the centre of the capital. Or at least Grens assumed the brownish water they were approaching was the river from Sven's illegible note, and that the bridge they were crossing was the one named for John F. Kennedy.

'Hotel Gaweye, sir. And sir.'

The taxi driver pointed to a building jutting out of the riverbank just where the bridge stopped. One of few tall buildings, an elongated complex that could have sat in any western city without attracting much attention, but here that was about all it did – stuck out. Shouted too loud. Didn't fit. Just like its soon-to-be guest Grens, who also didn't fit in.

'I'll pay.'

Ewert Grens stretched out a beautiful banknote from a bundle he'd quickly exchanged on his way out of the air terminal – a picture of a woman in a fluffy headdress that transitioned into a richly patterned boat surrounded by fish. Bright colours. A banknote that was stiffer than the ones he was used to.

'No, no, sir. Too much.'

The driver shook his head while Grens held out his hand. Five thousand West African francs, about seventy kronor.

'Please. Take it. You drive so much better than I do.'

The beautiful banknote changed hands, and just as Grens was about to put his wallet back into his inner jacket pocket, the Swedish official held something out to him.

'My various numbers. If you'd like to have a coffee, at the hotel or in town, just give me a call, and I'll find time between meetings.'

A business card. At the top stood the blue shield with three golden crowns and in slightly larger text 'Ministry for Foreign Affairs'; underneath were his name and contact information.

Ewert Grens stuffed it into his wallet.

'Thank you – but I'm not here to drink coffee.'

The government official nodded politely and headed for the hotel entrance, while Grens stepped out as the driver hurried around to open his door. Outside he was met by a hand wanting to say goodbye, still grateful for the tip in a way that embarrassed the detective.

'Frederick's my name.'

'Ewert.'

'Wow, that's hard. Eyert?'

Grens smiled and shook his head.

'Evvyytert?'

And nodded a bit at the taxi driver's second attempt.

'Good enough, Frederick. They had a harder time in the States. They ended up calling me Jerry.'

'Jerry?'

'Yes.'

Frederick finally let go of Ewert Grens's hand and closed the back door.

'Jerry it is. You need a taxi, call this number.'

This business card was a bit simpler, a napkin with a phone number written in pencil. Grens put it next to the other one in his wallet – it felt important to treat the friendly driver the exact same way as the government official – and started walking towards the hotel that didn't fit in.

The wind was blowing.

Warm and intrusive – it was like passing the open door of an oven. Plus hot gravel swirled around inside it, landing in his eyes and mouth.

Hotel Gaweye welcomed you into a giant foyer. The largest he'd ever seen. A sparkling red carpet and leather furniture along the walls, seemingly pushed to the side, gave him the feeling of walking through an empty gym on his way to the desk that stood at the other end.

'Welcome.'

English with a French accent. A female receptionist checked him in, gave him his plastic key card, and then, as he was on his way to the elevator, stopped him.

'Mr Grens.'

He turned around, could see her holding out an envelope.

'This is yours, Mr Grens. Printed on photo paper. Just as the sender requested.'

Ewert Grens coaxed open the envelope with his index finger and peered inside. Perfect. Sven had done exactly what he was supposed to do.

The hotel's small shops pulsated, just like the reception area, with powerful air conditioning. Invisible fans hissed and dried the sweat on his brow. He picked up a toothbrush, toothpaste and deodorant from the shelves on one side of the wide passage, a white shirt, underwear and a pair of socks on the opposite side. The elevator took him to the fifth floor and a large room with wallpaper, rugs and flowers in the same red as the foyer. The colour scheme was supposed to be very stimulating. As if he needed that. He already had red in his chest, a blaze that wouldn't give him any peace until justice was served for the people found encased in flame retardant.

He sat down on a bed as soft as his corduroy sofa and looked out at the hotel's lights glittering in the Niger River. Fresh-cut flowers and beautiful views – a new surrealistic reality, which obscured people who survived off dry leaves.

'Hello.'

He'd been sitting with his phone in his hand, barely aware of making a call. Perhaps it was the loneliness found only in hotel rooms. Or perhaps it was the fire in his chest. And not that it mattered – but it felt good to hear Mariana Hermansson's voice.

'Ewert? I heard from Sven . . . are you there?'

'Yes. South America one year, West Africa the next. The criminal world shrinks and expands at the same time, Hermansson.'

He'd been the one who called. So she waited for him to continue. And started to speak only when she realised he wasn't going to.

'We have a credible tip.'

Grens listened to her calm voice, her Skåne accent by way of the rough suburb of Rosengård, where she grew up among immigrants from hundreds of countries. He'd always appreciated her southern way of speaking, but in this surreal reality he needed it even more.

'About the guide. And the part of the tunnel system he lives in. We've already started searching, Ewert, with the dogs, and we'll find him. Make him talk. Figure out who hired him, who followed him and dumped those bodies.'

This did nothing for the blaze in his chest.

It only made it burn more wildly.

Ewert Grens stood up from the soft mattress and walked out of the room in a hurry, as if on his way to some crucial meeting. Fires have their ways. He almost rushed out of the elevator and into the gymnasium-like lobby, made sure it was just as desolate as before. It was possible to order a cup of coffee while sitting in one of those leather chairs, and he chose a spot near the middle, with a good view of the whole reception area. Zofia had explained that her husband would arrive late before returning home to Sweden on one of his scheduled breaks, and he and his colleagues in the private security firm always stayed here during their stopovers in the capital.

Their paths would cross again. And they had to do so here – not in Stockholm.

The first time they didn't meet face to face. Just an absurd bit of dialogue over the phone in the middle of a hostage crisis in a high-security prison.

The second time they met in Bogotá under equally extraordinary circumstances, but no longer two express trains headed straight at each other. Hoffmann needed Grens's help, and they didn't fight each other, they fought side by side.

This time the opposite was the case.

This time in Niamey, it was Grens who, despite agreeing to never meet again, was seeking Hoffmann out. It was Grens in search of answers. And it was Ewert Grens who, if the answer he got was right, would need Piet Hoffmann's help.

Three empty white porcelain cups sat in a row on the table.

The detective had just ordered his fourth cup of Liberian coffee, deliciously bitter, fantastically strong, when he recognised someone coming through the entrance on the western side. There he was, Piet Hoffmann. One year later. He'd let his hair grow out over the lizard tattooed on his head, so long that even the tail of the lizard that crept down his neck was covered. In addition, he was sporting a soft beard. Different corners of the globe demanded different looks. But the way he moved, the hardest thing for a person to change, which Grens had learned to recognise during hours spent with surveillance cameras, that belonged only to him. And now Hoffmann did what he always did when he stepped into a room – read it, surface by surface, always ready for danger, ready to act. Until his eyes froze. On an older man drinking coffee in a leather armchair. Grens saw Piet Hoffmann jerk unconsciously, trying to make sense of the scene again. With the same result. The man in the leather chair was someone who didn't belong there.

'What the hell . . .'

And then moved quick across the giant lobby.

'. . . are you doing here?'

'Good evening, Hoffmann.'

'Ewert Grens – in West Africa?'

'Yes. I'm on vacation.'

'Vacation . . .?'

'Just like when I took that sunny vacation in Colombia. You know, places you just sort of end up in.'

Hoffmann nodded towards the armchair opposite Grens.

'OK?'

Grens nodded back.

'It's you I'm waiting for.'

His appearance might be different, but the clothes were about the same as the last time, albeit in colours more suited to this continent. Brown boots, beige jeans and a sand-coloured vest with a lot of pockets, which hung over a T-shirt that looked very white against his deep tan. Last time he'd seemed tired, older than his years. Now he seemed younger.

'So, Grens, this . . . vacation? When will you be done with your sunbathing?'

The detective looked over at the golden clock sitting on the wall above the front desk.

'Thirteen hours. If I'm lucky. Then I fly home.'

'Were you planning to sleep before that?'

'Not much.'

There was a small bar in an area on the other side of the reception desk. Grens hadn't seen it before, and that's where Hoffmann disappeared to, returning soon after with two full glasses in his hands.

'I remember you prefer coffee. Black. And that you're not much for alcohol. But this time, I thought this might suit you better. Bantu beer. You get used to it.'

'Bantu beer?'

'Instead of wheat and barley and rye, it's millet. Gluten free. If you're wondering.'

Grens watched Hoffmann lift his glass, take a swig. Then he screwed up his courage and drank, too.

Different.

Not unpleasant. Not even unexpected.

But different.

'In Colombia, I had you drinking sugar cane. And you were hooked. Now I'm tempting you with gluten-free beer.'

'Well I did what I could to kill you once . . . so I suppose you're entitled to do the same to me, Hoffmann.'

Then they both fell silent. Drank, swallowed, waited. The same disturbing, embarrassing silence as in the hallway of Hoffmann's house, in front of Zofia, who'd had no desire to talk to or look at him.

In the end, it was no longer possible to stare into a beer glass or past each other.

No longer possible to avoid the subject by cracking jokes about vacations and beer.

Piet Hoffmann could feel it. The fire.

'OK.'

The one burning in the chest of the large older man, a rage that could not be hidden.

'Why are you here, Grens?'

The detective didn't answer.

With words.

His fury – sitting across from someone he'd decided to trust though he was still afraid he was wrong – stood in the way.

Instead, he answered by taking out the envelope he'd been given when he checked in, the copies Sven sent at his request. By opening it and pouring some of the contents onto the table, making sure a few remained inside, that he wouldn't use yet, maybe never.

'I don't understand – what's this about, Grens?'

Four photographs. All in colour, the kind that you usually see in black and white. They'd landed between them, next to the empty coffee cups and almost empty beer glasses. The last was upside down, the detective leaned forward and turned it over.

'This.'

He pointed to the picture. And immediately wished he hadn't.

'Them.'

Now it was Hoffmann who leaned forward. To see better.

'About what, Grens?'

Because what he was looking at didn't seem possible.

'*About what, Grens?*'

Because if it was what he thought it was, it was about war. And what would a Swedish detective have to do with that? Because only a war created images like that. Bodies. Lined up. Sixty, maybe seventy.

'You're trying to count? Sixty-eight. And those, Hoffmann, those piles of clothes belong to another five.'

A port. Hoffmann was sure of it. Maybe even Värta Harbour in Stockholm. With empty cargo containers stacked on top of each other. The bodies were placed in front of them.

'Last night. Or I guess perhaps early this morning. We found them. In that.'

Ewert Grens pushed the next photo forward. The one that had ended up balancing on a coffee cup. A picture of a container with an opening cut into its side. If you looked carefully, as Hoffmann did, you'd see eyes staring back at you from inside.

'I still don't understand, Grens. Not what this is about or why you're sitting here showing it to me.'

'You'll see. Just look at my last photos.'

The detective made room in the middle of the table for the photos. On the left – a close-up of the fabric of a jacket's shoulder split open. To the right – a close-up of a satellite phone. Grens kept looking at Hoffmann's face, trying to read it, interpret his response when the pictures were turned over.

Nothing.

Either because the former infiltrator was as unmoved as he seemed.

Or he was acting as skilfully as he used to every day in order to survive in his old life. That's the mantra Hoffmann had built his entire method of infiltration on. *Only a criminal can play a criminal.*

'The phone was sewn into a jacket that belonged to one of seventy-three refugees who suffocated in a container while being shipped to Sweden. We lifted two prints off that phone and found two matches. One set matched the refugee. One set was yours, Hoffmann.'

Now.

Now the reaction came.

From a person who wasn't pretending.

Piet Hoffmann's face shifted from unmoved to present to dismayed to tormented. He understood now what these pictures represented. What those two pairs of fingerprints meant. And he made no attempt to conceal that the phone in the photograph had a story that included him.

'The refugee?'

'Yes?'

'The one with the jacket. Who had the phone.'

'Yes?'

'What did he look like? Where did he come from?'

'West Africa, according to our medical examiner.'

'Age?'

'Not certain – but the medical examiner estimates thirty, give or take a few years.'

'And was there a woman, around the same age, from the same part of the world?'

'There weren't very many women, that's usually the case with refugees. But you're right – there was one who could have been with him.'

Piet Hoffmann's face didn't change. His tormented expression was frozen, and his face so recently young, seemed as old as Grens.

'In that case . . . those are my fingerprints. Because until a few weeks ago that was my phone.'

He stood up and started pacing through the desolate lobby – worried and stressed. Then he stopped for a moment, then started again.

'I need another one of those. Should I get one for you too?'

Hoffmann nodded towards the beer glass, and Grens nodded back. By the time he came back one glass was already half empty.

'You know what I'm up to down here?'

'I know what your wife reluctantly told me. A private security firm on assignment with the UN. Protecting transports. Lawful work. That's about all.'

Ewert Grens had never taken Hoffmann for the type who needed alcohol to stay in control. He didn't seem the type to lack the courage to look at himself. But now he downed the second half of the glass in one swallow.

'The UN doesn't have the mandate to protect itself in some areas. Can't meet fire with fire. Which meant that before they had this contract with a South African security firm they ended up losing every transport. Those poor UN muppets in their blue helmets couldn't do more than this . . .'

Hoffmann shrugged his shoulders, theatrically, threw his arms wide to reinforce his point.

'. . . and no food made it to its destination. But since day one, the day we started protecting them, it went from not a single grain making it to its destination, to every single one arriving. We all have military or police backgrounds. And no problem using our guns. We don't lose transports.'

Grens hadn't touched his Bantu beer. So when Hoffmann grabbed it and drank that one too, he had no objection.

'I can understand attacking a food transport if you're hungry. And sometimes that is the reason. I can even understand an attack whose purpose is to take the food and resell it, make some money. You know my history, Grens, so you know I've earned money like that. But I'll never understand attacking those transports just to destroy them. Just to increase the stream of refugees. The worse the food crisis becomes, the more people there are that want to flee. The more refugees there are, the more money those human smuggling fuckers make.'

He moved closer.

'And this, these pictures, Grens, are what connects my job – however strange it may seem – to your question.'

Now he turned over the four photographs, one at a time, until only their white and empty backs could be seen.

'Because one of the men who attacked our transport this morning, who I had to kill in self-defence – you remember Grens, *you or me, and I care more about me than about you, so I choose me* – he was someone I recognised. A human-smuggler. I met him before. When someone asked me to carry out a task.'

Ewert Grens considered turning the pictures over again, letting them lie there until Hoffmann was forced to tell him everything. There was no need. Other images were emptying out of the man who sat opposite him. Images from Zuwara, a Libyan port city on the Mediterranean, another spot the security firm employees occasionally stopped over at between missions. It was also the city that was the entry point for the Libyan route – the port human-smugglers used to reach Europe. That's where Piet Hoffmann was when he was asked to leave his hotel and protect a refugee couple who were about to hand over their final payment to representatives of a smuggling organisation. Forty-five hundred dollars' worth. For them – an incredible sum. Two years of work, day and night. A sum that equalled stage 2, 3 and 4, the continuation of what started in the back of a truck in Niger and four days' crossing the Sahara Desert.

'I'd been working in that part of the world for almost a year, trying to *prevent* human-smugglers from destroying food to increase their profits, and now I was suddenly supposed to just look on while someone handed them money. The young refugee couple was paying for a voyage in a crowded fishing boat across the Mediterranean to the Italian border, to the EU border. Paying for a trip in a crowded truck from Italy to Poland. And then passage in a packed container from Poland to Sweden. It sounded crazy. It was crazy. And when I saw them, Grens, so fragile, so . . . I explained as much to them, in spite of my promise to someone, I couldn't in all conscience participate. But they told me they'd do it *with or without* my help. They didn't seem so fragile any more. They seemed proud, strong, full of hope.

I changed my mind, Grens. I did what I was asked to do. I watched them hand over their life savings in a dirty envelope to two smugglers, I made sure they were guaranteed a safe trip.'

Piet Hoffmann stared at the upside-down photographs. It was as though he suddenly was emotionally, not just intellectually, aware of what he was saying. How things had ended for the people he was talking about.

'I even . . . when it was done. After they paid. And we were saying goodbye.'

Then he picked up one of the photographs.

'I gave them my satellite phone.'

It showed bodies in rows, spread out on the asphalt.

'Just to be safe. In case anything were to happen.'

And it was as though he wanted to jump into the picture, to Stockholm and Värta Harbour, and find the ones he was talking about, offer them a hand and help them up, warn them about the journey he played a small role in.

'Two smugglers took their money at that fucking meeting, both North Africans, probably Libyan. One of them died this morning. I recognised him. The same type as me. With the kind of scars a guy like me might have. He had all his fingers, but he was missing half his ear. And he was there as security, to make sure everything went right. My type is never interesting – we're there for the sake of others. Whereas the other guy . . . well, he was interesting. Clearly the leader, the man in charge, spoke surprisingly good English, heavy accent, but good. Well-mannered and dangerous at the same time. Reminded me of the ex-KGB I infiltrated when I was undercover in the Eastern European mafia. The ones who had to go into a new line of work after the Wall fell. This guy could have been one of them. You know, when a system collapses, they become dangerous – they're intelligent and have the right contacts. He might very well have been an interrogator in the Gaddafi regime, he's the type. The type with no god to fight for any more, so he fights for money. The way I understood it, he was responsible for that leg of the refugee journey, the stages that started in Zuwara and ended in a refugee campsite outside Frankfurt or Borås. Or like that – in that photo there – as an unmoving pile on the ground, who's already paid and no longer has any value.'

He crumpled the paper up in his hand, then looked at Grens, realised what he was doing, and started to straighten it out again.

'Leave it, Hoffmann. That picture has done its job.'

So they sat in awkward silence again. Both of them knew that the detective believed the story this former criminal told.

'Who?'

And since he did – he had to ask the most obvious question.

'Who asked you to help the refugee couple?'

Hoffmann stayed silent.

'I'm here as a police officer, Hoffmann. I'm investigating a mass murder. I need to pull on every string I can to try to figure out which way to go. I'm looking for the bastard in Sweden who stole their lives and their deaths. And you're the only one who has a name that might lead me further up that chain.'

'I can't say.'

'Why?'

'I just can't. But I want to make one thing clear to you, Grens, those photos make me regret getting involved. Regret I helped them, against all my instincts. You can't combine goodness with evil, it doesn't work.'

'I don't follow you.'

'As soon as good intentions commit to evil acts, it ends badly. The person who asked me to do it, to assist, behaved like I used to. Every time I've infiltrated a group at your bidding, I've believed I was doing something good. Thought I was helping the police with something important. I was going to expose evil. And every time I've only made it worse, or made it worse for me, for us, my family.'

'I still don't understand.'

'I can't say more than that.'

They were no longer alone in the lobby. An older couple, Americans by their accents, settled down in the leather armchairs behind them. Ewert Grens leaned forward and whispered.

'Who are you protecting, Hoffmann?'

'Do you want another beer?'

'Who? Look at the dozens of people in that picture. And you – you refuse to talk?'

'I've seen worse. Join me on any of my transports. After my leave, in a couple of weeks, I'll take you. You'll see people dying of starvation, from violence, everywhere. This whole country is one big fucking graveyard.'

'You think you can make me give up, Hoffmann? Who are you protecting – and why?'

The elderly couple, trying to catch their attention, raised their glasses, obviously hoping for some small talk with strangers. Grens nodded kindly, then turned back to Hoffmann with body language that signalled leave-us-alone.

'I would have told you, Grens, if it had been *me* who took the initiative to help the refugee couple. But it wasn't. And if I describe the circumstances, then I'll have to reveal the person who persuaded me to do this. I will never expose that person to risk – never again. Because human smugglers are no joke to deal with.'

'So you'd rather be a suspect for a massacre than give me the name of the person who can back up your story?'

'I was asked to help. I had the possibility to do so. End of fucking story.'

This time the silence was not awkward. They just sat in their leather chairs staring at each other angrily. Two people whose paths had crossed by chance again, both longing for tomorrow's aeroplane, which would carry them thousands of miles north, carry them home, from the beginning of a refugee's journey to the end.

Staring.

While Ewert Grens tried to make sense of this obstinacy.

And suddenly he did.

I will never expose that person to risk – never again.

'Zofia.'

It was that simple.

'Zofia. *She* wanted you to be there as a safeguard for the refugee couple with the smugglers.'

Piet Hoffmann had worked as an infiltrator for over ten years, first for the Swedish and then the American police, exposing violent and highly dangerous organisations. His entire existence, the prerequisite for his survival, was based on his ability to hold a mask. Always be somebody else, always use lies as a tool.

It didn't matter now.

Ewert Grens could see he'd guessed right.

Zofia Hoffmann was the link to the human smugglers.

'Talk to me, Hoffmann, goddammit.'

The American couple next to them laughed, toasted, had managed to ingratiate themselves with some other hotel guests who were much more fun than the Swedes, focused only on each other. Piet Hoffmann looked at them, it could be that easy – travelling abroad. For him and Zofia and their boys, showing a fake passport to a customs official was the same as being on the run, living to survive. When these two years were over, the length of his contract with the South African security firm, he was going to stay in his house in Enskede, that was all the adventure they needed.

'Hoffmann, for fuck's sake! I no more believe Zofia is responsible for human-smuggling and mass murder than you are. I understand you don't want her dragged into this. But I *have to* know what you know. And I have to talk to her about what she knows. In order to clear your names and find out who's really responsible. Once I've done that, when you are debriefed, my notes will go in the trash, and no one will ever read them.'

'I've heard that before.'

'Not from me – when *I* handle what we call excess material in an investigation, it never becomes general knowledge and never gets out. Listen to me now! I won't get Zofia involved in this investigation. Nothing will happen to her. Nothing will happen to the boys. You have my word on it.'

Always alone.

Piet Hoffmann breathed in, breathed out.

Trust only yourself.

That's how he'd lived. Survived. But his mantra changed when he got involved with the detective sitting across from him. He'd come to understand that if you don't trust other people, you can still *choose* to do so. He'd chosen to trust Grens in Colombia. And now the mantra had changed again. Now he was *forced* to trust him. Trust that Ewert Grens would look out for his family. He knew as soon as he admitted Zofia's part in all this – that she was the link – that he was exposing his family to danger.

'Zofia.'

Hoffmann was still whispering, despite how loudly their neighbours laughed and toasted each other.

'She asked me to go. I don't exactly know why, I didn't care, you can ask her that. But the connection between the refugee couple, my phone, and my presence there, had something to do with her job. At the school where she works, our children's school, she teaches a few classes in French for unaccompanied refugee children. It was for the sake of one of them, a child who'd made that same trip, that I assisted the Nigerian couple – made sure they weren't fooled or robbed.'

For the first time since Grens placed four photographs on the table, Piet Hoffmann seemed to relax. He leaned back in the leather armchair, his face softened slightly, didn't seem quite as old.

He seemed to think giving the detective the next link in the chain meant this was over.

He had no idea.

'I have another mission, too. Which will only happen *if* I strike you off the list of suspects.'

'If?'

'If.'

Ewert Grens spoke more loudly, the merry group next to them had stood up and was headed for the bar behind the reception desk.

'You met the smugglers who guaranteed a safe trip that was anything but safe. You saw the man you describe as the leader. So for my sake I want you to do what you do best.'

'What are you trying to say, Grens?'

'I want you to look him up again. Infiltrate the organisation that young couple gave their money to. Find out the name of the Swedish contact person, whoever's profited from the people who suffocated in a container in Stockholm. You get me that name, Hoffmann, because I once travelled to Colombia for your sake. You asked how you could thank me. I told you I might have an answer one day. Here it is. Infiltrate them, ingratiate yourself, find that bastard's name. *Then* your debt will be paid, and you can go back to what you're doing now.'

Piet Hoffmann was armed. Ewert Grens had noticed the contours of a holster for a gun and knife under his jacket, his standard equipment, as soon as the former infiltrator stepped into the lobby. But despite the rage in Hoffmann's eyes, which at one time might have meant violence, Grens wasn't worried.

They weren't enemies any more, and never would be.

'No.'

'I want to catch that bastard.'

'Not even for your sake, Grens.'

'I want to catch their Swedish contact because that's my job. I can't do shit about the profiteers down here, that's somebody else's responsibility. But I can lock up whoever is operating in my territory and leaving mass graves in their wake.'

'Let's try this again – no.'

'No?'

'I'm never working for the Swedish police again. Nor any other police outfit, never.'

'This isn't the same as last time. We don't need you to unmask the whole organisation.'

'Have you already forgotten, Grens?'

'All you have to do this time is get me a lead on the name of the person in Sweden.'

'Because if you remember, then you must also remember that this never ends well. Isn't that true, Superintendent?'

Piet Hoffmann pushed his palms forcefully against leather armrests as he stood up.

'I just started a two-week leave. Then it's three months to the next one. That's what my contract looks like – four trips home a year. I have a ticket booked on the same plane as you, and I'm going to see my family. So tomorrow we'll be sitting next to each other eating plastic-wrapped plane food. You said it yourself, Grens. It's not my job to catch them, it's yours. Have a nice evening.'

And as he walked away through the deserted lobby, towards the front desk, and the hall that led to the elevators, he never looked back. Despite Grens's angry eyes drilling into him.

Sometimes a goodbye is just a goodbye.

A HOTEL ROOM IS a strange place. Four silent walls stand guard over a bed – usually the most intimate of places, where each night you meet your imaginary life in dreams – but this bed had yesterday hosted a stranger, and tomorrow will hold another.

Ewert Grens loathed hotel rooms.

Since Anni's illness, and eventual death, he'd chosen to live alone. He preferred it. He didn't need other people. But in a hotel room, loneliness was never beautiful – it was as ugly, sad, as imposing as those who feared it imagined.

He couldn't relax, definitely couldn't sleep. He sat down on the bed with the remote control in his hand and clicked, clicked, clicked his way from world to world, never registering any of them. It wasn't just the solitude dancing around and scoffing at him. Anger danced next to it, irritation and resignation just behind. Piet Hoffmann had stood up from the leather armchair and walked away. The only one with any access to the smugglers, who'd even met their leader and knew where he was. The only one who both the European and American police considered the most skilful infiltrator in the world, and therefore had the capacity to coax and dig up a Swedish name.

And who, despite all that, wouldn't do it.

Grens couldn't stand it any more, rode the elevator down to the hotel entrance, wandered out into a West African night that was still oppressively hot and much darker than other capitals. No neon signs flashed here, there weren't lights on in every window of every home – there was nothing artificial to make the darkness lighter like in the sky above Stockholm.

He started to walk. Not knowing where, just straight ahead, trying to force what rushed around inside him into temporary stillness. A street called Boulevard de l'Independance. Not much traffic, even though he was in the part of the city his map – which still lay in his hotel room – called downtown. Nor were there many red lights hanging at the intersections here, instead there were roundabouts, and when he walked straight across one he realised he was on a new street. At least according to the sign. Place des Martyrs. And maybe he should have turned around here, traced his way back, probably, and probably would have if his phone hadn't started ringing.

'Good evening, Ewert. I'm . . .'

Mariana's voice. According to the number on the display, she was calling from one of the police station's landlines.

'. . . putting you on speaker phone.'

Despite spending last night making her way underground through Stockholm, she was still at the office late. He smiled. Though of course she couldn't see that.

'I'll start with the container company. After that I have another thought to run by you. Then I'll hand you over to Sven for a report on the guide.'

They were both still there. And it didn't make him smile any less.

'The container is owned by a transport company in Gdansk. And that's also where the container was last emptied of goods. According to the available paperwork, it should have been left empty. From everything we and the Polish police have been able to gather, nobody in the company knew the container was being refilled with people.'

Grens listened to someone in a police station in Stockholm, where, as a police officer, he'd learned each street by heart. But here, in a different reality, he was trying to figure out where he was – turned around, turned around again.

'Are you listening, Ewert?'

'I'm listening.'

'It sounds like you're waving your cell phone around, it's breaking up a bit.'

'I got turned around. Now I'm not any more. Go on.'

One more turn.

And he decided to continue straight ahead for a while.

'I had another thought, Ewert. Somebody I'd like to look into more closely.'

'Oh?'

'The mortuary technician. The woman who found the first two bodies in the morgue.'

'What?'

'I want to poke around a little. She might know more than she's letting on.'

'No.'

'No?'

He remembered a pair of warm eyes.

A smile.

One that made even an old detective comfortable in the company of the dead.

'She's not mixed up in this.'

'Ewert, the bodies were found in *her* workplace.'

'Yes – and she called it in. Why would she do that if she were involved?'

'It would not be the first time a guilty person made sure they were included in our investigation by pretending to help. In order to maintain control. Observe. She was the one who gave us the list of all the people with keys, from the medical examiner to the guy who refills the coffee machine. And we interrogated every single one – *except her.* We never investigated *her* motives or alibi.'

Ewert Grens wanted to hang up and shout instead, loud enough to reach all the way to Mariana and the police station.

If she's involved – why did she call me? At home? Why did she put her hand on my arm? Why did I like her smile so damn much?

'Ewert?'

Sven's voice, it sounded tired, he obviously wanted to head home to his townhouse and Anita and Jonas.

'Yes?'

'Let's move on. Is that OK?'

'I'm listening.'

'We had a setback a few hours ago.'

'Oh?'

'We went back to the tunnels – and found him. The so-called guide. Near where our tip indicated. Dead. His heart punctured. Very little blood – a thin and sharp weapon. A professional hit. A killer who knows a small knife is much more effective than a large one that might bounce off a rib.'

Ewert Grens stopped.

Dead?

Him too?

'Ewert – they're not just planning to dump every body in the container one by one. They're tying up loose ends, eradicating any risk they might be discovered. We're sure it's the right person – in his little crawlspace in the tunnel wall the dogs found a large amount of hidden cash. New numbers series, money he must have got hold of recently, probably compensation for guiding those bodies through the tunnel. But even without the money we *know* it was him – his clothes and body had traces of ammonium phosphate on them. The flame retardant. He must have helped to carry them all the way from the pickup point.'

They're tying up loose ends, eradicating any risk they might be discovered.

Another link to the Swedish contact had been cut.

And suddenly his irritation caught up with him. The feeling he had temporarily managed to suppress started spinning around inside him.

He changed his mind.

He wasn't done with Hoffmann. He hadn't even started. If he couldn't convince the infiltrator by asking nicely, or even pleading, then he'd have to use another method.

Force him.

'Jerry?'

Grens didn't hear the first time. Somebody was shouting, but not at him.

'Jerry? Here! It's me!'

That voice. It was familiar.

He turned in the direction it was coming from. A car parked on the other side of the road.

'You lost, Jerry?'

Lost. Yes, he most certainly was. And he supposed he was Jerry.

It was the same taxi that took him from the airport to the hotel. The energetic driver with a gentle touch on the wheel. Grens walked over, the door to the passenger side was already open.

So they drove back. While Frederick – Grens had remembered his name, which pleased them both – laughingly explained how the street they were on changed names six times in just a matter of a few kilometres. At the hotel entrance they had the same discussion as last time about money – the taxi driver didn't want anything for the ride, but Grens insisted and put another five thousand West African francs into the driver's breast pocket.

Ewert Grens was still just as convinced.

If being nice didn't work, if begging didn't work, then only force remained.

He checked the lobby first, still just as empty as before, then had the front desk call Hoffmann's room, no answer, then looked into the bar.

There he stood.

A glass of Bantu beer in hand. In conversation with a huge blond man, much bigger than Grens himself, and with a heft that came from muscle.

The detective approached them, trying to catch Hoffmann's eyes.

'I'd like to talk to you for a moment.'

White walls. White counter on the bar. White air conditioners on the white walls. White TV on in the white bar.

Grens didn't see any of it.

'I'd like to do it now, and alone.'

'I'm in the middle of a conversation. As you can see.'

'Finish it.'

The huge blond man whose beard was as wild as Hoffmann's, seemed to have understood what Grens said, and it seemed to amuse him. He also seemed a bit drunk.

'So you have friends here, Koslow? Introduce me.'

From Denmark.

Copenhagen accent, Grens was sure of it.

'The name's Detective Superintendent Ewert Grens. I'd appreciate it if I could borrow your friend for a minute.'

The Dane stretched out a hand as huge as the rest of him.

'I'm Frank. Detective, you say? What the hell's my good friend done now?'

A loud laugh, husky from too much alcohol.

'This time, it's not about something he's done. It's about something he's *going to* do.'

Hoffmann and the Danish man, Frank, looked at each other, raised their glasses, toasted and drank. They hugged each other, and Grens thought he noticed a kind of intimacy between them; *Good luck in Zarzis – good luck with the wife*, and then while the Dane ordered a new beer, Hoffmann left the bar with the detective and settled down in the same seats as earlier.

'Koslow? So that's what you go by these days?'

'My mother's surname. One of many identities I've used over the years. I thought it suited this life, and it's actually one of two names I bear – along with Hoffmann – on a passport that's not false. Now that I'm walking the straight and narrow. And one thing you should know, Grens. You saved my life once. Maybe even twice. But you will never address me in that way again. Are we clear?'

Ewert Grens had heard Piet Hoffmann make threats before. And seen the consequences of that.

He had also received threats over the years and seen the consequences of that.

Therefore he could choose to challenge it.

And, in a way, would do so.

Soon it would be his turn to threaten Hoffmann.

'What you said. How you too used to earn money by reselling things. Drugs. That's what you were talking about.'

Piet Hoffmann nodded. That was exactly what he'd meant.

'But that's not entirely true, is it, Hoffmann?'

'Excuse me?'

'That you *earned* money selling drugs.'

'You've seen my record. You know it's true.'

'I mean – you're *earning* money on it. Still.'

Hoffmann leaned back in his armchair, shrugged slightly.

'What the hell are you talking about?'

'About this.'

From the inner pocket of his heavy jacket, Ewert Grens took out the envelope with four pictures of bodies. But that's not what he was searching for. It was something else, photographs and an excerpt from an international investigation, which he'd left in there last time, hoping not to use them.

'I've seen your damn pictures, Grens. They shook me, as you noticed. However, I'll have to thank you for your generous job offer, but no.'

'You didn't see them all.'

He now spread the envelope's remaining contents, which Sven sent here and instructed the hotel staff to print, across the table in front of them.

'What do you say about this, for example – a suitcase you might recognise?'

The first picture. A suitcase. The one Piet Hoffmann had packed in Colombia before his trip home, gone through customs with it, and then, on his way to prison, persuaded Ewert Grens to keep it in his office at the station.

'I didn't know what you asked me to do, Hoffmann. So there it stood in my little cupboard, stuffed between the uniforms I never use.'

Grens held up the next picture. A scan of a page from a preliminary investigation.

'Until this popped up from another case. A collaboration between Portuguese, Spanish, Dutch and Swedish police forces. And there in the middle of the investigation – a photo of a bag identical to yours! A narcotics ring that was taken down while smuggling via southern Spain and Gibraltar and Faro in Portugal. In the preliminary investigation the detectives were able to figure out how the drugs were being transported from South America. In *completely odourless* suitcases. Where the leather itself was made of cocaine, which a chemist had melted down and removed the scent from. If you look there, Hoffmann, on the next page, you'll find even more pictures of seized goods. All those suitcases are identical to the one I kept in my office for eight months.'

Piet Hoffmann let out a long, deep sigh, which seemed to emanate from his gut.

And then he laughed, not loudly, the kind that was as much *with* as *at*.

'Well I'll be. Our detective figured that out, too.'

'Yep. I didn't just figure it out. I *allowed* you to do it, even though I knew all this before I gave the bag back to you. Take a look at my very last photo . . . I promise, there are no more. I've documented how I scraped off a very small sample of the suitcase, which I keep in a plastic baggie in my office. And next to it, you'll see another image of where I've lifted a set of prints from that handle of the bag. Yours, of course.'

'So? And what does that prove?'

'That I thought you were worth it. A starting capital, since the police forces in two different parts of the world used you and threw you away the moment you became a liability. But it also shows I have something to hold you with – if I have to.'

Hoffmann laughed again, but with a slight change of tone, a touch of menace.

'If I go down for that, Grens, so will you. Since you kept it hidden rather than reporting it.'

'Maybe, maybe not. It'd be almost amusing to find out who the court chooses to believe. The detective superintendent who claims he's just now realised he was tricked. Or the ex-con who's left his fingerprints on it, just like he left his fingerprints on a satellite phone that was sewn inside a dead man's jacket. And *if* we both go down – who has more to lose? The old man with no family? Or the man a generation younger with a wife and two little boys who are trying to acclimatise to freedom in Sweden after years on the run for his sake?'

Grens knew in his heart that the Swedish police had already used and destroyed enough of this man sitting across from him. Nevertheless, Grens had made the choice to continue exploiting and destroying Hoffmann, to risk his life.

He'd learned this much as a police officer, always have a back-up plan in case of emergency.

And sometimes that's what happened.

An emergency.

'Hoffmann – I *will* report you. I *will* put you behind bars. You *will* be locked up for many years. If I have to.'

Piet Hoffmann sat quite still. He was used to weighing truth against lies, had often walked that thin line himself. And he did as before, let out a long, deep sigh. This time in resignation.

'Two weeks.'

'What?'

'As of tomorrow, I have two weeks' leave waiting for me. I'll give you that time, Grens – but not a minute more. Otherwise, I'd have to tell my employer or Zofia what's going on. And you – you burn what's in your safe box. Deal?'

'The faster I get that Swedish name, the faster this is over.'

'Grens. Deal?'

Two people who didn't trust anyone, but from now on they would have to trust each other.

'OK. *Then* I'll burn it.'

Ewert Grens reached his hand across the table, slowly and deliberately tearing up the photocopies that lay between them. It wasn't what Hoffmann meant, he knew that, but it was an attempt to show his goodwill. He started to rise and was halfway up when Piet Hoffmann put a hand on his arm, pushed him back down.

'One more thing, Grens, before you disappear into your room.'

The hand stayed there and Grens let it, even though that kind of touch felt like a blow and made him want to fight back.

'You think I'm going to infiltrate them? Seriously, Grens, in a couple of weeks? You have no idea what real infiltration work requires, what it's built on. Trust. The kind neither you nor I have. Slowly you build trust, do things to deserve it, use it to get what they don't want to give you. It cost me nine years to reach the heart of the Polish mafia, get all the way from Stockholm to Warsaw and a meeting with the Roof, the leader. It took me three years to reach the shadows in Colombia, gain access to the most inaccessible parts of the jungle. Grens – two weeks are all I'll give you, and how far that will get me you can calculate for yourself.'

'This is a much simpler organisation. We know that from experience. Human smugglers are divided into much smaller units than South American drug cartels.'

As he spoke, Grens stared at the hand on his arm, making it clear he didn't much care for it, so Piet took it away.

'Going undercover like that, it's . . . do you like food, Grens, making really good food?'

'Excuse me?'

'Infiltrating is like French slow cooking. But what you're asking me for is a hamburger at a fast food chain. And the kind of criminals who need to be infiltrated have one thing in common – they don't like fast food. They prefer slow cooking.'

'Then you'll have to work another way. And call it something else.'

'Such as?'

'Collision.'

'Collision?'

'Confrontation. The opposite of time. A surprise attack that opens all the doors at once.'

'And how, Superintendent, am I supposed to do that?'

Ewert Grens stood up again and no hand stopped him.

'I don't know. That's your job, Hoffmann. But I know more than you think – infiltration that takes a long time is built on lies, and what you have to do is give them some kind of time-sensitive lie, the kind that won't last long. That *will* end up being revealed. And *when* it is, not *if*, you have to be ready. Otherwise you die. Or they do.'

THE BED IN HIS room wouldn't need to be remade for the stranger who would sleep there tomorrow. Grens couldn't sleep, it was meaningless to even try. Maybe it was the heat. Or the energy it took to wrangle Hoffmann into doing what he wanted, and which had been replaced by emptiness when Grens succeeded. Or maybe it was being on the hunt for people who let others suffocate in containers. Or maybe it was the desolation of meeting a warm smile in a morgue, which now had to be investigated – the insight that *if* he met her again before this investigation was over, it would probably be across the table from her in an interrogation room.

All of it. At the same time.

So he returned to the darkness outside. It was his only night on this continent, and he walked the streets of the capital, ordered a glass of orange juice in a small café, a bowl of palm nut soup at a simple bar. And everyone he met was kind. Like a long line of Fredericks, but without taxis. And they seemed to live by a different clock – no one was in a hurry to go home, if there were customers, there was also time to serve them another portion. So when at five o'clock, with an hour left until dawn, he ordered a three-round-tea in a restaurant with just a couple of tables that was about to close, he was greeted with a smile and told to sit down. Three-round-tea used the same leaves each time, but got ever weaker, and that was compensated for by ever increasing sugar. The smiling restaurant owner explained, in an English that wasn't easy to understand, that the first cup tasted bitter like death, the second was mild like life, and, if you held on, the third slid down as sweetly as love.

Around seven o'clock he returned to the hotel. Relaxed and not nearly as tired as he should be. A morning with enough time for freshly brewed, strong Liberian coffee, before he had to go up to the room he'd do anything to avoid and pack his simple hand luggage and check out. He sat down in the lobby in a leather armchair, but closer to the front desk this time – you've got to mix things up. And ordered his coffee. Two cups from the start, might as well.

They were delicious, just like last night.

He'd just waved for a third cup when a familiar face gestured to the armchair opposite him.

'We meet again, Superintendent. May I sit here?'

The Foreign Ministry official. From the taxi. The one with the very proper business card.

'Thor. That's my name. No need to pretend, I see you desperately trying to remember.'

Grens smiled.

'Why not, give me some company, Thor.'

The light-coloured linen suit hung perfectly without clinging. Ewert Grens stared at it wistfully.

'Next time I'm here. I'll know how to dress.'

And shrugged his shoulders in his too heavy and too dark jacket.

'Or how not to dress.'

He ordered his next coffee. Two just like last time. One each.

'I'm waiting for my ride, Superintendent. I've been sitting outside the entrance for . . . well, almost half an hour. They can come in here and get me instead. That's how things work here. You have to adapt to it.'

'Early meetings?'

'UN representatives, Niger's Interior Minister, and Doctors Without Borders. We, Sweden that is, have requested a report on the situation while I'm here to see what they're talking about.'

'So you're some sort of . . . one-man delegation?'

'What you have to understand is that we have neither embassy nor consulate here. Nobody wants to open one in this part of the world. Swedish ambassadors would rather sip on sake in Tokyo or bustle from one DC cocktail party to another with a *New York Times* tucked under their arm. I'm one of those who picks up the slack for our Stockholm-based ambassadors. An expert. That's what I'm called.

Expert on humanitarian aid. Quite a big wad of cash – twenty billion from the Foreign Ministry, plus whatever comes through Sida. In my case, it's about deciding how we best invest in Niger, Burkina Faso, Togo, Benin and Mali. I've done this for many years – travelled to the poorest countries in West Africa – because no one else at the ministry wants to do it. Even though we could *really* make a difference here, unlike so many other places.'

'Don't forget your coffee. It's getting cold.'

'I help people. For real, Superintendent. And I've tried to do so from the start, even from a distance. I've tried to run projects that take on huge issues, but shockingly few of my colleagues in Stockholm care about those who need everything – education, housing, infrastructure, food. So instead I do it here, in a country where the life expectancy is very low – half of this country's population is under the age of fifteen. Half, Superintendent!'

Ewert Grens drank a third cup. He himself was close to retirement age and hated it. Lived in a country where the number of retirees was rising so fast it threatened the whole economy.

The world, it only got weirder.

'So they flee, Superintendent, it's no surprise. The fishing boats in the Mediterranean are filled with refugees that come from here. I see it all the time, smugglers recruiting their customers, getting paid out in the open. Risk free. It didn't used to be like that. It's a consequence of how Europe toughened their asylum policies.'

The civil servant looked sincerely committed. As if what he was saying was more than work for him. More than just wearing the perfect suit.

'And you, Superintendent? Have you found the answers you came here for?'

'I got exactly the answer I came here for.'

'So you learned something about who's responsible for the dead people in a container in a *Swedish* port?'

'I don't know more, yet. My trip here was more about methods and staff allocation.'

The official made it clear he didn't understand the last bit, and was about to ask a follow-up when he was interrupted. By a young man in a uniform with no insignia.

'Mr Cirrata?'

Grens guessed it must be the driver, he was even holding a sign in front of him as they often did – in sprawling, block letters.

'Seems that our paths are diverging again, Superintendent. I too am headed home tomorrow – just a quick visit. Have a good trip.'

The official stood up.

'Cirrata, Dixon?'

And then smiled a bit at Grens's question.

'The name of the UN representative I'll be meeting. As I said – things don't exactly run smoothly.'

Dixon smiled again, but he didn't make it far before he stopped and said hello to someone else. Grens stretched up, trying to see who it was. Someone he knew as well.

Hoffmann, that was who the official was talking to.

'It's very sad that private security folks like you, armed to the teeth, are our only chance of getting food trucks through. These attacks are disgusting! Destroying food! I'll never stop being astounded by my fellow human beings.'

They stood close enough, and Thor Dixon was loud enough for Grens to hear. What Hoffmann said, however, he couldn't catch. Or maybe he made no answer, maybe his only reply was a nod.

'But don't misunderstand me – you're doing a fantastic job out there. Absolutely crucial. I hope you know that.'

Piet Hoffmann nodded again in response to the praise he and his colleagues had just been given, then they continued in opposite directions. The Foreign Ministry official towards the hotel's exit, Hoffmann towards the reception and Grens.

'Good morning. Have you been waiting for me again, Superintendent?'

They looked at each other hesitantly, yesterday evening floating like a cloud between them. And did what people do when they're trying to get closer – talked about something else.

'So you two know each other, Hoffmann?'

'Excuse me?'

'You and the Foreign Ministry fellow?'

'We've seen each other around. There aren't that many nice hotels to choose from.'

The cloud refused to clear. Grens had no choice.

'Yesterday, Hoffmann.'

He'd have to be the one to bring up what was on both their minds – after all, he was the one who came here with only one mission, and he was the one headed home again.

'I apologise. For . . . well, taking it so far. Maybe too far. But I . . . well, I had to.'

Ewert Grens gestured to the armchair across from him, just as he did yesterday, and Hoffmann made it clear he had no intention of sitting down again.

'You did what you needed to do.'

And maybe there was some hint of smile hiding on that tight face.

'You were able to reel me in in two meetings, Grens. You know how long it took Wilson? Four months. You got me to agree to be an infiltrator again after two meetings of twenty-five minutes.'

They didn't hug or shake each other's hands. But the smile – which Grens was sure he saw – it made him feel better about heading to the airport without Hoffmann.

'If you'll excuse me. I'm going to sit on the other side of the lobby. Alone. There's better reception there. I'm going to have to make a call, tell them I'm not coming home today, tell Zofia and the boys they'll have to wait three months.'

Ewert Grens was wrong. It didn't feel any easier.

'I'll . . . I'll keep an eye on them.'

'Grens, promise me one thing, that you'll stay the hell away from them, and from me when this is all over.'

'Your work will not affect them, Hoffmann, *that* I can promise you. OK?'

Piet Hoffmann didn't answer the older policeman who'd travelled halfway across the world to force him into infiltrating again. He walked away instead, over to the other part of the lobby, sat down with his back to the front desk. He'd promised never to do this to her again. Lie to her. Just to make it easier. Just to keep her from worrying.

'Good morning, my love.'

'Good morning, Piet.'

Zofia answered immediately. He could see her in front of him in the kitchen getting breakfast ready for everyone. He remembered how she'd described his nine-year lie, his double life in parallel worlds. For her and the boys – a husband and father, running a private security firm. And at the same time – he'd been a man immersed in the criminal world, risking his life every day on an undercover assignment for the Swedish police.

A betrayal greater than having another woman.

That's what she'd said when he was forced to tell her.

That the entangled lies were beyond her reach.

That another woman would have been simpler, she would have existed, you could have seen her, hated her, had a clear reason to leave.

She hadn't left, hadn't given up.

And since then he'd always told her the truth. Even when they were on the run, in the evenings while Rasmus and Hugo slept, discussing what it means to kill other people in order to survive themselves.

Until now.

'Zofia?'

'Yes?'

'I'm not coming home tonight.'

She didn't say anything. But didn't hang up. He heard her walking around the kitchen, a chair scraping, the clattering of a porcelain dish.

'Zofia?'

A toaster being started. Of all the sounds, how could he recognise that?

'Zofia? Talk to me.'

'You're not coming home?'

'The famine here is acute. We need to do another transport.'

'And when did you find that out?'

'Late last night.'

It was that easy. To lie. He'd assumed he'd be out of practice. But it came back to him as easily as if he'd never stopped.

'We're headed out on the first transport today. But I'll call you, just like always, every morning.'

More porcelain clinking. Maybe Rasmus's spoon on his bowl, always filled to the brim with vanilla yoghurt, or Hugo slicing his hard-boiled egg right on his dish.

'I'm putting you on speakerphone, Piet, in the middle of the breakfast table as usual – the boys just sat down.'

Her voice was neither annoyed nor disappointed. Neutral, that was how it sounded. Which was the worst.

'Hello, my boys.'

'Hi, Papa!'

Rasmus. But not Hugo.

'Are you there, Hugo?'

'Mmm. I'm here.'

Always so serious.

Their eldest son always understood so much more than he and Zofia realised.

'Good, what are you—'

'What time are you coming tonight?'

Hugo. As if he knew.

'I . . . have to stay. A little longer.'

'You're not coming home?'

'Hugo, I—'

'Are you coming or not?'

'Not tonight.'

A chair scraping on the floor again. Quick footsteps. And a door closing, probably the front door.

'Hello?'

'Hugo left, Papa.'

'He left?'

'Yes. He left yesterday, too. When you had to call back because you were shooting at each other. He sat on the front steps and waited until we went to school.'

Like a punch to the gut. And another one to the head.

Hugo had . . . heard the shots? Interpreted them? Had been worried?

Even Rasmus heard and understood. Or maybe Hugo told him later.

As parents they'd convinced themselves they'd been able to protect two small boys from the reality of the lives they'd led for so long.

But the whole time, they knew, understood.

For the second morning in a row Hugo had left the breakfast table, their daily moment of togetherness and he – just as Zofia said she used to – closed his eyes and pretended it was just an ordinary breakfast with an ordinary family.

Piet Hoffmann squeezed the phone.

He *had to* make it home.

He *had to* sit at that breakfast table, for real, just as he'd promised. Even if it was just one morning, one breakfast.

They'd already talked about it, he and Grens, when you have only fourteen days to infiltrate, get to the heart of a criminal organisation, you have to work in another way. Which of course was also true if you have only thirteen, twelve, or maybe even eleven days.

Collision.

That's how Ewert Grens put it.

Confrontation. The opposite of time. A surprise attack that opens all the doors at once.

Piet Hoffmann sat in that deserted section of the lobby with a silent phone in his hand, as if he could hold onto Zofia's and Rasmus's and Hugo's voices. He was going to leave immediately, head north to another place where the stream of refugees had left its traces. He'd already decided. If it was possible to implement the impossible in two weeks, maybe he could do it even faster than that.

PART FOUR

A PERSON LOOKS DIFFERENT from eight hundred and sixty-one metres away. Sharper.

His face was more elongated than he remembered.

His nose a bit wider, his chin weaker, his sideburns shaggy and with a smattering of grey that hadn't been obvious from just a few metres distance.

Piet Hoffmann squeezed the rifle in his hands. He read the thermometer that lay in front of one of his elbows – twenty-four degrees. He examined the single tree that stood far down by one of the harbour's piers next to a deserted warehouse – its leafy branches swayed, which meant a wind force of ten, maybe even twelve metres per second.

He turned the little screw gently, one notch.

TPR one. Transport right one.

Turned it again, one notch.

TPR one. Transport right one.

Perfect.

He had a clear view.

The rifle was loaded with the kind of bullet that made only a small entry hole, but, after a explosion, left a huge exit wound.

And he aimed, as he often did when he had time, at the point right between the eyebrows.

I remember how you, and the man I killed yesterday, waited for us.

Just there, outside that building, where you're standing right now.

I remember how you – in your heavily accented English, with its surprisingly good vocabulary, and the grammar of someone who was well-educated – took that young couple's life savings and guaranteed them and me safe passage for the whole of their journey.

Piet Hoffmann felt it every time.

How strange it was to be so close to someone through his rifle scope.

As if he were standing beside the man he was aiming at, part of the object blinking its eyes and wetting its lips with the tip of his tongue.

It was not often Hoffmann used the bipod. But with a wind that reached the roof he was lying on in erratic gusts, hitting both him and the sniper rifle, he did. And then – wary movements as he followed the man who was now back in the big room.

Hoffmann had never been inside.

Neither had the two refugees. They weren't allowed access.

The smuggling organisation's headquarters.

That's where the man he was aiming at was walking around. Really more of a hall than a room. But sparsely furnished with simple desks and equally simple chairs and shelves. Once upon a time it was probably a warehouse or factory of some kind – heavy iron beams hung like parallel bridges in the air above the man's head.

He'd introduced himself, they all had during their exchange, and Hoffmann was trying to remember his name. Neither the smuggler he killed yesterday nor his more eloquent boss had a name he could remember. He couldn't even remember the names of the refugee couple. He hadn't been that interested. Didn't know he'd need to.

But I do remember how excited the young woman and man were, almost giddy. Even though they'd just finished a four day long, non-stop journey through the desert.

I remember where they were looking – forward, not back.

Possibilities, not problems.

A new life, not the old one.

There was another room adjacent to the hall. That's where the smuggler headed now. Hoffmann left the head and its wrinkled forehead, aimed instead at the door the smuggler was opening. Armoured. Heavy. The sort of door that led to something valuable.

The man unlocked it with a key and disappeared. Piet Hoffmann waited.

The smuggler would soon come out again, the rifle scope would keep following his face, as it gradually got more moist, a shiny film of sweat despite the late evening.

One minute. One minute more.

Whatever he was doing behind that safe-like door, it took time.

Hoffmann's hands shook a little in the fickle wind, but he never lost his target through the scope. With the change in wind came the smell of cooking. A few metres in front of him, at the western edge of the hotel roof, two rusty chimneys pumped out the scents of the restaurant kitchen – fried meat, probably lamb.

It came unexpectedly, a sigh from so deep inside it filled his entire stomach and chest and pressed against his throat.

As when you're filled with longing.

Right about now he would have been landing at Arlanda airport, in another hour he'd be in Zofia's arms, sitting on the edges of two sleepy boys' beds, listening to their slow, even breathing.

But it had turned into another kind of trip. Helicopter. The South African they called Rob – who regularly lent his air fleet to the private security firm when a transport needed guarding from above – had, in exchange for a good amount of American dollars, personally escorted Hoffmann to Libya. Without asking any questions that couldn't be answered. They crossed the Sahara above a route traversed by camel caravans for hundreds of years, and landed just outside Zuwara, the port city he'd described to Grens as the most popular human smuggling gateway to Europe on the Mediterranean Sea. Grens – who'd sent Hoffmann here – was probably at this very moment landing in Arlanda, maybe passing by the baggage carousel and heading towards the Arlanda Express train and Stockholm. Headed home, unlike him.

That deep sigh again, it grabbed hold of him, shook him from inside as much as the wind did from outside.

Hugo's voice.

It had said everything. Meant everything.

His father should be there.

Piet and Zofia Hoffmann's firstborn, who understood so much, also needed to know he could keep sitting at that same breakfast table, that his new old life was real, would continue to be real. They belonged there. Without the trust of his two sons, their father's life meant nothing.

There.

The steel-plated door was opened and closed again. Hoffmann waited until the leader turned around, then he put his scope back on his forehead, got in close to the skin, still a shiny sweat, which had begun to flow from his temples and down his cheeks. When the man had walked all the way back to his desk, Hoffmann pulled the bolt upward and towards him, thinking of a young, giddy couple.

You're no longer alive. No longer breathing.

Can't smell, see, hear, feel.

You don't exist.

Because what that man promised – that man walking around behind a window exactly eight hundred and sixty-one metres away – wasn't worth shit. You took my hand, you piece of shit, you took their life savings, and you let them die.

Piet Hoffmann squeezed the weapon.

The trigger.

He had a clear shot again. Right between the eyebrows.

And he thought as he'd taught himself to think.

You or me.

And I care more about me than about you, so I choose me.

EWERT GRENS YAWNED, STRETCHED a little, rolled over the much too soft edge of the brown corduroy sofa, and, still half-asleep, sat up. He'd travelled straight from Arlanda to the Kronoberg police station, lay down without even taking off his jacket, just to rest for a minute – and apparently fell asleep. Missing a night on another continent had led to the sort of sleep he seldom experienced, deep and dreamless.

He stared unseeingly out through the window at the courtyard of the City Police station, waiting to wake up. It was a beautiful day. Sunny with no wind, but still cool out, he was wearing the right clothes again.

The coffee machine in the corridor was humming and puffing as it sometimes did when it was close to done. Button 38, black, two cups. Button 39, with milk, one cup. Button 40, with milk and sugar, one cup. He knocked first on Mariana Hermansson's door, then Sven Sundkvist's, they both looked at him and his small tray of steaming plastic mugs, and he didn't need to say anything. They left whatever they were doing and headed to their boss's office for a morning meeting.

'Hoffmann, Ewert?'

'Hoffmann.'

In the time it took Grens to knock back two cups of coffee and his guests a half-cup, he recounted his meeting at a hotel in a West African capital that neither Mariana nor Sven could find on a map, or had even heard of.

'*The* Piet Hoffmann, Ewert?'

'The Piet Hoffmann.'

'And you believe him?'

'Yes. I believe him when he says he's down there doing something legally for once – that he doesn't have any connections with those smuggling organisations. I believe he was acting on behalf of his wife, who was in turn acting on behalf of one of her students, when he helped that young couple hand over their life savings. And I believe his claim that he gave them the satellite phone for emergencies and urged them to sew it into the fabric of the jacket. A new and unused phone. That's how Hoffmann and his City Police handler Erik Wilson worked here in Stockholm, and how Hoffmann and his DEA handler Lucia Mendez worked in Colombia.'

Detective Superintendent Grens understood that he had to wait for them to catch up. He himself had spent a day and a very long flight arriving at these conclusions – Sven and Mariana would need a few minutes.

'Hoffmann always had access to several phones. And always carried several SIM cards. When you've been living a certain way long enough, you don't give up those habits lightly. It becomes a part of you. You become a part of them.'

He yawned again, apologised, and considered telling his colleagues about how their boss walked through the African night trying to escape a hotel bed that scared the shit out of him. But he didn't. Fear was too intimate. It was like love. If you share it, you expose yourself, make yourself vulnerable.

'The fingerprints on the phone we found in the jacket of the dead young man were Hoffmann's. And they led us to the starting point of the refugees' journey. Now we know how the trip began. But we know nothing about how the trip ended. About the smuggling organisation's Scandinavian branch. About who tried to camouflage bodies in foam and went to the trouble of dumping them in Stockholm's various morgues instead of simply burning the contents of the container – like most killers would. About who got paid, *here*, who's sitting around counting their money in our city, waiting for the next load of people.'

'The phone you're talking about, Ewert . . .'

Mariana Hermansson had put a folder on the rickety coffee table when she sat down in one of the visitors' chairs.

'. . . it's – still – all we have.'

Now she threw the coffee cups and an empty aluminium tray that had once held a small prepackaged cake into the trash, then spread the contents of her folder across the empty surface of the table. Documents that looked like the kind of phone call lists that it had become increasingly difficult to access since the telecom companies chose to hinder police investigations by repeating the word integrity.

'One of our newly employed forensics technicians, Ewert, has done some amazing work.'

'Who?'

'Does it matter?'

'It matters.'

'Yes, I suppose it does, doesn't it, Ewert? It's nice to know if you're appreciated by your boss, for example. Right?'

She looked at him. As only she could. A demanding look. And she was right. He was bad at showing appreciation, giving praise. It sounded . . . yes, insincere. Always stuck in his mouth.

'If I may continue, undisturbed?'

That look again.

It saw straight through him.

He was quite fond of it.

'Continue, Hermansson.'

She grabbed the documents, held them up.

'The satellite phone Hoffmann gave the refugee couple was the same Japanese brand that many terrorists have used recently. We do come across it sometimes in our investigations but rarely manage to get access to it. We don't have those kinds of resources. Or – we *didn't* have those resources. Because our new technician broke in. I don't know how, but he did. He created a key code and decrypted the phone – was able to look straight into the satellite network. Therefore, we know it's only been used a total of eight times. Once for an outgoing call. Seven times for incoming. The outgoing call was made, according to our technician – Billy is his name, by the way, if you're still wondering, Ewert, and he's all of twenty-eight years old – in a warehouse in a port city called Zuwara, somewhere along the Libyan coast.'

Zuwara.

Ewert Grens stopped listening for a moment.

The port town Hoffmann had told him about. The place he was headed to. Where he probably was right now.

'That outgoing call, it . . . are you with me, Ewert?'

'What?'

'Are you following?'

'I am.'

Mariana Hermansson took a deep breath and started over.

'The outgoing call was made sixteen days ago from a warehouse in an African port city on the Mediterranean. Late at night, 23.42. One minute and twenty-two seconds long. And it was made to – and this is the interesting part, Ewert – to *the same* number that later accounts for all seven incoming calls. Not a single one was answered. Just like the last one you yourself saw and didn't answer. Seven missed calls from one and the same unregistered number. Calls made *after* this container came ashore in Sweden. With the dead already inside it.'

The next document was actually in seven parts – one for each incoming and missed call. The eighth document summarised them with purple coloured lines and rings on a map of southern Stockholm.

'The lines here, Ewert, in purple – yes I know, I didn't have any other pen – correspond to the outer boundary of an area that covers only a few square kilometres. An almost triangular frame with Nynäsvägen bordering the east, Sockenvägen to the south and west, and Enskedevägen to the north. Inside the triangle, Ewert, you'll see seven just as purple rings. Those seven missed calls. The seven places where those calls were placed from.'

'The same number?'

'Yes.'

'From the same geographical area?'

'Yes.'

The detective superintendent looked at Hermansson, then at Sven who nodded slowly.

They all had the same thought.

'The couple had someone waiting for them.'

Sven put it into words.

'Someone who missed them.'

Ewert Grens stayed in that corduroy sofa for a long time after they left.

He didn't want to go over to his desk with its huge collection of yellow sticky notes, which always piled up during an investigation. Phone numbers scribbled down by some poor schmuck at the switchboard or in the department hallway, messages from pushy journalists seeking answers investigators didn't yet have. In the end, he'd take care of them in the same very satisfying way as always – push them all bit by sticky bit across his desk and into the bin.

He had more pressing things to do right now.

Because someone was making billions off the flow of refugees through strict border controls.

Because criminals rarely get caught the first time and therefore repeat their crimes.

Because the Swedish smuggler probably wasn't just waiting for the next transport, he'd surely *already* received containers filled with people.

Grens recalled his conversation with Piet Hoffmann in a deserted hotel lobby – that it had been for the sake of an unaccompanied refugee child, *who'd made the same journey*, that Zofia asked him to assist the refugee couple.

That's just how it was.

That's where his search would take him next. The refugees who had made the same trip in a container and disembarked at Värta Harbour – alive – had seen the faces of the people who opened and closed those container doors. And might be able to identify employees of the organisation responsible for a mass grave. But voluntarily stepping forward was the same as risking it all. It was therefore Ewert Grens's task to track down whoever was anxiously still calling, and who *might have* made the same trip themselves.

The detective superintendent started to rush through the corridors towards Bergsgatan. All his fatigue forgotten. With every step he became more convinced that someone knew what one of those bastards looked like. And he was pretty sure where to start searching.

In the area on Hermansson's map with all the purple rings.

The same area where he'd found himself two mornings ago.

The same area he'd already planned to interview someone later today.

The area where the Hoffmann family lived.

PIET HOFFMANN LAY EVEN closer to the two rusty chimneys than he had the night before. The restaurant kitchen puffing in his direction smelled different in the early morning. Fried lamb and spices had been replaced by freshly baked bread and *bazin*, and also that cumin-spiced soup.

The hotel's flat roof with its view over Zuwara would soon be hot against his stomach as the sun slowly climbed a clear blue sky. He balanced on his elbows and aimed his sniper rifle at the same building as yesterday evening. Five faces were squeezed into the magnification of the scope. That's how many he'd seen through the window on the second floor – but he guessed there was one more. Because the five men occasionally turned towards the part of the room Hoffmann had started calling the Safe Room yesterday – the safe-like door was open, and they seemed to be talking to someone who was inside. There were six, maybe seven people. Two of them bodyguards, judging by their outfits and equipment. He'd been prepared for this number of them.

He slid down the fire escape on the outside of the building, which led him to the top floor and another wide-open window – to his own hotel room. He placed the weapon in its case and hung the *do not disturb* sign on his door, left the room and took the elevator down to the entrance – unfortunately, where he was headed, he'd have to go unarmed.

A morning walk through the beautiful narrow streets of a busy port city. Ten comfortable minutes to enjoy the gentle sea air before the arrival of intense heat. Or that could have been the case. But this was something else entirely. A walk straight into a deliberate collision.

The tall iron gate that separated the street from the harbour screeched as it glided up, just like the last time he'd found himself *inside* it – just a half-step behind two refugees who relied on him for protection, as they handed over a brown envelope to the man with a wide nose, weak chin and shaggy sideburns. In the middle of the night, Piet Hoffmann had suddenly remembered his name. He'd been sleeping restlessly in the way he often did these days – he and Hugo were both the type to push their sweaty sheets onto the floor during the night. At around three, as he groped for the pillow that had somehow slid away into the darkness, in that state between waking and dream, the name materialised. Omar. That's how the smuggler had introduced himself last time. It was Omar he'd been aiming at.

And it was Omar's car he was approaching now – the one the front man had arrived in yesterday evening when Hoffmann was watching from his vantage point on the roof. A car parked near the lowest step of the worn concrete staircase that led up to their headquarters, reminiscent of the military vehicles elite soldiers used in active war zones. Designed to handle both shelling and mines, equipped with thermo-cameras to navigate through smoke bombs and live fire, which even had a small shooting hatch you could open in the windscreen to return fire.

Apparently, Omar didn't feel particularly safe.

That's the kind of man who's hardest to convince, takes the longest to win over.

Piet Hoffmann looked around, then dropped when he saw the coast was clear, crept under the car near the front left wheel. Connected a small GPS with a powerful magnet. It was always good to know where the boss was.

He got up, brushed off the fine-grained sand, which covered everything with a layer of dust.

The room he'd been monitoring and was now heading towards had a window with a small ventilation hatch at the bottom, and it was through that he detected a very familiar smattering of sound. He pushed open the unlocked front door – they weren't expecting visitors – and quietly climbed the stairs to the second-floor headquarters of this North African smuggling organisation, and the sounds he heard got louder.

A currency counter.

The reward for all their extensive criminal activities. That moment when all your cash is placed into the top of the machine, counted, sent to the tray at the bottom.

Hoffmann stood motionless outside the last door. He could hear their voices. Almost touch the cigarette smoke. Feel the vibrations of fans spinning high in the ceiling.

And then he did as he always did when it was a matter of survival. Breathed in, breathed out, pulled the air deep into his diaphragm until it turned to stillness. Gathering all his thoughts, all his vigilance, into the here and now, as he put his hand on the door handle and pushed down.

He knew that he had no choice.

He knew this was the only way to reach these kind of people fast.

He had to confront them.

———

The larger room of the smugglers' headquarters was filled with thick tobacco smoke and sweaty faces and eager voices trying to be heard over a machine counting tens of thousands of dollars and millions of West African francs. Piet Hoffmann stepped straight into the room and headed in the direction of Omar, who was casually leaning back in a chair with one foot on a desk. The two younger men closest to him stood up immediately, while the two Hoffmann assumed were bodyguards acted the part – cutting off his path and pulling out their weapons. One pistol, one revolver. Only one man remained in his seat, and in a way Hoffmann knew this meant he was pretending to be unconcerned – the man with the weak chin. Omar. With a discreet nod, he indicated to his bodyguards that they should search their uninvited guest, and afterwards another nod said the uninvited visitor could approach him.

'I recognise you. We met before – a month ago, was it? If you want to meet . . .'

Omar spoke just as calmly and in the same flawless but accented English as last time, with his head slightly bent forward. The look in his eyes could mean almost anything.

'. . . we'll do it out there – just like always when our passengers purchase their tickets. No matter who they have accompanying them.'

He nodded a third time, which meant *get the fuck out of here.*

Piet Hoffmann didn't leave, he stood where he was and deliberately lowered his voice – less risk of it breaking, of revealing what an impossible balancing act this actually was.

'I think I'll stay here. And you, Omar, if that's your name – you have a choice to make.'

One second.

'Either hire me. Or . . .'

A lie that will be tested in a single second.

'. . . I kill you . . .'

The time it takes for someone to weigh, evaluate.

The rest, the other time, is what it takes to make a decision, act.

'. . . too.'

He hadn't even finished his sentence before the two bodyguards stepped between him and the leader's desk, a wall of adrenalin and rage, while the other two ran over to Hoffmann and grabbed each of his arms from behind.

'Now let's see here . . .'

Omar's voice was still just as calm – Hoffmann was sure it was *feigned* unconcern.

'. . . what exactly are you saying? Am I getting this right, you walk in here and, and, how shall I say this, you *threaten me*?'

Piet Hoffmann stayed centred in that way that meant survival.

And therefore visualised his own death.

'Yes. I'm threatening you, Omar.'

Then Zofia's death, Rasmus's death, Hugo's death. He had to feel it – fear.

'Because I want you to listen to me, Omar.'

His own fear worked inversely – it forced him to act.

Because the person who has everything to lose is always the most dangerous.

'And if you don't do what I want, Omar, I will kill you. Just like your co-worker did when *he* didn't listen to me.'

'My co-worker?'

'Yes. Exactly.'

Piet Hoffmann relaxed, stopped resisting for a few seconds. And at the very moment the young man holding his left arm also unconsciously relaxed, let go. Long enough for Hoffmann to reach into his hunting vest and take out a USB stick.

'I'm pretty good with a sniper rifle. And that's what I use these days. I've mounted a camera on it.'

He threw the USB stick onto the desk. It landed not far from Omar's hand.

'On that little piece of plastic you'll find three short films. The first one is twelve seconds long and gives a pretty good picture of how I finished off one of your employees yesterday – he was with you the last time we met.'

Omar finally showed some reaction. Not much, but it was enough. His eyes roamed, not long, but clearly. He stretched his neck slightly. And his breathing temporarily became uneven.

The men in the room had known their colleague had been shot. Now they also knew by whom.

'He was shot while attacking a food transport that it was my job to protect. In the left temple. Distance – three hundred and twenty-four metres. He never should have bent down to pick up that grenade launcher. And after you've watched that, Omar, as a bonus, take a look at the other two movies I recorded using the same rifle. One filmed last night from fourteen hundred and fifty-three metres, *a clear shot* if I'd taken it, at a beautiful farm outside Zuwara – my target was your wife standing at her kitchen window, specifically her forehead. And another from eight hundred and sixty-one metres away – that was filmed a couple of hours later from a hotel roof of this very room, my rifle scope focused on you and that same point in between your eyebrows.'

He smiled at the armed and ready bodyguards who separated them.

'And your other . . . well, co-workers, the ones who are supposed to protect you, were standing outside the entrance of this building not paying nearly as much attention as now – because they didn't notice a damn thing.'

Hoffmann stretched out and pushed the piece of plastic across the table with a left hand that lacked an index and middle finger. Damp marks on the surface of the plastic from three fingertips as he dropped it in front of Omar.

'I could have killed you – one shot, one hit – but chose not to. That's why you're alive. And why you're going to hire me.'

They threw themselves at him. Eight arms pushed Hoffmann down hard onto the floor, while Omar slowly stood up and grabbed the revolver from a well-worn leather holster clearly visible beneath his white shirt. They tossed him down because Piet Hoffmann let them do it – even expected and prepared for it. Omar pushed the steel barrel of the gun against the soft skin of the forehead and stared into his eyes, which he'd learned was the best way to reach and control another person's soul. Hoffmann met those eyes with a cockiness he didn't really have, but *had to* convince them he did. The more clearly he imagined Zofia and Rasmus and Hugo dying, the less important his own death seemed, and the more strength he found to meet and return Omar's intense look. And, after what he guessed was forty-five to sixty seconds, the pressure on his forehead decreased slightly. The need to figure out who this person was who came bursting in here claiming he killed one of the members – who had even shown a willingness as recently as yesterday evening to kill one of their leaders – was far greater than the more natural response of meeting a death with a death.

'Who are you?'

Omar didn't scream, he wasn't the kind. In control. Even when he turned his gun and pistol-whipped Piet Hoffmann in the head.

'Answer my question, please.'

Another hit. Against the hairline, where forehead met temple.

The blood ran down both of Hoffmann's cheeks, dripping onto the concrete floor.

'Who the hell are you – and why in hell would we ever consider hiring you?'

His stare that had to remain steady.

He had to direct it at those eyes that demanded answers.

Just like he had to direct his words.

'Who am I?'

For as long as he could remember he'd always used the name that best suited his purpose. He'd been so many different people, crept into bodies with one identity and crawled out of them with another. After Erik Wilson recruited him in prison, and as he gradually transformed himself into an infiltrator with a serious criminal record burrowing his way into organised crime in order to unmask it, he'd assumed the code name Paula. When he was forced to flee, and ended up working undercover for the DEA to take down a South American drug cartel from inside, he became El Sueco in the jungle and Peter Haraldsson at home in Cali – the city he lived in with his family. Lies, truth, it had been difficult to know where the line ran, to even remember if there *was* a line.

Now he was going to use one of his real names. The time was too limited to create a background story tight enough to hold up to questioning. He'd have to use the same name, the same identity as when he was hired by the South African security firm. He would, for the first time since he infiltrated a criminal network, do it under the name he was born to.

'Piet Koslow.'

Omar pistol-whipped him – again. A horizontal motion that cut the cigarette smoke in two, a stroke that landed just above the right ear.

'Who the *fuck* is Piet Koslow? And *how the fuck* are we supposed to use him?'

The five faces Hoffmann had studied through his rifle sight belonged to the five men holding his arms, holding his legs, manhandling him. Now a sixth person stepped into the human-smugglers' headquarters. From the adjoining room with the open safe-like door, which these five kept turning and talking to earlier, though Piet couldn't make out to whom from the hotel roof. Footsteps with hard heels bounced against the concrete walls, shoes that were quite different from the mix of trainers and worn men's shoes that Hoffmann stared at from his place on the ground so far. Another leader of the organisation. You could see it, feel it. Someone with power, and in charge of what they stored in the Safe Room – and the currency counting.

Hard high heels, a woman's shoes.

She was short and smelled of expensive perfume, dressed in a blouse and long trousers, glasses with gold-plated metal frames – surely they *weren't* solid gold? – which she pushed up into her shoulder-length dark hair. Thirty, thirty-five at the most. She reminded Hoffmann of the women Zofia was friends with when she studied economics at Stockholm University, single-minded and academic and beautiful in a way that was very self-aware.

The Accountant.

That's how he'd think of her.

———

'So you think we should hire you?'

She spoke softly, almost a whisper.

And she had green eyes.

He saw them as she leaned down towards him.

'Yes. I do.'

And her calm was different to Omar's, she wasn't pretending. She didn't need to, those who are convinced they're superior don't.

'I don't believe in religion. Do you, Koslow? If that's really your name.'

'That's my name.'

'I don't believe in religion – and I don't believe in ideologies. But you know what I do believe in?'

She didn't look away from Piet Hoffmann as she pointed to Omar's desk and the USB stick, and through some barely noticeable gestures managed to make her colleague understand she wanted a computer to plug it into.

'Money. I believe in money, Koslow. What do you believe in strongly enough to make Omar and me even consider hiring you?'

———

Hoffmann was just about to answer when Omar asked her to come to his desk and watch what was on the computer screen. At least that's what Hoffmann assumed was said in Arabic, a language he didn't know – not the Libyan dialect or any other. And while the two leaders bent over in concentration and followed the sequences recorded by a sniper's webcam, he looked around carefully.

New computers at every work station.

Binders and filing cabinets neatly arranged.

Excel sheets spread across the desktop.

A professional organisation, like many businesses in the underworld, making sure to record income and expenses. The prerequisite for various actors working together towards the same goal, making sure everyone got their share of the profits. You have to know how much money is circulating in order to maintain trust. That's how the East European Mafia had worked in the Warsaw headquarters and with its partners across northern Europe. That was how the South American drug cartel was held together across its chain of employees, from production to transport to consumption.

'You want to know . . .'

'Shhhhh.'

'. . . what I believe in?'

'Not yet.'

The Accountant used her right index finger in a way Hoffmann had only seen among mafia bosses demanding obedience. Wagging it slightly in the air. Left, right, left. And this time it meant *stay on the floor and shut up*. He wondered if she'd seen someone else do it and purposely copied it, or if it just came naturally in that kind of hierarchy.

She turned back to the computer and pulled her shiny glasses from her hair in order to get a better look. The screen reflected in them. So the three sequences recorded by Piet Hoffmann were – as he watched them from on his back – mirrored there, but significantly reduced in scale. Still clear enough as the Accountant and Omar, who never exchanged a word, continued to replay them. Once. Twice. Three times. And when they, for the fourth time, moved the time marker backwards and watched as their employee had his head blown off, and saw Omar and his wife recorded through that same rifle scope, it was clear they'd concluded the claims of their visitor on the floor really *were* true.

'A strange way to try to show us your power.'

The Accountant looked at him as she spoke, her eyes still just as calm and arrogant. But now there was also a restrained and ticking aggressiveness, a dark emptiness to drown in – one that wasn't there before.

The four employees holding him securely were all capable of killing him, just like Omar.

But *she* was truly dangerous.

'If that's what you were going for.'

Hoffmann shook his head slightly.

'No. Not power. It's not about that.'

'Proving that you can kill us, that's power. Just as Omar could choose to discharge his weapon into you while you lie there – powerless.'

Her whispered English was just as competent and grammatically correct as Omar's. But lacked the heavy North African accent – she spoke as if she'd been educated abroad.

'And maybe we should do that, Omar? Pull the trigger? Just because we can?'

And when she smiled a little too long, with lips as thin as they were taut, she really seemed like a person who would give that command – just because she could.

'Not power – trust. That's what I wanted to show.'

'Trust? By coming here and trying to . . . threaten us? OK. Fine. Here's what we're going to do – if I don't like the next sentence that comes out of your mouth, then I *will* encourage Omar, really urge him, to pull the trigger. I think you can tell by now that's how things work, right? And then, when my suggestion has been followed, I'll contact the police sources we work with. I'll explain you broke in, an unlawful intrusion. So we had to do it in self-defence. And we'll double their salaries this week for cleaning up what's left of you. Are you absolutely sure – before you say anything more about trust – that you understand that?'

This was the moment when everything would be decided.

It was now that all he didn't have time to build would be examined and judged.

'Yes, I get what you're saying. Because, just like you, I believe in money. And I believe both you and me could make a lot more money for that currency counter if we worked together and chose to trust each other.'

In the past, with time on his side, he would have worked with the police authorities to build a credible backstory. His Swedish handler Erik Wilson had transformed Piet Hoffmann into Paula by changing his police records, making him a suspect for much more dangerous crimes, and even changed his sentence to make it longer and created false medical reports to indicate he was a psychopath – fostering the myth of his potency.

But he didn't have access to those kinds of methods right now.

So he had to give them something else – which attracted them as much as a false façade.

A true one.

But with false content.

'Trust. Which becomes cooperation. Which becomes money. But *how* we do it, and *why* we do it – that I can only tell the two of you. You and Omar.'

He didn't need to understand Arabic this time, what the bodyguards said was quite clear.

Do not under any circumstances be alone with him.

'I can only tell you what I came here to say if the others leave the room. You and Omar will understand why. And if I'd wanted to kill you, I'd have done it . . . You saw the films, right?'

Her thin, taut smile became even more aggressive, an even blacker hole, as she stretched out an open palm to Omar and waited until he put his revolver in it.

'Ah, Koslow . . .'

Now she didn't even whisper. Her voice was quieter than that, and yet at the same time not a word was lost, nobody in that room had any doubt where she was headed.

'. . . I changed my mind. I won't encourage Omar to pull the trigger.'

Then everything happened fast.

'Because I'm going to do it all by myself.'

She cocked the revolver.

'Because I don't much like you or what you have to say.'

And put her forefinger softly against the trigger.

'So Koslow . . .'

And squeezed it, all the way.

'. . . goodbye.'

A bang like a howl, echoed in the big room.

She had discharged close to Hoffmann's right ear, a shot that grazed and injured his cheek.

'Now you know, Piet Koslow. Who I am.'

That quiet voice crept around the room, and she stared at him with an aggressiveness that could no longer be hidden. She cocked the gun again, and pushed it against his forehead, just like Omar had.

'My colleagues who are holding your arms and legs will leave us now and close the door behind them. And you'll stay where you are, and I'll stay where I am, aiming at you, and you can tell me why you came here. If I'm interested, you will continue. If I'm not, I'll fire again. And I won't move the gun.'

'He died because we knew.'

Piet Hoffmann tried to meet her eyes as she spoke, but the hand and arm that held the weapon were in the way. But that made it easier to throw her off the track. The time-sensitive lies that he usually avoided, because they didn't last for long, but which were now the only tool he had to build his façade.

'We knew? Who is *we*? Knew *what*?'

'In the same pocket where I kept the USB stick there's a folded piece of paper. It's my contract with the security firm that was protecting that food transport. You can get that verified. They'll confirm I work there. And *we* knew about your ambush. We knew where it would take place, how you were going to attack and destroy our trucks, we even knew which weapon you'd be using to destroy the food and increase the flow of refugees.'

She pressed the gun's steel barrel harder against his forehead.

'How?'

But the finger that rested against the trigger stayed frozen.

'How did you know?'

'We've known before every transport for the last few months. By the time we departed we knew the site, the strategy and your capacity. You haven't been able to take a single grain from us, have you?'

'You're not answering my question. *How* did you know?'

'That's why I wanted to talk to you two alone – one of your employees is leaking information.'

The barrel had slowly dug deeper into his skin, and small and hesitant drops of blood started to drip down his face and onto his chest. But the pressure seemed to decrease slightly when she lifted the forefinger of her other hand into the air, and made that same small gesture as before, left right left.

As if in the midst of that whispering calm she'd started to feel a little worried and unconsciously returned to a familiar signal of her power.

As if she was listening.

As if she might even be taking a bite of the lie he was feeding her.

'We knew because my bosses, who plan the routes, are all experienced military personnel. Former officers. The type who find information, assess it, use it. One of your guys is leaking. That's why you need me – a leaker of your own.'

'Who?'

'I don't know.'

'Who do you think?'

'I don't know. Yet. And even if I did know, I wouldn't tell you. *Until we start working together.*'

Piet Hoffmann took a deep breath before continuing with this ticking time bomb of a lie.

'I've got two weeks' leave from my regular job. We're all scheduled in shifts. You can check that with your sources. So I can work for you here, on site. Call it a trial period. I can take part in your normal work, and in the meantime I'll use my access to look for your leak. And if you've come to trust me by the end of these two weeks, if I've won you over, we can keep working together, and when I go back to the food transports I can give you our routes, type of vehicles, weapons, schedules. All you'd need for a successful attack.'

Two weeks.

That's how long this lie needed to hold.

In order to carry out his mission. In order to survive.

'And honestly – it hasn't been going that well for you lately, has it? Every attack on our trucks has failed. But if you had the information I'm capable of giving you, then you'd start being successful again, and again, and again, and you could keep doing what you did before, increasing the flow of refugees.'

He wasn't prepared.

As she rapidly moved the gun from his forehead and let the barrel rest against his cheek like before. And pulled the trigger.

The ensuing silence had nothing to do with the unreadable way both she and Omar stared at him without speaking. It was that annoying tone – a monotonous ringing that had echoed inside his head since the last shot – that now abruptly ceased because the hearing in his left ear was gone.

'Why should I . . .'

She pressed the gun again against the same small sore on his head.

'. . . trust someone who comes here uninvited trying to sell out their employer?'

But this time he couldn't stay still, he was forced to readjust his head so he could catch what she was saying with his good ear.

'Like I said, I believe in the same thing as you. I believe in money.'

'Mmm. The difference between me and you is that I don't believe in snitches.'

'I'm a mercenary. I'm hired to do what I'm good at – if I'm well-paid. Right now I'm employed by a South African security firm that has a contract with the UN. But I could be employed by you both. And make twice as much. No matter what you think about it, no matter if you like me – you'll make money on it too. You'll save by not having your employees killed by a man like me. And you'll earn a shitload of money when you're able to start taking out food transports again and increasing interest in your work.'

The moment.

Now it was back. Now it was hers.

'Well?'

The same moment Omar had just faced – it always came down to this when everything was said and done.

'What do you say? What . . .'

The moment it took to test a temporary lie.

'. . . do you both say?'

The time it took to weigh it, judge it.

Piet Hoffmann observed her as doubt challenged trust. He knew how it worked.

The rest of the time was what it took to make a decision, act.

Then she decided.

Then she took her finger off the trigger.

Then she lowered the gun, secured it.

Piet Hoffmann stayed on the floor even though she no longer held a weapon on him. He saw a woman with green eyes and a rigid smile looking at a man with a weak chin and shaggy sideburns. And it was as if he could hear their silent conversation.

Omar said: I don't trust the intruder.

The Accountant said: the intruder could be useful.

Omar said: *if* it turns out the intruder doesn't work at the security firm – then he has to die.

The Accountant said: *if* the intruder is telling the truth – this could mean an enormous amount of money for us.

Omar said: it feels wrong – I don't like security risks and the intruder *is* a risk.

The Accountant said: it's a risk worth taking – we have been losing manpower and money since they started guarding those food transports, and it will be your job, Omar, to keep a close eye on the intruder, keep him under your control.

––––––––

The light fell so beautifully through the big windows. And when the Accountant and Omar each lit a cigarette, smoke rose slowly towards the ceiling and those heavy steel beams.

Piet Hoffmann stood up and drops of blood ran down from his forehead and head and temple. He lost his balance for a moment, confused by the absence of hearing in one ear, almost fell, and was forced to grab onto a desk for support.

No one had said a word since she lowered her gun. The silence could mean almost anything.

'Well?'

Hoffmann looked at the two leaders of one of Libya's most successful and fastest-growing companies. The kind that dealt in people.

'Fourteen days. That's what you get.'

She was still whispering. Put out one cigarette and lit a new one. And the smoke didn't climb as high as before – it danced around and around and that was beautiful too.

'You shot a man on that film you made us watch. You'll be his replacement. And you'll share your salary with his widow and five children. In forty hours you'll take your seat on the next fishing boat out of here. It always departs at midnight, and it'll be crowded, and the passengers will be hungry – it can make things unpredictable. We used to give them some food while they were waiting for a ride – made them feel taken care of, like they were in safe hands and heading for something better, and the word spread that this was a good place to go. That's no longer needed. They're so desperate they fight to pay us.'

There was a small pile of napkins between two computer screens. Piet Hoffmann reached out and grabbed them, pushed them hard against the still bleeding wound on his head.

'Your maiden voyage, Koslow. One mistake will be your last.'

He was in.

They had listened to his temporary lies, judged them, and chosen to believe them for now.

Collision, confrontation, they'd opened the door to a criminal network he planned to unmask. But the short prep time also meant he too would be unmasked. And when, not if, he was, he had to be ready.

Because that moment would mean a death sentence.

His death sentence.

Again.

'EWERT?'

If only he'd been just a little bit faster.

'Ewert, stop.'

Just past the coffee machine, and the copier, and then a couple more doors to the stairs and the lift at the end of the corridor, maybe five or at most six quick steps left and he could . . .

'Ewert Grens. I see you. Come back. I want a progress report.'

Detective Superintendent Grens wasn't known for avoiding conflicts. Rather, he usually sought them out, even needed them. *At least one conflict a day.* It was late at night a few years ago, they were all tired, gathered in his office working on a difficult investigation when Grens realised this about himself and verbalised it for both Sven and Mariana. *I'll be damned, but I think I feel better after a fight, gets the blood rushing, I feel more like myself, more alive, does that make sense?*

'Ewert? Turn around. Come here.'

But this conflict was one he did *not* want to have.

Didn't have the time or energy, not now.

The conflict about Piet Hoffmann.

'Ten minutes, Ewert. That's all I need. A short report on where we are. What we know. Because every note on your desk from some journalist trying to hunt you down and which will be pushed straight in your trash – yes, I was in your office and saw this for myself – is something that *I* will have to take care of. After a report, you're free to go . . . well, wherever you were going.'

Grens had almost made it all the way down the corridor of his department when his boss called after him. Erik Wilson. The police officer who was Piet Hoffmann's handler for many years, who slowly made Hoffmann into one of the world's foremost infiltrators, who was still closer to him than anyone else. And who had the most beautiful smile when he realised that Piet Hoffmann, who after returning to Sweden and serving his most recent prison sentence, had decided to never commit crimes or risk himself or his family again. The only person who, therefore, who really *shouldn't* know that Ewert Grens, one of Wilson's subordinates, had flown to another continent and temporarily forced Hoffmann back into a life as an infiltrator.

'I'm coming.'

So when Grens passed the copier and coffee machine and headed back in the direction of Erik Wilson's open door, when he started telling his boss about a mass grave and that there was someone in Sweden profiting from the stream of refugees, and that this person was the focus of the investigation, through all of this Grens made sure to avoid any mention of a trip to West Africa or the meeting he had had with their shared acquaintance. And there was some irony to this situation. Because Erik Wilson for many years had been the one who would do anything to protect and shield and fight for Piet Hoffmann's life. He'd made sure that Hoffmann escaped the mafia's death sentence in Sweden by helping him flee to Colombia. He'd even persuaded Grens to go to South America to make sure that Hoffmann and his family continued to survive. Ironic because now it was Grens who'd taken over Wilson's job, motivating Hoffmann to infiltrate a criminal organisation and risk his life on behalf of the police. *You know how long it took Wilson? Four months. You got me to agree to be an infiltrator again after two meetings of twenty-five minutes.* Because Ewert Grens – according to Hoffmann – was in a way better at Wilson's job than Wilson himself.

'And that's all, Grens? You're searching the ports, shipping agents, tunnel system, morgues, bodies?'

'Yes. That's all.'

Ewert Grens stood just inside the door of his boss's well-appointed office and met Erik Wilson's eyes. Held them. He did what he accused Wilson and all other handlers of infiltrators and informers of doing for so many years. Lied. Withheld information. Allowed lies and truth in the same police corridor.

'So if you'll just keep your press conferences as far away from my group of investigators and this station as you can, Wilson. Give us a reasonable amount of time, and we'll track down the bastard in Sweden who's making money off dead people.'

Grens had privately asked Nils Krantz, the forensic technician who'd lifted two sets of fingerprints off the satellite phone hidden in a jacket, to keep it to himself for a while. And the forensic engineer who analysed those fingerprints and confirmed a hundred per cent match with an ex-con named Piet Hoffmann. And lastly, behind the closed doors of both Sven's and Mariana's offices, he'd asked them to keep quiet about the trail that led him to West Africa.

'A reasonable amount of time? What does that mean? How long do you think I should sit around before I phase out your investigation team, Ewert, and form something bigger? Seventy-three unsolved murders have a tendency to increase the number of questions day by day, press conference by press conference.'

'Two weeks.'

'Two . . . *weeks?*'

'Yes. I'll have a name for you by then, someone who's guilty, someone you can arrest. If you let me work in peace, in my own way.'

'And what exactly, Ewert, are you basing this timeline on? Two weeks can be a helluva long time for a police chief to stand in front of the microphones repeating that we have the situation under control, especially if it turns out that's not the case.'

On your protégé and friend.

On Piet Hoffmann.

On the only collaborator I won't mention to you, not now, not later.

'I base it on collision, confrontation.'

'On what?'

'On the extraordinary skills of my colleagues.'

'I'm not following, Grens.'

'You don't need to. Trust me, Wilson, didn't you learn how important that is when *you* served as a handler?'

A few minutes later, Grens was able to slip out of the station and drive away. According to the counter on his dashboard it was just eight kilometres to Enskede, the suburb where the Hoffmanns' house and

Zofia Hoffmann and her sons' school were located. And at this time of day, on his way out of the inner city, the highways were almost deserted, a short drive, and he was stepping out into a schoolyard that looked like every other. Two-storey red-brick buildings on the right side that held the middle school and the cafeteria and the administration building, on the left-hand side, a one-storey building which seemed to be for the younger children, and in the middle one of those buildings put up to meet a temporary need, but ends up painted over and permanent ten years later. It was there he was headed. And stopped halfway across the asphalt yard to study a group of children divided into two teams throwing a ball back and forth. The same game he himself played half a century ago. It made him strangely happy to see it hadn't yet been replaced by electronics and digital voices coming out of game consoles.

He was about to move on when he saw something he recognised. *Someone* he recognised. A way of moving that was very much like his father's – as if the nine-year-old boy, who had now seen Grens, had unconsciously copied it.

Hugo.

It had been a year, the boy had grown, but it was him.

Ewert Grens raised his right hand in greeting but received nothing in return. The boy had seen him, recognised him, but chose to pretend otherwise.

Hugo's mother, Zofia Hoffmann, was supposed to be in one of the smaller classrooms in the middle building, according to a helpful woman in the school office which he'd called on his way here. The detective walked down a corridor which, after just a few steps, he was sure smelled of mould, and counted the closed doors, stopped in front of the fourth one on the north side. There was a small window in the classroom door. Zofia stood inside the room, visible in the middle of the glass, writing something in bright red letters on a whiteboard, erased them with a rag, then started writing again. French, that much Grens could see. And a total of seven students in a classroom with places for ten. The clock above her head showed only five minutes left of this class, and he decided to wait until then. Stand there and watch this pantomime, her mouth moving without any sound, her arms explaining what she couldn't convey with her voice.

That's probably why he saw her. Really *saw* her.

Saw what he hadn't seen during his strained visit in the family's hallway – it was now completely obvious.

The bell rang. A beautiful little melody, not at all like the arrogant tone he remembered from his own school days.

Seven students. All boys. Speaking in a language that was neither Swedish nor French as they passed by him. They were older than the other pupils in the schoolyard. Grens was no good at ages when it came to children, but he'd guess fourteen, maybe fifteen years old.

'Hello.'

He hadn't knocked. Instead, without warning, he stepped into the classroom as she gathered up the scattered papers left on the desks.

'Grens?'

'I'm sorry to disturb you. Again. But we have to talk, you and me – again.'

She didn't look very happy. Nor did she seem stressed, afraid, angry, which she had at their last meeting. Tired. Almost sad. That was what she radiated upon his arrival.

'Very well.'

She gestured to the empty desks. The only seats available. So he squeezed into one of them, in the front row. The chair was too low, as was the desk, but if he twisted his body in just the right way his throbbing back and too-stiff leg would be able to take it.

'I didn't realise it last time. In your hallway. Everything went, well . . . wrong. My visit. But now, when I've had time to study you through that window, and in profile, it's quite obvious.'

'What?'

'Your condition, Zofia.'

She looked down, not for long, but long enough, and seemed temporarily shy.

A reaction that didn't suit such a strong personality.

'Congratulations, Zofia. Right?'

'And you . . . just *saw* it? Even though I'm barely showing?'

'Yes. The way you stand, how you move, even how you breathe.'

She observed him. Her shyness gone.

'No one else knows, Ewert.'

'Excuse me?'

'Not the boys, not even Piet, not yet. I was going to tell him when he came home on leave. He was supposed to come home yesterday, but didn't. Something about . . . extra work.'

Now it was Grens's turn to look away.

From shame.

'You have to understand, it's still so new. Only the third month. I barely notice it myself.'

And she had no idea. He could see that. But while she spoke, she put a hand on her stomach, cupped it.

'Promise not to say anything, Ewert. I want to give the news.'

Ewert Grens nodded. And for a moment felt excited. For their sake. Without knowing why.

'I promise.'

Another child. It just felt right.

'The calm, Ewert.'

'Excuse me?'

'Everyday life. Piet promised no more infiltrating, no more death, chaos, fleeing, no more risking his life for the sake of the authorities. That's when I decided. Or, my body apparently did. Another baby. Piet's wanted another for a long time, but it wasn't possible. I just couldn't get pregnant. My age, I knew that . . . but it wasn't that. The calm. The not having to live like that any more. I relaxed. Another child, I don't know, I know it sounds corny, but it feels like this baby is an unintentional symbol for all that. Of Piet's promise. Our new life. Do you understand, Ewert?'

Grens looked down again. Ashamed, again.

Until he felt something else.

'So you mean . . .'

Pride.

'. . . that I know about this before *him*?'

She nodded.

'Yes. You know before my husband. Even though we weren't supposed to keep secrets from each other any more.'

The tiny desk was extremely uncomfortable. A piece of hard wood
to sit on and another to lean back against, and a pair of hard metal
pipes to tie them together. Grens couldn't understand how the students
were able to sit still, he himself felt the need to move continuously,
swinging back and forth, stretching out and in again.

'Zofia?'

'Yes?'

'The day before yesterday?'

'Yes?'

'We need to talk a little more about it.'

She looked at him, the shyness was now completely gone, he saw
the powerful, competent, fearless woman he remembered.

'You were looking for Piet. I gave you the name of his hotel. That
should have sufficed.'

Her voice was cold. And the closeness they'd just shared was long
gone.

'It's not enough.'

'I told you then, Ewert, and I'll say it again – you're not part of
our life any more.'

'It's not enough, because I'm convinced you didn't tell me the whole
truth.'

'The truth – about what?'

He stood up, sitting had become unbearable. Neither his back nor
his leg could handle going back to middle school.

'When I went to your house, to you, remember how thirsty I was?
I'd worked through the night, gone through a tunnel that led to a
container in Värta Harbour where seventy-three people were slowly
killed. And I think, unfortunately, that you're mixed up in it.'

'What exactly are you talking about?'

Her surprise was genuine.

Ewert Grens, after forty years of interrogating deceitful, despicable
and uncommunicative criminals, had become rather good at reading

the micro-expressions that revealed a lie so much more clearly than words.

Zofia Hoffmann had *no* idea what he was talking about.

'Ewert, what are you trying to say? What . . .?'

'A container full of dead refugees from West Africa. And there's something you're not telling me.'

'About what? Telling you what? When you arrived two mornings ago and opened the door to our home, *even though you said you'd never come there again,* I hadn't even had time to read the news, no matter how big it's become since then. And even if I *had* heard about it, it has nothing to do with me.'

'You work with unaccompanied refugee children.'

'Yes. And . . .'

'Wasn't the group you were just teaching refugees?'

'That has nothing to do with you or your investigation.'

'Yes. It does. I want to know *who* and *how.*'

Ewert Grens had been careful to close the door behind himself when he stepped into the classroom, but now he checked again to make sure it was really shut tight. No sound leaking out or in – he couldn't even hear the steps of two girls passing by. He also wasn't recording this conversation or even taking notes. This meeting was between him and Zofia, and he wanted her to understand that.

'I know you asked Piet to help a refugee couple who were paying for a trip from a port city called Zuwara in Libya.'

She didn't say anything. Just stared at him in confusion.

'And it was no regular trip, Zofia – they were going to be smuggled into Europe, eventually into Sweden. I know that because that refugee couple were suffocated in that container. And Piet's fingerprints were on a phone sewn into one of their jackets. And Piet wasn't able to explain sufficiently to me *why* he helped that couple.'

When she got up from her narrow seat, she wore another face – tense, pale, almost crumpled from a mixture of dread and panic.

'Ewert . . . what . . . I don't understand. *I just don't understand.* What are you trying to tell me?'

'I'm trying to say I know you didn't know when I stormed into your hall and started asking about Piet. But, in spite of that, I'm not leaving here until I've got all the circumstances explained to me – how did you end up asking Piet to help two refugees that are now dead?'

'*That* refugee couple? Was in *that* container?'

'Yes. And I want to know why you asked Piet to help them. I want a name. Something that might lead me to another name or at least a description.'

'That refugee couple?'

'Yes.'

'*That* container?'

Then what she was saying ceased to be audible. She leaned back against the whiteboard, slowly slid down the wall, and sank down onto the floor with her head between her bent knees.

She wept.

First cautiously, trembling, then with more force. Her shoulders shook, and she made a sound that reminded Grens of when parents visited their children in the morgue.

He felt uncomfortable. Awkward. Didn't know what he should do, or how he should do it. They'd hugged several times during the trip from Colombia, because of trust and a kind of closeness, but this had nothing to do with joy. To put a hand on her arm, or stroke her hair, or hold her, it felt wrong.

So he let her cry. Until she didn't need to any more.

'One of my students. A boy.'

She stayed on the floor with her head bent, looked at him when she spoke, her voice as thin as it was bare. He handed her the last paper towel he could find, taken from a heavy metal container on the wall.

'We talked about how he came here. Just me and him. A private conversation, I sometimes have them to get closer to my students, it's easier for them to relax when they're alone with me. Otherwise . . . they are so, well, practised is probably the best word, at being on their guard.'

She wiped her eyes with the rough paper towel and it ended up soaked and stained black by her mascara.

'My student is fourteen years old. And he told me all about his journey. It started on the back of a truck, driving through a desert, then onto a crowded fishing boat across the Mediterranean, then into the back of a semi, then a container over the Baltic Sea. And then, the next time we spoke, he told me about a young woman, his cousin, who was going to make the same trip with her fiancé. He was so excited for them to come. So worried that something would happen, and they'd get hurt.'

She tried to get up, but tottered, and Grens stretched out a hand and gently pulled her up. She was looking for a good place but ended up where she was, leaning back against the whiteboard, but standing this time.

'I knew that Piet, and the rest of the security forces, sometimes stayed in the same port city that my student described to me. And I was lucky. They were there at the same time. Piet was about to look after the young couple, for my sake. Or maybe for my student's sake.'

'And now *I* want to speak to your student.'

Ewert Grens was having trouble finding the right tone of voice. She'd just wept from sorrow and probably guilt, he knew her and had always thought highly of her, and what she'd done for the man she loved. But he was here as a police officer. And he was investigating who was responsible for murder. He needed answers, had to have an answer.

'And I want to do it alone, like you.'

She might be weak, dizzy, empty. But that didn't change anything.

'No.'

When she shook her head, she did it with dignity and conviction.

'You won't speak with him alone. I won't even tell you who he is. What he said to me – he said in confidence.'

'I'm investigating a mass grave.'

'You won't get anywhere with him. You represent exactly what he's learned to avoid.'

'I can force you, Zofia.'

'You can't force me to do anything. I've also lived on the run. I too know how it is. Like my student, I've learned to take anything to protect what I have left, and no bastard is going to take it from me. That's who I am. Inside. *Me*, Ewert.'

And it was at that moment that she switched from defence to offence.

It was as though she suddenly stood a little straighter, her cheeks gained back their colour, her voice went from thin to firm.

'*Now* I understand.'

This version of Zofia Hoffmann would never sink to the floor.

Instead, she took a step forward.

Didn't just meet Grens's eyes, drilled deep into them.

'How else would you have got Piet to give you my name, my part in this?'

She lifted her arm, pointed an index finger at him.

'You didn't just talk to him, like you said, that never would have been enough. You went down there, Ewert! To the hotel I mentioned. And somehow you forced him. You were the one who made Piet stay! You were the one who made him call me and give me that line about the extra transport, made him lie, despite the fact that we don't lie to each other any more!'

She slapped him.

With the hand that she'd been pointing with.

Ewert Grens's cheek burned.

'My husband isn't home with me and my sons on his two-week leave, instead he's far away, doing something that you're *making* him do. He's working with you. For you!'

She slapped him again.

His other cheek.

Now both sides burned, but Grens didn't move.

She was right of course. He deserved it.

'What's he going to do for you?'

'The same thing I want you to do. Help me track down the bastards you should be hitting.'

'I need to know if you're putting him in danger. You hear me, Ewert? If Hugo and Rasmus's father is in danger, hurt, while he's helping you out a *little*.'

She looked away from him for a moment, and it was a relief not to have those eyes drilling into him so terribly. She was looking at the wall, most of which consisted of windows. Towards the schoolyard. It was breaktime. Outside, her children were running around, Piet's children.

'They need him more than ever. Especially Hugo. He needs his father.'

Then they drilled into him again. She looked at him, into him.

'Do you understand, Ewert? Do you understand what I'm telling you?'

'The only thing Piet is helping me with is finding the person or people who are responsible for suffocating the young couple that you tried to help. Whoever's profiting from this endless chain.'

Now Ewert Grens turned to the window and the schoolyard.

'So, Zofia . . .'

It was easier not to give her the whole truth.

'. . . there is no danger at all. He's tracking down a name. That's all he has to do. I promise you – he is *not* in danger.'

PIET HOFFMANN ROCKED A little on the soles of his feet, from heel to toes and back again, as he stood at the far end of the rough stone pier in Zuwara's port. A half-step more and he'd fall down into the glittering, clear, deep blue waters of the Mediterranean.

The angry wind around him clashed with the obstinate heat and felt almost gentle and friendly as it danced against his skin.

He closed his eyes.

Salt drops landed softly on his face. A few long-beaked gulls screeched at him.

It felt easy to breathe.

Easy to forget why he was here.

'Koslow.'

The short, slender woman in her high heels, expensive clothes and gold-rimmed glasses that she wore like a golden diadem in her dark hair.

The lanky, unexpectedly wide-shouldered man with a weak chin and shaggy sideburns.

The Accountant and Omar.

At the edge of the docks, a few hundred metres away, with the two bodyguards on either side.

'Let's go.'

The Accountant's English had more of an Oxbridge ring to it than Hoffmann realised while pressed down on the floor of their headquarters. Whereas Omar's North African accent felt even more awkward and hard to understand when he repeated and amplified her command.

'For God's sake, Koslow, let's go *now*.'

Piet Hoffmann opened his eyes a little bit at a time. Blue as far as he could see. And then even more blue.

He was on a tour of Zuwara's port, to learn where all the smuggling organisation's transport boats and storage spaces were located, in preparation for the next round of refugees embarking at midnight, headed for the open sea and Europe, which Piet could almost sense, with a little imagination, on the other side of that endless blue. They'd watched him closely the whole time, constant surveillance, and it was even more obvious how the lack of solid preparation made this work even more precarious and dangerous, where the slightest misstep meant death. And that he, that this, that everything sooner or later was going to break and it was all about being ready for it *when* it did. He needed a few minutes by himself to think and plan, and so he'd said he wanted to feel the ocean, see the waves, out on the pier, did they mind? The Accountant had shaken her head lightly, which meant sure, as long as you're visible, so we can keep our eye on this person we hope will give us what we need – and who we've now confirmed via our sources, does actually work for the South African firm protecting food transports, but still don't know exactly who he is and where we stand with him.

The wind ruffled his hair a bit.

A few last drops of salt water against his forehead and cheeks.

He was ready and turned back to where they waited impatiently. He'd done what he always did during infiltration, when you can't write down or photograph or say anything – he'd drawn a mental map. Which no one else could access. Memorised the harbour's formal roads and informal shortcuts, estimated the distance between hangars and cranes and fences, counted the cars and trucks and dockworkers who appeared to be in constant motion, placed the small boats and fishing boats and those two that were a bit bigger and might even be called ships.

Because when it was time to run.

He had to know exactly where and how.

'Over there.'

They'd started walking back towards the western side of the harbour, and Omar pointed to a badly painted fishing boat that had been dragged onto land and was resting in a rickety wooden cart.

'One of our spares that we use when there's particularly high demand. Room for two hundred fifty in every departure. And it's made, well, at least thirty trips.'

'Thirty-seven.'

The Accountant didn't need any documents, nor any computer when she corrected Omar.

'With an average of two hundred and forty-four travellers.'

'All at once? In . . . that.'

Piet Hoffmann stood in front of a boat that wasn't much bigger than the fishing boats he saw as a child making their way between the islands of Stockholm's archipelago. Twenty, maybe twenty-five people seemed like a more suitable number of passengers.

The Accountant adjusted her glasses, they didn't hold her hair up like they should.

'Two hundred and forty-four is no problem if we pack them tight enough. Every extra refugee is pure profit once fuel and personnel are accounted for.'

When they stopped next time, the boat was perhaps slightly less old-fashioned, but still resembled the last one – a fishing boat with a peeling hull in bright blue and white, a slightly rounded cabin in the prow. It once had glass in its windows, but now only shards stood at their corners. In the aft of the boat there was some kind of stand made of fused iron pipes, probably something that could be draped in plastic and offer cover from the elements.

'We bought this one recently. Ten thousand dollars, twice what they cost just a year ago – but just like the tickets we sell, an increase in demand always drives up prices, and a skilled businessman takes advantage of it.'

The Accountant laughed weakly at him, a joyless, closed smile that Hoffmann recognised from other people who'd made it to the top of criminal organisations. First her silent index finger, left right left, little wiggles in the air, and now that fucking smile – he was sure of it, there must be some kind of universal language of power in criminal hierarchies such as these, which developed independently of each other.

'You won't find a serious fisherman along this coast who can compete with a net and its catch – not when they can sell their ships to us for the equivalent of several years of work.'

He tried to meet her eyes.

But it was impossible with that smile in the way.

'Tomorrow night. That means in . . .'

She looked at her phone.

'. . . thirty-six hours. This will depart again. With you onboard, Koslow.'

She walked over to the boat, which creaked each time the waves knocked it against the docks, and leaned over the railing.

'You might call us a niche travel agency. Our product is Germany and Sweden. That's what separates us from the others, that's why refugees stand in line to hand over their money to us. We take them to their dreams – trips to the most attractive and valuable destinations.'

And she patted the boat. Almost lovingly. Her palm against the hull like a rancher patting one of his breeding horses.

'We arrange their entire trip. Once they pay they don't have to worry any more, we take care of all the details. Every step from here to Munich or Berlin or Stockholm is included. The refugees know that, they want that kind of service. Who wants to get stopped at the border of Hungary or end up in the Czech Republic or Poland or some other EU country that doesn't even accept their allocated quota of refugees?'

The Accountant looked proud, her smile warm and sincere when she was describing smuggling people as a business venture, her lips were less taut, when she said words like *niche* or *details* or *business idea.*

'By the way, aren't you . . . Swedish?'

'Yes. But nowadays I work here. In Africa.'

'Omar and I visited the capital once. Stockholm. Beautiful city, lots of water, like here.'

Stockholm.

Her voice, eyes, lips reacted to the name of Hoffmann's hometown like they did to her business terminology. With warmth, sincerity. Stockholm was money. Stockholm was the other end of the chain. The Accountant and Omar's trip to the north had to have been for a meeting with their Swedish contact, perhaps even on site, where their customers were unloaded and the trip to Sweden ended. They must both know the identity of their contact.

And Hoffmann knew exactly where that information might be found, in the records a professional criminal organisation keeps in order to avoid distrust and fragmentation among the various members who demand their share of the profits.

Headquarters.

In a smoky, impersonal room Piet Hoffmann first observed through the scope of his sniper rifle – hidden somewhere among those new computers, binders, files and Excel programs was the name Ewert Grens wanted, Piet Hoffmann's mission.

It took half an hour to walk through the rest of the area – it was clear that the large, hangar-like building at the far west was the final destination of the tour. A warehouse built to store goods before loading them onto ships, which had once made this one of North Africa's most important port cities – now another kind of goods was waiting to be loaded.

Twice their walk was interrupted.

They'd stopped by the shipyard to greet some men in overalls with oil on their hands – another one of the organisation's newly acquired fishing boats was being patched up there, and as soon as it was reasonably seaworthy it would help them meet the exploding demand of the hunger season – when two men in uniforms climbed out of a police car and purposefully sought out the Accountant. She laughed, tossed her long hair so the scent of her perfume surrounded them all, and took the men aside. Before their tour Piet Hoffmann had seen her go into the room with the safe-like door and fill six brown envelopes with bills from the currency counter. Now she handed out two of them. They fitted snugly into inner jacket pockets of the two police officers' uniforms. Civil servants doing what everyone else was, adapting to a new system, accepting bribes to make a living. Hoffmann saw it in the drug jungles of Colombia as well as in Poland's amphetamine factories, the simple rules of organised crime – if it's going well for you then it's going well for your contacts, people willing to stay silent or hide things or falsify documents as long as they feel like they have a stake in your success. If they're happy with you, they won't want you going down, they'll want you out making money so they'll get paid even more.

The next break came when they reached the harbour's smallest pier, rusty metal fishing boats packed tight with wooden ones and even a few hard plastic boats, the common denominator being that they were all in even shittier condition than the ones Hoffmann had already seen. He counted seventeen. Their competitors who, according to the Accountant, operated only one transport vehicle each and had no access to a chain of service nor took any responsibility for the rest of the journey – from start to final destination. Their services were directed towards a clientele fleeing starvation in even more haste, who either lacked the money for more elaborate travel arrangements or didn't understand that a cheaper ticket meant a less attractive relocation site. The interruption occurred when they were at the far point of the pier, and Omar's phone rang. He answered and, after realising who it was, turned away so he could continue speaking. His voice lost some of the self-assured, aggressive quality that he usually tried to radiate, and his English became easier to understand, he seemed to be making an effort to be understood. It was something about an upcoming meeting, that much Hoffmann was able to pick up. And given the nature of Omar's voice – a meeting with someone important, someone with more power than Omar and the Accountant. Omar even straightened up when he answered the next question, now and then throwing a worried glance in the direction of the Accountant, who nodded, trying to calm him down. But he also performed impressively as he arranged a meeting without mentioning a place or a time, nor a single name – so if anyone were to intercept and write down what was actually said, and had no access to tone of voice and body language, then the conversation would seem to be about nothing.

'We're almost done, Koslow.'

Behind them fishing boats bobbed up and down in a sea as salty as it was sparkling.

And in front of them, they met the intrusive stench of urine and perspiration, and the odd feeling that body heat was streaming out through every crack of the dark building.

This was the one the Accountant had pointed to.

'Now you've seen everything you need to know in order to do your job – except our customers. The most important aspect of every business. Without consumers, there's no revenue.'

She nodded towards Omar, who was dragging apart the two doors to an apparently empty warehouse, then he stepped in and gestured for Piet Hoffmann to follow.

And he saw them.

The building whispered with people's breath.

Packed in, curled up, silent on the hard concrete floor.

Hundreds of people.

When Hoffmann's eyes adjusted to the darkness, he also noticed the armed guards, one sitting on a pallet at the northern end of the warehouse, one leaning against the metal wall that faced the south.

'Almost every day, sometimes several times a day, trouble arises. They're frustrated. Warm, dirty, hungry. They don't want to wait any more.'

Omar's eyes had been following Hoffmann, staring at Hoffmann, in the same way ever since he watched the contents of the USB stick, a sniper rifle aiming at his own head from almost one kilometre away. Hostility. Suspicion. It was the Accountant, her desire for even more money to count and enter into her ledgers, that had given Hoffmann the opening for what they were calling his maiden voyage. She wanted to take a chance. Omar didn't. His eyes followed every step Piet Hoffmann took, always mistrustful, just waiting for the slightest mistake to betray him.

But Omar's gaze shifted now back and forth between the refugees packed tightly at his feet and Hoffmann, and his expression changed for the first time.

From hostility to contempt.

'Well, they'll have to wait. Because *we* have to wait until we have enough to fill a boat. No transport takes off until it's completely full, more than full – and we don't have the time or space for the fights that break out when they're hot and hungry. If we have to shoot, we shoot.'

And then from contempt back to hostility.

'That means you too, Koslow.'

'I should take the shot if I have to?'

'Yes.'

'Or that *I'll* get shot if *you* have to?'

'That too. And dropped in the Mediterranean.'

The stench of urine and sweat could be shut out. It didn't exist, if Piet Hoffmann didn't want it to. But it was harder with their breathing. People who breathe are alive. And therefore can't be thought away. But he forced himself to look past them, through them, out over the large warehouse. Tried to imagine the huge space as if it didn't contain several hundred packed together bodies.

The walls of white-plastered concrete slabs hid a steel frame.

A square pillar every fourth metre held up the beams that held up the rest.

Hoffmann counted quickly – if the posts holding up the pillars were four millimetres thick, you'd need two hundred and fifty grams of det cord for each one. A total of five kilos. In order to be sure the entire structure collapsed it had to be pushed in two directions – the plastic explosives would have to be placed on opposite sides with double the amount so that an explosion would simultaneously push the iron beam to the bottom right and to the top left.

More information to file away in his mental map. The sort of thing that's good to know in an emergency.

'You look thoughtful, Koslow?'

'Yes, I'm thinking about the people in here. The refugees.'

'Unsure if you can shoot them?'

'Unsure if I understood you correctly – that we're waiting for more?'

'Many more.'

'Who are *also* going to fit onto the boat we looked at?'

'Squeezing them onboard is the least of our problems. Keeping them from panicking, making sure they stay calm, that's your job, Koslow. And *if* anything arises, you take the shot at any mother, father, child, or whoever the hell else might risk our transport. You do it here, on the dock, out on the sea. Once they've paid, once we receive our compensation, it's always more important to protect the boat than the goods we're shipping.'

Omar spoke loudly, in a shrill and raspy voice that could be heard by anyone in this overflowing warehouse. And it was clear that at least some understood what he said, a confused undulation made its way through the crowd, when he said *take the shot* an elderly man screamed, and a young woman stood up and started running towards them in worn shoes, climbing over legs and shoulders and hips. Not until a guard took a second shot into the air above her head did she stop, and then a particular kind of silence fell, hundreds of people focused on not making sound.

'Our record, Koslow, on boats of that size, is four hundred and sixty-four. We plan to break that tomorrow. By at least twenty. There are those who don't like how we push the limits. People in upper management. They have a policy, rules and regulations, that we, unlike the competition, will never risk sinking. But those of us on the ground usually ignore that. Why should we be different? And what they don't know won't hurt them. Right? Twenty more, that's eighty-five thousand extra dollars.'

'Ninety thousand.'

The Accountant didn't even look annoyed when she corrected her colleague. She even smiled her warm smile, the real one. When she turned to Hoffmann, she was smart enough to lower her voice.

'With those numbers you should be able to figure out how much an *entire* boat is worth, before expenses and profit-sharing. And understand why I'm hoping you'll contribute information that helps us to preserve and maybe even increase those figures, and why it's so important to me.'

Hoffmann nodded as if he understood.

He didn't understand shit.

Animals.

The people he looked at, the people who were looking at him, after a few days in this heat and under these conditions started to smell like animals, they were watched like animals, held captive like animals, valued like animals. They'd paid to get to a place where their lives would have more dignity – and the moment they handed over their money that very dignity was taken from them.

That was the moment Piet Hoffmann realised it, the moment he made up his mind.

Finding that name for Ewert Grens, leading the Swedish police to the Swedish contact, that was no longer enough. Not when the people who thought money was more important than human dignity would just be able to find a new Swedish contact to send refugees to – to continue treating people like animals, even suffocating them during transport.

He decided to collect on a debt that could never be repaid. In the only way possible – take the lives of those who took the lives of others.

But these smugglers weren't going to die physically, they'd die in another way.

He'd take away everything they cared about – their money and their ability to make more money. Sometimes you have to take *everything*.

It's a death that lasts longer, that eats at you a little bit every day.

A BLUE AND WHITE plastic band fluttered and whistled in the wind. And an empty cargo container with a square hole cut into one side. The only thing left. The only reminder of the most terrible sight he'd ever seen in his forty years on the force.

While all around him life bustled on in Värta Harbour just like usual.

Gulls screeched. Cranes, like huge fishing poles, caught and hauled up pallets and containers. Trailer trucks rolled onto ships that would soon depart, eventually disappearing into where the cloudy sky met the cold waters of the Baltic Sea.

Ewert Grens didn't really know why he returned. There were no new answers here. But he couldn't stand to be at the station any more either.

He'd sat at his desk, drunk three cups of black coffee to sharpen his mind, while scanning all the technical reports.

He then moved to the break room and ate dry cinnamon buns, while examining the forensic analysis.

He'd gone back to his office, put on a Siw Malmkvist cassette, and lay down on the worn corduroy sofa while reading through the interrogations Sven and Mariana had carried out.

Then restlessness had driven him here.

To the crime scene.

And the only thing that happened was that the sorrow and anger came back with the same intractable force, as when they first opened the container, when he – convinced he couldn't feel any more – cried the silent tears that had been so deeply lodged inside him.

Now they came back again. And, like before, he climbed over the plastic tape and walked away a bit, sat down on the hard asphalt to try to create some sort of distance.

Fucking hell.

Fucking.

Hell.

Seventy-three people.

And they were lying in there, enclosed in metal, packed on top of each other.

'Ewert?'

His cell phone had started ringing. And for some reason he answered it.

'Yes, this is Ewert Grens.'

'It's me, Zofia, I . . . oh, how are you, is everything . . .'

'Just the reception. I'm outdoors. It'll get better soon.'

She probably realised it wasn't the reception.

And it felt good not to care.

'You called, Zofia. What's this about?'

'I need the number.'

Grens covered the microphone and swallowed whatever the hell it was he needed to swallow.

'Which number?'

'The number, Ewert, to the phone that was sewn into the jacket. Which had Piet's fingerprints on it.'

His voice felt almost stable again.

He cleared his throat.

'Why?'

'I just talked to . . . the person who *you* wanted to talk to.'

'And?'

'I'll tell you if you come here. To our house. Piet's taught me enough to know I shouldn't entrust this kind of information to the phone lines.'

Ewert Grens remained on the asphalt.

The wind blew harder and the plastic tape no longer whistled, it rattled loudly, trying to tear itself free.

He missed her. The one who used to wait for his weekly visits at the nursing home that you could just make out on the other side of the strait. He'd accepted that he had to live separately from the one he loved, that's just how their lives turned out, but he hadn't learned how to bear the loneliness her death had left inside him. He needed her now. Needed to hold her, kiss her cheek, talk to her, and know she might understand. Often that had been enough – just saying things out loud and in her silent face he'd discover his own thoughts.

Grens got up and grabbed one end of the plastic tape that was about to break free, pulled it tight and fastened it with double knots. And as he walked to the car and drove through the inner city of Stockholm towards Enskede in sluggish afternoon traffic, his thoughts lingered on Anni, struck by how light it always felt to think about her. They hadn't completely lost the chance to share their lives after she was injured so young and shrank into her own isolated world – they'd still had each other. If he'd been forced to choose, he'd choose the life they ended up having together over never having met.

He parked outside the Hoffmanns' gate and through a sparse spot in the hedge saw both boys in the neighbour's garden. He counted six heads running around in short-sleeved shirts playing what seemed to be a game of football.

Zofia opened the door before he was halfway up the front steps. She was reserved and worried during his last visit to her home, had wavered between exhausted and aggressive at the school – now she seemed filled with purpose.

'Come in, let's sit in the kitchen, follow me. You can leave your shoes on. Coffee?'

She poured two large glasses like the ones they have at the café on Bergsgatan opposite the station. Black for Grens, a lot of milk for herself.

'Amadou. That's his name, Ewert. My student.'

She cupped her hands around her glass, as if trying to soak up the heat.

'I had three classes with him today – he's in a group of seven students, all from West Africa with French as a mother tongue. Our first class was the one when you arrived during this morning. The second and third were a double class that I finished right before calling you.'

There was a piece of paper turned upside down between them on the kitchen table, with ragged edges as if it had been ripped from a notepad. She grabbed it, held it as if she hadn't yet decided if she wanted to show him.

'I always gather my students' phones into a small basket before they enter my classroom. Not everyone does, but I demand their full attention, and you can't get that if they're fiddling with their phones. And today, after your visit, I couldn't stop thinking of another phone – the one sewn into the jacket. With Piet's fingerprint on it. So in the afternoon break between the last two classes I checked Amadou's list of outgoing calls. It was short. He'd only called four different numbers. Twelve times to the family home where he lives. Twice to one of the other students. Five times to me. And seven times to an unlisted number.'

Seven calls.

To a nameless phone number.

Grens might be getting just a little closer to the person who was calling the dead.

'The number, Ewert. To the phone in the jacket. I'd like to compare it to the one on this piece of paper.'

Another half cup of coffee.

Grens called Mariana and asked her to give him a phone number found in eight different places in the case file.

He then put the newly scribbled note on the table next to Zofia's, and she turned hers over. An identical set of numbers.

'Now we know. Now you know, Ewert. And I know you have to talk to him.'

Her voice and movements hadn't changed – she was still focused, had temporarily let go of her aversion to the man who'd prevented her husband from coming home.

'But let *me* go to his group home and pick him up. You'll learn so much more from him if *I* ask him to talk to you, if he knows I'll be sitting next to him. He's intelligent, empathetic, charming – but getting a residence permit is a long process that makes people cautious.'

Grens nodded. Her suggestion was a good one.

'One thing, Zofia.'

'Yes?'

'Does he seem to know that his cousin is dead?'

'No.'

'Do you want me to tell him? Unfortunately, it's something we police officers have to do sometimes. I've become somewhat used to it.'

She laid her hand on top of his, not long, but long enough for Grens to remember what it felt like to be touched.

'Thank you. But I have to tell him in order to convince him to meet you. He'd be terrified if you, a police officer, started your inter-rogation-like conversation by informing him that one of the few he holds dear is dead. However, there is something you can help me with, Ewert.'

'What's that?'

'I have no idea how long it will take for me to convince him to come with me – so I'm going to call Rasmus and Hugo inside and tell them I'll be gone a while, and you'll be here. I'd appreciate it if you could stay until I get back. I don't like leaving them home alone – I haven't really got used to the idea that we're safe here yet.'

They *had* been playing football on the other side of the hedge.

Sweaty, with grass-stained knees, the two boys sat down at the kitchen table on either side of Grens, while Zofia closed the front door to go and pick up another boy just a few years older than Hugo, a boy who was forced to learn how to survive without parents. And if the much older detective superintendent felt uncomfortable or awkward earlier that day trying to decide whether to hug a shocked mother, he now found himself completely lost as to what to do with her sons.

'Ah.'

They watched him, waiting for more.

'How, umm . . . how was school today?'

They looked at each other. That's what Mum usually asked. And Dad, too, in the morning over the speakerphone. But a police officer? Why would a police officer want to know about their school day?

'You must have done something?'

It wasn't exactly going well, this conversation with two boys who hadn't seen Grens in over a year. He didn't have the knack. He'd spoken to Jonas, Sven's son, a couple of times this spring. That was all. The only practice he'd had.

'OK . . . maybe you're thirsty? I'm very good at making coffee. But you probably don't drink that? There's water. Maybe some juice or milk in the fridge.'

'Hungry.'

The younger one, whose name was Rasmus, six or seven years old, had a serious look on his face as he turned to Grens. Things were developing. They had a topic of conversation.

'So you're . . . hungry?'

'Yeah. We usually eat when Mom comes home from school.'

'OK . . . and what do you eat?'

'Pancakes.'

'Pancakes?'

'Sometimes we eat pancakes.'

'OK. And where can I find those?'

'We make them.'

'You make them?'

'Mum makes them and we help.'

'I'm . . . not good at that sort of thing. Pancakes, and what have you. I'll be honest, I'm not good at making food at all.'

Rasmus jumped nimbly down from his chair, pushed it over to the sink and climbed up – was barely able to reach the handle of one of the cabinets on the wall, opened it and took out a bag of flour.

'And we need eggs. Two of them. And milk.'

It happened fast. One of the boys already trusted him.

Somewhere in his chest Ewert Grens softened as he realised how Rasmus found it completely natural that Grens was the only adult in the house.

'Flour. Eggs. Milk. Then we have everything? You're the expert, Rasmus.'

'Butter, too. And salt. And this.'

From another cabinet, further down, the boy took out a waffle iron. Grens was sure that's what was being placed on the counter.

'Do you know what, Rasmus? I don't think that's for pancakes.'

'Yes it is.'

The little hand swung the top of the waffle iron up and down, up and down, like a big mouth opening and closing.

'You see, Ewert? We put the batter in here. And close it, let the appliance swallow it. Wait a while. Then we get pancakes.'

Ewert Grens pushed the heavy waffle iron further in on the counter, it was too close to the edge and could fall.

'OK.'

He plugged it in where the electric kettle was usually connected.

'You're right, Rasmus. That's exactly what we're going to use. Because today we're making chequered pancakes.'

There was a heavy plastic mixing bowl in the same cupboard as the waffle iron, and both the ladle and the mixer were in one of the cutlery drawers. Rasmus's small hands and Grens's much bigger ones stirred the ingredients, with a short break while the detective took off his jacket and threw it onto the back of the chair next to Hugo.

'Ewert?'

Now it was Rasmus's turn to interrupt the stirring and mixing.

'Yes?'

In a voice as serious as the one he'd used to say they were hungry.

'Are we related now?'

'What?'

'Are you kind of like our grandpa now?'

'You know he's not!'

This was the first thing Hugo had said since Zofia left. Grens didn't care about the tone, or that the older brother was upset, the important thing was that he was getting closer.

'No, I'm not your grandfather. Not anybody's, actually.'

'Our uncle, then?'

The little brother hadn't been discouraged by his big brother. He was still as eager, as anxious to make contact.

'Are you, Ewert? Like an uncle?'

'No. I'm not an uncle either. I'm not really anything to you.'

'Because you can be, if you want. We don't have a grandpa or any uncles. All our friends do.'

Grens wished he shared Rasmus's enthusiasm. It sounded so good. Being related.

'Maybe you don't have a grandpa now, but you must have had one in the past?'

'No. Or I never met one.'

This time Hugo turned when he interrupted the conversation.

'Yes, Rasmus. We have one. But you don't remember. You were too little, that was before we . . .'

Hugo met Ewert's eyes. Perhaps in some kind of shared understanding.

'. . . moved. Before that sodding Colombia. Then Grandpa visited sometimes.'

He was nine years old. And not used to using swear words, that much was clear, he took too much, striving to make a word he hadn't really mastered sound as natural as it could. Grens remembered their first meeting in Bogotá's airport. Hugo had already been the more watchful of the two brothers back then. Just before their flight took off for Stockholm, and with their father's help, Grens made it clear to Rasmus he knew his name was Rasmus and not Sebastian, and then he'd turned to the quieter, taller boy.

So that must mean you're name is . . .

Hugo. I never liked William.

And I've never . . .

That's when Ewert Grens leaned closer, whispered right into the boy's ear.

. . . liked Ewert. But your name is your name. And so you become your name in the end.

And they had smiled at each other. They had a secret.

Now Grens sat down on the chair next to Hugo, wrinkling the jacket as he leaned against it.

'Hugo? I know you saw me in the schoolyard when I was visiting your mother, but you pretended not to recognise me. And I understand that you're a bit, well, worried that I'm here rather than your mum. But do you remember, Hugo? Do you remember the airport? We had a secret, you and me. We still have that secret together – you are the only person in the world who knows I don't like my name. I've never dared to tell anyone else.'

Grens put an arm around him, squeezed him gently.

And it didn't feel awkward, or wrong.

Then he got up and helped Rasmus lift the chequered pancakes out of the waffle iron one after the other. Until the glass tray – which he was quite sure was ovenproof – was full and they put it in the oven at 150 degrees so that all ten pancakes would be evenly warm.

'I'm good at washing up.'

So Hugo finally got up – squeezed into the narrow gap between Grens and his little brother and reached over to the mixing bowl where the batter had been, then the ladle and the whisk that were covered with a sticky film.

Hot running water and a lot of garishly green dish soap combined with Hugo scrubbing with the dish brush, then rinsing and scrubbing and then holding up the bowl for inspection until Grens nodded, which meant it was very clean, and then carefully placing it on the dish rack to dry.

'So I guess you know my dad?'

Hugo didn't look at Grens when he asked. It was probably easier for him that way, avoiding Grens's eyes.

'Yes, Hugo, I do.'

'And how often do you meet?'

Grens hesitated.

How are you supposed to answer a question like that?

Never.

And also two days ago.

'Not often. We . . . mostly spent time together back then. In Colombia.'

'I don't want to talk to Dad any more either.'

Ewert Grens turned off the running water, placed his hands on Hugo's skinny nine-year-old shoulders, and gently turned him around so they could face one another.

'What . . . are you trying to tell me?'

'That I don't want to talk to Dad since he might not come home.'

'Hugo, I don't understand.'

'I heard them talking. Back in Colombia. Late at night. When they thought I was sleeping.'

'Talking?'

'About things Rasmus and I weren't supposed to know. About people who died. And about how Dad might die, too.'

Grens ran a hand over Hugo's hair. That too didn't feel uncomfortable or wrong.

'Have you told your mum? That you were listening during those nights? That you're worried that your dad isn't feeling good?'

'She lies too!'

'Lies?'

'Not about other things. She never lies about other things. But about this. About Dad. So we can't talk about it.'

He didn't try to leave, didn't break free.

'Mum and Dad lie. And Dad hides things. I'm the only one who knows where he's hiding them.'

'Hiding?'

'Yeah. Just like he sometimes doesn't tell the truth.'

Ewert Grens stood at the sink of a home that wasn't his and realised he'd just been entrusted with the entire universe of one young person. A person who wasn't nearly as small as his parents believed. Who listened, put things together, arrived at his own conclusions, which he didn't like.

'You say that your dad is lying. That your dad hides things. But if you don't talk to him about it, he'll never know.'

'I'm *not* gonna talk to him. Because I heard a shot.'

'A shot?'

'Yes.'

'And when did you hear . . .?'

'In the morning. Mum puts the phone on the table, and when we have breakfast we talk to each other. With Dad. But you don't just hear his voice. You hear everything. Sometimes it's the prayer calls. Sometimes it's just loud, people screaming, maybe a car driving too fast. The last time we talked it was a shot. Last time *I* talked to him. Then I went outside and sat on the stairs.'

'What was the shot you heard, Hugo?'

'Just before he left. That's why he hung up. Because they were shooting. Because it was dangerous.'

Nine years old and incredibly aware of what was happening to his father.

He'd started to understand when they moved to Colombia, maybe even earlier. He didn't know exactly what his father did, didn't know an infiltrator risked his life every day, but Hugo had understood enough to be angry – a boy should be protected from thoughts like that, who might not be able to endure much more.

They set the table. Grens lifted down plates and glasses that were high up, Rasmus placed the knives and forks and put a spoon into the jar of strawberry jam, Hugo folded red and blue striped napkins and put them under the silverware. They'd already eaten two pancakes each when Ewert Grens became aware that Hugo was running a hand worriedly over his cheeks, back and forth. And his breathing had become uneven, shallow breaths interspersed with deep ones for no obvious reason.

'Hugo?'

'Yes?'

'Are you OK?'

The hand on the cheeks again. At the same time, the deep breaths returned.

'Hugo – what is it?'

'Nothing.'

'Answer me.'

Grens took the boy's other hand, the one that wasn't on his face. Held on tight. But not too tight.

'Hugo?'

'I know why you're here, Ewert.'

Hugo's eyes. They sought out Grens's like before.

'And why's that, Hugo?'

'Dad. That's why.'

He stopped squeezing Hugo's hand.

But it remained in his.

Hugo didn't move it.

'Something with Dad. First the shot, then he didn't come home, then Mum's voice and face. And now *you're* here.'

The eyes of a worried and wise nine-year-old met his, demanding answers.

'Is something going to happen to us, Ewert? Something bad?'

'KING OF SPADES.'

Rasmus's voice was completely neutral as he said it.

King of spades.

Ewert Grens looked at the just as neutral seven-year-old eyes. Expressionless.

Or as close as any eyes could be.

'King of spades, you say?'

'King of spades, I say.'

Grens turned to Hugo instead. Those eyes were more readable. Satisfied. That's how he looked.

'What do you say, Hugo, do you believe your little brother?'

'I don't believe anything. It's your turn. You have to decide, Ewert. Do you pass? Or do you cheat?'

The detective superintendent studied the upside-down pile of playing cards. Then the backs of the four cards Rasmus was clutching in his hands, and the two in Hugo's hands. He himself held nine cards. He was definitely in last place.

'I would *not* want to meet you two in an interrogation room.'

Rasmus's neutral look. Grens tried to pierce it, get behind it, but couldn't penetrate it. Over the years he'd become quite good at interrogating murderers, hit men, drug barons, mafia bosses. Reading their unconscious body language, picking apart their frustrating silence, dismantling lie after lie. This expertise was no help now. A seven-year-old boy didn't move, think, or talk like a criminal. And when he lied, he did it better.

'I don't know Rasmus, but I think I'll say . . . doubt it.'

'You *think* you'll say it?'

'I am saying. Doubt it. Show your card. I think you're bluffing, and you're going to have to pick up that whole pile on the table.'

'Wrong, Ewert. Again.'

Rasmus stretched out a hand and turned over the card he'd just put on top of the stack.

King of spades.

Just as he claimed.

'There you go, Ewert. Pick them up, all of them.'

Two siblings, both so pleased with themselves. Their opponent who sat between them at the kitchen table suddenly had nine *plus* eight more cards in his hand. Or hands, he had to use both. An opponent who was far behind in a game where the goal was to have as few cards as possible, preferably none at all.

'Rasmus? Hugo? I am appointing you as my assistant detectives – next time I'm in an interrogation room trying to crack a criminal I want you by my side. They won't fool you. You, on the other hand, will fool their shirts off their backs. Just like you're doing to me.'

Ewert Grens smiled, his chest and stomach felt warm and fluffy, a kind of calm he almost never achieved. They'd eaten pancakes with strawberry jam, all ten, did the dishes and tidied up, and when Rasmus went and grabbed a deck of cards, it felt completely natural to sit down at the kitchen table again and listen to Hugo's recitation of a lot of rules the detective had never heard of.

He had no family of his own. And couldn't imagine being part of one. But it was surprisingly moving to have this small insight into what having a family might be like. Even though the reason he found himself here came from the very worst of circumstances. Or, maybe, those circumstances were why it affected him so much.

'She's coming!'

As soon as the gate opened, Rasmus heard the steps he'd recognise anywhere, at any time, and rushed through the kitchen and the hall to meet them on the staircase outside.

'Hi, my darling.'

His mother's steps.

'This is Amadou, he's going to chat with us tonight, talk a little bit with me and Ewert.'

Grens lingered at the kitchen table, gave them time to take off their shoes and coats – she'd bring the boy he'd never met to him, not the other way around, better not to risk scaring him any more than he already was.

'Have you said hello to our guest, Hugo?'

Zofia waited until Hugo met Amadou's outstretched hand, then gave her son a hug and asked him to go to his room and take Rasmus with him.

'We'll sit in here. Are you thirsty, Amadou?'

She spoke in a mixture of Swedish and French, skilfully weaving together the two languages in a way that made them complement each other, so that everything was comprehensible to everyone and no one was left out. Amadou nodded and Zofia poured orange juice into one glass and water into another, placed both next to where he sat down.

'Hello, Amadou. My name is Ewert. I think Zofia told you why I'm here.'

Grens spoke in Swedish, but the boy didn't seem to fully understand. Until Zofia translated into French, and he nodded gently.

'She may have also told you a little about what I do?'

The boy nodded again. He looked younger than the fourteen years Zofia said he had. And he'd been crying. His eyes were swollen, red-rimmed, tired.

'About why I wanted to meet you?'

Short, skinny, few signs of puberty, which would probably hit soon. He was clearly connected to the dead refugee couple. His skin colour, his build, he probably came, as Zofia claimed, from the same place in West Africa as the refugee couple, and could be related to one of them.

'So if I . . .'

Grens waited until the boy stopped staring down at the table with eyes as red as they were unsure.

'. . . say container, Amadou, what do you say to that? *Container ship?*'

He used the English word, and the worried boy seemed to understand.

'Container ship?'

'Yes.'

The boy turned to Zofia.

'*Porte-conteneurs?*'

'*Oui*, Amadou. *Porte-conteneurs.*'

And he really thought hard, leaning his forehead to his palms with his elbows on the table. So anxious to do the right thing.

'I think . . . when they opened the container, I'm thinking about . . . Zofia, *joie*, in Swedish, what is it called?'

'Joy.'

'Joy. I remember being happy.'

Grens had expected many things. But not that. He continued in Swedish, and Zofia translated it into French and then Amadou's French replies back into Swedish.

'Did you see who opened the container when you arrived?'

'Yes.'

'A face, multiple faces?'

'One face. The one who opened it. There were several. But I could only see one.'

'And what do you remember when you think about it?'

'What I said. Joy. When I think about that face – all the fear that I had disappeared, we had arrived. I think of it as a good face.'

A skinny boy who repeatedly said the word joy.

But looked crushed.

'I know, Amadou, that Zofia told you about your cousin and her husband.'

He'd just received news of a death.

'Because she was your cousin, right?'

'Alyson Souleymane. That's her name.'

He stared down at the table, like before.

'Was her name.'

Grens was in no hurry. It took the time it took. Until Amadou was able to look at him again.

'The same last name as me – Souleymane. Her husband's name is, *was* Idriss. Idriss Coulibaly. I have a picture. Zofia asked me to bring it. I couldn't carry much with me, when I came here. One photograph of me – you see, I'm standing there – and of Alyson, she's there, and of Idriss and Alyson's sister. It was a beautiful day.'

The boy handed over a wrinkled photo whose colours were already starting to fade. Four young people laughing at the camera, they were sitting on a piece of cloth on the ground eating something, it was evening and the flash from the camera reflected in their eyes. Grens couldn't be sure, because the quality wasn't good enough, but the two Amadou called Alyson and Idriss had a striking resemblance to the two found in the morgue.

'Alyson and Idriss, you say.'

'Yes.'

'Can you . . . Amadou – is there anything you know about Alyson's body, or Idriss's body, that could help me to make sure they're the ones who . . . are no longer alive.'

'How they look?'

'Yes. Something that can't be seen in the picture.'

The boy did like before, rested his forehead heavily in his hands while he tried to remember. Ewert Grens was looking for something, anything, that Sven and Mariana could compare to the forensic report on the two bodies – something that strengthened Amadou's credibility, and thus the credibility he might need later as a witness.

'She has . . . *had* an injury. Alyson broke her foot once. Right foot. We climbed a high tree, we were picking leaves when one of the branches broke. She fell, she was in pain for a long time, I think she still was when she left. She never said anything, but I could see it.'

'Good. Good, Amadou. A broken foot always leaves traces. Anything else about Alyson? Or something you might remember about Idriss?'

'His throat. It was as if someone had cut off a piece of his skin.'

'Cut off?'

'Yes. And then pasted over an equally large piece that was lighter.'

Grens considered putting his hand on the boy's shoulder, for a moment, maybe even on top of the boy's hand. But decided not to. He knew from his own experience how wrong that kind of touch could feel, how something meant to comfort or give strength could feel intrusive instead – sometimes take rather than give.

'That's very good to know. You've helped a lot, you've helped *me*, Amadou. I'm pretty sure what you're describing is the same pigmentation I saw when . . . that we can use for identification. To see if this is your cousin and her husband. Your friends.'

The orange juice glass was empty and Zofia took it to the fridge to refill it, while Grens tried to stretch out his body, these kitchen chairs weren't meant for an old man with a stiff neck and an equally stiff left leg. He waved his arms over his head, swung his heavy body back and forth, twisted his head. And in the corner of his eye he saw something that shouldn't be there. *Someone who shouldn't be there.*

Hugo.

At the far end of the hall – if you looked just right – reflected in one of the kitchen windows.

There he lay, the elder of the Hoffmann brothers. On the floor. Curled up by the wall.

Eavesdropping.

Without knowing he'd been discovered.

'Zofia?'

Grens pointed towards the hall.

'I'm going to the bathroom. It's out there, right?'

Zofia nodded and Grens stood up.

'Then we'll talk some more. You're very helpful, Amadou. And you're going to help me a bit more, since you're so good at observing and remembering – try to tell me what another person looked like.'

He'd been moving while he was talking, two quick steps until he stood in the hall.

'Hello, Hugo.'

A pair of surprised eyes – a spy who had no idea he'd been discovered.

'Ewert, I . . .'

'Take my hand – I'll pull you up.'

Grens offered his hand and was careful to speak quietly – Hugo needed to understand that this was between them.

'Hugo, you're not supposed to hear this.'

'No . . . but it's important.'

'Take my hand and stand up.'

'This is about Dad. I just know it. It always is when there's talk in the kitchen and we can't be there. So I *have to* listen.'

'But that's not the case tonight. This isn't about your dad. This time you shouldn't listen for Amadou's sake. OK?'

Stubborn. That's how the older Hoffmann brother looked as he lay as still as a stick on the floor. But Ewert Grens was just as stubborn. So the outstretched arm hung in the air between them. Until Hugo sighed, let himself be pulled up.

'Stay in your room with Rasmus until we've finished talking. Then Amadou and I will leave and you can hang out with your mum as much as you want.'

Grens lingered while Hugo disappeared up the staircase to the second floor of the house. He opened the bathroom door, flushed the toilet and let the tap in the sink drain before returning to the kitchen table and another boy.

'Joy. I think that's what you said, Amadou. *Joie*? That's the French?'

Amadou nodded.

'*Joie*.'

'You felt that when the container was opened. When you were released.'

'Yes. Joy.'

'Can you describe the face that gave you that joy? Which was the first thing you saw when the container door was opened? You said there were several people, but you could only see one.'

They waited while Zofia translated.

First, Grens's question, then Amadou's answer.

'Describe? What do you mean?'

'Man or woman?'

'Man.'

'Same skin colour as you, Amadou, or as me?'

'Like you.'

'Dark hair or light?'

'No hair.'

'Beard, moustache?'

'Bit of a beard. A few days of not shaving.'

'His mouth?'

'Normal.'

'Nose?'

'Normal.'

'Eyes?'

Amadou was just about to answer, just as bluntly as before, when he stopped and looked away.

'Amadou, the eyes, do you remember them?'

The boy turned to Grens for a moment and pointed to one of his own eyes.

'They had different amounts of black. That middle part. I don't even know what that is called in French. The part that gets bigger and smaller depending on the amount of light.'

'*Pupille?*'

Zofia pointed to Grens's eyes.

'The black inside the brown of your eyes, and inside the blue of his, right? If that's what you mean, it's basically the same in Swedish. Pupil. Pupils, if there are two.'

'Yes. *Pupille.* The man who opened the container had blue eyes like the detective, but pupils of different sizes despite the same amount of light.'

'Different-sized pupils?'

'Yes. One eye had a large pupil, one eye had a small pupil. The whole time he looked at me.'

Grens put a hand on Amadou's shoulder now. And the boy didn't react or show any discomfort.

'You are extremely helpful, Amadou. A face with pupils of two different sizes is a face we can search for. You and I will meet again. I'll bring a sketch artist with me. And then you'll tell her everything you remember as well.'

So young. And he'd made the same trip as the seventy-three who never arrived. The only witness to the single verifiable face on Swedish soil.

The only clue that might lead a detective superintendent to the smuggling organisation's top person in Sweden.

'Amadou?'

'Yes?'

'We'll soon be done for today. Just one more question.'

'Yes?'

Ewert Grens really had no idea why he said it. He didn't have the time. It wouldn't help him.

But for the boy in front of him.

For him, it might help. Might mean something.

A kind of dignity.

Perhaps that was what Grens wanted to give him.

For that roaring pit of grief inside the skinny, sunken chest, which leaked out no matter how brave he was, no matter how much he wanted to do the right thing, being questioned just an hour after learning that his loved one had died.

'Alyson's family. And Idriss's family. How can I find them?'

'Find them?'

'I'd like to let them know. I'd like to inform the relatives of the people who arrived in the container. And the two names you've given me are the only ones I have so far. I've told many people about the death of a loved one – and I've learned that there is something worse than knowing. And that's not knowing.'

The boy who'd lived longer than most other boys his age looked at Grens.

He understood. He agreed. He wanted to help. But slowly shook his head.

'I can't. I don't know how to find them. I've never met Idriss's family. And Alyson, she's my cousin, but . . . her family and my family, everyone's fled somewhere else . . . you don't always know where people end up, not there.'

Amadou then drank a third glass of orange juice, and Grens said yes to a final cup of coffee and one of those cheese sandwiches left over once the three boys no longer had room for more. As he was leaving, the detective put his hand on Hugo's shoulder – he'd started to really get the hang of it, almost felt natural – and thanked him for an interesting game of Cheat and swore he'd take his revenge next time.

Rasmus followed him out the door and about the time they reached the gate, he threw his arms around the neck of a completely unprepared Grens. Whispered in Grens's ear that people could be related in lots of different ways, and he'd *actually* heard that there were more than just grandpas and uncles there were also part-time-grandpas and chequered-pancake-uncles.

And it was, *actually*, absolutely true.

Amadou had agreed to let Grens drive him back to his group foster home, had assured Zofia he was no longer afraid of this officer. And when he was settled in the passenger seat and Rasmus and Hugo had returned to the house and the kitchen table – you could see their bobbing heads through the kitchen window – the detective asked Zofia if he could talk to her for a moment before they parted ways.

'You and Piet have got good kids.'

'Yes. I know.'

'And they'll both be very proud big brothers in six months or so.'

'Yes. They will.'

'I can already see—'

'What do you *really* want to talk to me about, Ewert?'

She looked at him, impatient and demanding. She'd already told him not to intrude on her family further. A couple of hours as a babysitter for her sons hadn't changed that.

'Say what you want to say. So I can go in again. And you can leave.'

It had been a long time since Ewert Grens felt afraid. Of anything, at all.

That's what happens when a person loses everything that matters to them.

But now he was. Afraid. Too afraid to figure out how to say what he was thinking. Afraid she'd take it in the wrong way.

'Hugo.'

'Yes, Ewert – what about Hugo?'

'He's quite the kid.'

'What *about* Hugo?'

Just like before with Amadou. Ewert Grens didn't really know why he was saying this, why he spent time and energy on something that he didn't need to concern himself with, something that wasn't his responsibility.

Nevertheless he did. Because he couldn't help it.

'Hugo doesn't seem to be feeling great.'

'I know.'

'He's worried. And we talked quite a bit. I think . . .'

'Ewert – what's so hard for you to understand? I told you not to get involved! You took our lives away from us, for many years, until we took them back. We were fine until you showed up the other day, even after you promised you never would. That part of Piet's life was supposed to be over for ever!'

She'd screamed that last sentence at him.

Amadou had started to follow every move from the passenger seat, as were two little heads from on the other side of the kitchen window.

'Just listen to me for a minute, Zofia.'

'I don't need to listen to you.'

'Hugo understands much more than you may think, he's aware of what happened – and what *is happening* – to his father.'

'Hugo hasn't quite adjusted to the move in the same way Rasmus has. I know that. It's always been like this. In Colombia, too. It simply takes him longer. He never accepted—'

'He hears things and puts them together. He understands, Zofia.'

'—our new life, maybe it's like that when you're the oldest. And it's my job to take care of them. Make sure he slowly adjusts. My job, Ewert – not yours!'

Again, she shouted the last bit.

Amadou jumped in the passenger seat, and the two heads in the window ran towards the hall and the front door, before Zofia stopped them with the wave of a hand, directing them inside again.

Ewert Grens walked the last bit towards the car, then around it, and opened the door to the driver's seat. He had been afraid of her reaction. Worried that his words would fall flat. And they had. It had gone just as badly as he'd feared.

'Zofia, I think he needs help. From someone else. Sometimes you need it. For example, I have a colleague named Sven with a phobia of

death. I've never met a police officer who's more afraid of dead people
– I don't understand how he managed to get into the academy. So I
sent him to therapy. And it did him good, it seems like . . . Zofia, look
at me, I think Hugo might also need professional help. That's what I
wanted to say. That's all.'

She was silent as he climbed into the driver's seat, as he put on his
seatbelt, as he turned the ignition key. Until he grabbed the gearstick.
Then she knocked on the window and waited until he rolled it down.
She patted Amadou's cheek, then leaned in as close to Grens as she
could get.

She didn't scream any more, this was worse. A quiet, ice-cold voice.

'Ewert? You don't have any children, that's why you can't understand. You have destroyed what was finally starting to feel normal.
Please leave here. And never come back.'

THE LIGHTS WERE ON in only a few of the Ministry for Foreign Affairs' many high windows. A beautiful building, proud, maybe even grand. At one time the palace of a prince. It had stood for over two hundred years, radiating power. Solemn. Stable. Stern. Those were the words that Grens's exhausted mind tried to grasp hold of.

He'd stopped near the middle of Gustav Adolf's Square, near the statue of a verdigris-green and pointing king atop a horse. He'd kept the business card in his wallet, high quality paper with a blue shield and three golden crowns printed on it – it was exactly where he left it, next to the other less luxurious business card he'd received at the same time. The taxi driver Frederick, his name and number pencilled onto a napkin.

Now he picked up the expensive business card again, ran his fingertips over the raised print, and called the same number he'd called half an hour earlier.

'Detective Superintendent Grens here. I'm outside.'

'I'll come down. We can sit in my office. It's quiet, and definitely more private than a bar across the street or the cafés that stay open late on Drottninggatan.'

Thor Dixon looked just as cosmopolitan in the context of the Swedish capital as he had in Niger. Those grey eyes were just as sharp and clever; his hair, the same grey, lay in perfect waves without seeming newly combed; his slim body wore another suit – slightly darker – but it too screamed of taste and class.

As they shook hands at the doorway to one of Sweden's political centres, it felt as if they'd met many more times than in a taxi on their way from an airport and then briefly in an air-conditioned hotel lobby. Grens had experienced that before – how meetings in other places, in other realities, made more of an impact, as if you, without knowing it, needed each other more.

The stone staircase echoed and had worn, slippery steps. They climbed three floors up and turned into a deserted corridor, where the door stood open to the Foreign Ministry official's office.

'Sit down. And I'll arrange something to drink. Mineral water? Whisky?'

'Coffee.'

'At this hour? Aren't you planning to sleep this evening, Mr Grens?'

'Coffee puts me to sleep. Coffee wakes me up again.'

'Coffee it is.'

Dixon moved to a sideboard with a thermos and porcelain cups, and Grens looked around. The office seemed as stern as the rest of the building. Heavy furniture from another era. The room lit by impractical lamps, whose bulky shades drowned out the light bulbs inside. Walls lined with paintings, all of which seemed to be by the same artist, with two exceptions – two documentary-like photographs were hanging in beautiful frames behind the desk. Pictures of big white buses driving along a gravel road somewhere, and when the detective leaned in closer, he saw red crosses on their roofs.

'My mother.'

Thor Dixon had noticed Grens inspecting the only thing in the room that seemed personal and not inherited from a predecessor.

'She was rescued by those White Buses. April 1945. Norwegian, five years as a POW. She ended up in Sweden. Fourteen years later, I was born. I often stand here and just look sometimes, sink into those black and white photos, imagine her sitting in one of those seats. What a terrific job they did! Truly, those white buses were a relief organisation that made a difference. Saved lives! My mother's life. That's probably why I work in this building. Do what I do.'

The detective caught a lovely whiff of the coffee that stood on a silver tray on a rather low table. He sat down in a sofa with red and gold stripes – a glossy fabric that would have fitted in in almost any castle. About as far from his own tired corduroy sofa as you could get.

'Thank you for letting me stop by at such short notice.'

'I told you. You can call any time you like for a drink. Even though I meant in Niamey when I said it, still the offer stands.'

Grens took a drink — it *tasted* lovely too — and gestured towards the window and the still not quite dark summer night sky outside.

'You're working late.'

'I often do. I landed at Arlanda a couple of hours ago. And, to be honest, I don't have much to go home to. No one is waiting. So I'd rather sit here. Without this, Superintendent, not much would feel particularly meaningful.'

Ewert Grens nodded.

He could have said much the same thing.

He knew how big an empty apartment could feel, how odd it was to find it impossible to relax in a bed chosen and adapted specifically for his back — while an ugly, old corduroy sofa that was too small, and too soft, and too tight, and stood in a boring office in a police station, put him to sleep like a baby.

'You gave me this. If I wanted to drink coffee. But also if I needed your help.'

For the third time that evening, the detective superintendent picked up the fancy business card.

'Now I do. I need your help.'

Grens placed the card between them on the coffee table, like a ticket or an IOU about to be redeemed. Then he related carefully chosen details about the investigation to the official responsible for the area where seventy-three dead refugees came from — if an outsider feels included they're more willing to invest time and effort, Grens had learned that over the years. And the furrowed, but elegant, face transformed into an expression that was equal parts sorrow and rage.

'I . . . it makes me so bloody angry. How can I help you? Whatever you need. Anything I can.'

Ewert Grens wasn't sure how much to say about the bodies dumped in the morgue. This detail was still being withheld from the press and public. And he wanted to keep it that way. No unnecessary intrusions into those tunnels until every inch had been investigated thoroughly.

'Two of the dead — we think we know their identities.'

The detective superintendent handed over a handwritten note that bore two names.

'Alyson Souleymane and Idriss Coulibaly. Those are their names. I want to inform their relatives. Make sure their bodies are transported home to their loved ones. So they're buried by the people who care about them, who miss them.'

'These two were found in the container?'

'Two of the dead. And you regularly meet with local politicians, relief organisations, UN employees, government officials down there. You have access to whatever structures exist in a very chaotic country, you have the contacts. While I – I don't even know where to begin.'

The man opposite Ewert Grens was a diplomat. Used to negotiation, weighing every word. He'd noticed that the detective hadn't answered his question about the container, and instead repeated his previous words – *two of the dead*. But he let it pass.

'You say you don't know where to begin, Grens – but I can tell just looking at you how important this is. Why? How could notifying and delivering bodies to relatives in West Africa help you find whoever's guilty?'

'This isn't about that. Not everything in an investigation pushes you forward. The person or the people responsible for this catastrophe didn't just take their lives, they took their deaths, too. It's part of my job to give them back.'

Grens had already been thinking about it on his way up that stone staircase.

How the whole building lacked sound. Just the faint noise from the evening traffic out on Central Bridge, that was all. Nothing from inside. Corridors, stairwells, offices – not even a whisper. And as Ewert Grens and Thor Dixon quietly scrutinised each other, without taking a drink or scraping their feet, the silence started to feel as solemn as the palace itself.

'I believe you, Superintendent. You'd like to give them back their deaths. And yet – I can't help feeling there's something more. Something else driving you. I'll help you regardless if I can, but I am still wondering what this is all about. Why do you *really* want me to devote my time to turning Niger's bureaucracy and their at best insufficient documentation upside down?'

Really.

In suspecting more, Thor Dixon had stressed the exact same word Zofia had a couple of hours earlier. Grens didn't like sharing the details of his investigations, even with his own boss, but giving this official a little insight, building a sense of confidence, would be to the benefit of the detective.

'There's a boy. He's related to one of the dead. I just met him. And I have never met anyone who seems so . . . abandoned. I think – well, I'm not completely sure – but I think he might feel less alone if he knows that I . . . that *we* tried hard to locate those relatives.'

The cosmopolitan diplomat nodded, slowly.

'Thank you. Then I have two reasons to make these calls. And I must say I find this all quite unexpected. I didn't think the Swedish police went about their investigations in such an, well, emotional way.'

'It *is* unexpected. For me too – believe me. Guess I'm getting old. But don't tell anyone – we don't want to confuse my colleagues after all these years.'

'About what, Superintendent?'

Grens emptied his cup and put it on the silver tray, before getting up and saying thank you. They were halfway down the stone staircase when Thor Dixon slowed a bit.

'We hear things around here. And we heard you found some of the bodies. In unexpected places.'

Ewert Grens stared straight ahead while he walked. He didn't want the official to see he wasn't getting the whole truth.

'Really?'

'In the morgues of more than one hospital. Several bodies. That had been hidden there. Is that right?'

'Unfortunately, I can't comment on that.'

'You just commented on it, Superintendent. In the morgues? In that case, I understand what you mean by giving them their death back. What I do not understand, however, is how the bodies ended up there. How someone could get them inside.'

'Unfortunately, I can't comment on that either.'

'People on the inside? Hospital staff? Morgue staff? Who else could—'

'Sorry, Dixon.'

Just a few steps left down that echoing, slippery staircase. And all Ewert Grens could see was a woman's warm smile.

'But you won't get any more out of me.'

'Then you should know, Superintendent, that this tragedy has had consequences for my institution as well. Never a quiet moment. Phones ringing off the hook – journalists *demanding* answers. When of course we don't have any!'

The last step on the stone staircase wasn't far from the front door that led to Gustav Adolf's Square. But far enough for the detective's walk to be interrupted three times. First when he gently grabbed Thor Dixon's arm and spoke without looking at him.

'OK. I'm asking for your help, so let's say this – you *will* be getting the answers to those questions very soon.'

Then when they reached the single visitors' chair that stood in the entrance hall.

'Because we have a witness. The boy I spoke about. The one whose relatives I asked you to find. We have something concrete to go on. We're getting closer to the bastard who's making money by transporting people in cages.'

The last time Grens stopped, he'd just put his hand on the door's heavy handle.

'This boy made the same journey. But unlike the others, he survived. He saw the individuals who closed the container in Gdansk and opened it in Stockholm.'

PIET HOFFMANN LAY ON his stomach on the flat roof of the hotel. A dry, mild evening breeze swirled around him as he balanced on his elbows and aimed the sniper rifle at the window he was becoming quite familiar with.

Zuwara's highest point. And a perfect view of the Accountant in his night-vision scope.

For a couple of hours, she'd been sitting at one of those simple desks, making notes, sorting papers, counting money, entering numbers into a computer and printing out documents, and now, as she pushed her glasses up into her hair, she seemed to be done. She'd been in constant motion until now, and when she stood still, he was able to magnify her face even more, get close to the skin, to every micro expression. Calm. That's how she looked. Satisfied. Lovely in a way that was unlike the other beauty she possessed, which seemed so self-evident to her and to everyone else. Soft. Kind. Not like earlier in the day. Alone in headquarters she'd let go of that distance, calculation, no longer on guard against everything and everyone.

Soon she walked out of his sightline, in a direction he could no longer follow. This time he knew where – he'd been pinned to the floor with Omar's revolver against his temple when he heard and saw her heels coming towards him the first time. The Safe Room. That's where she'd gone, to the thick, safe-like door, which she was probably closing and securing with several locks.

There was a buzz inside his jacket.

Hoffmann raised his upper body slightly and fished out a phone from deep inside his pocket, glanced at the display, and the monitoring system for the GPS attached to Omar's car.

The vehicle had started moving about an hour ago. The coastal road from Zuwara to Tripoli. It had stopped halfway at, according to the satellite image, what seemed to be a petrol station and was parked there for fourteen minutes. Now – that's why it had buzzed – the car was rolling again at a normal speed eastwards, along the coast headed towards the capital.

It could have something to do with the call Omar got early today when they were far out on the pier.

Submissive.

That's how he'd sounded. A voice that's temporarily lost its confident, aggressive tilt. An upcoming meeting, Hoffmann was convinced that's what he'd heard. And based on the change in his voice – a meeting with his superior. Sure, he could be headed to Tripoli in the middle of the night for a mistress or a brothel or a party at a restaurant or anything else the likes of an Omar might get up to. But the likes of an Omar never signals submissiveness in a conversation about those things. And he'd also spoken English, even tried to dampen his heavy accent. The trip *made sense* together with that conversation, Hoffmann was sure it was that meeting Omar was on his way to – leaving Zuwara and headquarters with a boat just a day from departing would not be something a control freak does unless forced to, ordered to.

And suddenly, Piet Hoffmann realised something.

Now.

His opportunity was now.

With Omar almost in Tripoli, and the Accountant having locked up for the day, the direction of the night changed. It had arrived significantly earlier than Piet Hoffmann had expected but now was his chance to sneak into their headquarters without being discovered. In the hours before sunrise he would search for the information Grens needed, and while he did so he'd prepared a death – the kind that was only possible for those who valued money higher than life.

He'd already planned it on his first night on the roof – and had written down – *what* and *how*.

Bump key
Interpreters
Leaf springs

Resin
The Dane
T-beam
Det cord
GSM-controlled ignition switch
Giraffe
Metres per second

Now he also had *when*.

Time always ticked by more quickly when it was limited.

And Hoffmann had no idea when another opportunity like this would arrive, the Accountant out of headquarters and pathologically suspicious Omar at a proper distance. But he did not – even though he was in a hurry, even though his whole body wanted to rush over there – let himself get sloppy with the last of his security checks.

So he reviewed the display of his phone – made sure Omar's car was still moving at the same speed towards the city limits of Tripoli.

So he again searched the port area through his night-vision scope – made sure the only armed guards in the vicinity were the two smoking by the entrance to the warehouse with over four hundred refugees inside it.

So he crawled back over the raised edge of the flat roof and peered over it – making sure that the brawny man, one of the bodyguards Hoffmann challenged at headquarters, was still waiting down on the street in his car. A shadow on Hoffmann. They still didn't trust him. But a shadow that wasn't well-trained. Easy to detect, bored, lacking focus. Nevertheless, from his place in the front of the hotel, in a Ford Mustang opposite the entrance, it would be impossible for Hoffmann to walk out without being noticed.

'Piet?'

She had answered immediately.

'Is that you?'

'Zo, were you awake?'

He hadn't really been aware he'd taken his phone again, and it wasn't to check for a third time if Omar was still on his way to Tripoli

– instead, he had pushed one of his few pre-programmed numbers. To Zofia, to Hugo, to Erik Wilson. Only those three, in that order.

'Yes, I was awake.'

'And the boys?'

'They're sleeping. I just heard Rasmus snoring. And Hugo was shouting something in his sleep as he does.'

Piet Hoffmann was about to expose himself to the kind of danger that might mean death. That's why he sought out her voice. That's what he always did to sharpen his senses – if he was close to her, close to the boys, he had something to lose.

'Zofia, I—'

'I know why you didn't come home.'

'These extra transports, they—'

'I heard it as soon as you called. You were lying. But I didn't know why. You used to be an expert liar, Piet, lying to me day in and day out and I didn't have a clue – you've lost your touch.'

'I . . . Shit, Zofia, I had to.'

'I know that too. I talked to Ewert Grens.'

'Grens?'

'Yes.'

'Why did he . . .'

'Just do what you need to do and come home, unscathed, on your next break. OK? Grens promised me that you weren't in danger. Is that true?'

He was lying on a roof in North Africa. He had one hand on his sniper rifle. He was infiltrating a criminal organisation with none of the prep he needed.

'Yes, that's true. A simple job, Zo. Not at all like before. Absolutely no danger.'

'Now you're lying again.'

It had never felt this hard before.

And when she hung up and her voice was ripped away – he'd never felt so alone.

Home. He had to get home.

He wormed and crawled his way to the fire escape on the side of the hotel, which connected the roof to the top floor, and in his room he retrieved his packed tool bag and climbed up again, it was possible to do it all while staying hidden behind one of the thicker smokestacks. But to get out of the hotel and past Omar's scout in the Mustang, he would have to use another way.

Across the roof. The fourth building on the right. That was his destination.

He hunched down and sneaked towards the backside of the hotel and in the opposite direction of the armed guard, to a place where the roof of the next house stood just a few metres below. The two properties were separated by a dark alley, he took a deep breath and jumped and felt the hot stench of garbage streaming up at him from the giant waste bin behind the restaurant kitchen four floors below.

The fourth building he landed on, each a few metres down and a few metres away like a giant staircase, had a neon sign on its roof – HOTEL written in red and yellow letters. And next to it, a hatch that led down to the top floor. That was his goal. There he'd be able to exit this hotel without the guard seeing him.

He moved quickly after that, but without running and with a preference for the wider alleys – in the narrower ones, he risked running into small crowds, which always stood around outside on cool nights like this. The pleasant breeze became more of a driving wind as he neared the water – the sea called to him and the waves did their best to intimidate the docks and piers with hard waves.

The harbour area, like the rest of Zuwara, was not well lit, and it was easy to climb the high fence with his tool bag and sniper rifle case. The building that held the smugglers' headquarters, which he'd peered into so many times from the hotel roof, was completely dark except for a dim porch lamp over the front door of one entrance. Piet Hoffmann bent down before going into the perimeter of the light, did a final check on Omar. The monitoring system on the phone display confirmed the car had arrived in Tripoli, and according to the coordinates, it was parked in front of one of the capital's most expensive restaurants. Omar *was* really there. Omar *was* meeting someone who considered himself important enough for that sort of place.

Hoffmann made another call to a number that wasn't saved.

'Hi there, this is Piet Kos—'

'My friend! My best fuckin' friend who saved my life!'

'—low here, I need your—'

'My fuckin' saviour! *Whoohohoho! Whoohohoho!* My hero!'

'—help. Where are you?'

Hoffmann was hunched down, whispering in the dark outside a building he was about to break into. While the voice on the other end of the line was a slurring Danish accent, singing off-key, maybe dancing. Frank. Who was doing exactly what he promised. Pushing away the emptiness inside, escaping the thoughts that it seemed best to keep running from.

'Where am I?'

Piet Hoffmann turned down the phone's volume before answering.

'Yes?'

'I told you. Fuckin' Zarzis in Tunisia, Koslow! North Africa's most beautiful beaches just lying here waiting for you. Are you on your way here? *Whoohohoho!* Almost two weeks left, you and me here, you and fuckin' me and—'

'Zarzis. Three hours by car to Tripoli?'

'Two when I drive!'

'I'd like you to go there now. Are you sober enough for it?'

Frank let out a noisy, drunk laugh, but caught himself quickly. As if he suddenly understood the seriousness in Piet Hoffmann's voice. And when he spoke again it was in another voice.

'I can drive. No problem. Whatever you need, my friend, anywhere, anytime, you know it.'

'There's a car parked outside Al Mahary Hotel. Armoured. Heat camera and sprinkler and shooting hatch in the front window. I'm sending you a picture of the man who owns it, taken from the scope on a PSG-90 rifle. I'm pretty sure he's – Omar is his name – eating dinner with somebody. And when they've finished eating, and maybe had a drink in the bar, they'll sleep in rooms at that hotel – they never would have gone to such an expensive restaurant if it weren't at that hotel.'

Piet Hoffmann's young Danish colleague paused, his heavy breathing almost drowned out by the music in the background, *malouf*, violins and sitars and drums and flutes and a woman singing fatefully, beautifully.

'A picture taken with a rifle scope?'

'Yes.'

'I thought you were headed home, Koslow? To the wife and kids? Because, unlike me, you *have a family*?'

'Didn't work out. I ended up in Zuwara. I had some things to do here. Could you go there for me, to the car and restaurant and hotel?'

'I'm there in two hours and fifteen minutes. You'll know whoever this Omar is hanging out with by tomorrow morning.'

Seven steps to the stairs and three steps up.

The front door was grey metal and had a bolt lock of the same make and size as the door on Piet Hoffmann's hotel room. This afternoon he'd gone to a small department store near the centre of Zuwara and bought an iron file and three small rubber rings that were used in moped engines. When he got back to the hotel, he'd filed down some of the seven sharp teeth on his hotel key. Lastly, he'd flattened the metal piece close to the key's head, and attached the three rubber rings there. He now pushed the key into the headquarters' cylinder lock and hit a small hammer on the key head so that it first went into the lock and then, with the help of the rubber washers, bounced out again. On the third blow – that was usually enough for the vibrations to push the locks springs in an almost vertical position – he turned the key as he struck, and literally felt the little pins fall into place. *Bump key.* Just as easy every time, no matter the country or type of lock, and always left no trace.

The stairs to the second floor were built of coarse, unpainted wood and creaked with the same whiny squeak as a staircase in another reality – the stairs between the kitchen and his boys' bedrooms in a house in a quiet neighbourhood south of Stockholm, which he missed every day and every minute.

No one was watching.

Just as he'd ascertained from a roof eight hundred and sixty-one metres away.

Not inside headquarters or out.

He stopped in the middle of the big room under the solid, transverse T-beams, calculated the distance and room height in whatever dim light made it through the windows. He then began walking along the chalk-white walls that framed what was once a factory. In his hand he held four white, centimetre-sized microphones. Interpreters. That's what he called them. He placed them one in each corner, found holes and cracks where they melted into the white.

Everything that was communicated verbally in here would be recorded and translated.

He continued towards the Safe Room, it was there behind the thick security door that the answer to Grens's mission was to be found.

There were two ways in. Either use a crowbar to cut and bend the doorframe and then a hacksaw to clip the uncovered bolts until the door could be pushed open. Or drill a small hole above the lock and pick it until nine springs clicked into place.

And it wasn't until he arrived at the entrance to the Safe Room that he decided which method was best. When he examined how the safe door sat in its frame, and how the doorframe sat in the wall, it became clear that the damage done by a crowbar and hacksaw would be too difficult to disguise later. Picking a lock took longer than forcing it, demanded fine motor skills that were almost beyond him, but there was only one burglary technique that would keep the Accountant and Omar from discovering the infiltrator trying to destroy their organisation from the inside.

The drill in his tool bag was small and neat, and he knew exactly where to direct it above the lock. It had been quite a few years – long before Zofia, when drugs and the money to buy them was the focus of his life – and it cost him half a kilo of Polish amphetamines to buy a lesson from Sweden's premier locksmith. But he'd learned exactly where to drill a hole and insert a thin iron tool, learned how to reach the leaf springs that controlled the lock's nine discs, and how much force to use on them, and how to wait for the rattling noise he heard right now – which meant that the door was now unlocked.

He was in.

And once he pulled the picked open door shut, then he could reach up and turn on the ceiling lamp.

There wasn't much to the room. Seven or eight square metres. But with two cabinets that contained everything he needed. A filing cabinet, which took up most of the wall, and a safe sitting in the centre of the room.

He started with the safe – even though he wouldn't break into it now, he had to do that last, when his mission was over, and it was time to disappear. But in order to get into it, to take what was inside and force these fuckers to die a little bit every day, he would need the combination. The string of numbers that opened the lock. This safe was designed like many modern ones – a digital display and keypad had replaced a rotating dial. But that was perfect. A lit display screen showed the four or six or eight or ten digits that the owner chose as their key. So Hoffmann hid the smallest webcam on the market in one of the crevices in the wall and angled it towards the front of the safe, which meant the next time the Accountant entered her combination it would be recorded and saved. Into Piet Hoffmann's phone.

The lock on the filing cabinet was simpler – he was able to skip it completely.

With a heavy jerk he pulled the metal filing cabinet away from the wall, turned it, and with a hammer and awl prised open a space big enough for the bolt cutter to squeeze in and start chewing its way through. A couple of minutes were all he needed to cut a hole large enough to fish out the first section of hanging files. He spread the documents across the floor. Afterwards, when he was done, it would be as easy to turn the filing cabinet around, push it against the wall, which would hide the hole from behind, while the hanging files concealed it from the front. Unless you were looking for it, there was no reason to inspect the back of the cabinet. There'd be no trace of what he'd done, as long as he put the cabinet back exactly where he found it.

He started reading only after turning off the ceiling lamp – now that he didn't need overhead light, it was safest to use his torch for the close-up work. In the night of a North African port city light always found a way to slip out and reveal itself.

Hoffmann flipped through the documents one by one, each labelled in the corner with a small octopus head. He didn't find much that was more interesting than that symbol, which he assumed was a logo connected to the organisation's name. The entire first section of hanging files consisted of formalities – insurance terms on leased cars, warranty certificates for dishwashers and computers, receipts for office supplies, copies of rental agreements for the harbour buildings. Nothing that led him to a Swedish contact. He carefully pulled another row of hanging files out of the hole he'd cut and started flipping through them as well. Same result. Nothing that had anything to do with the man or woman Ewert Grens was hunting.

A glance at his phone – forty-two minutes had passed since he entered the Safe Room. About twenty minutes per section. He counted another five sections of hanging files in the cabinet, so he needed about one hour and forty minutes to skim them all.

He'd reached the middle of the third section when a familiar feeling hit his gut. Excitement and satisfaction at the same time. A feeling that climbed from its place inside him, up into his chest and stayed there. He held the documents that quite possibly constituted an opening.

Now we're getting somewhere.

day	unit	stage 2 + 3 + 4	zuw1 12,5 %	zuw2 12,5 %	lam. 5%	sal. 8%	A C C 15%	bank 5%	gda 8%	trans balt 7%	C C 25%
2 May	404	1500 $ + 1000 $ + 4000 $	328 250 $	328 250 $	131 300 $	210 080 $	393 900 $	131 300 $	210 080 $	183 820 $	656 500 $
5 May	423	1500 $ + 1000 $ + 2000 $	235 937,5 $	235 937,5 $	95 175 $	152 280 $	285 525 $	95 175 $	152 280 $	133 245 $	475 750 $
9 May	444	1500 $ + 1000 $ + 3500 $	333 000 $	333 000 $	133 200 $	213 120 $	399 600 $	133 200 $	213 120 $	186 480 $	666 000 $

Piet Hoffmann read page after page with columns summarising one hundred and fifty-seven smuggling trips from Libya all the way to Sweden or Germany.

And he read them again.

And again.

Now we've got them, Superintendent Grens.

Little by little the numbers and abbreviations started to make sense. Several years of records for a criminal organisation, revealing how they distributed their profits between various shareholders. He'd seen this kind of layout a few times before when he'd come in contact with human trafficking networks. And it seemed to be just as useful for those making money transporting people for another reason.

Day, the column to the far left. The date the transport departs. In the earliest documents, from a couple of years ago, when their organisation was just starting out, they filled a boat with refugees about every third week. And in the latest document, detailing the last few months – which Hoffmann now held in his hand – departures had increased to twice a week.

Unit, the next column. Product. It could have been toothpaste or potatoes or furniture. But in this printout the unit represented the number of people.

Stage 2 + 3 + 4, third column. The price per refugee for the trip over water and land. With a basic rate for the first two stages, smuggling refugees into the EU, and with different prices for the final stage – the most expensive being for destinations in Germany and Sweden. Which, according to the Accountant, meant offering a complete package so the customer wouldn't have to worry about anything.

Then nine columns of profit distribution by percentage. After several readings, Hoffmann was absolutely sure that *zuw1*, *zuw2*, *lam*, *sal.*, *ACC*, *bank*, *gda*, *trans balt* and *CC* represented code names for various participants.

Nine owners who operated a company that could never be traded on the stock exchange. But who kept detailed bookkeeping of all their income because suspecting you weren't getting the right cut would end in violence and violence has consequences – it cost money and attracted the wrong kind of attention. This type of information was the best way to prevent a breakdown in trust, clear numbers that everyone could count for themselves, distributed on paper and therefore easier to destroy after reading than digital files.

Piet Hoffmann placed the documents on the floor and turned on the ceiling lamp for a moment while taking pictures with his phone camera, the only way to get enough light to make them legible in a photo.

The same nine code names at the top of each page.

One of them – Swedish.

Who are you?

What do you call yourself?

How big is your share of the profit made from every person who has struggled for breath in those sealed containers?

There were another twenty-two pages in the same folder, which he didn't have time to read – despite his conviction that he'd found the very heart of what he was looking for. He'd already used up too much time. But he photographed them too, to look through later.

And just as he was finishing that, about to move on to the fourth row of hanging files, he heard something.

Rubber tyres rolling over fine gravel on asphalt.

A car. And it was slowing down. Very close.

Omar? No, he was far away, even if he'd turned around and drove back here immediately after the last time Hoffmann checked his position. The guards posted at the warehouse where four hundred people sat waiting? No, they wouldn't have driven the short distance that separated the two buildings. Dockworkers? No, there was no reason for dockworkers, or the people who ran the cranes, or who loaded and unloaded goods, to be here in the middle of the night.

Piet Hoffmann turned off the lights in the Safe Room and crept out into the main room, over to the row of windows near the entrance.

There *was* a car down there.

Parked just outside.

And through the windscreen he saw her.

The Accountant.

Did she forget something? Or had he been discovered? Hoffmann ran back across headquarters towards the Safe Room and started gathering up the documents, stuffing them back into hanging files, and putting the files back in place through the clipped-open hole. He pushed the cabinet back against the wall, dropped the loose piece behind it, and made sure the hole was hidden if someone were to open and look in from the front. When he was satisfied, about to hurry out of the narrow room, several metal pieces glinted at him from the floor, metal filings from the cabinet. Too many to pick up. He kicked at them, scooted them with his feet and hoped they were too small to be noticed when spread out. He grabbed his tool bag and slammed the door from the outside, pulled out the long metal tool and heard the lock click into place again. Lastly, he rubbed a piece of resin onto the thin borehole over the locking mechanism, the brown colour filled in and covered.

He'd chosen the only possible hiding place on his very first visit, while lying on the floor with a gun pushed into his forehead, he'd stared up at it. One of the T-beams that crossed the room high above their heads. He put the tool bag and rifle case onto his back and jumped up on one of the desks, then from there onto the underside of the coarse iron beam, grabbed it and lifted himself up. As long as he lay very still on his stomach, the beam was wide enough for only one shoulder to protrude.

He heard the door of the entrance three floors down open and close again.

Her steps on the stairs.

Her breath as she entered the main room of the headquarters and turned on the lights.

Her mumbling to herself as she wandered around the room below him.

If she were to look up. If his chest or knee or feet made even the smallest sound against the cold steel. It would be over.

Frozen.

Piet Hoffmann lay completely frozen.

Until he was sure that her steps had disappeared and were nearing the Safe Room. Then he twisted his neck, leaned slightly in order to follow her with his eyes.

She never seemed to notice the refilled drill hole. She also didn't appear to have noticed the pieces of metal on the floor. The safe. That was her destination. He could see her back from his position halfway up to the ceiling, cursed that he hadn't turned on the camera. Next time. Then the combination would be filmed and sent to him.

She opened it, examined something on the bottom shelves, and took out her mobile phone. Pushed a single number, that much he could see. A saved number.

Her voice wasn't friendly, nor was it unfriendly. She seemed slightly annoyed to be here in the middle of the night. She spoke in Arabic, and since the electronic interpreters he'd placed hadn't been turned on yet, Hoffmann didn't catch much. But maybe enough. He heard her say the name of the voice at the other end, *Omar*. He heard her rattle off some numbers, that much Hoffmann knew, large numbers that matched the organisation's income. He heard her say *Tripoli* in a way that convinced him that it wasn't Omar who had requested the numbers, it was the man or woman whom Omar was meeting in the capital right now and who, despite the late hour, had demanded to hear them.

Who made Omar sound so submissive earlier in the day.

Who was important to the smuggling organisation, maybe even its leader. In that case, according to the documents, only two code names got a bigger share than *zuw1* and *zuw2* – the two Hoffmann guessed were the Accountant and Omar.

The code name *ACC*. Or the code name *CC*.

It *might* be one of those two Omar was meeting in Tripoli, who'd requested the Accountant go here and give them a verbal report. Hoffmann thought of his Danish friend, driving at high speed from his beach paradise, and his trip was now even more important.

A few minutes later, the Accountant concluded her conversation, said goodbye to Omar, another one of the few phrases Hoffmann had managed to pick up, *ma'a salama*. He stayed on the T-beam until he was sure her car had left the port area, then for a second time he put the thin metal device in the drill hole above the Safe Room's locking mechanism and opened the heavy door to the heart of the smuggling organisation. One last inspection – everything looked good as he picked up the metal filings he'd kicked around when he was in a hurry, no signs left of an intruder. He was about to close the door when something caught his eye. There. In the far corner, partly hidden by the filing cabinet. One document stuck out. He hunched down and picked it up. It was the document he'd just photographed! When she arrived, surprised him, and he was in such a hurry and almost pushed the hanging files through the hole and shoved the filing cabinet against the wall – he must have lost it, run out without realising it.

And she – she hadn't noticed a thing.

How unbelievably lucky.

Hoffmann pulled the cabinet away from the wall, put the paper back in its place, returned everything to where it should be, turned off the light, and locked the door. His work was done here, for now. On his way down the stairs his phone buzzed. A text message from Frank. there in ten minutes. He checked the phone's display – the car was still parked outside the luxury hotel. And Frank was perfect for this, much better than Hoffmann himself would have been – a Danish tourist who Omar had never seen before and with no connection to his new employee.

The wind was blowing harder now than it had been when he arrived. Cool, pleasant air that woke him up. He guessed he had about an hour's work left here, then a brief nap until dawn, followed by a meeting with the Dane who'd hopefully have both a name and a picture to get Grens a little closer to the Swedish contact.

Piet Hoffmann started with the microphones – he would place a total of eleven electronic interpreters: the four already inside head-quarters and the rest at various spots in the harbour. He hid the fifth near the headquarters' entrance, the sixth and seventh behind the big warehouse, without the two guards noticing him, the eighth on the long side of the warehouse, the ninth and tenth on two of the piers. The eleventh interpreter he hid under the roof of the fishing boat cabin, which would depart in less than twenty-four hours with him onboard.

It felt strange to stand on that deck in this dense darkness and feel the waves cradling him. In this space, in this small shitty boat, four hundred and eighty-four people would be packed and transported like cattle.

I don't believe in religion. I don't believe in ideologies. I believe in money, Koslow.

Four hundred and eighty-four human beings who were already waiting not far from here.

Worth the two million one hundred and seventy-eight thousand dollars altogether.

For just this trip.

Then he repeated what he had done when he peered into the warehouse that smelled so strongly of terrified refugees. He calculated how many explosives he would need to blow it up – the best way to take the only thing those who traded lives for money actually valued. One and a half metres of det cord per boat should suffice. In addition, he only needed a GSM-controlled ignition kit. All the fishing boats had a fuel cap. First you tie square knots of the det cord, several of them, until they form a clump. But not so big that they don't fit into the tank, where you secure them with tape high up. For detonation a simple bulk text message will blow all the boats into the air – at the same time.

One step left. The giraffe. The way out if all other ways are blocked.

That's what it looked like – the harbour's tallest lifting crane. With both bags on his back, he balanced on one foot at a time as he climbed up one of the legs of the giraffe – criss-crossed steel rods. Halfway up he reached the body of the giraffe, or the driver's cab, and then continued climbing up the giraffe's neck, or the upper part of the crane, on towards what reminded him of the head, the bulge where the last bit of steel turned downwards towards a hoist hanging as freely as a giraffe's tongue.

It was there at the head of the giraffe that he stopped, looked out over the harbour, the whole of Zuwara. And there under the cover of night's darkness, which would soon be broken by morning light, he took the bag off his back, opened it, and peered at the contents – the sniper rifle, his handgun and the boxes of ammunition. Around the steel rods of the giraffe's head he affixed four leather straps, running them through the metal loops at the corners of the tool bag.

This was it, impossible to detect from the ground, this was where his fully packed bag would hang – the only way out if no other way was left.

Always alone.

He knew how it worked.

Trust only yourself.

THE SUN HAD BEGUN its slow trip across a blue sky. Bringing with it the sweltering heat as early morning turned to late. Piet Hoffmann closed his eyes. It felt so good to rest for a moment, to let his cheeks soak in the warmth and pass it on to the rest of his tired body.

The old Roman city of Sabratha was halfway from Zuwara to Tripoli. That was where they'd meet. At a World Heritage Site, an amphitheatre that looked like a forgotten set piece built a few hundred years after the beginning of the modern era. A tourist attraction with few tourists these days, and among the few who were wandering around its pillars and landings, a Swede and a Dane would blend in.

So strange.

European civilisation was born here.

But now people were fleeing this place for Europe.

Frank had texted he was a few minutes late, so Hoffmann was waiting for him on one of the stone benches in the ruins of the ancient theatre. Now he saw the long blond hair and the reddish red beard approaching, the powerful steps of a twenty-eight-year-old in extremely good shape. They hugged each other as always, and Hoffmann waited until those muscular arms stopped squeezing the breath out of him.

'Here. A tourist map and a few brochures. Hold them, and look down at them every now and then while we talk, pretend we're here for the architecture and history, instead of discussing what you saw in Tripoli.'

Piet Hoffmann nodded towards an older couple photographing each other in front of one of the amphitheatre's openings, a window that framed a view of the sea. He pretended to photograph Frank, before moving on to the next row of thousand-year-old pillars and staircases.

'I was sitting at the bar in Zarzis when you called. They have a house wine, red, that tastes like life, Koslow. Do you hear me, *life*? It wakes you up, you laugh, believe in a tomorrow. I left the other half of that bottle. Or the second half of the second half, if we're being precise. Two hours and thirteen minutes to the position you specified. Al Mahary Hotel. Paid for a room and sat down in the lobby with a cup of coffee. Then another. And another. I thought I'd missed them. But at six thirty this morning the first bodyguard arrived. Dark suit, in good shape.'

'Bodyguard?'

'Bodyguards, two of them, so ridiculously obvious, only the wide-legged stance and the sunglasses were missing. They read the room, made a call. Fifteen minutes later a man walked down the hotel staircase, gave his room number to the maître d' then continued on into the breakfast room. Room 702, said in English with German accent. Ten minutes later the man in your photo arrived. Omar something or other, right? Headed to the breakfast room as well, Room 612, if I got the Arabic right, settled down at the same table as the first. Then I went in and sat down two tables away. Both ordered scrambled eggs and black coffee. The German – he *was* German – said that yesterday was enjoyable, and your Omar said he was looking forward to continuing their work together. Meaningless courtesies. Whatever was important had already been said far from other ears the night before.'

'If the meeting was about what I think it was about, then I think I know what was said. But German? Are you sure?'

'Completely sure. I'd know that accent anywhere, I'm a Dane after all, Koslow, we're neighbours. And not just some regular German guy. Most don't travel with bodyguards.'

Four older men in shorts with very pale legs walked by in front of them. All with SLR cameras on their stomachs and bright straw hats on their heads. Besides the couple Hoffmann already nodded to, they were the only visitors in sight. It had only been a couple of months since ISIS lost control of this historic city. Making it a tourist destination again would take time.

'There were ten of us eating breakfast at the time. I pretended to be in a hurry, satisfied with my half a cup of coffee. While they were still working on their eggs, I stopped to chat with the maître d' and peeked into his book with the list of guests who were eating. Room number and name. Everything was there in neat rows.'

'And?'

During their conversation Frank kept moving his fingers up to a folded piece of paper sticking out of his chest pocket. Now he unfolded it and handed it to Hoffmann.

'In room 702, a man named Jürgen Kraus. The only German-sounding name on the entire list. And this is what he looks like.'

A picture that was probably taken with Frank's cell phone lying at a slant on the breakfast table. A coffee cup and a salt cellar covering part of his face, but his squinting eyes and straight nose and narrow lips were sufficiently visible to be compared to other pictures.

CC?

Or *ACC*?

Or someone else?

Regardless, he had the first name and first face outside the group working the North African end of the refugee chain. Someone a Swedish police officer could look into in order to get closer to the name he wanted. Piet Hoffmann fiddled around with his phone, pretending to take a few more pictures, before entering the phone number he'd memorised for Detective Superintendent Ewert Grens. But just as the phone connected and started to ring, Frank grabbed hold of his arm.

'What's this all about anyway?'

'What?'

'This, Koslow. What you're doing here.'

Frank handed over another picture – the photo of Omar that Piet Hoffmann sent him.

'Nothing.'

'Nothing?'

'Exactly.'

Frank smiled. Not spitefully, but not ready to let the matter pass either.

'Listen – I'll help you, no matter what this is about. You know that,

Koslow. But this picture was taken through a rifle scope from at least six, seven, eight hundred metres away. If this is *nothing* – you don't just aim sniper rifles at people. Right? Plus, just a few days ago you said you were on your way home to your family – and now you're here in fuckin' Libya spying on Germans with bodyguards and meeting me in a tourist trap.'

Piet Hoffmann had no desire to answer. He wasn't sure he even wanted to hear how it sounded out loud.

'Soon. You'll get your answer. But first I have to make a call.'

He lifted Frank's hand off his arm and entered the Swedish detective's number again.

———

Half a century. When you really counted it. Just over fifty years since a fourteen-year-old Ewert Grens sat in a classroom like this one.

Now another fourteen-year-old was sitting here. Very different from the Grens who exists now, or the Grens who existed then. Amadou was short and thin, while Grens had always been taller and wider than his classmates. Amadou was shy, anxious, while Grens used to have a social ease he'd almost forgotten. Amadou spoke French, and a bit of English and Swedish, while Grens had always spoken the working-class Swedish of the southern suburbs he'd grown up in.

But they had one thing in common.

They both, no matter what, never, never, never gave up.

Grens took his father's beatings until he had to choose whether to give up or fight back. He decided never to take shit from anyone, no matter the cost – and God knows it had cost him. Amadou had accomplished the impossible, decided to leave a life of immense struggle and used the power of that decision to propel himself all the way here.

Perhaps that's why the fourteen-year-old boy trusted the sixty-four-year-old man. Because he did trust him. Ewert Grens could feel that what began between them in Hoffmann's kitchen, a sort of conversation, had turned into a cautious trust. When the sketch artist sitting across from Amadou asked him to describe the face in more detail, pressing him about the nose and forehead and hairline, Amadou glanced towards the detective, seemingly waiting for an approving nod before trying to describe it again.

A face the boy, spontaneously and bizarrely described using the French word *joie*, joy. A person employed by a smuggling network who earned his money transporting desperate people in closed containers. In an insane world where good and evil were constantly in flux, that face, the one who opened such a container, could mean joy.

Grens took a step closer from his place at the whiteboard in order to get a better look. The sketch artist, a woman in her forties who freelanced for the police, and who Grens had requested because she made witnesses feel comfortable, had been able to draw about half the face of joy using Amadou's memories. The features could fit any number of faces. Except for those eyes. They had different amounts of black inside their blue. Different-sized pupils. One large, one small.

'That's what I see every time I dream.'

Amadou sought out Ewert Grens's approval, like before.

'Usually in the morning. Before I wake up. I see them staring at me.'

The different-sized pupils were already a more specific observation than Grens and his colleagues got out of the vast majority of witnesses. After a brief conversation this morning with Errfors, who noted he was a medical examiner and not an eye specialist, Grens learned that if pupils differ by more than one millimetre, it may be congenital, that is, genetic, or could else have occurred later in life and be a sign of a disease of the brain or blood vessels or nerves. The detective superintendent, therefore, took a step back against the whiteboard, so as not to disturb the process of illustrating the second half of the face. His eyes wandered along the walls, and he realised this classroom was usually for much younger children – the collages and poems written by hand were probably made by children of eight or nine. And he wondered how the sketch emerging from the directions of another young person would fit in there, a picture of a participant in one of Sweden's largest massacres.

He never answered his own question. His phone started ringing from inside his inner pocket, and he apologised and walked out into the corridor.

'Yes? Grens here.'

'Good morning, Superintendent.'

The first call since they'd gone their separate ways in a West African capital.

'Good morning, Hoffmann.'

'I sent you some photos late last night. Have you taken a look at them?'

'Not yet. I started my day at the school.'

'School?'

'Another time, Hoffmann.'

The wind was blowing on the other end of the line. The only sound Grens could actually make out. He tried to imagine Hoffmann in front of him, somewhere near the Libyan coast. Maybe that was what he heard – the sea.

'Then I think you should, Superintendent. The documents I sent contain code names for the nine leaders of the organisation. And I'm sure one of them is your Swedish contact.'

Ewert Grens had seen at breakfast that he'd received a number of MMS. But he hadn't connected them to Hoffmann, and decided to look at them later since he was short on time. He put on his reading glasses and clicked on one, which according to the timestamp arrived at 03.21.

'Are you looking?'

'I just opened the first one you sent.'

'At the top left corner you'll see an octopus head. This appears on all of their documents. I'm guessing it has some connection to the name of the organisation. All criminal networks have some ridiculous, but carefully chosen name – hard to understand why people who live off other people's death and shit and suffering would even care what they called themselves. Under the octopus head, Superintendent, you'll see the columns that show the percentage shares of all the main players. Everything is recorded. Every dollar is distributed between those columns. Each one is self-sufficient, each carries out their part, rewards his employees, links in a chain that have to hold. Two we can rule out. I took pictures of other documents that I went through in my hotel room – records of payments to police officers and customs officials that leave me fairly certain that the first two, *zuw1* and *zuw2*, represent the Accountant and Omar, who are responsible for the port in Africa. That means the Swedish contact you're after, Grens, is one of the other seven.'

Ewert Grens was again struck by how surreal this reality was. Or perhaps it was the opposite – how real the surreal was. As when he found himself in the middle of a painting of everyday life in a port with dozens of dead bodies in the foreground. Here he stood in a school corridor, surrounded by the voices of children inside their classrooms and out on the schoolyard. Having a conversation with a man in the middle of the chaos of human smuggling. Which was represented by columns of money. Shares in a business that dealt in people who sometimes lived, and sometimes died.

'I photographed more documents which I didn't send last night. But I have them if you want them. Some are about an armoured boat. Which apparently comes here and picks up the money once a month. About how it's sent to be laundered by a banker in Malta, and then sent on to an account in Qatar. With one full fishing boat every third day, they have an income between twenty and twenty-five mill per trip, can you imagine, Grens? The boat that, according to their book, will be arriving in just a few days, collects around twenty million dollars that they keep in a shitty little safe!'

Grens suddenly had to put a hand onto the wall. For support. Until he could regain his balance again.

The surreal reality.

Those eyes staring out from a container in Värta Harbour – that's what was inside the shitty safe Hoffmann was talking about. Souls moved between closed metal boxes that altered only their shape.

'One more thing, Grens.'

Hoffmann seemed to change his location, maybe now facing the sea – at least it sounded like the wind had increased.

'I *might* have a name for you. Not sure which code name it corresponds to. A Jürgen Krause. German-speaking. Checking out right about now from a luxury hotel in Tripoli. I have a picture of him that I'll send immediately. Another little thread for you to pull on.'

A group of students was moving from one classroom to the next at the other end of the dim hallway. Suddenly one of them stopped, his backlit face hard to make out, and turned to Grens, trying to meet his eyes.

Hugo.

It was definitely him.

Grens waved. And the silhouette waved back.

'Don't hang up yet, Hoffmann – I think I see someone you know.'

The detective started to head for that waving hand, and it started heading for him. When they were standing opposite each other, Grens kept the phone angled from his cheek so Piet Hoffmann could hear.

'Hello, Hugo – you'll never guess who I'm talking to right now?'

The boy shrugged his thin shoulders.

'Who?'

'Your dad.'

But he didn't look as happy as Grens had expected.

'Here – you can talk to him.'

He handed the phone to Hugo – but he wouldn't take it. So it hung in the air between them.

Too long.

'Ahh, he . . .'

So Grens lied while looking into Hugo's eyes.

'. . . was running late for his next class.'

And then he couldn't stand the silence.

'Well, you know . . . kids, Hoffmann. Otherwise – everything good with you down there?'

'Everything is good, Grens. And you're lying as badly as I do these days. We'll talk later.'

———

Piet Hoffmann squeezed the silent phone hard, as if it could answer his questions. Grens *had* lied. He was sure of it. Hugo had been standing next to the detective, and he'd refused to talk to a father he hadn't seen in three months.

Maybe just for that reason.

Hugo knows as well as I do – I should be there, not here.

'What's up, Koslow?'

Frank had been waiting in one of the thousands of empty seats in the amphitheatre, where it was much hotter than here. The wind didn't blow as hard inside those stone ruins.

'Yo, you there? How come you look so fuckin' lost?'

Piet Hoffmann sat down next to his Danish friend, without answering, it was none of his business.

He looked lost because he was.

'I asked you already, Koslow, what the hell this is about. Why are you here instead of at home – like you should be – running around pointing your sniper rifle at people? It's about time you answered my question.'

Frank was a madman. Frank wanted to fill the emptiness with chaos. But he was no idiot.

And he hadn't lost his ability to feel, on the contrary, he felt too much.

'What's this all about, Frank?'

'Yep.'

'Doing the right thing.'

'Right, Koslow?'

'We make our money protecting food transports, and when the grain actually makes it to its destination, we're delivering hope. But the ones who destroy that grain, they make their money on the opposite – taking that hope away. That's what *their* business is. Hopelessness is what starving people feel when they decide to flee. And the German in Tripoli. He's part of the organisation behind the latest attack. Maybe many of the attacks.'

A young Libyan couple were now the only other visitors at this historical site. Hand in hand, they wandered through the columns, comparing them to images in a thick book, running their fingertips over thousand-year-old irregularities, then approached to ask for help with a photograph. They posed in front of one of the openings that were like windows to the green sea, and as soon as they said thank you and headed for the amphitheatre's upper level, Frank continued.

'So the German is . . . according to you . . . partially responsible for the attacks?'

'Yes.'

'And how the hell do you know that?'

'I just know – can you trust me on this one?'

Frank inhaled and exhaled slowly. Twice. Then he met Hoffmann's eyes.

And nodded.

'Fine. I'll trust you. And now? I have the feeling you're not done with me. So what do you need?'

'I want you to go look up an old acquaintance of mine in Tunis. Eight hours there by car, eight hours back.'

'Who?'

In every part of the world that Piet Hoffmann had worked, he'd cultivated a certain kind of contact. So-called fixers, who would rather call themselves station agents – running the kind of stations where the goods that can't be found through official channels stopped over for a while; who conveyed transactions between faceless buyers and sellers.

'When you get to Tunis, go to Le Grand Café du Theatre and drink a cup of coffee at one of the tables at the very back – one that's shaded by the yellow umbrellas and large green plants. Always a lot of guests, a good mix, no one who'd get excited about a bearded Dane.'

At home in Stockholm he'd go late at night to a small cliff called Fåfängan, and there, out of the boot of a car, he'd buy what he needed for the next day's crime from a man named Lorentz. In Colombia, the station agent was named Cesar and worked in Bogotá behind the graffiti-covered façade of a grocery store called the SuperDeli, which sold weapons and car bombs and could even tattoo the dead. Here, his name was Rob and his front office was a café in the capital of Tunisia – the South African who fixed a tool bag filled with interpreters and web cameras and even found a helicopter to take him to his destination, all of it lightning fast.

'Robby will find you – you don't need to search for him. He'll sit down at your table and have a cup of tea, and you'll discuss the weather. When his cup is empty, he'll leave a black bag on one of the chairs. A new tool bag with three hundred metres of det cord, twenty

230

GSM-controlled ignition kits, and a Radom gun. It's already paid for. When you come back to Zuwara, I want you to wait for a couple of days or until I give you the go-ahead. And then you'll place the contents of that bag according to my instructions. The gun is yours in the meantime, you may need it.'

Frank's pale face had already started turning pink under the bright sun. So the colour of his cheeks didn't reveal if he was eager or excited. But his breathing, and his eyes, and the way he held his upper body tightly did.

'Shit, Koslow – what the hell did you do before you started working security on food transports?'

'You don't wanna know.'

Frank had heard the chaos, heard the life.

And smiled expectantly as he put his arm around his Swedish friend.

'You're right, Koslow. I don't wanna know. And I'd bet there's not many besides your wife who do, am I right?'

'What are you doing here, Ewert?'

Hugo had let the phone with his father's voice on it hang between them in the dusty air of the school corridor. Until Grens – who never lied because he'd decided long ago not to do it, no matter how hard that made his life – had actually lied. Pretended Hugo wasn't standing there refusing to take the call.

'I had to talk to Amadou again. And with your mum.'

'Mum is angry with you.'

'I know. She told me that.'

'She's angry with me, too.'

'No. She's not. Your mother loves you and Rasmus more than anything else in the world.'

'Yeah. But she *is* angry with me. Just like she's angry at you. Because only you and me, Ewert, tell the truth about Dad.'

The backpack that hung off of one of the boy's shoulders had a name tag sewn onto it.

HUGO. In proud capital letters.

'You see, Ewert?'

Hugo ran his finger along the letters on his backpack, as if he was writing his name over again on top of them.

'It should say William, right? Even though I never liked it. Both you and me, Ewert, know that's more true.'

The detective superintendent turned the boy's backpack slightly to get a closer look, scrutinising it before saying anything.

'What's more true, Hugo?'

'William. He's been around almost as long as Hugo. But maybe it's good? That it says that?'

'What's good about it?'

'That you and I have a secret together. About our names.'

'That I never really liked Ewert?'

'Yeah. That you never liked Ewert, and I never liked William. Not even my teachers know that was my name for so long that I almost forgot Hugo. And I don't like Hugo any more, not even Mum and Dad know that. Only you know, Ewert. Just like I know about your name.'

Talking to Hoffmann, seeing the evidence of how people locked into a metal box were transformed into numbers and profit had made Grens dizzy. He'd had to lean against the wall for support. Now that dizziness returned. More unfamiliar feelings pushing their way inside. Such as being close to a little boy. Such as the responsibility of hearing and responding to such a clear cry for help.

'I didn't want to talk to Dad just now. And I don't want to talk to Dad in the mornings any more either. When he calls. We always did before. At breakfast we put the phone on the table. Talked to each other.'

Grens put the backpack back in its place, making sure it hung firmly on the boy's thin shoulder.

'I *know* your dad wants to talk to you. And, Hugo – I really think you should talk to him next time. It would make him happy. And if you want to talk to me *too* sometimes, that would also make me happy – you can call anytime.'

The superintendent glanced at a clock that seemed as old as the walls it hung on, brown clock-face and long, ornate hands that marked the minutes and hours. He should go back to the classroom where

Amadou sat with the artist who was sketching the face of joy, the face of a member of an organisation that left lifeless bodies scattered behind them.

'I saw that you had your own phone. But not Rasmus, right?'

'Just me.'

'What's the number?'

'Mine?'

'Yeah.'

'Zero. Seven. Three. Nine. Three. Two. Seven. Seven. Seven. Eight. Eight.'

Grens turned around, Hugo shouldn't see what he was doing.

Until the phone rang and the boy answered. And heard Ewert's voice.

'Hello, Hugo – now you know what my number is too. Save it. Then you can call whenever you want.'

Grens then followed the almost bouncing steps that disappeared down the corridor.

And when Hugo turned around and waved, Grens waved back.

At the very moment, his phone started to ring. It looked like it could be a government number. A new glance at the school clock with its ornate hands before deciding he had time to talk.

'Grens here.'

'This is Thor Dixon, you asked me . . .'

'Great. Thanks for calling. How's it going?'

The grey-eyed Foreign Ministry official who was as comfortable travelling the world as Grens was on his morning walk to the police station.

'I have the contact information you requested. For the young man and young woman from Niger. The families of Alyson Souleymane and Idriss Coulibaly. You'll receive them immediately by email.'

Death notifications.

They were a part of a detective superintendent's everyday life.

Ewert Grens had reached the age of sixty-four, delivered this terrible news hundreds of times, before realising this kind of message served another function – giving people who had lost their lives their deaths back to them.

'Thank you. That means more than you realise. I'm about to go and meet the boy I told you about. Maybe he'll feel slightly less alone after this.'

'There's no need to thank me, Superintendent. We are both in government service.'

'I owe you one.'

When Grens opened the door to the classroom they were sitting exactly where he'd left them. Amadou leaning forward slightly with his elbows on the desk, the sketch artist with her left hand holding a pen, working on another layer of the face.

He did his best to sneak in, trying not to disturb their concentrated collaboration – Amadou describing the next detail and the next without the artist even having to ask for them. A sketch which, when Grens got a look at from a distance, reminded him of all those phantom pictures – harmless, clinical, made up in a way that had no feeling to it. This became even clearer as he wandered around the classroom again staring at the collages of nine-year-olds. Illustrations of people and monsters who looked considerably more terrifying than the man who – along with a German name, and some documents describing the profit-sharing system of nine owners – was still his best link to a real, and yet surreal, mass murder.

IT WASN'T OFTEN EWERT Grens visited the cemetery twice in the same week. But he needed her. Even if she was lying under a white cross and had decided to no longer exist. With so much death over the past few days, and so many children putting their trust in him, he wanted something besides walls to lean against, if he was going to stop the spinning inside him.

He and Anni would always share that – life and children and death.

The detective had left Amadou and the sketch artist shortly after lunch with the picture of a phantom rolled up in a cylindrical document holder. A face that was then scanned into a computer and with a few clicks transformed into a digital file. Next it was sent to every police officer and customs official and even to many bus and taxi drivers. And as he sat there on a park bench, reading and rereading an engraving of her name – ANNI GRENS – he considered whether or not to send a copy to the major newspapers. To be honest he hadn't always got along so well with journalists, and lived by one rule: tell them as little as possible about as little as possible. But sometimes the press was a good tool. If time was too short. Or feelings running strong. And this hunt couldn't go on much longer, he knew that. It took up too much space in his chest, which already had a hard enough time holding a heart that pounded too hard.

Grens ran his hand along the top of the white cross, smiled at her and whispered, as he always did, *I know you're not here any more but I don't care*, and walked across the lawn towards the northern entrance of the cemetery where his car was parked.

He'd asked Mariana to stay later for an evening meeting, and when she knocked and stepped into his office, she arrived with all the energy he didn't have. He had no family of his own. He also knew that a few hours with children who asked you to be their grandfather wasn't the same as having one. But the two people he spent year after year with in this building. Mariana Hermansson and Sven Sundkvist. Loyal, capable, humane. They were as close as he got to family.

'I think Hoffmann was right, Ewert – what he sent us is already yielding some answers.'

Mariana had spent most of the day interpreting and exploring the MMS files that Grens had forwarded her.

'If we start here. Do you see? The octopus in the top right corner.'

She had a folder with her when she arrived, now she opened it and placed its contents on the rickety coffee table, which had stood in this office as long as the worn-out corduroy sofa and the shelf with the ancient cassette player.

day	unit	stage 2 + 3 + 4	zuw1 12,5 %	zuw2 12,5 %	lam. 5%	sal. 8%	A C C 15%	bank 5%	gda 8%	trans balt 7%	C C 25%

'The same symbol on each new page. The one Hoffmann assumed was connected to the organisation's name.'

She circled the little black octopus with a red pen. Several rings on top of each other. As if she were tying it up in ever thicker twine.

'Nine actors sharing the money, of which one – code name *CC* – receives the lion's share of the profit, twenty-five per cent. Nine actors. Are you following me, Ewert? An octopus has eight arms. Plus a head. Eight arms to carry out the work – while the head thinks, leads. *CC is* the leader.'

'With all due respect, Mariana, I'm not interested in the leader. We'll allow our European colleagues the honour of locking the leader up later. My interest is solely in the Swedish contact. That's who I want to find.'

'Yes.'

'Yes?'

'Yes, Ewert. Exactly. I think *CC is* the leader. But I think *CC is* also the Swedish contact.'

Ewert Grens was a large man. When he moved inside a small space it took up a lot of room. Now he got up out of the corduroy sofa and wandered back and forth between the desk and the windows, trying to pace his way into an answer.

'This Swedish contact person – you think they're the leader?'

'Yes.'

'Why?'

The detective superintendent had paused temporarily at the window, it was easier to meet Mariana's eyes from there.

'I think, Ewert, that Piet Hoffmann is right about his other assumption as well. I believe, like Hoffmann, the more I turn and twist what we have here, the code names *zuw1* and *zuw2*, which share twenty-five per cent, are in charge in Zuwara where the trip takes off. And I think, also like Hoffmann, that the German, whose name and picture we have from a meeting in Tripoli, is one of the leaders of this criminal network.'

'Why?'

Mariana Hermansson smiled. Sixty-four years old and still so irritatingly impatient. So she paused intentionally. He'd repeat himself soon enough.

'*Why*, Hermansson?'

She considered waiting longer.

Another time.

She'd work on training him some other time.

'We know from Hoffmann that the trip is divided into four stages. That the smuggling organisation gets paid for part two, three, four. Their business idea is to offer a final destination of the buyer's choosing. I think the ones who are keeping the biggest cut of the profits and call themselves *ACC* and *CC* are the contact persons at those final destinations – Germany and Sweden. It's logical. Those who get paid the most are at the beginning and end points of the journey. Those in the middle get paid less. And – I don't think for a minute that the octopus's head, the leader with the code name *CC*, is personally travelling to North Africa and taking the risk of meeting the other members. That's what a leader does in the early stages, when contacts are being made and power structures being set. At this stage, however, that's what the second-in-command does. Like a German who takes fifteen per cent of the profit and calls himself *ACC*.'

While she was talking, Ewert Grens had started pacing again.

Back and forth. Back and forth.

'*If* you're right, Hermansson.'

His heavy breathing fogged up the window whenever he reached it.

'*If* the entire organisation is led from here.'

And bumped against the desk as he turned there.

'*If* those responsible for that fucking hell in the container . . .'

When Mariana, as a rookie cop, first got to know Ewert Grens years ago during a trafficking investigation, the detective superintendent with the most informal power in the police station, she'd met a person who was constantly angry and always made other people uneasy. That wasn't the case any more. Since coming to accept the injury and death of his wife, realising that it wasn't his fault, he rarely unleashed that stubborn aggressiveness.

'. . . *if* those, Hermansson, who take life and death . . .'

But now he did.

With a fury that made even Mariana – who never backed down, who was the only one allowed to challenge him – afraid.

'. . . *if* they're here, Hermansson, in Sweden . . . my God, I thought I'd have to be satisfied with hacking off one of the arms of that octopus. *If* you're right, then I'll be damned . . .'

Then he rushed over to the foggy window.

Tore it open.

And shouted out over the desolate courtyard of the police station.

'. . . the whole head will be chopped off and the rest of it will rot and die!'

And it echoed out there, weakly.

Until the faraway voice ceased.

Until there was complete silence.

Mariana saw her boss begin to shake, his back and shoulders trying to hold back what needed to come out. She'd only seen him like this once before. The day his wife, Anni, died.

'What is it, Ewert?'

She knew he didn't like to be touched. So she let him be. Even though that seemed most appropriate.

'Ewert?'

He closed the window. Turned around.

'I . . . don't really know.'

And she thought that maybe it was because she was here. That's why he dared to lose his self-control.

Because he depended on her, he could be small and naked in front of her.

'There . . . there's no dam inside any more. It won't stop pushing and grinding and tearing. It just goes on. As if the mass grave was what . . . as if the two hundred and thirty-two murders I investigated over forty years . . . as if those seventy-three coming all at once just won't fit.'

He walked towards the visitor's seat and sat down.

'Sometimes, Mariana.'

Sank down.

'Sometimes I miss her so.'

Suddenly unspeakably tired.

And it was obvious the conversation was over.

On the outside. Inside it would go on.

She left the rest of her papers on the coffee table without comment. He'd go through them later, stay overnight as he often did, review the investigation material and sleep for a few hours on the corduroy sofa. She didn't tell him that their German colleagues had started an investigation based on the name and picture Hoffmann sent, or that the tips were streaming in from witnesses all over the country convinced they'd seen the real version of that phantom, that she'd issued a nationwide alert and put the call out on Interpol's many wanted lists, and that her investigation of the mortuary technician had become very interesting. Under that gentle and friendly surface was a whole other woman. He'd read all of that for himself soon enough. So she put her hand on his arm and then briefly on his cheek and whispered that she knew tomorrow they'd get even closer to the guilty one.

THE SEA WAS AS black and troubled as the darkness that surrounded them.

Twelve minutes to midnight.

Until departure.

Until his first voyage as an armed guard on a fishing boat that could sink at any moment.

Piet Hoffmann had never seen human beings transformed into nothing as he did now. Four hundred and eighty-four bodies packed onto a boat intended for less than a tenth of that number. So desperate that they'd risk drowning to avoid starving.

They'd been collected at the warehouse and led in a long phalanx through the harbour area – like a silent millipede hidden by the Zuwara night. The first were packed into the boat's limited cargo space, down a rickety wooden ladder; the rest were pushed onto the deck, pressed hard against the railing to make more space, more space, more space, and when the last were forced on board with whips – lashes that cracked against thin backs – Hoffmann left his position.

'Maybe that's enough.'

A few quick steps over to Omar, who had returned from Tripoli this afternoon to oversee this record-breaking boat that would give them record-breaking income.

'What – Koslow?'

'That there.'

'What do you think you're doing, Hoffmann, on your first voyage, telling me what is and isn't *enough* when you know you're on thin ice with me anyway.'

'The whips.'

'Most effective method. If you really wanna pack tight.'

'We're not transporting animals.'

Omar held up his whip, dangling it dramatically in front of Hoffmann.

'No, they're not animals, Koslow. They're weight. And it's our job to get as much of it onboard as we can without sinking.'

Then Omar whipped again. Illustratively. A few times on the gravel-covered asphalt of the harbour, and a couple of times against the backs of those stuck between the dockside and the boat, unable to move either forwards or backwards.

That crack as it split the air.

An oxtail whip.

Hoffmann was sure of it.

'And by the way.'

Omar scratched his weak chin with the back of his hand.

'You're wrong, Koslow. They *are* animals. But with one difference – a cow doesn't pay.'

Many years ago, when Piet Hoffmann was in a reformatory institution, he met with a prison psychologist who told him his problems were based on a lack of *impulse control*. That's why he reacted with violence first and thought through things afterwards – against anything and everyone that he didn't trust. But that was a long time ago. Swallow it, keep all that shit inside, wait and keep waiting until you can strike back a single time with the power that only someone with very good *fucking impulse control* has. So, therefore, he just smiled at that weak chin, nodded, and tried to imagine the piles of cash that were being whipped into that boat, which the Accountant would count and record and put into a safe, whose number display was being recorded by an invisible webcam, by noon the next morning.

A couple of minutes after midnight the boat departed.

Hoffmann had already chosen his place during his tour of the harbour yesterday – he was going to sit on the roof of the cabin, the captain beneath him inside, and the other guard at the far end of the prow of the narrow deck. He justified it as giving him the best view of the stressed, hunted, unpredictable herd of human beings.

That was true.

It was also true that it was the only space big enough to avoid breath on the back of your neck, on your throat, on your cheeks.

Only here, on the cabin roof ringed by a low metal edge, which formed a small fence, would he be undisturbed. No risk of exposure when he opened his phone. Only here could he carry out his mission – guard the refugees – while performing his real task – monitoring the display of his phone, which guarded the safe.

According to their schedule, they'd travel north for five hours, and when they got close to the oil rigs on the other side of the water, which were technically in Italy and Europe, they'd dump their whole load and turn back and five hours later drop anchor in Zuwara with an empty boat. With a loaded rifle resting across his thighs, he turned back towards the harbour as they pulled away, keeping his eyes as long as he could on the streetlights and restaurants of the coastal city that wouldn't go to sleep for another few hours – regular people living regular lives while four hundred and eighty-four other human beings made a record crossing on a dark fishing boat headed out onto the night-black sea.

If he didn't look down. If he stared straight ahead and let his eyes wander between black sea and black sky. For just a moment he could be almost anywhere, have as much time as he pleased.

That wasn't the case.

He was sitting on the roof of a cabin in a fishing boat, guarding people. They were just a few minutes from this journey's destination. In the middle of an endless sea, no land in sight – that's where they'd stop and let down ten rafts that were packed flat in a box under the deck, and which inflated automatically when they hit the surface of the water. Rubber boats, each of which could hold twenty-five adults. And tonight would have to hold twice that.

Through the journey, Piet Hoffmann had continued to perform his double mission – to resolve conflicts between people pushing into each other by screaming and showing them his gun. All the while regularly checking his phone's screen, which lay next to one of his legs, making sure not to miss it should the Accountant, like last night, decide to go into work a little earlier.

They had arrived.

The dull thumping of the diesel engine quieted, as it was used now only to keep the boat stationary. He realised just how dangerously low the boat was sitting – with the water no longer pushed aside by a strong forward movement, you could see how heavily laden they were, how close they were to sinking.

There weren't many women on board – Hoffmann guessed about thirty. They climbed with silent concentration down onto the first rubber raft using an old and wobbly rope ladder. Then came about the same number of children, the older ones holding onto the younger ones' hands, and last came the terrified, screaming babies that fathers balanced over the railing as if they were considering dropping them down. Until Piet Hoffmann left his place on the roof, squeezed between those tightly packed bodies, and explained how they could climb halfway down and hand over the smallest children to the out-stretched arms waiting to receive them.

When it was the men's turn to start filling up the rest of the rubber rafts, fights started to break out. Everyone wanted to secure their spots simultaneously, and Hoffmann and his fellow guard were repeatedly forced to use mild violence to separate those tired, hungry, scared refugees who were finally acting like the animals they were treated as.

Between the sixth and seventh raft, the captain told them to stop while he got the engine going again. He was moving the boat a few hundred metres east and throwing the last four rubber rafts down there. Piet Hoffmann was able to climb back up to his place on the roof again, and had barely sat down and switched on his phone when the first interpreter, the one he'd placed at headquarters just outside the entrance in Zuwara, sent him an alarm.

A diffuse, crackling sound turned into a much more obvious one – a locked door being opened. Then steps on the stairs. Some heavier, as if the full foot were being put down, some lighter as if just the sole of the shoe were touching the stone. Until the next interpreter, the one he placed at the inner entrance, took over. More steps. More voices.

A woman's voice, the Accountant, he was sure of it. Then a man's voice, also somewhat high. Omar. And then two more, deeper, the two bodyguards. He checked the time – twenty past five. They were starting early.

The next time the interpreters reacted, it was easy to follow the course of events.

As if he were with them inside that big room.

The scrape as they filled the top tray of the currency counter. The shuffling sound as each banknote was counted and packed. The squeak of the container at the bottom of the machine being pulled out and emptied.

He could even see the thick smoke of cigarillos slowly winding up towards the ceiling fans.

When the currency counter fell silent and the last bundle was taken out and bound with a thin strip of paper, Piet Hoffmann switched the program on his phone – he no longer wanted to listen, he wanted to see. Now the Accountant would go into the Safe Room. Now she would open the safe and lock up this voyage's profit until an armoured boat picked up the entire contents.

The video on his phone was perfectly sharp and filled his whole screen.

And he didn't even have to wait.

The Accountant's hand moved from one edge of the image to the other, and the rings on her fingers sparkled as she put in the first digit.

4.

And the next.

5.

And the next.

2.

Number by number until she'd pressed the safe's buttons a total of eight times.

Hoffmann looked down at the almost two hundred men still standing on the upper deck, then at his fellow guard at the railing, then at the captain in the cab beneath him who was busy pouring hot water warmed on a simple gas stove into a dirty porcelain cup with instant coffee.

None of them seemed to have picked up on what he was doing.

He folded his phone and turned it off.

Now he had her code to the safe.

Delilah.

That's what she went by these days.

A woman who drove a man to madness in a very famous song. A character in the Bible who tricked a man for the sake of her people.

And it sounded like a flower. Like a beautiful flower, and so she'd decided to believe she was beautiful until she was.

She didn't really like these early mornings. But in the hours after one of those crowded fishing boats departed, it was easy to get up before dawn. She'd become better at it over the years, taking advantage of life, maximising her day.

The last bundle of cash just fitted onto the lower shelf. With three and a half weeks' income counted and packed, the safe was stuffed to the limit. Twenty-five million dollars. One more trip, three days more, and it would be emptied to make way for next month's cash, and the contents would be sent to Jazmine. Under the protection of a security company that specialised in transporting profits from refugee organisations along the southern coast of the Mediterranean.

Laundering dirty money until it was clean.

That's what Jazmine did for all of them at Lombard Bank in Malta, before transferring it forward.

They trusted each other unconditionally – the young woman from Zuwara, who saw her mother and father shot dead by power and decided to take that power back for herself, and the equally young and equally orphaned woman from Algiers – and they had since they were roommates at Cambridge. Two foreigners on scholarships, given an opportunity they hadn't even dared to dream of. In those first years after graduating with a degree in international economics, they'd worked at the same bank in Paris, she and Jazmine. They got decent wages, continued to climb the social ladder. But at some point, it wasn't enough. Despite a life that offered so much more than what she'd grown up with. She wanted more, so much more, and it was then that she changed her name from Farrah to Delilah and decided to choose to be beautiful. With one hundred and seventy thousand migrants leaving Africa every year through Libya's ports, and as one of the leaders of an organisation that sent an ever increasing percentage of them, her early estimates had shown that she needed just five years with twelve and a half per cent of the profits. If the inflow of products – people, refugees – remained constant. If the relationship between demand and access to a new life also remained constant. Five years, and she'd wrap up her role and cash in for ever.

She counted the days – every day. Seven hundred and twelve left.

The door of the safe was sluggish, she pressed it with both hands as usual, making sure it was properly closed. Just two people knew the eight-digit code. Herself and Omar. She was in charge of finances and the contracts that were prerequisite for working freely within this port area and in other crucial locations. Omar was responsible for security. Together they formed the two most important arms of the organisation – without them, without the beginning of the trip, there would be no profit for the other arms, even the organisation's head.

Outside the Safe Room, she heard Omar laugh. Loud and long. He had a nice laugh, one that charmed you, surrounded you. He sat in a cloud of cigarette smoke with his feet on the desk between his two bodyguards, as he often did. She'd got to know him well over the years. What initially seemed to her like sulking was mostly an old-fashioned informality. He was honest. Happy-go-lucky. Easy to read and easy to interpret. He really only had one defect. He liked money too much. So much that it made him stingy, and stingy people got stupid. He didn't understand where the line between being stingy and being thrifty stood, or how stinginess sometimes means less money, that it's always wiser to buy the best service, even if it's more expensive. The only time they'd really had a major disagreement was over something that concerned both of their areas of responsibility. The transportation of the money. She'd won in the end, but had to work hard to convince him that the security firm who retrieved their monthly profit was worth their fee – it cost more because of their professionalism and confidentiality and loyalty. Omar still hadn't understood that, not just material things have a price.

She left the Safe Room for a computer screen opposite Omar, the one that had become hers without ever making it explicit, and she started printing out Excel documents with updated profit and loss statements – they'd be sent on to the other members in paper form. The printer took an annoyingly long time to warm up, and then it frustratingly spat out each document one at a time, perhaps that's why her mind always floated away towards the future right about now. The future that would begin in seven hundred and twelve days when she gained access to her combined profits, which, like everyone else's profits, were hidden in the organisation's accounts in Qatar. She'd decided to invest half of it in property in Paris, and the other half in property in Nice and Cannes, but for herself she loved scrolling through the websites of property brokers in the Loire valley. She'd buy a big house there, far from the fakes of the Riviera and the snobs of Paris. That's where she'd earn her new money – but it was in Loire where she'd grow old.

The last copies were hers, and she always put them in the hanging files in the filing cabinet. She returned to the Safe Room and opened the cabinet with a key like a tiny harpoon with a long, slim middle and sharp teeth at one end.

It was after she had put half of the copies into their proper place and was about to start with the files hanging all the way in to the right, that she abruptly stopped what she was doing. That corner sticking up. Just a normal corner of a normal piece of paper. But for her it wasn't – it was a deviation from a pattern.

Her papers never lay like that.

She pulled out the entire hanging file from its steel rails and grabbed the corner, coaxed up the piece of paper. It wasn't just sticking up – it was filed upside down. The only document like that in the whole row, the whole cabinet. No matter which one she took out – none of them were standing upside down. With text and numbers in the wrong direction.

She studied it.

The same type of tables as on any other document in this half of the filing cabinet. Percentages distributed between nine units. Date of travel, number of passengers, ticket price each leg of the trip. Nothing else. Nothing that separated this upside-down paper from the others.

She didn't understand it.

Until she started to put them back.

The back. It wasn't completely white. Small traces of dirt. Like dark scratches on white. The paper had been where it shouldn't be. As if it had been taken out, put somewhere else or maybe dropped, and then put back again.

She shook, not from fear – from rage.

Only two people knew the code to the safe. Only two people had a key to the filing cabinet.

She turned back towards the large room, the cigarette smoke and the ceiling fans and Omar laughing with the bodyguards.

Don't you trust me?

After all this time?

After . . .

'What is this?'

She was barely aware of leaving the Safe Room, aware of placing herself in front of him and holding the piece of paper with the dirty back towards him.

'Answer me!'

And Omar looked sincerely surprised.

'Excuse me?'

'Why in hell have you been rooting around in what's mine?'

'What are you talking about, Delilah?'

'This!'

She turned over the document.

'So? A blank piece of a paper? That means nothing to me.'

'It says you opened my filing cabinet. It says you took out my copies and were so damn stupid that you dropped them on the floor and then put them back upside down.'

Omar took his feet off the desk and sat up straight in his chair while staring at a paper that was still just as empty.

'Delilah – what are you up to? Why would I get into your filing cabinet?'

'That's exactly what I'm standing here asking you! Why the hell did you think you needed to look at the latest transactions!'

Omar stared at her, at the paper, at her again.

And shrugged his shoulders.

'Delilah, that room is your responsibility. And this room is mine. I don't interfere with your room – and you never get in the middle of my room. That's our agreement. And I've stuck to that. So I'm going to have to ask you to run around and wave that paper in some other room.'

She was still shaking when she sat down beside him. But no longer just from rage.

'If it's not you, Omar.'

The hand that placed the document between them on the desk was trembling, even her finger as she pointed with it, shook.

'Then someone else has been inside the Safe Room. Someone else has opened the filing cabinet.'

The captain had stopped the boat a few hundred metres to the east, where it would circle until everyone was off, and as fatigue mingled with competition and fear, the shoving turned into ever more vicious punches. Everyone still on board, who hadn't already climbed down the rope ladder and started to float to the shores of Europe, could see there wasn't enough room for everyone in those four rafts. Hoffmann and his colleague threatened, fired warning shots and used escalating violence to separate the desperate men all trying to disembark at the same time. But it wasn't until the last rubber raft was filled to the brim – people piled on top each other, lying on each other, hanging off each other – that the real panic broke out.

Piet Hoffmann counted eleven men of varying ages still on board.

While the overflowing rafts sank deeper – the black water was just under their reinforced rubber edges.

'No – we're not getting off! None of us!'

The man who spoke was taller than his fellow passengers and stood in front representing all of them – French with a smattering of English.

'It's full. Full! And we paid! We are entitled to seat! But there is none!'

He had realised what Hoffmann realised, what everyone realised. Those last twenty refugees who'd been pushed and whipped onboard, the ones that made this a record-breaking number, were too many for those already overflowing boats.

'They're going down!'

The captain leaned out of his cabin as he shouted at Hoffmann and his colleague.

'And it's your fucking job to get them there so we can drive home!'

With Hoffmann still in his position on the cab, it was the other guard who was closer to the rope ladder.

And who began to speak.

'You heard him – down you go.'

He also aimed his automatic weapon at the man who spoke for those who were still on the boat.

'Otherwise, I'll shoot you first. Then the others. Please pass my message to them.'

'We're not climbing down. None of us! We'll die! The ones on the rafts will die!'

A boy in his early teens, gangly and with feet that had outgrown the rest of his body, sneaked over towards the speaker and stopped right behind him, ready to jump in and defend. Father and son, Piet Hoffmann was sure of it – they belonged together in that obvious way he belonged to his own sons.

'You have to drop more rubber boats. And if there aren't more, you have to solve it. It's your responsibility! Yours! We have paid to go to Europe, not to fall into the water and drown!'

The speaker's body language couldn't be misunderstood. He refused to move. Just like his son. Just like the other nine men who'd formed a human wall in a semicircle behind him.

Just then, one of the men down below lost his grip on the edge of the rubber raft and fell.

Into the troubled waters.

He shouted and waved his arms, he couldn't – just like all the others – swim.

Those who sat closest to him stretched out his hands, urging him to fight, fight, and when after half a minute he managed to grab hold of them he pulled so hard that more almost fell out. Not until he calmed down, stopped screaming and thrashing, did those outstretched arms slowly pull him up, but not all the way, that was no longer possible – there just wasn't any room left. So he was forced to hang there, over the rubber edge, while four hands held onto his soaked T-shirt.

'You go down!'

The other guard had temporarily turned his attention and his weapon towards the rubber raft, but now he turned back to the spokesperson.

'Climb!'

'It's impossible!'

'Fucking climb!'

'You can see for yourself! It won't work! It won't work! Me, my son, everyone standing here . . . you have to get hold of another raft.'

The captain was tall and powerfully built with a bushy beard and shaved head. The kind of person that stands out. Nevertheless, while this conversation was going on he'd managed to leave his cabin and make it all the way over to the guard and spokesman, without anyone noticing.

'You're right.'

He said this as he put his hand on the shoulder of the speaker, acknowledging all of the men's concerns, and in a tone of voice that broke through the others with calm and authority.

'It *is* full, just like you said. The last raft has no room for you. So here's what we're going to do – you come with us, and we'll meet another boat in just five nautical miles. I'll contact the captain there – I know they have space on their rafts. Agreed?'

The spokesman was also large with a heavy way of moving, but now when he relaxed he became so much smaller, he'd fought for his life and won. His son smiled cautiously, and the nine standing in the protective semicircle spread out.

The captain returned to the cabin where Piet Hoffmann was waiting to praise him for how he'd handled the conflict. But the captain forestalled him, and his voice was very different now, not calm, but more like a cold hiss.

'Shoot them.'

That's why Hoffmann almost thought he'd heard wrong.

'Excuse me?'

'In a few minutes, when we've taken them away from the other boats, shoot the whole lot and throw them overboard.'

The bald head disappeared into the cabin, and the fishing boat jerked slightly as the throttle was pushed upwards. Then he returned, still with that hiss.

'We told you the requirements. You have to be ready to take a shot if the time came. Now it's fucking time.'

Hoffmann grabbed the edge of the cabin roof, jumped down onto the deck, and landed opposite the captain.

'We can solve this some other way.'

'They paid for a one-way ticket. Not a return trip. *Shoot them.*'

'I don't shoot people who aren't threatening me.'

Piet Hoffmann breathed in, breathed out.

So many times he'd found himself in this situation.

So many times he'd killed for his own credibility. Never be questioned. An infiltrator's first rule.

Now he was on his way there – again. Where he didn't want to go. Kill. Or be unmasked.

He tried to go back to the mantra he'd used during his undercover work in the mafia of Sweden and in the drug cartels of South America.

You or me.

And I care more about me than about you, so I choose me.

But then he'd been facing other criminals. Who were also a threat – killers, people with blood on their hands – who lived by the same rules.

But that wasn't the case now.

These people didn't want to kill, they wanted to survive.

'I don't shoot peaceful people like rats. So here's what we'll do – *I'll* pay the return trip for whoever is left.'

The captain stared at Hoffmann for a long time, without answering. And then he crossed the deck. Increasing his speed. Finally running to the other guard and grabbing his automatic weapon. It went so fast.

He shot the father.

He shot the son.

And then he slowly pointed the gun back and forth across the rest of the group.

'Throw the bodies over the rails.'

Nine men standing there in front of him, immobile, not yet having grasped what was happening.

'Pick them up and throw them.'

Now they did.

Or at least their muscles did, they shook and cramped while looking at each other and trying to make sense of this.

'Or would you like to wait while I shoot you all one at a time? And throw you over myself.'

None of them said anything. And yet they did. With confused, terrified looks.

Until two of them lifted up the dead teenage son, shot straight through the right temple, held him by his hands and feet as they carried him to the railing.

And then dropped him into the bottomless deep.

'Him, too.'

The captain pointed at the father, shot through the heart.

His body was much heavier, and it took four to lift him and roll him over the railing.

'And now you hop in after them.'

They were all silent like before and unmoving.

'Fucking jump!'

The captain started firing one shot at a time right next to them.

'Jump! Jump! Jump!'

One short and shrunken man was the oldest in the group. Hard to say for sure, but Hoffmann guessed he was around sixty. An eternity in the part of the world he came from, where half of the people died before reaching fifteen. His bare feet were bloody, tender, and he couldn't move as fast as he should with the captain's shots blowing splinters off the railings. Maybe that was why he was the first to jump.

Jumped, sank, and never came up again.

'Jump!'

The next one was significantly younger, probably around twenty, and when he finally surfaced, those long arms somehow fought their way over to the rubber raft, and someone grabbed onto an arm that held him up, but still outside the raft.

'Jump! Jump! Jump!'

The next one who went to the railing, balanced there with his arms outstretched in despair.

'I can't swim.'

'Then it's time for you to learn. Fucking jump!'

A shot next to his right foot, one to his left, the bullet burrowing into the wood of the railing.

'Jump or die!'

The third shot hit his lower leg, pulled him down, and he fell into the sea, which refused to release him. Piet Hoffmann breathed in through his nose, out through his mouth, like always when he sought composure.

He hadn't done the shooting himself. But it didn't matter.

He'd made the decision to not be discovered – yet – and therefore chose not to intervene. He'd let people die in order to take, from those responsible, everything they cared about, another sort of death that lasted longer, where you died a little bit every day.

He hoped he'd made the right choice.

EWERT GRENS HAD SLEPT uneasily. Even though he'd spent the night in his office on his corduroy sofa, which was as close to safe as he could get. That obstinate rage just refused to leave him alone, bouncing around inside him from chest to belly to chest again, and as soon as he fell asleep it crept in and disturbed his dreams. Around two o'clock, without being aware of it, he got up and went to that foggy window again, repeated his promise to the deserted inner court-yard how *that damn octopus head will be cut from those damn octopus arms*. A little later, at half past three, he grabbed two cups of black coffee from the machine in the darkened corridor and emptied them before even reaching his office, as good as sleep. Around five he gave up, he left the station and nicked a fresh newspaper from a stack on Kungsholmsgatan, then walked with it in hand to a late-night café near Fridhemsplan that had amazing cinnamon buns.

That's where he was when the call came in.

The call that in a few hours would have him opening another window and for a third time releasing his rage, though it would be mixed with even starker feelings.

'Ewert?'

The officer was calling from the emergency call centre. A clever woman with a pleasant voice.

'Yes?'

'We received an emergency call forty-five minutes ago, and I've discovered it's connected to you. I mean, connected to one of your investigations.'

'Yes?'

'A group foster home. Eastern Enskede. A place for unaccompanied refugee children. The director claims that you had contact with him as lately as yesterday. And the day before yesterday.'

'Amadou.'

'Excuse me?'

'That's his name. The boy who's connected to my investigation.'

The officer paused, and Grens could hear her typing as if looking something up on her computer.

'That's correct. The first call identifies him as Amadou Souleymane.'

'Identifies?'

'He was found in his room, in his bed.'

'What are you talking about?'

'He was dead. He *is* dead.'

Ewert Grens wasn't able to run any more. Not since being shot almost twenty years ago, two bullets shattered his left knee. After that night in a burning apartment in western Stockholm, followed by two months in the hospital, he'd become known as the limping detective who refused to use a cane. Now he ran. Without pain and without limping. He ran towards the police station and down into the large garage beneath it, and then to his car parked there. He called Mariana – she was asleep, but she could be ready and out the door of her high-rise apartment building by the time Grens drove by on his way south. Then he called Sven – who stood in his kitchen in Gustavsberg packing a lunch for Jonas to take on a field trip. Sven promised to jump into his car immediately.

The foster home business was run like many others, inside a normal house in a normal residential area. A narrow, serene street with two cars in every driveway and expertly pruned apple trees. So the four blue and white police cars, the dark blue forensic van, and the medical examiner's car with the Karolinska Hospital logo on it was attracting attention. Newly awake neighbours gathered in their bathrobes, talking in small groups to each other, peering, staring, speculating, and the arrival of Ewert Grens meant one more car to disturb this quiet suburb.

The house had five bedrooms, and four boys slept in each.

Two police officers, a young man and an equally young woman, were in the first patrol car to arrive on site, and now led Grens, Hermansson and Sundkvist to the right room.

Two bunk beds, a desk, a cupboard and a chest of drawers. That was it. Temporary, that's how it felt, furniture with no personality or history.

He still lay in his bed, the bottom bunk near the window.

Amadou.

A fourteen-year-old boy who no longer existed.

'I've only done a very preliminary examination. But what I see, Ewert, is as interesting as it is alarming.'

Ludvig Errfors still used a pocket-sized tape recorder to take notes that would be printed out later.

A bean-sized wound with jagged edges can be found on the anterior axillary line on the left side.

You didn't see them much nowadays, since phones had become the cameras you documented a crime scene with, the audio recorders that kept track of your descriptions, and the notepad that kept your notes.

Only a small amount of blood, roughly one cup full, on the chest and in bed.

Now he held up the tape player so that everyone could hear it.

Probable damage caused by a sharp object penetrating the left lung and heart.

It was bizarre to stand in this room, just half a metre from the bed, and see that fragile, hopeful, and as recently as yesterday, incredibly vivid face, and at the same time hear Errfors' dry observations, stating that this was no longer the case, that on the contrary this face was pale, still, hollow.

'The method he was killed by, Ewert. The murderer's modus operandi. A sharp and narrow blade that pierces more efficiently than a big knife. Right into the heart. Puncturing it. Leaving life rather than blood to run out.'

Unaware of Errfors' look, Grens turned to the bed and the boy who'd chosen to trust him. It was only now that he saw it – the white sheets lacked almost any traces of blood.

'An approach that is identical to what I found on the body in the tunnel alcove. The man you called the Guide, in our records too, it's the only name we have for him.'

'Identical method?'

'Identical.'

'As in . . . the same killer?'

'As in – even with this hasty initial examination, Ewert – exactly the same killer.'

There was an old hammock in the garden behind the house. That's where Grens planted himself when the medical examiner and the two forensic technicians politely asked him and his colleagues to leave the scene of the crime. It creaked and whined as he moved it. The cushions were damp after last night's rain, but it felt good to slowly rock back and forth, especially after his first run in twenty years.

The rage driving him since opening the container, that uncontrollable feeling, which he couldn't understand, had now transformed into something significantly more powerful.

Hate.

'Ewert?'

'Yes?'

'Are you listening?'

'I'm listening, Sven.'

'As I told you when we found the Guide. This is more than just dumping one body at a time to avoid detection. This is bigger than that – someone's tying up every loose end.'

Ewert Grens really liked hammocks, always had.

He should put one up at home, on his balcony facing Sveavägen, sit there and swing away from a bed that occasionally became a black hole to fall into.

'This boy, Ewert, the witness – it's the same philosophy. He'd become dangerous.'

'And how the hell did he become dangerous, if nobody knew about him!'

'Maybe when he met the sketch artist during school hours. Or he told his friends at the home. Or one of our colleagues said too much in the wrong place. Or when we sent out those press releases, someone started wondering where we got our information. Or—'

'Sven – enough.'

The trust he'd liked so much. The boy's eyes looking at him with that same confidence he'd seen in Hugo's eyes. That same fucking trust had led the darkness to Amadou.

It was my fault.

Grens swung the hammock back and forth, desperately trying to grab hold of something Sven had said, something he knew was important.

It was me who made him talk, had him describe a face that became a phantom, the only witness they had with first-hand knowledge of the smuggling organisation.

Swinging.

Back and forth. Back and forth.

Until Sven's comment sunk in and started to mean something.

'You said it, Sven.'

'What?'

'They're tying up every loose end.'

'Yes?'

'Zofia Hoffmann. She was our link to the boy. She brought us together, got the boy to trust me.'

He slowed with his feet, the creaking stopped, the hammock was still, and he climbed out. He was in Enskede, close to both Zofia Hoffmann's workplace and home, at one end of a triangle, and only a few minutes' drive to the other two points. He searched for her number in his notes, found it and called.

No answer.

He called again.

No answer.

Maybe she was walking across the schoolyard and couldn't hear it.

Maybe her first class had started, and she'd put it on silent. Maybe she was still annoyed that he was in her and her family's lives and was ignoring his call.

Maybe.

She could also be in imminent danger.

'You two stay here. Wait until the technicians and Errfors are done, then you go back inside and try to see whatever it was we didn't see the first time.'

'What about you?'

Sven shouted at the fleeing back of the detective superintendent.

'Ewert? Where are *you* going?'

Neither he nor Mariana received an answer because there was none. Because Grens himself didn't know where – Zofia Hoffmann's work or home?

He could see now that the threat to the Guide and Amadou was also an imminent threat to a woman he'd forced to participate in this. This meant it would be his responsibility if she was hurt. Rage and hatred mixed with fear, and kept him from thinking clearly.

That's why he ran again, for the second time in twenty years.

'I CAN'T GO TO gym class in my underwear.'

Rasmus threw his arms wide.

'Come on, Hugo, don't you get that?'

'Then you need to help me.'

The clean clothes were in the basket at the bottom of the rack in the laundry room. That's where they'd look first. He wished Mum were here. She'd know exactly where they were, and he wouldn't have to listen to Rasmus whining any more.

'Come on – help me then.'

But her classes always started early on Mondays and Thursdays. Before his own, which began at quarter past nine, and before Rasmus, who didn't start until around ten o'clock. On those days it was his job as big brother to make sure they both got to school on time. And also that Rasmus had his gym bag with him. His *packed* gym bag. Not like that time when there was a shoe missing, and Rasmus had to sit out, and Mum was annoyed because Hugo hadn't done what he promised. And now – now it was the sodding gym shorts that had gone missing.

'Hello – Rasmus?'

'I *am* helping.'

'Look like it then.'

He'd emptied the whole basket of clean laundry onto the floor, and together they inspected every piece of clothing, even looked *inside* the shirts and pants to see if those stupid shorts were hiding there. But no luck. They were just gone.

'What about the dirty clothes hamper?'

There were two hampers in the corner of the laundry room, one for darks and one for lights. Rasmus's shorts were yellow and green and who knew which one they'd be in.

'If you take the lights, I'll take darks. OK?'

'Mmmhmm.'

'OK, Rasmus? These are *your* shorts.'

'Ooooookaaaay.'

'You don't have to be so annoyed.'

They emptied the contents of the hampers into two large piles. Socks and sweaters and pants and towels and shirts and underwear and sheets and basically everything except a pair of green and yellow gym shorts. Now they started to look *inside* every garment again, to see if the shorts could have got stuck there. Hugo had just turned the first T-shirt inside out when he thought he heard something. From above – maybe from the kitchen or the hallway. He walked over to the basement door, which was slightly ajar and peeked out into the entrance hall.

'What are you doing, Hugo?'

'Shhhhh.'

'You have to help. Like you told me to.'

'I thought I heard something. Be quiet.'

They both listened.

And there really was a sound coming from upstairs. The front door.

Somebody was doing something with the lock.

'Did you hear, Rasmus?'

'Yes. The door, it's opening.'

'Mum has a class, why would she come . . . now?'

'Maybe she knows we can't find the shorts.'

'And how would she know that?'

'Maybe she . . .'

The door had been opened, now it was closed.

Then steps.

But not Mum's, she didn't walk like that, these steps were heavier.

'Who?'

'Shhhhh.'

'I'm whispering.'

'Please, Rasmus, be quiet.'

If he sat down on the floor. If he just craned his neck a little bit. And if at the same time he cracked the basement door a little, he . . .

There.

As he peered up through the small basement staircase, he could see a bit into the kitchen, and at the far end – at the door to the hall – someone was coming inside.

Black shoes. Black trousers.

Not Mum.

A man.

Hugo craned his neck even more, and if he just slightly pushed the basement door open without making it creak, he'd be able to see the rest.

Legs. Hands. Shoulders. Head.

Shit. *Shit.*

As if someone had kicked him. Hard, in the stomach.

Hugo was sure – that was exactly how it felt.

Because he recognised him. The man standing in their kitchen. Even though he'd never seen him in reality.

But he remembered.

Ewert had been sitting in their kitchen talking to Amadou when he discovered Hoffmann's eldest lying on the floor in the hall and eavesdropping. Hugo remembered how Ewert was nice about it, didn't tell him off, just said he had to stop listening and go to his room.

Hugo did. For a while. Then he'd sneaked down again.

That's when he'd heard Amadou talking. First a French word, *pupille*, which Mum said meant pupil, and then Amadou said the man who let him out of the container had different sized pupils. *One eye had a large pupil, one eye had a small pupil. The whole time he looked at me.* Hugo hadn't understood the thing about the light, still didn't, but he remembered the description of the eyes. He'd encountered them on the drawing Amadou and a woman from the police department had made together at school, which he saw when he stepped into the classroom to talk a little with Ewert – who'd quickly tried to cover it. And even though the rest of the image was no longer visible, the eyes were, and they'd stared at him.

That's the face he was looking at now.
In their kitchen.
The man in the sketch.
The man Amadou saw and recognised.

WATCHING THE SUN RISE.

It could have been so beautiful.

A fishing boat far out in the Mediterranean, a silence unlike anything else, dead calm.

Piet Hoffmann leaned against the railing, over it, staring down at the sparkling blue water as the prow split it, the diesel motor pushing them forward. It could have been so beautiful – but the only thing he could see over and over was a father being shot in the chest, his son shot in the temple, and how the two of them were hoisted up and thrown overboard at exactly the spot at the railing where he now stood.

The boat was halfway back to Zuwara, and a new day was dawning for an organisation even dirtier, shittier and more evil than any criminal activity he'd previously infiltrated. Here, life always lost out to money.

No one said anything. The captain stood in his cabin staring straight ahead, the other guard smoked his cigarette half-asleep on a wooden box, and Hoffmann alternated between his place on the cab and at the railing. No one said anything because they had nothing to say to each other. Even though everything inside him was screaming for answers. For punishment. For some kind of justice, the justice he'd always demanded so quickly when he was young, but which as an infiltrator he'd learned to wait for, and in waiting get so much more.

He made sure to turn his back while again reading the very excited text Grens sent late last night – the head of the Octopus might be in Sweden, the organisation might be run from there, and if so the detective was planning to hack it off, separate it from the rest of the body. As for Hoffmann, it didn't matter where the head was, he planned to cut off every arm.

The electronic ringing of a phone somehow didn't seem to belong on this calm expanse of water. Even less so in the midst of a smuggling operation that forbids telephones in order to minimise the risk of being traced. So as soon as the captain's phone rang, an angry sound that seemed to surround them all, Hoffmann realised something wasn't right. And when the captain threw a quick glance in his direction just a moment or two into the call, and then slowed down the boat and moved to the back of the cab to make sure no one could see or hear him, he knew for sure – this wasn't good.

Piet Hoffmann made his way slowly back towards the cargo hold, trying not to attract attention, then hurried down the wooden staircase to the narrow space behind the boat's engine. He squatted down and took out his phone, opened up the interpret program. The small and white microphones he'd placed in holes and cracks in the walls all around headquarters. If this was what he suspected – the call to the captain was about himself – then it was surely one of the leaders calling, and they'd be calling from headquarters.

They were.

Both of them.

As the interpreters recorded everything that was being said, and the software translated it from Arabic to Swedish, he was able to distinguish three clear voices. Captain, Omar, Accountant. And it was Omar who was speaking as the interpreter clicked into place at this crucial moment.

'*Infiltrator.*'

'*What?*'

'*The guy on the boat, working with you right now, he's an infiltrator.*'

'*Which one?*'

'*The blond. The European.*'

'*You're sure? An infiltrator?*'

Piet Hoffmann had been through this before. Unmasked. He knew what it meant. A death sentence. And from this moment on – kill or be killed. He knew when Grens forced him into this mission that this might happen, even assumed it would, but not so soon.

He didn't understand it. How did this happen?

Until the Accountant began to speak to the captain, and she described a piece of paper in her filing cabinet that was upside down and dirty on the back.

That paper.

Which he'd discovered just as he was about to close the door of the Safe Room. Which he dropped in his haste to hide from her on the T-beam.

That fucking paper had set off this whole chain reaction.

'Do not underestimate him, whatever you do. The information we just received directly from the top says that he's been a professional infiltrator for years – Polish Mafia and then South American drug cartels for the Swedish and American police. He's killed many times. So be very careful when you force him to tell you who he works for. Then throw him overboard.'

Piet Hoffmann was hunched down behind an old boat engine in the middle of the Mediterranean, and this information changed everything. For him, for Ewert Grens. Someone on the smuggler's payroll had access to classified documents from a Swedish police investigation. Grens had no clue that the head of the organisation was so far ahead of him, and with much more powerful connections.

The captain hung up, and Hoffmann was about to turn off the translation program when the Accountant and Omar continued their discussion. Loudly. The information about who he really was and what he was doing had shaken them, that much was clear. They were unsure of how much he knew, and how much damage he could do. And soon the Accountant made another call.

'I can't explain why – but I repeat we cannot wait two days.'.

The male voice on the other end of the line was so loud and shrill that almost every word could be heard.

'And I, Delilah, repeat we're departing in fifteen minutes. But not for Zuwara and not for you. We've got a pickup for another organisation in Algiers.'

And the Accountant spoke in that same unpleasantly calm tone she'd used while pressing a gun to Hoffmann's forehead.

'You'll have to reprioritise.'
'It's impossible—'
'If you want to keep us as customers.'
'Excuse me?'
'You heard what I said.'
'I heard what you said, Delilah. But I wasn't sure I understood.'
'Then I'll explain it to you again. You reprioritise. Or lose your best customer by far.'

The money shipment. That was what they were talking about. The transport that in a few days was going to pick up tens of millions of old dollar bills.

And the Accountant wanted them to come sooner.

Immediately.

'Do we understand each other?'
'Very well, if it's that important to you . . . we leave Malta in fifteen with a new heading – Zuwara.'
'Good. Now we understand each other. And what time will you be here?'
'Considering the current weather conditions.'
'Yes?'
'From here, across the sea, we have three hundred and ninety-four kilometres.'
'Yes?'
'Let's say . . . seventy-five knots on average. And even though we're armoured. We need to avoid the coast guards and pirates.'
'When?'

Hoffmann had heard about a company that picked up money all over the Mediterranean. He'd even worked on the food transports with a couple of guys who worked with similar companies – young men who rotated between security firms all over this region. Skilled and unscrupulous mercenaries, valued by both their employers and their employers' customers.

'At that speed, that distance, let's say . . . noon. That's when we arrive at Zuwara's port.'

Noon.
Hoffmann checked the time on the satellite phone.
09.00.

'And if you want to save even more time, you'll meet us down at the dock yourselves.'
'We'll be there. With the contents of the safe.'
'See you in three hours.'

He got up from his hiding place behind the engine in the cargo bay. He had to start *now*.

He'd have to expose his position, head up to the deck, even though they wouldn't leave him alone for long. But he had an advantage, and he was going to use it – neither the captain nor the other guard knew that he knew.

Three hours.
That's how long Piet Hoffmann had.
Precisely.

PART FIVE

THE FACE FROM AMADOU'S sketch.

It *was* him.

Inside their house. Here.

Hugo had been sitting on the basement floor for way too long, peeking up through the stairs and slightly open doorway. He couldn't leave. Couldn't even move. He was stuck. His arms and legs no longer did what he wanted them to.

The phantom from the sketch.

He didn't understand – what was he doing in their kitchen?

But he didn't really have to understand, because he knew this wasn't good. This meant danger. Sometimes you just know.

Slowly feeling returned to his body.

As if his breath finally decided to worm its way back into his limbs, through his blood and veins and muscles.

He very carefully closed the basement door, so that it hardly creaked at all. He placed each foot just as gently onto the floor as he walked through the narrow basement hallway in complete silence. He entered the laundry room and saw his little brother leaning over the large dirty clothes hamper, balancing on the edge, rooting around for his gym shorts at the very bottom.

'Rasmus?'

He whispered.

'Come on, Rasmus.'

'Who was it? And where did you go?'

'Nobody. But you have to whisper.'

'We were supposed to help each other!'

'Whisper – like me.'

'You're the one who said it! Help out, help out!'

'You *have to* whisper.'

'I need to find my shorts and go to school – class is starting soon!'

'Listen, Rasmus – this is how it is. We have to whisper and we have to hide.'

'What? Why should . . .'

Finally Rasmus started whispering. As if the word *hide* had made the difference.

'. . . we do that?'

'Just because.'

'Not unless you tell me why.'

Hugo grabbed his little brother's thin upper body and pulled him out of the laundry basket. The truth. He had to tell it like it was.

'Because what we heard is something dangerous. Super, super dangerous. OK?'

Rasmus looked at his big brother. He recognised that voice. This was no game. This was serious. *Whisper* and *hide* meant *dangerous*.

'Come with me. And don't make a sound.'

Hugo took Rasmus's hand and held it tight, something he used to do when Mum forced him. Now it felt natural. Together they left the laundry room, sneaked back through the basement hall, and into Dad's workroom.

There was a desk there, with a swivel chair. A big cupboard. And that was basically it. Hugo grabbed the heavy swivel chair and dragged it over the vinyl floor towards the cupboard, and then into it. The chair should stand in the middle of the space, while he climbed up and stretched his arm behind the shelf. If he twisted his arm and hand slightly to the right. There. A small lever. He pushed it down and heard a faint, extended electronic sound. The wall at the back of the cupboard slowly slid open, revealing another room. An even smaller room stood behind this small room. A secret room. Narrow, maybe two or three metres in length.

And it was as he emerged from that room, on his way to grab Rasmus and put back the desk chair, that he heard it.

The basement door. It was creaking.

The man from the drawing had heard them.

And was heading into the basement.

Hugo ran out of Dad's workroom, grabbed Rasmus by the hand like before and held his finger to his own mouth. Rasmus understood. He was supposed to be completely silent.

09.04

(2 HOURS 56 MINUTES REMAINING)

Piet Hoffmann stayed in that space behind the engine, below deck, calculating how much time he had, planning death. His own death. And how he was going to avoid it.

He'd chosen life a long time ago, and that meant when he'd been unmasked in the past he'd chosen other people's deaths. This time it was a little different. A few would die physically. The two on this fishing boat with him. The captain and the guard. And maybe a few more. But the Accountant and Omar were going to die the slow way, losing a little bit of their lives every day – taking away the only thing they really loved – money – and destroying the tools they needed to earn any more of it.

Also, there was the matter of timing, how different it would be on this occasion.

Three seconds, three minutes, it's an eternity when you can plan, be in control of everything. But three hours, technically so much longer, feels far too short when you're no longer in control.

Hoffmann inhaled, exhaled.

His firearm was still above deck, on the roof of the cabin. He wouldn't be able to use it. Probably wouldn't have anyway – bullets damaged bodies, and he had to keep the captain and guard basically intact if his plan was going to work. So death would have to arrive silently. He grabbed for the knife he always kept in his shoulder holster, ran his hand over the wooden handle he liked so much, and the blade that was sharp on both sides.

He'd been unmasked. They intended to execute him and throw his body overboard. But he had two advantages. They didn't yet know he knew. And – Omar's last order to the captain was to make him talk, get the name of his employer, so they wouldn't shoot immediately, he would be able to bide his time, lull them into security, and then strike.

It was time.

He stuck his hand in under the fishing boat's diesel engine and screwed a tap closed – switching off the fuel supply – then hurried to the narrow wooden staircase that led up to the sunlight. Only a minute, no more, then the engine would start to sputter and hack and the boat would lose speed.

Up on deck he returned to the same place he'd been just before sneaking down, leaning against the railing, and did his best to push away the image of a father and son heaved into the sea like so much garbage. Swept away. As if they never existed. Even the blood that bore witness to it had dried into the deck and was being cleared away by sun and sea and wind.

There, at the railing, he waited.

Until the engine ceased and the speed of the boat decreased.

Not acting surprised. But also not seeming indifferent. Piet Hoffmann turned to the cabin, saw the captain checking one gauge after another, then heading off in irritation towards the engine, which seemed to be the source of the problem. A glance towards Hoffmann who nodded back, friendly and normal, balancing on that thin line of time that was about to determine everything.

After the captain descended the wooden staircase into darkness, Piet Hoffmann headed for the cabin and the guard next to it – not so fast as to seem suspicious, but quickly enough to take full advantage of every second his opponent was alone.

It was unexpectedly easy to reach the guard. He just stood there with a barely noticeable smile, convinced that when the captain returned, the two of them would take down this bastard together, completely unaware that the infiltrator already knew he'd been compromised.

Hoffmann held the comfortable wooden hilt of the knife in his right hand, angling it upward from the wrist, hidden behind his forearm.

They looked into each other's eyes as Hoffmann stretched out and pushed the blade into the unprotected back of the guard, just between the ribs, like an embrace, a deathly one. It was important to end his life without causing too much damage to the body. No cut throats. Nothing that could be seen through binoculars.

Then he hurried towards the stairs that led to the lower deck. About halfway there he heard the engine restart, felt the boat begin moving slowly. The captain had found the source of the problem, realised the fuel supply was cut off deliberately, probably by whom – the infiltrator knew they knew. That advantage had been neutralised.

Hoffmann had only one choice.

He pressed himself as close as he could against the wall on one side of the stairway, could hear the captain taking the steps two at a time.

The knife arrived more from the side this time. Hoffmann struck the moment the captain reached the deck, and he had to repeat the move several times, damaging the upper body more than he'd planned.

He was still breathless, hunkered down next to the corpse, and probably risking the satellite phone by getting blood on it, but time was ticking and a call to Frank couldn't wait.

'I'm gonna need you to return that favour now. Big time.'

'I'm listening, my friend.'

'In just two hours I'll arrive at the port in Zuwara. I'll need you to be ready for my signal, and when you get it, head for the big warehouse.'

'Already, Koslow? You said a couple of days, maybe more.'

'Didn't work out. Is that a problem?'

'No problem. What's the signal?'

'You'll know it when you see it.'

He closed the phone and grabbed the captain by his arms, dragged the heavy body to the cabin – then did the same thing in reverse with the guard, dragging him over the deck and to the prow. Placing them both where he'd need to use them. It was absurd, inhumane and shameful, but it was their death or his own, and he had chosen theirs. He then did what he always did in order to keep going – focused his thoughts on his family, who were all in an entirely different reality. A life that was normal and safe in every way that his wasn't.

09.13
(2 HOURS 47 MINUTES REMAINING)

'What are we doing here?'

'We're going to—'

'And where . . . where are we, Hugo? I don't understand.'

'Shhhhh.'

Hugo held his finger to his lips. Rasmus was whispering, but he had to be even quieter now.

'OK?'

'OK. I'll super-whisper.'

Rasmus turned around in the narrow space, which was not quite completely dark, daylight from one of the basement windows sneaked in near the ceiling. Dad's stuff, he was pretty sure of that. Three briefcases on the floor, all identical. A white metal locker against one wall. A safe against the other. A rack hung with vests, the kind policemen wear in movies, the bulletproof kind.

'Hugo – what is this?'

'Dad's secret room.'

Rasmus lifted one of the briefcases. Not very heavy. But there was something inside, you could hear when you shook it. He touched the door of the safe, locked, and the door to the locker, unlocked.

'Don't open it.'

'Why?'

'Not now, Rasmus.'

Hugo's face was still serious. Not at all like a game. Rasmus took his hand off the handle to the metal locker.

'This room, Hugo, how did you know—'

'Super-whisper.'

'—that it even existed?'

'Dad has secrets. If you want to know what they are, you have to be good at sneaking. The first time it was at night. He didn't know that I was hiding in his workroom with the basement door open to listen while they talked about things I wasn't supposed to hear. I was lying under the desk and thought he would see me. But he didn't. He walked into the cupboard. And didn't come out! For a very long time! After that I snuck down almost every night when they thought we were sleeping. Sometimes they talked about things we weren't supposed to hear, sometimes they just went to bed. And sometimes, Rasmus, Dad came down here. I saw him stretch up. Pull on something. The wall slid open. And I tried it when I was home alone. Sometimes I just sit in here by myself. It's nice.'

Rasmus spun around again, searching for something without really knowing what. This was all there was. Briefcases, locker, safe, vests. And two children.

'And why are *we* in here now?'

'Somebody is in our house. And I think he's looking for us.'

09.18
(2 HOURS 42 MINUTES REMAINING)

Piet Hoffmann was holding onto one of the small, protruding handles of a circular wooden steering wheel. It looked like a miniature version of the helm a skipper uses to steer big ships. But this skipper was alone. In a small fishing boat. Far out on the open sea. Just over an hour and a half left to the harbour.

He'd moved back and forth between deck and cabin, cargo bay and cabin, engine and cabin. All the time checking the wind and water and holding course, while trying to find the solution with only the limited resources on board. He was pretty sure he'd finally found the answer.

First the bodies – he positioned the captain standing up inside the cabin. He found a rope at the bottom of the cargo bay and tied the captain by his legs and waist to the instrument panel. You wouldn't see the lower part of his body from land if anyone were to watch as the boat approached. With his face and throat undamaged, and his damaged upper body temporarily held together by the duct tape Hoffmann found in one of the cabin drawers, the observer would see a slightly pale, but present, captain leaning a bit against the cabin wall as he steered the ship. The other body, the guard, Piet Hoffmann rigged up at the front of the boat, in the prow. He pulled loose one of the iron bars on the roof of the cabin and threaded it through the guard's clothes – from the neck, down his shirt, down the back of the trousers, all the way out of one leg. Then pushed the rod down into a fastening eye on the boat deck. Used more tape to hold the lower body against the railing, the observer would see a guard who seemed alive and alert.

With the bodies in place, Piet Hoffmann hoped to win the crucial seconds he would need as the boat approached port. With Omar and his bodyguards still convinced they were the ones in charge.

Now he had to build the rest of it.

The diesel motor in the engine room. An old fishing rod leaning in the corner of the cabin. And the rectangular firelighter next to the gas stove where the captain warmed his coffee.

A surprise for them.

One that would allow him to temporarily disappear and reappear again.

09.53

(2 HOURS 7 MINUTES REMAINING)

They'd waited for exactly thirty-five minutes, in complete silence, almost without moving. Hugo followed the second hand on his wrist-watch, turn after turn, tick tick, and whenever Rasmus was about to start talking or moving, he'd squeezed his little brother's hand until it passed.

They'd heard the man from the sketch walking around in the base-ment. Back and forth, in and out of different rooms. Twice he'd gone into Dad's workroom and opened the door to the cupboard and closed it again. Then he went upstairs, luckily the basement door creaked loudly, so they always knew where he was. That's also how they realised he'd come back.

The man in the sketch.

The phantom.

He walked around out there, in the basement, in the workroom, even opened the drawers in Dad's desk, you could hear it. Opening, opening.

Then the cupboard.

It sounded like he'd stepped inside it.

And now . . . now he was right outside the secret room. Breathing. Opening drawers and cabinets there, too. Hugo squeezed Rasmus's hand as much for his own sake. As hard as he could. And Rasmus squeezed back.

As if they were quietly talking to each other.

Do you hear him?

Yes, I hear him.

Now it was Rasmus who squeezed Hugo's hand. Twice. And Hugo, who squeezed back twice.

I'm afraid.

Me too.

They held each other's hands, completely still now, eyes closed, counting the seconds.

Until he moved out of the cupboard.

Until you couldn't hear him breathing any more.

Until his steps echoed out of the cupboard, the workroom, the basement, and then the door creaked.

'Hugo?'

Rasmus finally whispered.

'Yes?'

'He's gone, right?'

'Yes. For now.'

'School is starting.'

'We have to wait.'

'I'm not supposed to be late.'

'Today you're going to be.'

10.04
(1 HOUR 56 MINUTES REMAINING)

Piet Hoffmann walked down the well-worn wooden steps towards the engine with a small propane tank and the hotplate in one hand and the fishing rod, tape, and long lighter in the other. He'd lashed the rudder, lowered the speed and made sure there was no oncoming traffic. He put the propane and the hot plate on the floor and used the rest of the tape to fasten the long lighter to the last step of the stairs, just above the simple gas stove. He then broke the fishing rod in the middle, took off the hook and wound the fishing line hard around the lighter's on-and-off switch. Then he opened the gas stove's tap, released the line on the rod and let it run as he climbed back up towards the deck. Everything was ready now. He could vanish into smoke and return when the heavily armed guards of the smuggling organisation were most confused.

10.29
(1 HOUR 31 MINUTES REMAINING)

Tick, tock.

Round and round.

Hugo still had his eyes on the second hand of his wristwatch, and he was sure the man from the sketch hadn't been down in the basement for twenty-five full laps.

He explained to Rasmus he was going to sneak out now – that's what big brothers did in situations like this. And Rasmus would have to stay hidden in the secret room – that's what little brothers do. He pushed a small red button that sat fully visible on the wall to open the door. It sounded just like before, a quiet buzzing as it slid open. And then he tiptoed out of the cupboard and workroom and all the way to the basement door. Where he stopped.

He'd done this before, and Mum and Dad hadn't heard him.

But it was different now.

Pressing down the handle, widening the gap without making it .creak, was so much harder with your heart flapping like a wild bird in your chest.

He didn't need much, just a centimetre maybe. And then he saw him. The black shoes and black trousers. The man from the sketch was sitting at their kitchen table talking on the phone. In English. And not very well – if Dad's vests reminded Rasmus of the ones from the movies, this reminded Hugo of how the bad guys talked in those same Hollywood films.

I wait.

Hugo was sure that's what he said. Then.

Empty.

Alone in house.

And that's when Hugo felt another kick in the stomach, just like before.

That's when it all became crystal clear.

The man from the sketch said *Zofia Hoffmann*.

And Hugo realised that's who he was waiting for.

Mum.

10.38

(1 HOUR 22 MINUTES REMAINING)

Piet Hoffmann stood next to a dead man in a tiny cabin, steering a fishing boat towards a North African harbour that was becoming more and more visible. The wind had died down, this sun had never seen a cloud in its life, and the seagulls circled stubbornly above – occasionally diving into eddies the boat left in its wake, while squawking and chattering.

A gas stove, a lighter and a fishing rod.

It was going to work. He'd turned his limitations into his advantage.

At that moment everything felt possible.

Then that fucking phone started ringing. The captain's phone. In the pocket of the dead man's trousers.

Piet Hoffmann let it ring. Twelve rings. Took it out of the pocket and checked the number. Same number as the previous call. Omar. By now the infiltrator should have answered the question *who do you work for* and been thrown overboard.

The phone rang again.

Hoffmann let the ringing die out, like before, but as it did he connected his own phone to the electronic interpreters hidden in the crevices of the walls of headquarters.

It *was* Omar. Piet could hear that clearly. And there was hardly any need for a translation function to understand Omar's fear and rage because the captain didn't answer. It was obvious he didn't know what was happening on that boat. Where there shouldn't be anyone left to damage their organisation. Then it was the Accountant's turn to call. The captain's phone, still no answer. And then she called the person responsible for the transport, coming to pick up the contents of the safe. Even the Accountant sounded stressed, that calm voice she used, no matter the external pressures, sounded forced, irritated.

'I need an answer!'

Hoffmann again heard that harsh, loud male voice at the other end.

'The answer is that we're keeping to our timetable.'
'And?'
'We said three hours. We stick to three hours.'
'What does that mean?'
'The weather hasn't changed. We're holding to seventy-five knots on average.'
'What time exactly?'
'An hour and . . . let me see, fourteen minutes until we arrive in Zuwara.'

Piet Hoffmann turned off the translator – he'd heard what he needed. Zuwara's port grew ever nearer. He guessed he had ten, twelve minutes left.

If he managed to surprise them, disappear and reappear, he'd have about an hour.

It might still be enough.

10.47
(1 HOUR 13 MINUTES REMAINING)

Ewert Grens had probably never been in a teacher's office before. And even though half a lifetime had passed since he'd left the compulsory part of his schooling behind, he still felt incredibly guilty when he'd knocked on the door. This had once meant a frightening kind of authority. This was where you were called to await a reprimand. It was outside these windows he made himself as small as possible when he was late. From here, notes were sent home to be signed like official court documents.

This morning he had arrived with another feeling, which he'd also prefer to be without.

Worry.

Because Zofia Hoffmann was in grave danger.

Because he had no idea how she'd handle the news that one of her students had been murdered in his bed.

A few hours ago he'd waited in the entrance to the staffroom, and she approached from inside with books and folders under both arms, on her way to today's first lesson. She had looked at him with equal surprise and embarrassment and asked what he was doing there, and before he could answer, explained she was already late and hurrying towards her classroom. He'd followed her, opening doors to the dull corridors and picking up the papers that occasionally slipped out of one of her folders, and before they were separated asked for a meeting with her when she was done with her class. Of course, he could have asked for her time right then, immediately, which was more common in police affairs. But he preferred to have a pretext to stay here, guard her for a couple of hours, keep an eye out for what might be nothing more than an imaginary threat.

He had stationed himself on one of the benches in the schoolyard, where he could see straight into her classroom without being seen, and then after the bell rang he'd returned to the staffroom and sat down in a sofa that was almost as worn out as his own. Her expression as she arrived expecting a cup of coffee and some small talk with her colleagues and realised that the superintendent was still here, still expecting to talk to her, was as gloomy as it was irritated.

'OK – what are you doing here, Grens?'

'We have to talk.'

'I asked you to stop interfering in our lives. And still you persist in doing so.'

'A talk. Which needs to happen in private. We need to go somewhere where we'll be undisturbed.'

She unloaded her books and folders into a basket that resembled the one he and Anni had once dragged into the forest for early autumn mushroom picking. Then Zofia poured coffee into a giant mug with her name on – pointedly not asking him if he'd like any.

'OK, a talk, Grens.'

'Soon.'

'What's it about this time?'

'I'll tell you. When we are alone.'

Zofia pointed to a small room used for phone calls, two doors down from the staffroom. It allowed for private conversation in an environment that didn't welcome it. As they headed there one of her colleagues stopped them, apologised for pulling her aside. Grens stepped away a bit, still watching her – it didn't take long, they didn't say much to each other, but Zofia's body language conveyed it all.

Resignation.

A teacher temporarily switching to her role as a nagging parent. She entered a number into her cell phone.

'Apparently they're not in school.'

She glanced at him in a way that was no longer a rebuff, but rather in search of sympathy, pulling him in.

'Rasmus. And Hugo. That's what my colleague just told me.'

'Oh yeah?'

'They haven't arrived yet.'

'What time . . .'

'Their classes already started. But neither one is here. And Hugo isn't answering his phone.'

Her irritation was palpable.

'Rasmus has gym first thing every other morning. And I've explained to Hugo he has to help Rasmus pack his bag.'

Ewert Grens looked at her, trying to hear what she said.

What she was really saying – without herself being aware of it. Hugo and Rasmus hadn't come to school. They couldn't be reached.

It didn't make sense.

Her children had nothing to do with this. *She* was the link to the dead boy, the one who might be in danger as smugglers tried to cover all their tracks.

It didn't make sense. And yet.

Grens just knew.

'When and where did you talk to them last?'

'At home. Around eight. I start early a couple of times a week.'

'And they're alone?'

'Yes. Since their father wasn't able to come home like he should.'

Her irritation was back and aimed squarely at him.

But this time he hardly noticed. Because the only thing that mattered now was keeping her from realising what he was thinking.

'Stay here. Take care of your students. I'll go and fetch them.'

'You?'

'I have time.'

'Why would *you* go there?'

She grabbed his arm, pulled on his coat jacket.

'Ewert? What's going on?'

'Nothing. I just want to be helpful.'

'Why are you here? What did you want to talk to me about?'

He didn't answer her, he was already on his way.

He was running again, just like this morning, again unaware of the pain that should have penetrated his every thought.

10.52
(1 HOUR AND 8 MINUTES LEFT)

Hugo closed the basement door just as carefully as he'd opened it, without a squeak. And it would have been so nice to just lie down and close his eyes. That's what he did when he was little. If he was afraid, or sad, he used to close his eyes and keep them shut while Mum and Dad took care of whatever he was afraid of or sad about. When he opened them again everything was OK.

Now he was the big one. He had to take care of it.

Even though fear and the urge to weep almost overwhelmed him.

First, he needed his phone. If only he could find it. Damn telephone. He'd had it when they started searching the laundry room. He remembered that much for sure. Was it in there? He sneaked in, good thing he'd got so good at sneaking around after Dad. Not even the slightest sound. That is until everything happened at once. The phone started ringing! Not as loud as usual, something must be lying on top of it, dampening the sound, but loud enough for the phantom to hear.

It kept ringing and beeping as he passed by the washing machine and shower and dryer. When he reached the hampers he could even hear the vibration. He rummaged in the dirty laundry he and Rasmus had spread out on the floor, searching, searching, until finally he found it. Beneath a wrinkled bath towel, or maybe a large hand towel. And silenced it as he picked it up.

Three missed calls. All from Mum.

And now he had to make a call. Not to Mum. Not to Dad. They couldn't help him. But to the very last number in his contact list, a man who could help.

10.55

(1 HOUR 5 MINUTES REMAINING)

'Yes, hello – this is Grens.'

The detective had just turned onto the quiet, narrow street that led to the Hoffmanns' house.

'Ewert . . . it's me.'

'Hugo?'

'Yes.'

The discomfort he'd felt leaving Zofia arrived again at full force. Even more powerfully.

'What do you need?'

Grens tried to listen to the sounds behind Hugo's whispering voice. There were none. The boy must be indoors. In a very quiet room.

'Ewert?'

'Yes?'

'Somebody is here. Inside the house.'

The superintendent had reached the front gate, was about to park outside it, but changed his mind, made a U-turn. If what he suspected was true, if Hugo was right, Grens didn't want to announce his arrival.

'Who, Hugo? Who's in your house?'

'The man from the sketch. The pupils. The one Amadou caught sight of.'

'Are you sure?'

'Yes.'

'And how do you know . . .'

'At first I only saw his trousers and shoes under the kitchen table. But I snuck over to the basement door and saw him, saw his eyes. It's him.'

'It's him?'

'Yes.'

'OK. Then you need to . . . is he still there? In the kitchen?'

'That's where I saw him.'

'Hugo, listen, you—'

'And Mum isn't home.'

'I know, she—'

'But he's waiting for her.'

'What's that?'

'I heard it.'

'Heard?'

'He said so when he was talking on the phone.'

On the next street, parallel to the Hoffmann residence, Grens was able to park without being seen. Hugo's breathing followed him through the phone as he started walking.

The man Amadou identified.

Who became his death.

If it was him.

If that's who was inside the house.

'Hugo?'

No answer.

But it sounded like the boy was also on the move.

'I'll be with you soon, Hugo. Now you need to be really clever.'

A quiet, buzzing sound. And then finally Hugo's whisper.

'I'm back with Rasmus. We're hiding.'

'How is your little brother?'

'I'm hugging him in my arms.'

Grens crossed the neighbour's garden and made his way through a hedge to reach the Hoffmanns' property. He smiled, briefly, and it felt good. What a beautiful string of words. He'd like to do the same. Hug both boys in his arms.

'It's good you're whispering, Hugo.'

On one side of the house a window stood slightly open. A bedroom, to judge by the furniture. He searched for something to stand on, turned a tin pail upside down, if he climbed on it, he'd just be able to squeeze into the window and heave himself over the frame.

Even while cooking chequered pancakes for them, the detective had thought that these were two little boys that didn't need any more bullshit in their lives, any more and it would be devastating. And now those same little boys were hiding from a suspected murderer in their own home.

He stretched, loosened the hook and pushed up the window, braced himself against the frame and heaved himself inside.

It was surprisingly easy to get over and into the room. And now he too whispered.

'I'll be with you soon, Hugo.'

'Where are you – is it far away?'

'Just a little longer. Just stay where you are. And keep holding Rasmus in your arms. Promise me.'

'I pro—'

Then silence.

'Hugo, hello, where did you go?'

'He's here, Ewert. Close. He must have heard the phone ringing. He's in here, in the basement, where we're hiding.'

11.01

(59 MINUTES REMAINING)

He jumped over the rail as the boat with its disconnected propellers passed by the inner pier of Zuwara's port. Dived from the aft into blue-green waters. Not far from the armed guards of the smuggling organisation.

The fishing boat glided forward that last bit, loaded with fuel, towards the concrete dock. Piet Hoffmann floated in the water holding half the fishing rod, letting the line run freely, while the boat bounced against a pair of buoys before coming to rest, as if it had a will of its own.

He waited until the bodyguards jumped on board. Until they discovered that the crew – the captain in the cabin, the guard at the prow – were no longer standing of their own accord. Then Piet locked the fishing reel, stopping the line. And with a jerk, the lighter's button was pushed down, turned from off to on.

Felt like a fish had taken a bite.

And the explosion was immediate.

A powerful shockwave and a furious, intense fire. Thick, black diesel smoke poured out. What he'd been waiting for. It was like the mushroom cloud that followed a nuclear test. It surrounded the boat, engulfed the whole harbour.

Now he would be able to swim ashore unseen, make his way to the crane, climb up to the head of the giraffe. Reach the case that hung there – his only way out when there was no other way.

11.09

(51 MINUTES REMAINING)

Hugo held Rasmus close. He did what he told Ewert – what Ewert told him. Hugged his brother in his arms.

While the man from the sketch walked around the basement again.

The sound of footsteps.

He wasn't giving up. He was getting closer.

This time it was louder when he opened the cupboard, he wasn't nearly so careful as he searched the shelves and ripped open the drawers. And when he was finished, he didn't leave, he just waited. It sounded like he was slowly pulling his nails back and forth against the thin wall.

Hugo squeezed and squeezed his little brother against him, and their hearts beat in a wild rhythm all their own.

Those eyes and those pupils were out there.

Just an arm's length away, on the other side of a wooden board.

Time had no meaning. Which happens sometimes. It became impossible to know if a lot of time had passed – or none at all.

Then there was another creak. The basement door was closing. And then those damn steps, those damn steps fell silent.

Hugo wasn't brave enough to call again.

No no no no no no not again.

But he had to.

'Ewert?'

He whispered as quietly as he could. And when Ewert answered, he whispered too.

'Yes?'

'Where are you, Ewert? He . . . was here. But now he's gone.'

'I'm in the house. In your parents' bedroom I think. But I'm not sure I understood where you and Rasmus are. In the basement, is that right?'

'Yes. In Dad's workroom. Inside the cupboard, or behind it. In a secret room. You can't find it if you don't know about it.'

Ewert still whispered. And now, it sounded stern. Not angry, not that way, but more firm like Mum and Dad were sometimes.

'Hugo, I want you to listen. You can't move from there – at all. Do not leave Rasmus. Don't call me or anyone else. Your only mission is to sit in that secret room until your hear from me again. Do you understand what I'm telling you, Hugo?'

'Yes.'

'If you do as I say, everything will be fine. OK?'

'OK, Ewert.'

11.14
(46 MINUTES REMAINING)

The grey-black smoke that had enveloped everything was slowly thinning out. Piet Hoffmann climbed up the crane, the giraffe's legs, body, throat. The cries of the gulls had been replaced by the voices of Omar and the Accountant. Confusion. Chaos. Perfectly suited to this work.

The fabric case hanging from the leather straps on the giraffe's head. He unpacked his sniper rifle and the boxes of ammunition, left his pistol inside for now, and started up the translation program on his phone. Now the microphones he placed in the shipyard and on the pier were the electronic interpreters he needed to capture the enemy's communication.

'What the fuck is going on?'

Omar had reached the floating, burning wreck of the fishing boat. And he shouted at one of the guards who hadn't quite made it to the boat yet when Hoffmann triggered the explosion, and so was still alive.

'We don't know. Something just—'

'And the Swede?'

'He's not on board. Not alive anyway.'

'Are you . . . are you sure?'

'We searched the entire boat. What's left of it.'

'We need reinforcements! Now!'

Piet Hoffmann pointed the sniper rifle to the place where he thought he might see them. Through the scope he was able to get up close, could see Omar taking out his phone to call for reinforcements.

He couldn't allow it to go through.

11.17
(43 MINUTES REMAINING)

Since Anni died, Ewert Grens hadn't felt responsible for the life of another person. Hardly even for his own. And now suddenly he did. Two little boys had decided to trust him. And for some reason, they'd reached a detective who thought he was unreachable. They'd talked to him, looked at him, and it meant something. Even though nothing really mattered these days.

But the tenor of that responsibility – which initially opened up a heart that had been closed for too long – changed when another boy who'd also chosen to trust him ended up dead in a bloodless bed. What had felt light and easy, suddenly felt heavy and hard.

It was as though they were inside one of those video games the kids loved to play.

Trapped in a make-believe world.

The bad guy – the murderer – had struck once and he would strike again. The innocent – the children – were being hunted while they hid in a secret room. And one player had to solve it all, and when he did, the game would restart and life would go back to normal.

That's how it felt.

That's *not* how it was.

They were all trapped, all in the same place. The murderer, his prey, the player. That much was true. But this world was real, this house existed, nothing was pretend, and every action would have consequences that couldn't be undone.

He, of all people, knew what that meant.

What it was like to be close to somebody, feel responsible for her life, and fail to protect it – what it was like to watch the woman who meant everything to you slowly disappear. So as the detective superintendent crept out of that bedroom in a house that belonged to a family he wasn't even part of, to confront a murderer who was here to kill again, Grens had just one concrete thought, one plan – never again watch while a life he was responsible for was lost.

He would rather lose his own instead.

Shouldering that burden a second time – he didn't have the strength, not in body or soul.

He instinctively ran his hand across the worn leather holster, a cross beneath his jacket. The gun was strangely light in his right hand, he'd experienced that in those few moments before he was about to take a shot, how the weapon became almost weightless when it was really needed.

Grens opened the bedroom door gently, carefully. His work as an investigator was about arriving at a place after a crime was committed, interpreting it, puzzling out what had happened, seeking answers to why people were injured or killed long after. Now he stood in an unfamiliar house, doing something he'd never done before in his long career as a policeman – confronting a killer *before* a murder took place.

One step, then one more, through the hall where Hugo just a couple of days earlier had eavesdropped on them.

Ewert Grens paused, now *he* was the eavesdropper, but all he heard was the clock ticking loudly on the kitchen wall, the fridge humming along, a car out on the street honking at something.

If he stood right here, leaning just a little towards the bathroom where he'd flushed to cover for his talk with Hugo, he could see the short staircase leading down to the basement.

They were there, the boys. And they were his responsibility.

His.

The detective superintendent pressed himself against the wall, and along it.

Into the kitchen. That was where Hugo had seen a pair of black shoes and black trousers, which belonged to a familiar pair of eyes.

That was where he had to go.

Ewert Grens summoned all the courage he could, all the anger, all those terrible years in the pit of his stomach, until he had the strength to take that final step. Around the corner, where the hall turned into the kitchen.

He held his gun at shoulder height and maybe it shook a bit more than when he was younger.

A sweeping movement from one side of the room to the other – kitchen table, cabinets, stove, counters.

Empty.

Maybe Hugo imagined it all.

As children sometimes do.

Grens exhaled, a bit. Relaxed somewhat. Dropped his guard.

And that's when a heavy blow hit the back of his head and he fell – headlong – onto the kitchen floor.

His face took the brunt of the hit.

Something in his cheek was crushed. A few teeth were loosened in the upper jaw. The tip of his chin made a crunching sound. But he didn't feel the pain of any of it. Just like this morning when he started to run for the first time in decades.

He lay there as the next blow hit higher up on his head, a third on the crown.

A pair of hands grabbed at him, at his jacket, turned him around.

Ewert Grens lay on his back unable to defend himself and saw what Hugo had seen before he hid, what Amadou saw and what led to his death – a pair of eyes with pupils of different sizes. The man was unexpectedly similar to the phantom in the police artist's sketch. Hair so short it was almost a buzz cut, a tiny nose, uneven teeth, a few days of stubble on his chin. And what he held in his hand reminded Grens of a tool he'd once used in woodwork class, what they called an awl, basically a handle with a long, sharp metal tip attached. A weapon that created deep wounds with clean edges, penetrated lungs and hearts, left behind only a small amount of blood on the chest and in the bed – about the amount that would fill a coffee cup.

And it was odd.

What Ewert Grens felt was something like disappointment. Of all the damn feelings.

As if all that worry in his long life had been completely unnecessary. Not because he'd been worried about death itself, that wasn't it. That was the emptiness. That was the great silence. That was nothing. But day after day, as long as he could remember, he'd been plagued by fears of dying, or rather fear of the moment before dying, the moment when he realised death was imminent. That feeling, knowing that he would know no more, feel, think, see, hear, smell, taste no more. When consciousness became conscious that the functions of the body were about to cease. That anguish. That last, hellish bit of anxiety.

But all he felt was – nothing.

A man, a murderer, stood over him with his sharp weapon in hand, poised to strike Grens in the heart, and yet – nothing.

11.19
(41 MINUTES REMAINING)

Piet Hoffmann didn't want to take a shot – thereby revealing his position – until it was absolutely necessary.

Twice, Omar dialled a phone number, without getting through. On his third attempt he managed, and Hoffmann waited. Until he couldn't wait any longer. The reinforcements finally answered.

And the shot had to be taken.

But it was still too easy to die immediately, physically.

So Hoffmann aimed at the cell phone. And when the shot hit its mark, not only was the phone blown away, so was Omar's hand.

11.20
(40 MINUTES REMAINING)

It was a disappointment that the moment before death wasn't worth a life of worrying. But also a surprise. And it was also exactly like the cliché. Time slowed down to almost nothing. A second stretched out endlessly as his senses took in the world one last time.

Ewert Grens stared at the sharp end of a long metal tool pointed at his chest and heart. And he knew exactly how, what, when. The tick of the kitchen clock was as loud as a drumbeat, the light above the stove brighter than the sun, the breath of his killer stank more than a garbage dump.

All of it, one last time.

Then he saw something more. There. *There.* At the same height as the blade, behind it, just a few metres away. A movement. A person. Hugo.

And a weapon.

Hugo was holding a gun in his nine-year-old hand.

That was why that distinctive bang drowned out everything else, and his every thought became incomprehensible and unnecessary.

Hugo had fired the gun. Ewert Grens saw the recoil knock the boy onto his back, heard just as clearly how the shot grazed and scratched the kitchen fan before embedding itself into the wall.

Hugo had fired the gun, and he'd missed.

But it was enough time for the man above Grens to jerk back and turn around. And for the detective to grab hold of the phantom's leg, twist it, push him away and then down onto the kitchen floor. Sufficient for the awl to fall out of his hand, and for Grens to pick it up, raise it high, and plunge it into the man's heart.

11.21

(39 MINUTES REMAINING)

The shot at Omar's hand changed the conditions. Hoffmann's position had now been revealed. So he took five more shots. Two shots at the bodyguards on either side of Omar. One shot at the guard running out of headquarters. And two shots at the guards outside the warehouse, who were in charge of the refugees waiting inside for the next departure on the next smuggling boat.

He needed Frank. Who was doing exactly what he'd promised. Watching for a signal, and once the boat exploded, moving to the position behind the refugee warehouse with phone in hand.

'You ready?'

'I know what you mean by obvious signal now, Koslow. No way I could've missed that.'

The cloud of smoke had almost dissolved, and from his spot on the crane Piet Hoffmann searched for his Danish friend through the rifle scope, without success.

'Frank, can I count on you now?'

'You insult me by even asking the question.'

'Good. Then this is what I need you to do. Now that the guards are neutralised, I want you to gather up the refugees, I'd guess there are fifty, maybe seventy-five inside, and move them a good distance away. Then I need you to return to the empty warehouse and prep it. Two hundred and fifty grams of det cord wrapped around each column. If we're going to level the place, we'll need force from two different directions – the explosives have to be placed at double points to push the iron beams down and to the right and up and to the left.'

'How long do I have?'

'A helluva lot less than you need.'

'The usual, then.'

From the top of the crane, his view of the sea was magnificent. Hoffmann stared into its endless waters and still couldn't see the money transport boat.

'One more thing, Frank.'

'Yes?'

'Watch your back for Omar – the guy you were trailing in Tripoli – and the Accountant, a woman, mid-thirties. They're the only ones left out there, but don't shoot to kill if you run across them. They're mine. I'll take care of them. And I want them alive.'

'And if I have no choice?'

'You have a choice. OK? However, you have no choice when it comes to those refugees. They're already afraid and worked up and now, with the chaos, they'll be panicking – but you still have to get them out of that fucking warehouse. Before we blow it to high heaven.'

11.22

(38 minutes remaining)

Dead.

Ewert Grens put a gentle finger on the inside of the man's wrist, no pulse. And then just for the sake of it, despite already being sure, he put two fingers on the side of his windpipe.

For the first time in his life, he had killed someone.

Four years ago, he believed he'd killed someone, when he gave the command to shoot Piet Hoffmann during a hostage crisis at a high-security prison. But he had later found out it wasn't true.

Now he had killed for the sake of Hoffmann.

And Grens didn't feel a damn thing. Everything he feared – guilt, shame, angst at ending a life – was completely absent. *You deserved it, you bastard.* You took a child's life, and you almost took the lives of two more, and you were about to kill me to do it – your right to exist in this world, to live, had ceased.

He hurried to the basement staircase. To Hugo. Who stood there, pale, shaken, but still grabbed Grens's outstretched hand.

'Rasmus?'

'Downstairs.'

'Show me.'

On his short walk through the basement he called Sven who, together with Mariana, was still at the crime scene at the group foster home – Grens told them both to come here now. And before Sven could even ask a follow-up question, *what happened, Ewert*, he'd hung up.

'Here, Ewert. Or . . . there.'

Hugo had guided Grens into his father's workroom and pointed to one corner.

'Inside the cupboard. In a secret room.'

The detective helped the nine-year-old boy move a desk chair into the cupboard, and watched the slender back climb up onto it and pull a hidden lever. As the wall slid open to reveal a secret room, Rasmus ran out, paused for a moment when he saw Grens's beaten up visage, but threw himself around Ewert's neck anyway, with a mixture of laughter and tears.

Grens held him tight, while turning back to Hugo.

'What is this?'

'It's Dad's. But it's secret.'

'But *you* knew about it, Hugo?'

'You can't tell him. OK?'

Grens looked at that serious young face. And nodded

'Was this where you found the gun?'

Hugo opened a metal cabinet that reminded Grens of a gun safe.

'You see? There's more. And knives. And a grenade, I think.'

Good God.

Hoffmann kept all this just one floor below the kitchen table where his children ate breakfast every morning?

The everyday tools and life of an infiltrator. In addition to the gun safe, there were a few briefcases, a clothes rail with bulletproof vests of significantly higher quality than what the police had access to, and a safe with a security code.

The everyday life of an infiltrator – but it was a long time ago, Hoffmann. Another life. A promise you gave to me, to your family.

A promise you broke.

'Did you already know, Hugo, that the gun was in there?'

'Yes. I've known for a long time. I go in here sometimes.'

'But how did you know . . . you could shoot it?'

Hugo stared down at the floor as if he were ashamed.

'I googled it. The pistol is called Radom, it's Polish like Dad – or like Dad's Mum and Dad. You can see how to shoot it on YouTube. I've never tried, I promise, Ewert. But I remembered. And it worked.'

Ewert Grens looked around one last time. Sven and Mariana weren't far away, a couple of minutes and they'd be here. He took Hugo and Rasmus by their hands and gently guided them out of the secret room.

'Hugo? I want you to put the pistol back exactly where it lay. And make sure everything else is exactly like it was before, too. And close the door from the outside, you know how to do it.'

The boy was telling the truth, he'd been in this room many times before. He knew the location of every item and made sure to reset the security code on the safe, which the detective had fiddled with, back to all zeros.

'That's how Dad keeps it.'

'Good. Because this is what we're going to do. Now we don't just have a secret together – we have a *huge* secret. Hugo – you can't tell anyone what happened upstairs. OK? You were never there. You never did anything just before he ended up on the ground. Promise me?'

'I promise.'

'You were very brave, Hugo – a hero! You and I will talk a lot more about it later. I'll never forget, you can be absolutely sure of that. But if we tell anyone else right now things will get . . . complicated. More complicated than necessary. For Mum and Dad.'

'I won't say anything. About this.'

'And you, Rasmus – when it comes to the secret room, you'll have to do what your big brother has been doing – know about it, but never talk about it.'

Rasmus had been holding Grens's hand this whole time. When he answered, he squeezed his fingers as hard as he could inside that much bigger hand, as if to emphasise how important this was.

'I can be quiet, *too*. I understand things, *too*.'

'I know, Rasmus.'

Grens gave the boy a hug and let go of his hand. A hug. He couldn't remember the last time he gave one of those.

'And you stay here. In the workroom. Don't go up until I tell you it's OK. Do you promise – again?'

'Promise.'

They said it at the same time. Ewert Grens smiled, then headed for the stairs and up to the hall and the kitchen where he'd meet Sven and Mariana. There was a dead man lying up there. A phantom. He knew now that man did a lot more for the smuggling organisation besides just opening container doors. He was the hit man tasked with tying up their loose ends. Who had killed the Guide and Amadou with the same tool he aimed at the heart of the detective. Working for the Swedish contact person, or if Mariana was right, for the leader of the entire organisation.

11.26

(34 MINUTES REMAINING)

Headquarters. That was where Omar fled, according to the microphones. Where, with the help of the Accountant – she'd been there the whole time, according to those same interpreters – he slowed the bleeding from the stump where his hand had been. So that's where Piet Hoffmann ran as soon as he climbed down from the crane.

There was only one entrance. The stairwell. He had to find another one. The façade was uneven and full of holes and, like so many other buildings in the area, not well maintained. Which suited him perfectly. Climbing three floors up on protruding bricks was nothing compared to making his way up to the giraffe's head.

Omar was lying on one of the desks in the large room.

A bloody bandage pressed to the point where his left arm ended.

That was about as much as Hoffmann could make out through the window from the best place he could find to stand on. The wall was even more crumbled here, he was able to ram half a foot into one hole.

He searched the room for the Accountant, and the door to the Safe Room seemed to be open a little. He took out his phone and connected the webcam inside – it had previously conveyed with perfect sharpness as her fingers danced across the safe's display inputting the code.

No connection. No transmitter, no camera.

She had discovered it.

Of course.

Probably changed the code.

And with the money transport boat approaching, whose security personnel were as skilled at using violence as himself, there was only one option left to him.

Collision, confrontation. It had opened the door for him.

Now it would open the window.

11.30
(30 MINUTES REMAINING)

Ewert Grens was sitting at the Hoffmann kitchen table as Sven and Mariana's car parked in front of the gate. He'd just made it. In the span of a few minutes, he was able to grab a pair of tweezers from the bathroom cabinet, and after a few failed attempts, he managed to grab onto the bullet embedded in the concrete wall next to the kitchen fan. Now it lay in the inner pocket of his jacket, and it would remain there until he drove over Väster Bridge on his way back to the police station. One good throw out the car window, and the story of a nine-year-old and his pistol would end at the bottom of Lake Mälaren.

From a promise in Africa to a bullet in a wall in southern Stockholm.

He'd promised to keep an eye on this house. Promised nothing would happen to Hoffmann's family while he was working for the Swedish police.

Grens was hit by a wave of exhaustion, the pain started to pulsate in his ravaged face.

A little boy had chosen to confide in an old detective he barely knew, told him he heard shots through the phone when Dad called. Now he'd heard the same thing in his own home, in a place that should be the very definition of safe. Had even seen a dead man on the kitchen floor of his family's home.

I'll take care of you, Hugo, make sure you get the help you need.

The front door opened. He recognised Sven's quiet steps and Mariana's more energetic ones. Their ways of walking were very like their personalities.

'I'm in the kitchen. First right.'

They stopped at the door, near the kitchen counter and dish drainer, and looked around the room.

A dead man on his back.

Their boss in a chair next to him, his face badly beaten.

'Ewert, what, what—'

'You two take care of this.'

'—happened?'

'And do it fast. An immediate crime scene investigation. And—'

'You have to go to the hos—'

'—question me immediately. So you know exactly what happened. The people who live here don't need us in their lives a minute longer than necessary.'

I I . 3 2

(28 minutes remaining)

The first three shots broke through the glass window. The next hit Omar in the right knee – with one hand gone and one leg unusable he wouldn't be going anywhere. Piet Hoffmann had gloves on, but still cut both of his palms as he braced them against the window frame and jumped into the big room of headquarters. A second later and he reached the Safe Room and the door, which stood ajar. Collision. Confrontation. His gun in one hand as he grabbed the door and pulled it open.

There she sat, on top of the safe.

That expensive clothing, those golden-framed glasses, her cutting look. And the revolver, which she'd pushed into his forehead until it bled and then taken a shot next to his ear deafening him temporarily on their first meeting – she was pointing it straight at him now.

'I shoot as easily as you, Koslow. Just as willing. Just as quick.'

Two muzzles. Two deadly weapons with the safety off.

'But I don't have as much to lose. I know about you now. Wife. Small children. I'm on my own.'

'You're sitting on your kin. Money. Without it you're as dead as your guards. And as far as my family is concerned, mine is far from here, and completely safe.'

She was strangely calm.

'If you say so.'

As if she knew something he didn't.

'Completely safe. Are you sure?'

As if she really didn't have anything to lose.

'If you shoot I shoot, Koslow. And we both die. So I'll count to five. That's how long you have to get out of here. Then we'll both leave here alive.'

She wasn't desperate. Nor was she afraid. Which complicated things.

'Five.'

To kill her would be easy. But she was supposed to live. Die, but gradually.

'Four.'

She wasn't bluffing.

'Three.'

He was sure of it.

'Two.'

He had to make a decision. Now.

'On—.'

A shot. Someone had taken one.

The bullet pierced her eye, and she fell forward. Someone had taken a shot – but it wasn't Hoffmann, nor the Accountant.

'She was dead serious.'

The voice came from the window he'd just entered.

'You heard her? You wanted her alive. But . . .'

Piet Hoffmann turned around. Frank. Outside the window with his foot probably lodged into the same hole, with one arm draped inside far enough to take the shot.

'. . . she *would* have shot you, Koslow.'

She was serious. Spoke the truth. She didn't live for religion or ideology – only money, and she was prepared to die for it.

For the money in the safe in front of him. Hoffmann input the eight-numbered code. It remained locked.

'You just shot the code.'

'What?'

'Frank, she was the only one who knew the new code.'

The man with the bushy hair and the wild beard shrugged his shoulders.

'Then you better . . .'

'And what are you doing here? Your job is elsewhere!'

'The refugees. We have a small problem. They won't leave the ware-house.'

'Without the code, we have more than one problem. I can take care of the safe if you give me a few metres of det cord. And you take care of *your* problem, Frank. Shoot into the air, threaten them, do whatever you need! They have to go so you can prepare! Time is of the essence.'

Hoffmann helped him in over the remnants of glass. They tore off a piece of the hundred metres of det cord Frank had picked up from Rob in Tunis, then carried in his backpack. They took out one of the twenty detonators from their box, then tied up Omar just to be on the safe side before they split up again.

He had two options. The more thorough method would take longer, but he'd end up with all the money intact. Or a much quicker, more violent method, which would make a lot of noise.

The careful method was to drill a hole into the safe – through a layer of steel and then concrete and then steel again – fill it with a few hundred litres of water and push in a little bit of det cord. A sub-dued, nice little explosion that wasn't very loud. Which left everything inside intact. The money would end up wet and heavy, but still just as valuable when it dried.

The more violent method was to tape the det cord around the door to the safe, then wrap some around the upper hinge, around and around, and then the same thing on the lower hinge, and then connect it to a detonator. He'd have to cart out the still tied-up Omar before setting off an explosion that would knock out not just every window in this building, but every window in the building's vicinity.

Hoffmann checked the time. Twenty-five minutes remaining. The transport boat approaching Zuwara's port would soon be visible using binoculars.

Short on time, he chose the only alternative he could.

He had to carry out Omar, move the Accountant's body, and blow up the safe.

And hope that the twenty million dollars inside didn't burn up.

11.44

(16 MINUTES REMAINING)

Sven Sundkvist called for forensics and the medical examiner and reinforcements, while Ewert Grens called Zofia Hoffmann. In just a few minutes, the house would turn into a place where voices and wills and emotions competed for space with each other. That's why Grens repeated his order to be interviewed immediately, and why he sat at the kitchen table opposite Mariana in front of a mobile phone that recorded his every word.

MARIANA HERMANSSON (MH): I still don't understand, Ewert.
EWERT GRENS (EG): What is it you still don't understand?

Mariana Hermansson was fearless, uncompromising, always said what she felt regardless of the consequences. Tough, according to some. True enough. But always toughest on herself. She didn't need anyone to push her, she did that for herself. That was how she worked. She knew that about herself. But still. This situation was uncomfortable.

Sitting across from her boss, staring at his broken, bleeding, aching face, and asking the kind of questions an interrogator always asks a suspect with a dead person lying at his feet.

MH: You're sixty-four years old.

EG: Can't do much about that.

MH: Not in the best shape.

EG: I guess I could do something about that.

MH: And the man lying there must be mid-thirties, do you agree?

EG: Sounds about right.

MH: In good shape. Muscular. Right?

EG: So it seems.

MH: OK, despite this disparity in physical status, despite the blow you say you received on the back of your head, which caused a fall forward and the subsequent facial injuries, even though the dead man jumped on you and raised his weapon, this awl, which is highly deadly when plunged into the lungs and heart, just as it was in the murder of a fourteen-year-old last night, and a middle-aged man in the tunnel system – despite all that, you claim you were able to overpower him? Force him off? And, in defence of your own life, take his?

Ewert Grens heard what she said. And he knew how good she was. But not even she would find out what really happened if neither he nor Hugo told her.

EG: Yes.

MH: Yes?

EG: Yes.

MH: But how, Ewert? Where did the strength come from? How could you, from such a vulnerable position, a position where you were absolutely sure you were going to die – how could you overpower a significantly younger, considerably stronger man who's murdered several times before?

EG: There are some things, Hermansson, that are impossible to explain. I guess I had a little angel at my side.

At that moment Grens turned, perhaps unconsciously, towards the basement door, but Mariana Hermansson didn't notice.

SVEN SUNDKVIST (SS): Is it OK if I ask a question?
MH: Ask away. I have the feeling that he's already decided his answer, regardless of the question.

During the brief interrogation, Sven had, in anticipation of the forensic team, conducted his own examination of the kitchen. Now he pointed with plastic gloves on his hands towards the kitchen fan and the wall next to it.

SS: There's damage to the fan, in one corner.
EG: Really?
SS: A scratch that can be connected to a small hole in the wall.
EG: There you go.
SS: And when I bend down to the floor and skirting, I see particles there. Quite a few. Pieces of the same material that the wall is made of. Which I take to mean that either the Hoffmann family isn't especially good at cleaning or the hole is fresh.
EG: Is that a question?
SS: My question, Ewert, is if you were here when that wall was pierced?
EG: No.
SS: So you don't know anything about a fresh hole in the wall directly behind where you just killed a man?

Just as Ewert Grens turned to the basement door when he mentioned the angel, he now, just as unconsciously, let his hand slide down into his pocket, grabbed hold of a bullet that had just been fired. But neither of the other two participants in this interrogation noticed.

EG: That's right, Sven – I don't know anything about it.

11.54
(6 MINUTES REMAINING)

Sixteen million dollars weighs more than you'd think.

They fled through the gates of Zuwara's port in Omar's war-ready car, their bags filled with used dollar bills. About a million dollars, which had been on the bottom shelf, had burned up in the explosion – but they got most of this month's smuggling revenues, it was enough.

The transport boat with armed security personnel was visible to the naked eye now, gliding ever closer through the gentle waters of the Mediterranean. And it would get here just in time to meet what remained of a criminal organisation. Because Piet Hoffmann now opened his phone and sent a mass-text message to the GSM-controlled ignition sets Frank placed along with the det cord on every pillar of the warehouse and into each diesel tank of the smuggling boats and across the floor of headquarters. From a distance, it was almost beautiful to watch it all blown into the air at the same time.

11.57.

He'd made it.

Three hours was as long as three minutes or three seconds.

PART SIX

PART SIX

ZOFIA RAN TOWARDS HER rusty front gate, up seven steps that led to the house her family was only just starting to feel safe in, just daring to live a normal life inside, and there at her front door she was met by a stretcher bearing a dead body, covered by a sheet. And a thought passed through her mind. About normality, what it was. About how things like this happened in Colombia, when they were on the run – from a life sentence in a Swedish prison, from a death sentence from the Polish mafia, then another one from the White House, and then one more from a South American drug cartel – and in those circumstances she accepted the abnormal. Even expected it. But here, in their own home, in a suburb called Enskede, in the city she grew up in, she'd actually started to allow herself to think the normality was something real. So she wasn't shocked, had seen too much for that, lived too long in another world, but still her heart broke. For the boys. Her boys! Where were they? How were they feeling? What . . .

'In here, Zofia. But don't go through the kitchen, it's not quite ready.'

In the living room. That's where they sat. Each with his own half-filled glass of juice and slice of leftover pie. Rasmus and Hugo. And opposite them, Ewert Grens, with a face that was beaten to a pulp.

'I'd guess another half hour. Then we can leave you in peace.'

The detective superintendent refilled the orange juice to the very edge of the glasses, smiled at the two boys and headed for the kitchen, while Zofia sat down on the sofa and put her arms around them, pulled them close, and kissed their foreheads, cheeks, ears, eyes until they protested, and she had to let go just a little. She wanted to comfort them. Or maybe she was trying to comfort herself.

Mariana and Sven were still at the kitchen table where Grens had left them, each writing in their own notebook, standing up occasionally to look more closely at some detail with one of the forensic technicians.

'I thought of something just now when I was with the boys. Something Hugo said.'

Grens pulled out the third kitchen chair.

'He heard something when the phantom made a call. The dead man, that is.'

'Heard?'

'When the bastard sat down here at the kitchen table, waiting for Zofia Hoffmann to come home. Apparently he made a call. To someone in the organisation.'

Mariana flipped a few pages into her notebook.

'Do you remember Billy, our new wunderkind, Ewert? Who did the impossible – decrypted the code to the phone we found in the refugee's jacket, got access to the satellite network? I called him at the same time as the rest of the technicians. He was here while you took care of the boys. He drove back with his blue lights on to do an analysis of the dead man's phone. But his first attempt wasn't successful. He doesn't think he'll be able to break in. It was super-encrypted. We'll have to prepare ourselves that we might not get any phone numbers, or even a location or time, not for outgoing or incoming calls.'

'Then let's talk to Hugo.'

'You think he's up for it, Ewert?'

'He's up for it, Sven. Unless you have a better witness?'

They all three headed for the living room, where a mother and her children sat on the sofa, drinking juice and having a cosy afternoon snack. Or that's what it looked like when they knocked and entered. Not like two little boys recovering from the experience of hiding in a basement from a murderer, then seeing him dead on their own kitchen floor.

'I apologise, Zofia, but we need a little help from Hugo.'

Ewert Grens smiled at the boy he shared a secret with, a *huge* secret, while Zofia put her arms around her children once more, squeezed them close to her like before.

'No, I don't think so.'

'I know you'd rather we don't. But we have to.'

'Listen to me, Ewert! You can go to hell . . .'

'*I* want to, Mum.'

'Honey, you don't need—'

'I want to help, Ewert.'

Hugo wrestled out of his mother's embrace and leaned over the coffee table, towards Grens.

'I can talk. About what I'm allowed to talk about, I mean.'

The nine-year-old boy and the sixty-four-year-old detective looked at each other and Grens nodded, *this* was no secret.

'Hugo – we're trying to find out everything we can about the man who was here. And only you saw him. Heard him.'

'OK?'

'So I want to know at what time he made that call.'

'Time?'

'Yes. What time was it when you saw him sitting at the kitchen table talking on the phone?'

Hugo struggled. He wanted to remember. Wanted to help Ewert.

'I think . . . it was before I called you. And before Mum called – and I had to find my phone, which got lost in the dirty laundry while Rasmus and I were looking for his gym shorts, and there were three missed calls. So before your call. And before Mum's. But not by much.'

Grens looked at his own call history – 10.55, a call from Hugo. He then asked Zofia to check her last unanswered call. 10.47.

'How long is *not much before that*, Hugo?'

'Maybe . . . ten minutes. Something like that.'

'Good. Then we know. That's useful. And now, Hugo, I want to know one more thing. What did he say? Other than that he was waiting for Mum.'

'That's enough! You got an answer to your question, Ewert. Leave us alone now!'

The nine-year-old boy put his hand over his Mum's, to calm her, probably an echo of how she usually calmed him.

'Mum, it's OK. Like I said. I *want* to talk to Ewert. Because he was here.'

The adults exchanged a brief glance. And Grens realised what it was going on. She was fighting against her own guilt, thinking *I wasn't here when my sons needed me.*

'So what did he say, Hugo?'

The detective cut himself a slice of apple pie and held it in a napkin, and despite the pain in his jaw, he took a bite.

'Try, Hugo, try to remember.'

'English. That's what he spoke. But not good English. More like somebody who speaks another language. And some Italian words. I think.'

'Italian?'

'Yes.'

'Like what?'

'I think . . . bread.'

'Bread?'

'Ciabatta.'

Grens took a second bite of apple pie, nodded to Zofia, as if to say it tastes good.

'Ciabatta?'

'Yes.'

'Are you sure, Hugo?'

'Not really, but . . .'

'Can I come in?'

Mariana glanced from her boss to the nine-year-old boy.

'Hugo – could it have been *cirrata*?'

The boy did like before, thought for a long, long time, eager to be helpful.

'Yes. Maybe.'

And then he muttered it to himself, trying out how it sounded.

'Cirrata. Cirrata. Cirrata. Yes. I think so. I think that's what he said.'

'Octopus. The name of the organisation. An eight-armed octopus is called *cirrata*.'

Grens looked at her in surprise. She was good, he knew that, but not that damn good.

'Romanian, Ewert. The same language family as Spanish and Italian. And Latin.'

Of course. The detective felt a little ashamed he'd forgotten, like always. Because other people's lives didn't really interest him like they should. Romanian. Her second language.

'He said one more thing. That was connected to ciabatta. Or cirrata.'

Hugo's cheeks were starting to get back the colour they lost after he was knocked down by the recoil of a gun.

'It came after *cirrata*. He said *kapoot*. *Cirrata kapoot*.'

He turned back to Mariana, she understood the language, and she was the one who answered.

'*Kapoot?*'

'Yes. And I'm completely sure about that word.'

Mariana smiled at the boy, he should know he'd done well, then turned to Grens.

'And that, that means head of the octopus, Ewert.'

'What?'

'*Caput*. That's what it means. Head. And if you take it one step further – the abbreviation CC. *Cirrata Caput*. The head of the octopus.'

She picked up her phone, swiped through images of the documents Piet Hoffmann had photographed in a smuggling organisation's North African headquarters.

'And if you think about it – cap, as in capital cities, like capitolium, still the same language family. Places where decisions are made. There, Ewert, do you see at the top right of the paper? *CC 25%*. The one who gets the biggest cut. This backs up what we already guessed. The head of the octopus. In relation to the eight arms, which receive smaller shares. A head that decides and eight arms that act.'

'You mean he sat on this damn chair and spoke to the head of the organisation . . .?'

'If Hugo's memory is correct. And if we're interpreting it correctly.'

Ewert Grens stood up from the Hoffmanns' corner sofa.

Was it possible?

Had the man who killed Amadou, who tried to do the same to an old Swedish detective, been acting on orders from the top? Even reporting directly to the leader – from here?

Grens thought about the picture Hoffmann sent – along with the images of some business documents – of a German man in Tripoli, identified as Jürgen Krause. *If* the German did turn out to be the head of the octopus – why would a murderer sit here, in Hoffmann's home, sent to kill Zofia Hoffmann, and call *him*? The leader? In an international smuggling organisation where each country functioned somewhat self-sufficiently? This should have been a problem for the Swedish arm to solve.

Also, *if* Mariana was right then . . .

CC was the leader.

CC was also Swedish.

Ewert Grens walked out into the hall, entered the kitchen, and went over to peer out through the window. Early afternoon in a beautiful suburb. Just as quiet as it should be.

Now it was his turn to open the photos app on his phone. He didn't have many in there. He rarely took them. Never had – what happened happened, and if he couldn't remember it without a photograph, it must not have mattered. But this, he'd take a picture of, saved. The first person he'd ever killed. In this very kitchen. A person who spoke to his employer – probably the top person, a Swede – just shortly before his death.

The detective marked the image and pressed the symbol for send.

And then he called.

'Grens? Is that you? I don't . . .'

Piet Hoffmann was sitting in a car, that much was clear from the noise surrounding his voice.

'. . . really have time. I'll call you in a few hours.'

'You sound stressed, Hoffmann?'

'Sorry, can't do it. Talk to you later.'

'I just need you to look at one photo. Which you should be receiving right now.'

More noise, car sounds as Hoffmann moved his phone from his mouth and opened the message that had just beeped.

'OK. And?'

'The man who is dead.'

'I can see he's dead.'

'You recognise him?'

'No.'

'You're sure?'

'I've never seen that face.'

'Are you absolutely sure?'

'Absolutely. What's the connection? Who killed him? And where's this picture from?'

Grens turned around and stared at the small spot of blood that the awl had left behind. He wanted to scream. *Here, Hoffmann.* He was on your kitchen floor, next to the table where your wife and your sons eat breakfast every day while they talk to you. Your family. Who are sitting in the living room and who just helped me with my investigation because one of your sons saw and heard and tried to shoot that same dead man.

'Who killed him or where isn't important. What is important, however, is that he had direct contact with the leader of the entire organisation and is our best chance to find and identify them.'

That roaring, howling, speeding sound again.

As if Hoffmann looked at the photo one last time.

'No, Grens, I have never seen him. And now I have to get back to *my own* chaos. I'll be in touch.'

Ewert Grens stayed in the kitchen, near the bloodstain on the floor and the bullet hole in the wall. Something was gnawing at him. And it had been ever since Hugo's conversation with Mariana and those expressions in Latin.

Cirrata.

The word was familiar for some reason – but he couldn't quite remember why.

It gnawed at him.

AS SOON AS THEY drove Omar's car out of the area of Zuwara's harbour, Piet Hoffmann saw them. The refugees. Who Frank threatened, driving them off before prepping the large warehouse with det cord in order to blow it into the air.

He saw them walking along the highway, away from the destruction. And they were desperate. Screaming, crying, gesturing.

For a moment he didn't understand it at all.

Until he did. Because the world was a fucked up place where right became wrong and wrong, right.

He had destroyed the ability of deeply disturbed human traffickers to profit from the hell of other people's lives.

He cut off the smuggling organisation at its roots so it would never flourish again.

But when he did, he'd destroyed all the hope these refugees had for the future.

That's why they wept and cried out. And that's why he couldn't stop thinking about the sight of them. So after his confusing conversation with Ewert Grens about a dead man lying on a floor, and despite having made a significant part of the journey to Tripoli and the airport, Hoffmann hit the brakes and turned off on a side road wide enough to make a U-turn, ignoring Frank's protests.

When, after twenty kilometres or so back in the wrong direction, they came upon the procession of refugees on a country road, it felt to Hoffmann like he was meeting the pure grief of hopelessness itself. Even if that defunct organisation was planning to put them onto a boat that could have sunk at any moment, even if that organisation couldn't have cared less if they drowned, once they paid. Hoffmann knew all that, and that this particular Libyan route to Europe was basically closed from now on, which was a good thing, but when he tried to convince the people in the front of that procession in this fucked up place in a fucked up world all his reasoning fell flat. So he opened the boot and took out one of the two suitcases Frank had helped him fill while the explosion of the safe still echoed through headquarters. And mumbled something in a mixture of English and French about this being a lot more than what they paid to the smugglers, and they could go home and start over with it, or flee in some other organisation's boats across the Mediterranean, and it was their choice. There was enough money there for whatever direction they decided to go.

IT WAS AFTER THE X-ray and the examination of his wounded head at Karolinska Hospital, after he returned to his office at the Kronoberg police station, when he could finally lie down on his worn corduroy sofa, that he remembered. What was gnawing at him. Cirrata. Where he'd seen it, heard it. A hotel lobby in Niger. A driver in a uniform, holding a sign, asking for *Mr Cirrata*. And a Foreign Ministry official who stood up and thanked his companion. *Cirrata, Dixon?* And met the question with a warm smile. *The name of the UN representative I'll be meeting.*

Who was he going to meet?

Who was the UN representative?

Ewert Grens rushed from the sofa to the desk he rarely used. The top man. The smuggling organisation's Swedish leader. Had Dixon been headed to meet them? He found the business card with the government logo under a pile of unsorted and unopened mail and called. Once. Twice. No answer. The voicemail greeting was in English and Swedish, and Grens left a message asking him to call back.

Grens was impatient.

Paced his office as usual.

Until he couldn't wait any longer.

It didn't take long to Google the hotel in Niamey and it felt good to be able to call them right away. In his most proper-sounding English he asked to be connected to one of the guests at the hotel. Two misunderstandings and two wrong calls later, the chief of security at the hotel was satisfied that Grens was the Swedish police officer he claimed to be, and almost ready to violate the privacy of their guests, despite policy.

'A driver, you say?'

'A young man in a uniform with no insignia. At eight o'clock in the morning three days ago one of your regular guests – a Swedish government official named Thor Dixon – was picked up by this young man. I'd like to get in touch with that driver.'

'Why?'

'That's my business.'

'Do you want my help or not? There are many taxi services to choose from, and it will take me a number of hours to find the right one. That is, before I can locate this driver.'

'I want to know where that young man drove Dixon and if possible who Dixon was meeting with. I'm not interested in your guest, if that makes it any easier for you, I'm trying to find out more about whoever your guest was meeting that morning.'

The phone call didn't make his restlessness any easier to handle. Patience had never been Grens's strong suit. So he continued to pace across his office, between his desk and the window, between the sofa and the bookshelf. Until someone knocked lightly on his door, and a colleague whose name he couldn't remember peeked inside.

'You have a visitor.'

'Really?'

'Shall I show them in?'

'Depends on who it is.'

'A very young man. And his mother.'

A face appeared at about elbow height next to his colleague. Wearing a smile.

'Hugo . . .?'

'Hello, Ewert.'

'What are you doing here – at the station?'

'Visiting you.'

Zofia stood at his side, together they filled his doorway.

'He begged. He wanted to come here so badly. To you, to where you work. Is that OK?'

Ewert Grens smiled, more broadly than he realised.

'Welcome. It's not often I have such lovely visitors in this office. Or any at all, to be honest.'

He smoothed out the corduroy fabric of the sofa as best he could.

Gestured for them to sit down. And moved a pile of papers out of the visitor's seat before settling down across from Hugo.

'Ewert – that's not completely true.'

Zofia observed Grens, but didn't really meet his eyes, or at least that's how it felt.

'Hugo did ask me, that's true. But I too wanted to come here.'

'Yes?'

'Because I want to apologise. I . . . well, it was just so overwhelming when I got home. But I saw your face. And I see it now, black and blue and bandaged. I understood, I understand, that you were protecting my kids. Protecting me. That he was waiting for me, not you.'

She looked at him.

With eyes too weary to think of any more death.

'But it was you, Ewert, who . . . you saved my life. My boys' lives.'

'Well, it was actually the other way around.'

Grens winked at Hugo, without Zofia noticing.

'Other way around? I'm not following you, Ewert.'

'Hugo was the one who saved my life.'

It took a moment. Then she smiled. Even laughed a little. Nudged Hugo so they could both laugh at the detective's silly joke.

'I'm so sorry, Ewert. I acted stupidly. I said the wrong thing. You are always welcome. Whenever you'd like to visit. I know Hugo and Rasmus would appreciate it. I would appreciate it too – if you could keep in touch with them.'

Ewert Grens smiled. It felt good. One less battle in a day that was full with them.

'And . . . your health?'

He nodded towards her, wasn't sure Hugo was aware she was pregnant.

'Hugo knows. He's going to be a big brother again. We just talked about it. It was connected somewhat with this visit. And my health is fine.'

She placed her hand on her stomach, unconsciously, and Grens stared for a bit too long.

'We . . . were going to have one. A girl, it turned out. Fifth month. That's when Anni was injured. My wife. So it never came to be.'

'Ewert, I didn't know . . .'

'Sometimes things just don't work out. But now I've met two wonderful boys. Right, Hugo?'

Afterwards, he stood in the hallway watching them go for as long as he could, a boy and his mother headed off to eat cinnamon buns – Grens made them promise to try the café across the street – then he went three doors down to where Sven and Mariana were waiting.

'Sit down, Ewert.'

Mariana's cheeks were slightly red, and she frowned like she always did when they were close to a breakthrough in an investigation – when what she was holding inside felt too big, and just had to come out.

'Sven and I think we have . . . well, just listen, we'll take it step by step.'

A blue folder lay on the very ordinary table between three ordinary chairs. Despite being in this department for quite a few years now, Mariana hadn't done anything to personalise her office. Same furniture, same things on the walls as when she moved in, satisfied with what someone else had chosen to put in. Sometimes it made him a bit sad. But more often he felt pride to have recruited a colleague like this – even guiding her through the bureaucracy, past a long line of more 'qualified' applicants – someone who actually found the work itself, the investigation, more important than what rug she had on her office floor.

'Let's start with the now dead man who attacked you in the Hoffmanns' kitchen. No match in our records. But we did get something back from Interpol. Identical fingerprints and DNA linked to two unresolved murders in Italy and Poland.'

She'd been holding up the top document from the file, and now switched to the one below it.

'Then we come to the man Piet Hoffmann calls Omar, whose picture was taken through a rifle scope, and we learn, according to our Libyan colleagues, that his full name is Omar Zayed and he was once an official in the Gaddafi administration. Worked for the secret police, responsible for interrogation, torture, that sort of thing. One of the few that survived the purge and apparently found a new meal ticket.'

The next bundle was a bit thicker. A few papers stapled together.

'We've continued our investigation into several other people in parallel. Names that popped up now and then in connection to all of this. People previously unknown to us.'

'Go on.'

'First the mortuary technician. Name is Laura, age around fifty, and works in the morgue at Söder Hospital. And when we looked into her, she wasn't nearly as gentle as she seemed.'

'Oh?'

Ewert Grens became aware of his own uneasiness. And turned away slightly so Mariana wouldn't notice it too, how much he was hoping Laura wasn't the Swedish contact they were looking for.

'She turned out to have a pretty messy past. Maybe that's why she decided to go into working with the dead.'

'*Oh?*'

Mariana glanced at her papers as often as she did at her boss.

'We've investigated her as far as we can. And we're sure – it's *not* her.'

Grens felt that same soft lightness he'd felt when he was with the mortuary technician. And he didn't care what Mariana and Sven saw, since it was impossible to hide.

'So we had to move on. To the next name. If you look here, Ewert, at the first page in this stack.'

'Not so fast.'

The detective wasn't quite ready to move on.

'What did she do?'

'Who?'

'The mortuary technician. Laura.'

'Ewert, what does it matter?'

'I want to know.'

Mariana smiled.

At least, he thought she did.

'She got divorced. Then served eight months in Hinseberg Prison for assault.'

'Assault?'

'Yep. He should never have been unfaithful.'

Then it was Grens's turn to smile.

At least, Mariana thought he did.

'And now? Can we move on?'

'Yes, now we can move on.'

Mariana pointed to the stack of papers she'd just put on the table. On top was some sort of personnel list from the Ministry of Foreign Affairs. Several years old. Mariana pointed to a row in the middle.

'There. Do you see?'

Ewert Grens read it. A personnel list from the Swedish Consulate in Benghazi, Libya. And a name he recognised.

'Thor Dixon. He worked there during Gaddafi's time, Ewert. Prior to his years as a Stockholm-based expert for the West African ambassadors.'

'That's what they do in the Foreign Ministry. Move around. Work their way up the diplomatic hierarchy.'

'True. That's how it works. But look at this.'

The next paper in the stapled bunch.

A photo. Black and white. Taken from a newspaper. Two people staring into the camera. Suits, serious expressions, small flags on the top of the long conference table.

'Do you recognise them, Ewert?'

The superintendent put on his reading glasses, which these days he always kept in one of his pockets, and leaned in closer.

'No.'

'That one is Omar Zayed. To the left. And the man sitting opposite him, that's a young Thor Dixon. In an official photo. In an official context. But it proves something – they worked together. Knew each other.'

Ewert Grens didn't say anything. He wasn't really sure where this was headed. Or if he even wanted to know.

'Then we found this. It's from another newspaper article about a diplomatic meeting. Eight people in this photo. At the far left sit three men. Do you see who they are?'

It was the same time period. Maybe even be the same suits. Omar Zayed and Thor Dixon. But the third man, also in a grey suit and striped tie, around the same age as the other two, Grens didn't recognise him.

'Jürgen Krause. The man Hoffmann sent a photograph of, meeting with Omar in Tripoli. And who we think has the code name *ACC* in the financial documents. Second in command. Do you see the pattern, Ewert? That's how the organisation was built. With international contacts. Formal contacts that many years later became informal. A network that already existed. And geographically fitted the circumstances perfectly. A representative in place where the smuggling begins – and a representative in each country where it ends. *Zuw1* and *ACC* and *CC*. We now know *zuw2* also works in North Africa, so I would bet that when we decode the other names *lam* and *sal* and *bank* and *gda* and *trans balt*, some will have been diplomats connected during that same time period.'

Ewert Grens had listened. Everything she said made sense. And yet he still didn't understand it.

'Dixon?'

'Dixon, Ewert.'

'You're absolutely serious . . . Dixon?'

'Yes. Dixon. The head person, who might not oversee every detail of what the others were doing, but who made it all possible.'

The detective superintendent leaned back in the uncomfortable chair, readjusting his unsteady legs. There wasn't much more to do.

'And now? I suppose you already have a suggestion for the next step?'

Mariana put the short stack of papers back into a blue folder that could accommodate significantly more.

'Sven and I need your permission to request Thor Dixon's phone records. All of them. His private phones and those he uses as a government official. We want to see if we can establish a link to the organisation – perhaps he even spoke to the man in the Hoffmann's kitchen while Hugo was listening. Maybe Dixon personally gave him the order to kill.'

EVENING DARKNESS AGAIN. BUT this time he knew which one of those grand windows belonged to Thor Dixon. And the light was on. The government official was working late, like a detective superintendent usually did just a few kilometres from here.

Ewert Grens was a few minutes early, and he waited by the verdigris statue in the middle of Gustav Adolf's Square for Dixon to come down those heavy stone stairs and open the door to the Ministry of Foreign Affairs. Dixon had called back after the voicemail Grens left, sounded just as friendly and eager to help as before. Because that's what Grens had said – he needed help again into the investigation of the people killed in a container. Not that he was here to investigate Dixon himself. But that pleasant attitude, the comfortable way the Foreign Ministry official greeted the detective, invited him in, without a hint of hesitation or secretiveness, made Grens doubt if he was here on the right mission. Made him wonder if Mariana and Sven and his own interpretations of old articles and financial documents were the mistakes of overworked professionals eager for results, no matter the cost, impatient to make an arrest.

'This is turning into a lovely little habit. Evening visits from the detective superintendent. But . . . and I do apologise . . . what happened to you?'

Thor Dixon's voice didn't sound at all to him like someone who was guilty. Grens had learned the signs over the years.

'Thanks for meeting me so late – again. I appreciate it. And this . . .'

Grens threw his arms wide.

'. . . a little accident. The sort that police officers are prone to.'

It was as deserted and silent as during his last visit to this former palace.

Their steps echoed just as loudly in the corridors.

'And how can I be of service to the authorities this time?'

The government official had a thermos of coffee already prepared on the side table in the corner of his office. He poured one for Grens, black, handed him the porcelain cup with the official Foreign Ministry seal on it without even asking. Grens always wanted coffee, of course.

'With a few names. A few more names, that is. I think they might be people you know.'

'People I know? That sounds exciting. By the way, I'm glad everything went so well with the boy, the relatives he wanted you to inform are being told the news by some of my trusted African colleagues right about now. Maybe you could convey that to the boy, Grens, ease his mind, make him feel better.'

Ewert Grens took a drink of the black coffee and studied the official.

The boy doesn't feel anything.

Because he's dead.

And I'm here to find out if you had anything to do with that.

Thor Dixon met Grens's eyes, and if the official had some special reason to mention Amadou, perhaps testing his visitor, it was impossible to detect. Either Dixon was just as innocent as he seemed, or he was a damn fine actor.

'I'll tell the boy that. If I meet him again.'

Grens once again searched the official's face. Nothing.

Innocent. Or ice cold.

'Then let's get to the names I need your help with. First *his* name, the man standing next to you and some miniature flags in this photo, taken in Libya.'

Ewert Grens sat down on the visitors' sofa opposite Dixon, who in turn settled into a beautifully worn leather armchair that was as elegant as its owner and looked more like it belonged at the Opera Bar than in an office. The detective put the paper onto the equally stylish coffee table and pushed it over to the official, a copy of a photo from the newspaper article Mariana and Sven found in their research.

'You recognise him?'

Thor Dixon leaned over the picture.

'Could you possibly hand me . . .'

And pointed to the shelf behind Grens.

'. . . the reading glasses lying over there?'

Ewert Grens grabbed a pair of shiny metal glasses, which framed Dixon's grey eyes as he examined the photograph.

'Yes. I recognise him.'

'Yes?'

'Zayed. Omar Zayed. From my time as a diplomat whose responsibility was working against – or with, I suppose – the Gaddafi regime. How exactly does this assist you in your investigation, Mr. Grens?'

'That man next to you, Omar Zayed, has been identified as one of the leaders of the international smuggling organisation responsible for the dead people we found in the container.'

'Excuse me?'

'We know that with complete certainty.'

Dixon stared at the picture, resting his chin on one hand.

'Omar Zayed?'

'How well do you know him? How well do you know each other?'

'So Zayed was somehow . . . involved in this tragedy? This madness? And what exactly do you mean, Mr Grens? We worked together. It's an official picture from official negotiations. I didn't know him then. I don't know him today. But you think . . .'

'Another name we need to discuss.'

Grens pushed the next picture over the table, the one with eight people around a conference table, and pointed to a stocky man with a parting in his hair.

'That man there, sitting between you and Omar Zayed.'

'Yes?'

'Is he familiar?'

Dixon readjusted his glasses, which had slipped down a bit on his nose, then peered at a blurry image that was harder to interpret.

'Jürgen Krause. German.'

'It almost looks like you're shaking hands and hugging each other – are you?'

'This photographer would have some trouble finding a job these days . . . but yes, that's probably what we're doing – I've never been very comfortable with such things, but diplomatic negotiations sometimes call for it.'

'Krause has also been identified as one of the leaders of the smuggling organisation.'

'I don't quite follow you.'

'We are completely sure. Our German colleagues have already picked him up for questioning.'

Thor Dixon first studied the picture, then Grens, without revealing anything.

He wasn't worried, or angry, or outraged. He was calm. Just like an innocent man would be.

'That sounds quite unlikely. But if you say so. And I repeat – what exactly are you implying, Mr Grens? What does this have to do with me?'

'That's my question for you.'

'And the answer is the same – another official photograph from another official negotiation. A person I didn't know back then, nor do I know them now. I don't understand where you're headed with this, Superintendent.'

'I'm heading for this, an official meeting with official acquaintances later turns into unofficial meetings with unofficial acquaintances. Your official missions made the unofficial possible.'

Some photographs. A diplomat who pops up in a few too many places in the wrong kind of company. It wasn't much, yet. But if Grens had hoped to push him off balance, break him down, provoke some kind of confession, he'd have to wait. The diplomat sitting in front of him was cool, calm and collected. Waiting for the detective to continue.

'I have worked with good and evil my whole life. And I learned one thing, Dixon – there's no such thing. Neither one. Because this is how it works – most of the criminals I've caught have had crimes committed against them at some point in their lives. It's all about *when* you choose to look closely into a person's life. Where you decide to carve out your little peephole. If you choose a point in time where they're the victim, you define them as good. If you choose a point where they are committing their crimes, then they become evil.'

The sheets of paper on the table. Ewert Grens picked them up, was about to crumple them when he changed his mind, and instead held up, with a shaky hand, the picture that had all three men in it.

'Just like three people who meet at some point in their lives, officially or unofficially, with completely different agendas. Good or evil. Or good that becomes evil. It all depends on the moment when you judge their meetings.'

'Was there anything else I could help you with, Mr Grens? Any other name that might have brought you here?'

There was a pen on the table. The kind used to sign official agreements, a triangular tip that gushed out ink in clumps if you weren't careful. That was what happened now. Lots of clumps. As Grens pulled off the cap and drew a circle around one of the men in the picture.

'I'm not here for his sake . . . for Omar Zayed's sake – even though I probably should be. Someone else will have to take care of him. Or not. I'm also not . . .'

Now he circled the stocky, smiling man in the middle with a thick black ring.

'. . . here for Jürgen Krause. I believed I might be for a while. Thought when I gave his name to my German colleagues, they might end up taking down the leader of an international human smuggling organisation. But no, the one I want was here all the time. That is . . .'

It was time now.

Ewert Grens leaned over the table, and lowered his voice without being aware of it.

'. . . the end of the chain was right here at your desk, Dixon. I'm here for your sake. For your name. Because *you* are the leader they call CC, and for every refugee shipped across sea and land, who sometimes end up dead in containers, you get twenty-five per cent of the profit.'

Then he paused.

The detective superintendent had flung some very serious accusations around and the official just sat there, revealing *nothing*. Not fear, which he should feel if he was guilty, nor dismay, which he should have felt if he were falsely accused. Nothing. That was the whole of his reaction.

'The boy you asked about, Dixon. You referred to him just now that way – the boy. His name is Amadou. Do you remember? His name *was* Amadou. He's dead. Only six people knew he was the primary witness in my investigation. Amadou himself, Sven Sundkvist, Mariana Hermansson, a police sketch artist, Zofia Hoffmann and the Foreign Ministry official I'm currently talking to. Because I came here and told him in confidence. I have good reason to trust every other person on that list, except you. I believe you used information I gave you. For your own purposes. Had him killed, just like the guide we found in a tunnel beneath the streets of Stockholm, a man our forensic technicians can connect to both the container and the morgue. And the man who murdered them both lies here in Hoffmann's kitchen, where he too died – after speaking to someone he called Cirrata Caput.'

Grens pulled up two pictures on his phone. First the one he took of the man who tried to kill him, where the murderer had his own weapon plunged into his heart. Then the document that showed how nine people distributed the hundreds of millions they made from refugees.

'Cirrata Caput. CC. Do you see? At the top right corner.'

'Yes?'

'*You*, Dixon.'

'Excuse me?'

'You heard what I said.'

Just as unmoved. Just as calm. Even a careful smile.

'Mr Grens – you'll get no more coffee here.'

'Excuse me?'

'There will be no refills for you, Mr Grens.'

'I didn't come here to drink coff—'

'Because I'm sorry to tell you – I just don't understand what you're talking about, Superintendent. I'm a government official. My mission is to save people, make their lives better. I meet with those in positions of power on all of my trips, all of which are logged and registered. I don't know what you're up to – but you're trying to pin it on *me*, for some reason, scare *me*. But it won't work – I'm a diplomat, I negotiate with governments, I'm not afraid of meaningless words. And what you say now means nothing. So I'll have to ask you to go, Mr Grens. Go and seek your answers where you'll actually find them.'

The coffee cup remained empty.

Grens had done what he came to do. In the absence of evidence, he'd tried to push someone steady off balance.

Just like on his last visit, the two of them walked out side by side in silence, through the stone building, down the stone stairs, and out the entrance. And just like last time, Grens only spoke again when they were about to part.

'Sweden, Dixon, is a very interesting country. You have to go a few metres under the surface to smell the shit here. In some places they're not so good at covering it up, hiding it, so you smell the shit right on the surface. But no matter where you are, shit smells exactly the same. And I smell it on you, it's stinking up this whole place, and it makes me as ashamed as I am furious.'

'Have a pleasant evening, Mr Grens. I certainly plan to.'

Ewert Grens held the bronze handle of the door, but rage prevented him from pushing it down. And there was only one way left. Lay it all out. Take back the upper hand.

'I had a conversation last night with a contact of mine in North Africa, where this criminal organisation's activities originate. And when I listen to him, hear how it works, how cynical it all is, then I . . . well, it's not often I punch a man these days, but you're damn close to it, Dixon. What you're doing down there. Destroying their food, those food transports, making the famine worse, starving even more people so they'll flee. And all of it just to make some money.'

'What . . .'

The diplomat's throat flamed an angry red. And when he spoke, each word came out clipped off. Those grey eyes flashed for the first time.

'. . . are you talking about?'

'You sat with me in a hotel in Niger going on about goodness. Now you stand here lying about saving people's lives, making those lives better. All the while, you destroy their food!'

'What are you accusing me of? I . . . *of all people* . . . I *live* for this, Mr Grens! I'm ready to *die* for this! I told you already that without this work my life itself would be meaningless. You insult me! It's damned impertinent! Go now. Get the hell out of here!'

He lost his composure in the end. Not because of the charges themselves, but because of the detective's criticism of how they did their work, their methods.

For a diplomat who should always remain aloof, it was an extremely emotional outburst.

For someone who was guilty it came too late, at the wrong moment.

It puzzled Grens. Something didn't fit. Why did Thor Dixon unexpectedly lose his dignity and control, which he'd worked so hard to maintain – and why then?

It was cool outside, despite being June. Almost cold. Ewert Grens walked to the car parked outside the Opera House, but didn't drive to the police station or to his apartment – instead he headed for an address in Vasastan. One he'd never visited before. The front door to Thor Dixon's home. He planned to wait outside, sometimes staring up towards a dark window on the third floor. He was sure his visit to the Ministry of Foreign Affairs had begun a chain of events. And if it had, he needed to be prepared. This might be the head of the Octopus.

THOR DIXON DIDN'T NOTICE the car parked on the other side of the street as he stepped out of the taxi and headed for his front door. But it didn't really matter, the detective watching him had no idea what he was feeling or thinking. Only Dixon knew who he really was, and that's all that counted to him.

Good. Evil.

This was about doing the right thing.

He entered his comfortable early twentieth-century penthouse apartment, very roomy for a civil servant who lived alone, and headed for his office with the large desk overlooking the Vanadislunden Park. It was there that he was now sorting through two equal stacks of paper, documents usually kept in a wall safe hidden behind the bookshelf. Clear away a row of August Strindberg's novels, and there was the keypad that unlocked another life.

The first stack of papers, on the left side, contained Excel sheets similar to the ones Grens had shown on his phone.

day	unit	stage 2 + 3 + 4	zuw1 12,5 %	zuw2 12,5 %	lam. 5%	sal. 8%	A C C 15%	bank 5%	gda 8%	trans balt 7%	C C 25%

One hundred and seven documents corresponding to one hundred and seven fishing boats filled with refugees, who were transferred into trucks, or onto containers, whatever would carry them to their final destinations in Germany and Sweden. In the beginning there were just a couple of voyages a month across the Mediterranean, now there were a couple each week. The money transport was carrying over twenty million dollars these days. And a quarter of that was his.

In the second pile, which was the same height as the first one, lay one hundred and seven more documents.

But these copies were something else completely.

The heart, the heartbeat, of this his work.

What he lived for. What he would die for.

One hundred and seven deposits corresponding to each dollar assigned to *CC* after one hundred and seven smuggling trips. Each arm managed its own bookkeeping, its own profits, over the years. Thor Dixon knew very well that Omar's and Delilah's and Jürgen's motives were quite different from his own. Just like Angela's five per cent in Lampedusa, Ettore's eight per cent in Salerno, Jazmine's five per cent at Lombard Bank Malta, and the percentages that went to the companies responsible for the port at Gdansk and the transports across the Baltic Sea. For all of them, the money was everything. But for him, it was just these copies on his desk. Cirrata Caput. The head of the Octopus. A rather ridiculous name that Delilah laughingly suggested at one of their first meetings, but it stuck. He was most assuredly the head, the founder of the network who had linked all the entrepreneurs together, through his diplomatic contacts, at parallel meetings while on his regular work trips. Twenty-five per cent was what he kept for himself. And every penny of it – after he paid off the people at Värta Harbour and the person he brought in for special assignments now and then – was transformed into the documents in the second pile.

Because if a person has decided to flee, they'll do it no matter what organisation offers them transport.

When they choose us, I not only help the person fleeing get to a place where they can live a better life – afterwards, I return their money to a system that will help even more people.

The donations lying here in front of me.

That was something he couldn't explain to the detective superintendent pressing him for answers this evening. Who first guessed at the truth, then accused him of the grotesque crimes of other organisations, as if it were his fault the food transports were destroyed – the disgusting acts of smugglers, who were the exact opposite of everything Cirrata stood for. That he stood for. If he were to live like that – well, he might as well not live at all.

That's why he opened the cupboard now and grabbed a bag packed with a visa, a passport and a new identity, which had been sitting there since the first smuggling trip. And that's why he headed out of his apartment towards the lift.

Because no matter how carefully he explained all this to the detective, and the judicial system he represented, they weren't going to understand. Wouldn't try to. How could they? How could they know how much strength and love it cost to manage a journey from oppression to freedom? *I've* been working with these problems for twenty-five years. *I've* seen states collapse, systems fail and dissolve, refugees driven out, people dying while doing whatever they can to survive. What's one truck abandoned on the side of the road after dozens of people suffocate – when there are thousands headed up and thousands more to be helped? What's one suffocating container – when there are so many more arriving at port, giving those who flee and those who stay a better chance at a good life? And as for the collateral damage – one lost individual dying in a tunnel, one solitary boy falling asleep for ever in his bed? They're drops in an ocean of tens of thousands who are saved thanks to my work. Because what right do we have to bomb a place, leave only chaos in our wake? There will be no end to the refugee crisis. On the contrary, it will only get worse. And I – *I'm doing something*.

He turned off the light in the hall and locked the front door to his home.

For the last time.

EWERT GRENS SAW THE taxi stop outside, saw the official pay, then disappear through his front door. Then a third-floor light turned on, in the area Grens guessed was an entrance hall and then in a room that could be either a bedroom or an office. The kind of classic building, where all the apartments had vaulted ceilings. It reminded Grens of his own place on Sveavägen, not that far from here. He looked around before venturing to adjust the driver's seat and lean back more, convinced he had a long wait ahead of him.

Just then the lights were switched off again. In both rooms.

And his phone rang.

'Do you have a minute, Ewert?'

Mariana. She wasn't whispering, but her voice was unusually quiet and tense, and he wondered if she was aware of it.

'I'm sitting outside his home. And something just happened that I should . . . is it important?'

'Yes. This is important.'

'OK?'

'Thor Dixon's phone records. We got a warrant for all his numbers, even his private phone. The time at which one of these calls takes place is particularly interesting. Especially since the call came from an unlisted and unknown number. Incoming at ten thirty-seven this morning.'

'Ten thirty-seven?'

'Yes. Which matches up perfectly with Hugo's recollection. The time when he would have been listening to the killer on the phone in Hoffmann's kitchen. In addition, Ewert – he got another call from an unknown subscriber sometime late the night before. Around three twenty-two. According to the medical examiner, that's Amadou's approximate time of death.'

'I'll be damned. We didn't have much evidence. But we're starting to.'

'And there's more. Even better.'

Now the lights turned on in the stairs. Grens stared at the front door, which according to Sven and the condo board president was the only exit from the house.

'Are you listening, Ewert?'

'I'm listening.'

'We heard back from Niger. The head of security at the hotel in Niamey. He located that driver you were looking for. I've just talked to him about his morning pickup. The driver is absolutely sure that they weren't headed to visit someone at the capital building named Mr Cirrata. He's sure that was the name of the passenger he picked up and drove there – and which he has identified as the man in the picture you sent down. Thor Dixon.'

The front door. It was being opened.

By Thor Dixon.

With a suitcase in one hand. Heading for one of the cars parked along the pavement.

The meeting must have shaken him more than he let on. He was clearly in a hurry.

'I need you here, both you and Sven, *immediately*.'

'What's going on, Ewert?'

'He's leaving. Dixon. Headed somewhere. As soon as we hang up I'll call for back-up.'

The Foreign Ministry official put his bag into the boot. Which was exactly where Ewert Grens would start searching as soon as they caught this bastard.

THOR DIXON DROPPED HIS bag into his boot and closed the lid. The streetlamps on Vanadisvägen were surround by a halo of light – the misty air, almost fog. A June evening? Was it like this when he got home not long ago? He opened the driver's seat door and was about to sit down when one of his phones rang – only eight people had this number – inside his jacket pocket.

Omar.

Now?

'I've explained this to you before – you are never to call me at this number when I'm in Sweden.'

'It doesn't matter any more – it's over.'

Thor Dixon was standing with the car key in his hand, in the middle of the street, and almost in his car.

'Over? What are you talking about?'

'The boats, warehouse, headquarters, our dead employees.'

Omar's voice, it wasn't exactly panic, more pain, as if every word were being torn from his mouth with the greatest effort.

'All our shit burned.'

'I don't understand.'

'Right now I'm lying not far from the harbour, on a box that used to transport fish. Because everything, *everything*, was blown into the air. The whole operation – knocked out! We let in the wrong person. We made one mistake, but it was enough.'

Thor Dixon still didn't understand. But it sounded like Omar was about to end this conversation, like he didn't have strength for more. And between what was happening down there, and what just happened here – Ewert Gren's unannounced visit to the Ministry of Foreign Affairs and his many questions, statements, and finally that incredible rudeness – Dixon felt the night pressing in on him. And there was one thing he'd couldn't let go of, no matter how hard his diplomatic training tried to push it away.

'Omar? Before you hang up.'

Ewert Grens was being honest, sincere when he said it.

'Yes?'

'I want you to answer one question for me. One thing I can't get out of my head. A question someone asked me this evening.'

'Yes?'

'The food transports – the ones guarded by the private security companies?'

'Yes?'

'Who attacked them?'

'Who . . . what?'

'These attacks were perhaps the most urgent of all my missions on my recent official visit to Niger. I assumed it was the usual suspects. Pirates. Local, small-time gangsters. Or simply those hungry enough to do whatever it takes. Answer me, Omar. Who, who's been attacking those transports lately?'

'Why does it matter?'

'Who attacked those food transports before they were guarded? Who's tried to stop them now that they are? Who's despicable enough to take food from the people who need it most? From people who will die without it?'

'What does it matter – it's all over now.'

'That's why. Who, Omar? Surely it wasn't . . . *us*?'

Silence. A long one. As if his strength gave out, and he hung up.

'Hello, are you . . .'

'Everything.'

'Everything . . .?'

'Don't you remember? You said you wanted us to do *everything* we could to make more people choose to flee.'

'I meant we should offer them such attractive solutions that they'd see the opportunity for themselves. For a better life.'

'We did. Me and Delilah. *Everything*. Every arm is self-sufficient, right? That's how you wanted it. And that was our way of increasing profitability – motivational measures, and more people crammed onto every boat until they couldn't fit. We didn't create this never-ending crisis, we just made it a little more obvious that it was time to flee it.'

Then Omar really did hang up.

Who's despicable enough to take food from the people who need it most?

Or maybe the conversation ended because Thor Dixon threw his phone onto the asphalt.

We did . . . we just made it a little more obvious that it was time to flee . . .

Then Dixon slammed the car door – from the outside – and it might have been that he wept as he walked back to the house he lived in.

EWERT GRENS WIPED OFF his windscreen with the sleeve of his jacket, which was fogging up where his breath collided with summer. Otherwise, he had a good view from his car of the other side of the street – Thor Dixon was close enough for him to reach in a couple of seconds. The Foreign Ministry official had stood with the door to the driver's seat open, talking on his phone, and he seemed upset, tense, his arms sometimes gesturing wildly. *As if he were desperate.* Then he'd thrown the phone onto the ground with all his might – at least it looked that way from here – closed the car door and hurried back to the building he'd just left.

And when I compare what I'm seeing now with the unpleasantly unshakable official of our last meeting, it's like I'm watching a façade crumble.

The light in the staircase turned on, Grens even glimpsed the lift heading upwards.

Did he forget something? Did he suspect something? Has he discovered his pursuer?

Or did I do the right thing – did my little push work after all?

In that case, it's only a matter of time before he flees.

A detective superintendent who should go inside.

With the newspaper clippings showing contacts with a couple of the organisation leaders, and the phone records, and the hotel driver's witness statement, he had enough for at least an arrest. But he waited, shouldn't and wasn't going to do it alone. It was unnecessary and unprofessional when Sven and Mariana, according to the latest text message, were very close.

He tried to see into the stairwell, then into the apartment. It was as impossible as before. No curtains fluttered, no lights turned on.

Now. Over there.

The black Volvo with dual rear-view mirrors. Mariana at the wheel, Sven next to her. They rolled down the inner city street, parked a couple of spots away, and turned off the headlights.

Exactly five minutes.

That was how long they usually waited.

BREATHE.

Can't. *Can't.*

No matter how he struggles there's not enough air, no matter how he swallows and gasps it reaches neither throat nor chest, as if someone were holding him down, trying to suffocate him.

Thor Dixon hit the emergency button on the elevator and after a couple of failed attempts was finally able to force the door open, squeeze out onto the second floor.

It didn't help.

His breath takes nothing in.

There was a window ten steps down, in the small landing between the first and second floor, that's where he ran now. Opened it, let in the wind, the cool, the oxygen.

Closed his eyes.

Two conversations had changed everything. First, the detective asked a question that shook him to his core.

I live for this, Grens! I'm ready to die for this!

Then Omar sent him off a precipice.

Who, Omar? Surely it wasn't . . . us?'

Questions with the most terrible answers.

He couldn't bear it.

Cirrata, the organisation he'd created, responsible for the most terrible of terrible acts, destroying the only food there was. The opposite to the very essence, idea, existence of an aid organisation. To who he was.

I can't breathe.

The ultimate betrayal.

Delilah and Omar didn't understand what the system was built to do.

The one that always takes care of other people. That takes the living to a place where they can live a good life, gives the dead a worthy death.

I can't breathe.

Seventy-three bodies in a container. What if that's not all?

What if there's a number beyond what I can grasp?

I can't breathe.

How many starved after my colleagues attacked their food for profit?

How many people sank into the depths of the Mediterranean because we overloaded our boats just like all the other smugglers?

I can't. I can't. I can't.

Thor Dixon stood with his elbows on the window sill and leaned out.

It was clear to him now.

He had made the wrong decision based on the wrong premise.

If he had seen what he should have, what Grens realised in just a short time, he would have acted.

This is my fault.

He leaned out even further, in search of air, struggling to breathe.

All my fault.

Breathe in.

My fault.

Breathe.

THEY LEFT THEIR CARS at the same time, hurried towards the entrance. Sven had put in the four-digit code, given to them by the housing association chairman, and the beautiful and ornate front door, which consisted mostly of a glass mosaic, glided open.

They felt the draught as soon as they stepped into the entrance hall. Like a window had been left open.

There *was* an open window on the first landing. And the wind was banging it against its frame with every gust.

A way out. Which led to the courtyard behind the building and then to another building's courtyard and another.

Damn it.

They split up. Sven crawled out through the open window and into the darkness. Grens and Mariana continued up the stairs.

Two long, angry rings of the doorbell. Then another one.

But only silence from inside.

The detective superintendent was just turning around to head back to the car and to get his break-in kit, when Mariana tried the door handle.

Unlocked.

She signalled to him to come back, and they entered a long hall with their guns raised and ready, as they caught a glimpse of Sven through a window, as he disappeared between the courtyard's gates.

Abandoned.

That's what it felt like inside.

The hall led to the room Grens had tried to picture while peering in from the street. A place to work. A large oak desk, a bookshelf filled with Swedish classics that didn't look particularly thumbed through, a brown leather armchair, and on the walls black and white photographs of the White Buses, similar to the ones Dixon had at the Ministry of Foreign Affairs, where he'd admired and praised them as a relief organisation that truly made a difference. Mariana continued into the kitchen, and Grens stayed in the office searching for hidden spaces – if there were any, it would be in there.

As he passed by the desk for a second time he noticed two neat stacks of paper sitting side by side. Two stacks of very similar heights, Grens guessed about a hundred A4-sized sheets in each pile.

He did a double take.

On top of one of the piles lay a document similar to the images saved on his phone, the ones Hoffmann sent from the Zuwara head-quarters. He picked it up, examined it. It wasn't just similar – it was almost identical! Different numbers, but the same columns. He picked up one document after another.

All came from the same source.

Income reports from transport after transport of smuggled refugees.

All the evidence he needed.

The bastard would rot in his cell, and the detective superintendent would be the one to throw away the key.

Grens was about to flip through the second pile when he heard Mariana cry out.

'Ewert!'

He rushed towards her voice – still not really sure what awaited him, but he would understand, afterwards. Through the large kitchen and the even bigger living room, then into one of two bedrooms. Mariana had turned on a floor lamp and sunk down onto the double bed, wrinkling the shiny fabric of its bedspread.

'In there.'

She nodded towards a cupboard. The kind big enough to walk into. So Grens did. Walked in. And stopped short.

Thor Dixon hung from a hook in the ceiling.

A rope wrapped tight around his neck.

He had chosen – for some reason – to suffocate himself. Dying the same way as seventy-three refugees in a container.

WITH THE FORENSIC TECHNICIANS and the undertakers squeezed into Thor Dixon's large walk-in wardrobe, Ewert Grens wandered off alone through the other rooms of the apartment. The Foreign Ministry official left no note or explanation before taking his own life. Something must have suddenly become too heavy for him to bear. Something, or so Grens was guessing, connected to the smuggling business – the one documented by that pile on the desk. Or rather by one of the piles. There was another still unexamined stack next to it.

Grens went through the hall, passed the kitchen and the second bedroom, and stopped in the office.

Bookshelf of Swedish classics. The brown leather armchair. The heavy desk.

And – two piles of documents.

That was his target.

He'd already looked at the first pile, one hundred and seven sheets of profit-sharing reports that corresponded to each completed smuggling trip. Conclusive evidence for their investigation. In court it would be enough to link Thor Dixon to the criminal network.

However, that second pile.

He flipped through it for the first time.

Also, one hundred and seven pages. Each one numbered the same way.

Some form of receipt, he was soon convinced.

Anonymous deposits. Made to a variety of bank accounts.

Grens pulled out Dixon's chair and sat down. Uncertain what exactly he was reading.

If the other pile had been a record of payments, this pile seemed to be deposits – a new one for every payment received.

A sum equalling what code name *CC* received after each transport was soon paid out.

Enormous sums. Hundreds of millions.

Anonymous donations to a whole range of established aid organisations' accounts. The Red Cross, Save the Children, the White Helmets, Amnesty International, and more – almost every group seriously committed to helping people in need had received improbably generous donations.

Ewert Grens stood up.

Dammit – the bastard thought he was doing good work.

And immediately sat down again.

There was more.

Two documents. They differed considerably from the others in both layout and content, sticking out at the very bottom of the pile – highlighted with an angry green, sure to be found if someone like Grens was flipping through.

He pulled them out of the pile.

The first – dated several years earlier – was a copy of a power of attorney Thor Dixon acquired while establishing bank accounts in Qatar, where a banker at Lombard Bank Malta transferred the smuggling business profits.

The other – a transaction dated just a few minutes before Grens and Hermansson entered the apartment – was a copy of how Dixon, using that authority, just completed his very last coup. A coup that was as inventive as the rest of his illegal activity. The official simply used his power of attorney to first pledge all the assets of the organisation, and then, using those assets as collateral, had borrowed the corresponding amount, and deposited the money in various aid organisations' accounts.

Grens leaned back in the beautifully worn desk chair.

This was Dixon's suicide note.

The official had created his human smuggling business to help even more people flee. While the money, which would otherwise have gone to criminals, was paid back to on-site relief efforts.

Two birds with one stone.

Plus, *plus*, he'd planned from the very beginning that his employees' profits would be used this way as well. On the day this was over, the organisation revealed or broken apart, he'd embezzle the profits of his partners, whose names were Delilah and Omar and Jürgen according to Hoffmann, and they would have worked all those years for free. Everything had been ready. An emergency exit, a farewell, one last huge gift that just had to be activated.

Detective Superintendent Ewert Grens wasn't sure if he would ever find the strength to stand up again. Another day, and in another context, he might have been able to laugh at such skilful manipulation of society, because sometimes society deserved it.

But this bastard had gone around thinking he was a hero.

While they lay there. Trapped. Motionless. Stacked on top of each other.

While the Guide lay there.

While Amadou lay there.

They died for . . . this?

WITH HERMANSSON'S AND THE medical examiner's conversation still faintly audible in another part of the apartment, the superintendent left the desk and went over to the window overlooking the same street where he'd sat watch in his car. Opened the window wide, just like in the stairs. Let in a summer evening that would never really be completely dark at this time of year.

So that's why.

That's why I couldn't make sense of it, because he wasn't motivated by the same things as other criminals.

Why would someone let people suffocate in a container, then go to the trouble of making sure their bodies were taken care of in the right way? Why camouflage the smell in foam, then cut the bodies out and drag them through the tunnels beneath the streets and dump them in various morgues?

It was you.

And you were trying – when it all went to hell – to do the same thing as me.

Give them their death back.

HE WAS PLANNING TO surprise them. And he could feel it in his stomach. That longing. Walking that short distance from the rusty gate to the house where his real world existed.

He wasn't supposed to even make it home this time. But what was planned to take two weeks ended so much faster. Piet Hoffmann had just put his suitcase on the top step of the front stairs, started searching his pockets for his keys, when he heard a sound. From inside the house. A voice. A child's voice. He checked his watch. They shouldn't be awake yet. Not on a normal Saturday?

He looked around. The neighbours' car was parked in the driveway. As usual, on a weekend morning.

He heard it again. A child's voice. Rasmus. He was sure of it. And there, that was Hugo. Why were they up so early? He felt three things simultaneously. Worry – had something happened? Joy – he would get to kiss them, hug them that much sooner! And just the slightest amount of disappointment – he'd been planning to take his bag downstairs, take care of its contents, then wrap the presents he'd bought and make breakfast for everyone, all before his family stepped into the kitchen.

He gently pushed down the door handle and slipped into the hall. Surprise.

Felt even more intensely in his stomach.

They were all sitting in the living room as he rushed inside and hollered out loudly, but happily – guess who's here!

Of all the reactions, he got the last one he expected. They were terrified. Not just by his sudden entrance – Hugo screamed, and Rasmus hid, and Zofia stared blankly ahead, even after they must have realised who it was, that Dad was home.

His surprise stopped them short.

'What . . . is it?'

They were up too early for a day off. They reacted with panic and almost dread when he burst in on them like he always did.

'Zofia? Rasmus? Hugo? Did something happen? Why are you up so early?'

Zofia shook her head and tried to smile. Rasmus peeked out from behind the sofa. And Hugo tried to steady his voice.

'No, Dad, nothing happened. It was . . . a short school day yesterday. Sometimes you get more awake from that.'

After hugging them and saying everything had been much simpler and faster than expected with the extra food transport, he went to the kitchen to brew himself that cup of coffee he'd skipped at Arlanda in his urgency to get home. He stopped halfway, near the kitchen table. He was used to reading rooms, interpreting, preparing. But his own kitchen felt unreadable. A stain on the floor that hadn't been there before. And in the wall, near the kitchen fan, a new hole, not wide, but deep and with dimensions he recognised. Hugo followed him in, just half a step behind, and they looked at each other.

'Nothing happened?'

'Nothing happened, Dad.'

Ewert Grens lied for Hugo when Hoffmann called and the detective offered to hand over his phone. Now Hugo himself was lying. And not very well. At least not to a father who knew every detail of his face.

'Nothing? That stain wasn't here the last time I was home.'

Blood. It wasn't visible, but that was his guess. It looked like someone had recently tried to clean away a fresh pool of blood.

'Pancakes.'

'Pancakes?'

'Ewert was here the night Mum went over to pick up Amadou. And we made chequered pancakes. And Rasmus dropped a whole jar of strawberry jam, the glass broke.'

'And the hole?'

A bullet hole.

He could see it, the violence in the walls, how a place always carried traces of the violence that had taken place there.

And he sat down.

Hugo lying, that was one thing, children sometimes do so when they want to conceal a truth that was worse than a lie, just like adults. But maybe he was imagining it? Still affected by the explosions and bodies and chaos he left behind? A stain and a hole. It could have been the result of any number of wild childish games. And he was turning it into blood and bullet holes?

'I don't know.'

'You don't know how the hole in the wall got there?'

'Wasn't it always there?'

After a while, after his coffee, after he and Zofia held each other like they always did, after giving Hugo and Rasmus their presents – some plastic action figures he bought onboard the plane, which were apparently collected by children all over the world – he took the stairs to the basement, to his workroom and its cupboard and then to the room that stood behind it, which only he knew about.

That's where he carried the suitcase, one of two bags he brought with him out of the headquarters, the other one remained with that last group of desperate refugees.

To a secret room inside a cupboard.

Which he opened with a small lever high up on the right side of the wall.

A safe and a steel cabinet and a rail hung with bulletproof vests. That's about all that would fit inside. But if he moved around some of what he had stored in the cabinet and safe, packed it better, the contents of the suitcase would just fit.

Everything felt good again.

All that longing and joy that became worry when his wife and children responded so unusually to his arrival, and the confusion when his son lied to him about the odd traces of something in the kitchen. Now replaced by calm. In a body with a mind that was always, always prepared.

Until he opened the metal cabinet.

And saw the pistol on the top shelf.

It lay with the barrel facing outwards, not inwards like he always kept it.

Someone had been here.

A RADIANT MORNING.

Ewert Grens sat on a stone that supported his ageing body perfectly and stared out over the entrance to Stockholm's harbour. The water was absolutely still. Untouched.

It had been a week since his last visit to the nursing home, which he kept coming to because it was how he kept himself sane in a world that was anything but. Just him and Anni and a large, flat rock that time had carved and placed here just for him. Far from the paperwork he'd shuffled onto Sven and Mariana, and which was always the real ending of any investigation.

The only place that was his alone.

And where someone, dammit, was always interrupting him. Last time because the morgue personnel found one body too many.

'I want to talk to you.'

'Can it wait? I'm a little busy.'

'No.'

This time was probably his own fault – after all, he was the one who insisted on dragging Piet Hoffmann into all this.

'Very well, talk.'

'I just got home and . . . what happened while I was gone?'

'What do you mean?'

'Well, in my kitchen I'm pretty sure there's a new bloodstain. And on the wall, I'm pretty sure there's a bullet hole. And in my . . . I have a private room that nobody knows about, nobody *knew* about – somebody has been messing with my stuff. Grens – you promised to make sure nothing would happen to my family.'

'And I have. Nothing happened to them.'

'So how do you explain bloodstains, bullet holes, an intruder in my private room?'

'I don't know, Hoffmann. How do *you* explain it – maybe it means if you don't change, you might lose your whole family?'

Grens looked out over the water, following an archipelago ferry as it made a deep cut into the surface of the water. He'd done it again. Inserting himself into other people's business. But he couldn't help it, no matter how much he told himself he didn't want to live like that. Two little boys had ignored the distance he'd built around himself and wormed their way inside.

'Once a week, Hoffmann, I drive over Lidingö Bridge to the nursing home where my wife once lived. I sit outside it. Until I'm done. Because I have a connection to this place – to her. Do you have a connection to the house you're in right now? I'm trying to hold onto the only thing I've ever had. While you run from all you have right now. And I don't know which one of us is the bigger idiot.'

A cruise ship on its way to Finland floated by beneath him, looking like a giant monster that might swallow the archipelago ferry, and which definitely destroyed whatever peace was left on the water.

'I've seen your oldest son, Hoffmann. How he's changed in just a few days. Children are strange like that, they change so fast you need to be there to see them bloom. I've been watching what you should have watched. You missed when your son did something amazing yesterday. And you won't see it next time either. Don't you understand – *your* son would rather call me than you when he's scared.'

Grens wasn't sure if Hoffmann was still on the other end of the line. No ambient noise, no breathing.

'I have a rock, worn down by time. You have a family, Hoffmann. And it's soon getting bigger. Take care of them.'

But it didn't matter. He didn't have much more to say. So he said the last bit mostly to test out how it sounded, hear if it were true.

'I'm standing up now – I'm going to go and meet a woman named Laura, who I called yesterday evening, who has eyes that shine with intelligence and a mouth capable of the most gentle smile. She made me relax in a room of the dead, though I hear she has a very bad temper. And apparently she'd like to meet me too. Have you ever heard anything more ludicrous?'

YOU HAVE A FAMILY, Hoffmann. And it's soon getting bigger. Take care of them.

What the hell did he mean by that?

Piet Hoffmann stood in the kitchen of the only home he had and turned the tap on, let the water run into the sink until it was cold. He filled a glass, emptied it, filled it again.

The hole in the wall. The stain on the floor.

You were supposed to be safe. While I was fighting for my life for three hours, you were in another world, this world, which was safety itself.

So what is it I don't understand?

Hugo's lies. Rasmus's fear. Grens's fucking bullshit.

What am I not seeing?

Or is he right – am I losing my family? Am I like some cyst they'll surgically remove? Are they keeping me at a distance, as I always did with them?

He walked through a house he didn't recognise. Wandered between the kitchen and the living room, the living room and the hall, the hall and the kitchen.

And Hugo?

Why did Grens bring him up? Say he'd grown. Done something amazing.

What did that mean?

Piet Hoffmann kept wandering, troubled, restless. He couldn't stay still. All the longing and joy and peace he'd been looking forward to, which kept him going through that dark night on the Mediterranean, he couldn't access it any more. So he went back to the basement, down to his workroom, to a wall in a cupboard that slid open to reveal a safe filled with half of last month's smuggling profits, which a security company never picked up from Zuwara's port.

More than ten million dollars.

Money that would last them for as long as he could imagine.

How about that, Detective Superintendent, for taking care of a family?

TWENTY-EIGHT DAYS EARLIER

'ALYSON!'

I shout as loudly as I can, but I'm not sure she hears me.

'Alyson!'

The wind whips sand around us, as the pickup speeds across uneven ground, constantly slamming us against the truck bed – and it's as if the landscape we're travelling through cuts off every word I say and throws it to the ground long before it reaches you.

'You have to hold on!'

We're sitting near the edge of the truck bed with our legs sticking out, bracing our feet against the cab, and since we're eighteen people squeezed into an area that should only accommodate a few, it's hard to keep our balance as the vehicle careers this way and that. Four days. That's how long until we arrive. Until the first stage is complete.

'Like this, Alyson – look at me!'

She still can't hear me, but when I finally get her attention and we look at each other, it no longer matters. She smiles. I'm sure of it, even though she has a white cloth wrapped around her head and forehead and the rest of her face to protect her from the burning sun, covered except for a gap at the eyes. She's so happy. Just like me. All these days and months and years of longing, and now we are finally on our way. I stare back at Agadez, where we bought our seat on this truck bed. The city grows ever tinier as we head deeper into the desert.

I love her so much. And remember exactly when that feeling began. When we stood next to each other under the drying acacia trees and together picked the last leaves. The only thing left to eat. We decided then. We wanted another kind of life. We decided to go to Niamey. The capital, which we laughingly called a village sometimes, since its streets were unpaved and goats and cows wandered around eating trash, just like Filingué.

367

'Idriss!'

So strange.

I hear *her* voice.

When she shouts towards me, the words don't fall apart, don't drown in wind and sand.

'We're on our way, Idriss!'

I nod and laugh, even though I know she can't see it, waving is too dangerous, I might fall off.

Eighteen in the bed of a pickup truck with room for six people max. It works. As long as everyone decides it *will* work. Most of them, like Alyson and me, have travelled from Niger, two small groups came from Senegal and Gambia, and a few are from Burkina Faso and Togo. While we were waiting to board, I offered to be in charge of the water, and now the heavy red plastic can is squeezed between my knees. Sometimes we send it around a lap – only two gulps each, that's important, or it won't last until the next stop where we can fill it again.

For two years we worked night and day in Niamey, left our shack on the south side at dawn, crossed the Niger River along Kennedy Bridge and sold vegetables for Lawayli and his brother at the Marché Albarka on the north side, then after lunch we picked up trash on Boulevard Mali Bero, and in the evening we washed dishes in the kitchen of the Marquis Africa Queen restaurant. Two years and it still wasn't enough. The money still wasn't enough. So we went back to Filingué to persuade Alyson's aunt and my father to sell their animals. And they did. For our sake. They sold their only possessions of any value and helped us raise the rest of the money we needed. I think about them often as we drive through the night on the back of the pickup. Whenever we stop so the driver can rest, I hold Alyson's hand and talk about Libya and the Mediterranean and Europe and the rest of our lives.

'Idriss?'

The car's slowed down, the desert road has become even more uneven and heaps of sand drift over it.

For a while it's easy to talk.

'Yes?'

'You have . . . everything is where it's supposed to be?'

I understand exactly what she means. Even though no one else does. But that's the point.

Everything means all the money we collected to pay for each stage of this journey, minus the six hundred dollars we already spent for this ride through the desert. And *where it's supposed to be* means that the money still remains in the fabric of my trousers, shirt and thin jacket where she carefully sewed it in just a few bills at a time to keep them from becoming bulky and easy to discover.

'Yes, Alyson. Everything is where it's supposed to be. And soon you and I will be where *we're* supposed to be. In another part of the world.'

She looks at me and laughs, until I'm laughing too, until we're both laughing as we so often do, so hard that it's difficult to stop. The others on the back of this pickup shake their heads, but soon they can't help it, start laughing too. A strange sight – identical sand dunes, one after the other, and a pickup truck packed with people whose faces are hidden behind white cloth, all of them choking with laughter.

About an hour and a half later, I'm not sure, but as I try to read the sky based on the sun's location, the driver slows down for a second time. We pass by the bodies that a couple of the guests at the café in Agadez had talked about in hushed tones. I count up to thirty-seven, they're lying all over. Many children, that's easy to see, they're so small. Rotting and desiccated, most of them ripped apart by jackals. This was as far as they got, just past the Algerian border, when the engine on the truck they were travelling in broke down.

I grab Alyson's hand and squeeze it hard.

We were just laughing. We just felt joy bubbling inside us, as you do when you're finally on your way.

I look at her and she looks at me, while the driver speeds up again. Just three more days. Then we arrive in Libya and the port of Zuwara, by the sea.

I turn around one last time to see those scattered bodies before they disappear behind a sand dune.

Now we know.

That too can happen when you're on your way to another life.

And I'm so extremely grateful that our trip is different.

NINETEEN DAYS EARLIER

AN ABANDONED WAREHOUSE IN Zuwara's harbour, just a couple of minutes' walk from the dock and the water. We've been sitting here waiting for five days and five nights. In the beginning we numbered in the dozens, soon around a hundred, and now – I can't say for sure because it's hard to count people trapped in a huge space barely able to move – we number close to four hundred.

Which means we won't have to wait much longer.

The fishing boat will have to accommodate all of us, because we are all from countries south of the Sahara and the smugglers charge based on where you come from. Myself and Alyson and the others around us pay fifteen hundred US dollars each for stage two – crossing the Mediterranean. While those who started their journey north of the desert, like the Tunisians and Moroccans, often pay more, and the Syrians and Sudanese even more. The more you're able to pay, the fewer you have to share the boat with.

'Alyson?'

I hold her close, press her tight against me.

'Yes?'

'I think it'll be time soon. Seems like there's enough people now.'

She yawns, huddles into my arms.

'When?'

'Tonight. Not totally sure, but I thought I heard something. You should keep your shoes on, and jacket, it'll happen fast.'

It's dark in here, no artificial light at all, just the moonlight falling through the cracks between the ceiling and the wall, enough for us to see each other's faces, and hers is calm and expectant. We have been so careful. When, after four days of driving through the desert, the rusty pickup dropped us off a few miles outside Zuwara, we didn't do what everyone else did. Instead of heading straight to the harbour and a boat that was soon fully loaded and departing, we decided to wait for the next one – made our way to restaurants in the centre of the city, where we'd been told we could expect to find the people who worked in security. We were planning to meet one of them. A person we could trust, who would help us as we handed over all the money we had – payment for stages two and three and four. A person who could demand that every leg of our journey was assured.

'Idriss?'

'Yes?'

'Do you hear what I hear?'

'Yes, Alyson. Footsteps approaching the door. It might be time now.'

We already knew the name of our final destination – a country called Sweden. We went from restaurant to restaurant in downtown Zuwara and finally found the man who worked in security. Blond, maybe forty years old, but with eyes that seemed much older. He accompanied us to meet the representative of the smuggling organisation. He even gave us a satellite phone, in case of emergencies, which we used to call Alyson's cousin, a young boy named Amadou.

'Listen. Do you hear? It *must* be them.'

'I hear.'

'It's our turn, Idriss.'

She laughs, and I kiss her brow, cheeks, mouth. We stand up and the warehouse empties out quickly. Hundreds of people form a living train as they make their way through darkness, and no one says a word, no one even breathes loudly or scrapes their feet on the dock. This is how we've been instructed to behave, and so all of us, already willing to give up our life's savings to be here, do as they say.

'Idriss, you have to stay really close to me.'

She pulls me towards her, we have to stand for the whole trip in order for everyone to fit, and with every rock and lurch of the boat we're pressed even closer. After weeks or months of travelling, people who haven't had much access to water or soap take on a particular kind of scent. Alyson insisted after our meeting with the man in security that we take a detour to the beach, rinse off even though she knows the sea here isn't particularly clean. I protested, thought it was more important to get a good spot in the warehouse, but gave in when she explained it was for my sake, that she couldn't stand not wanting to let me in close. She bathed under the cover of darkness, dipped herself with her clothes on, laughing and splashing me, trying to pretend she didn't see the bloated bodies that had washed ashore nearby – two boats with a total of six hundred passengers had sunk recently, and no one cared any more about carting them away.

I try not to show her how worried I am.

But at least this boat looks like a real boat, which is good – less risk of someone stopping us far out to sea. We seem to be headed to one of the oil rigs just off the coast of a island called Lampedusa, and even though it feels wrong, I know that the boat was never supposed to take us all the way there. We'll be let down into life rafts and picked up by the people who work on the oil rigs – they usually call the Italian coastguard, who in their turn make sure the people are taken to land.

'Do you see what I see, Idriss?'

She's happy, I know it, and she kisses me often, her soft lips against mine.

'Yes.'

'The coast of Africa just disappeared.'

She kisses me until I grab her shoulders, gently turn her around.

'And there, Alyson, in the other direction – the open sea.'

'Another world.'

'*Our* world.'

SIXTEEN DAYS EARLIER

I'M SURE WE MUST have left the small roads and driven onto a highway. A constant speed, less stomping on the brakes. But still just as hot. We're in a truck that usually transports food products. I saw it as we stepped into the back of the truck, a big logo, a colourful image of canned soups.

One day and half a night.

That was how long we sat in the refugee camp at Lampedusa.

They took our fingerprints, then not much happened until we were taken to a boat even larger than the last one and transported to Salerno on the mainland.

'Alyson?'

'Mmm.'

'Are you asleep?'

'Almost.'

·'Good. Try to sleep. You need it.'

She leans against me, rests her head between my chin and throat. She makes me so calm.

I feel her breath, and it becomes my breath.

One night in the next refugee camp. Until a representative for the smuggling organisation arrived with one of the camp guards, led us to a parking lot and then loaded us into this truck where we are supposed to sit for two days. If everything goes as it should. We paid one thousand dollars for this. It costs the same no matter where you came from, except children ride for half price. It makes sense, they only take up half as much room. Sixty-five of us. I counted as we climbed in, and then again when we'd been driving for a few hours, mostly just to pass the time. Three children, five women, fifty-seven men. Approximately the same percentages at each stage.

I'm so glad I have Alyson, that she wanted to travel with me.

'And you, Idriss?'

'What about me?'

'Why aren't you asleep?'

'Soon. When we're . . . a bit further on our way.'

Two thousand kilometres through Europe, and I wish we could see some of it, how it *really* looks, if it's as green as people claim. Shut inside this truck we don't see any of it, can't even move. But it doesn't matter. The third stage is a short trip.

I'm not sure if Alyson has heard about the trucks that never arrive. If she has, she doesn't want to talk about it. Same as me. There are narrow openings that let air in. There's even a slight draught from the back doors. So I don't understand how it happens. Sometimes happens. That everyone in the truck dies. They suffocate. And when the driver notices, he abandons them on the side of the road.

I'll wait to sleep.

Wait until we arrive, until we're unloaded one last time.

Alyson is depending on me.

TWELVE DAYS EARLIER

THE VERY LAST TRIP. Then we arrive. That's how Alyson's cousin travelled, too. In a container that crosses the Baltic Sea every day, unloaded in one port then sent back empty. Loading us into one of them, making sure seventy-three passengers with no identity papers are guided through the port area in Gdansk under the cover of darkness, seems to be the easiest thing in the world for the smuggling organisation.

Despite that, the final stage is also the most expensive. Two thousand dollars each. Almost half of everything we made in Niamey. I don't understand why. Because it's not something that can be understood. Maybe a smuggler can just name his price once a person is close enough to their dream.

We waited in the harbour and the container for two days, and it was just as crowded as now – we almost sat on top of each other, and during the night we lay on top of each other. Packed as tight as on the truck bed through the desert, on the fishing boat across the Mediterranean, and in the back of the truck through Europe. Being lifted into the air by a crane and onto a ship was as unpleasant as it was wonderful. And when the heaving and puffing and roaring engine slowly started to move, we giggled out loud again, not caring what the others thought, the kind of laughter that leaves you soft inside.

That's how it feels to be halfway across the Baltic Sea.

Holding Alyson's hand.

Like there could never be anything better.

As if the man who locked the door to the container from the outside was right. He'd looked at us and whispered – in two days you'll land in Sweden, and the rest of your life will begin.

Anders Roslund on a series within a series – from beginning to end to beginning again

Recently, I opened a cardboard box and it transported me back in time twenty years.

To the world of crime novels as it existed then.

Both my sons were moving out, and we needed more boxes. At the far back of our storage space I saw one. If I emptied it we'd have one more. It happened to be the box where I'd collected newspaper articles back before my dream of becoming a published author became a reality. At the bottom of the box, under books on writing techniques and dictionaries, I found a newspaper supplement, an insert from one of Sweden's major newspapers. Dated 1998, it was an overview of Swedish literature at the time: the publishing houses, the next generation of writers. On its back cover, which I noticed just as I was about to throw it in the garbage, there stood a list of books – the top sellers in Sweden that month. I read it and was amazed. There wasn't a single Swedish crime novel, not a single Scandi noir in the top ten. There was historical fiction, chick lit, contemporary novels, satire. Just two detective novels – one British, one American. That's what it looked like just twenty years ago. I had completely forgotten – now every month at least half of the bestsellers are Swedish crime.

Twenty years ago the Swedish – Scandinavian – crime novel was suffering a slow death from its own repetition.

Whodunnits were being written over and over again.

And if that had continued, just one dominant approach to writing (which is neither more nor less important, that's just all that was being published), the bestseller lists in Sweden and around the world today would have looked exactly like the newspaper at the bottom of my cardboard box. There would have been a total absence of Scandinavian crime novels. But something happened around that time. A handful of authors rewrote the rules and breathed new life into a whole genre. I'm extremely proud to say that Roslund & Hellström was one of them.

Around the time I first met Börge, I was given the task of launching a new daily news show for Sveriges Television, which I eventually dubbed Kulturnyheterna (the Cultural News). And as my clever and wonderful editorial team and I built our programme, we did it from the same starting point that I approached Roslund & Hellström. Our programme's goal was to make room for new substance in a new form expressed in a new way. Plagiarising what already existed was an easy road to cancellation. The same was true for Roslund & Hellström. If we were to be worthy of being bought and read, we had to add something new, fresh; repeating what already existed was an easy road to ending up forgotten.

For many years I'd carried around preconceived notions of what this genre was. The Swedish crime novel needed to regain its broader base. The *who* in our books would be supplemented by a *what* and *how* and *why*, plus the *when* of the thriller. That's how I reasoned when I – who had always sought to understand and describe the driving forces behind violence – met one of the founders of the newly established, non-profit organisation KRIS, which rehabilitated prisoners. Börge and I clicked both as people and storytellers and agreed to write from the platform I introduced:

We would have half fiction and half fact – entertain the reader while at the same time giving them insight into worlds we both knew so much about, but few others had visited.

We would write our books as ensembles – changing perspective frequently, never letting a single detective drive the story from the first chapter to the last. Instead, what drove our criminals would be described just as clearly as their investigators. Therefore, each book would have a secondary main character other than the detective superintendent (who would be number two in each book) – the actual main character could be the victim or the perpetrator (and often both at the same time), and it would be around this character's universe that the story spun.

We would use the novel's ability to function as social critique, which in our country for some unthinkable reason was going to waste – there it lay like an untouched tool on our writing desk and we, along with a few others, were grateful to have it. The crime novel is the perfect place to entertain, while also holding up a mirror to society.

And – we formed a partnership and would write crime novels together, at a time when authors didn't collaborate, and publishers weren't looking for duos. It was so unusual that when I suggested that we mark our shared authorship by removing our first names – away with Anders and away with Börge – Sweden's most dominant online bookseller explained it wasn't possible, their computer system simply couldn't manage two surnames with an '&' in between! So 'Roslund & Hellström' was standardised on our debut book *Pen 33* as 'Anders Roslund Börge Hellström'. After it became a success with both critics and readers, and won the Glass Key award for best Nordic crime novel, the online booksellers found a way to accommodate our names for the next book. And nowadays, with so many writing as partners in the crime genre, I'm often asked by both Norwegian and Danish journalists about how we inspired writers all over Scandinavia, and it makes me very happy. For two such thoroughly untrendy people as Roslund & Hellström, there's a special kind of honour in finally creating one.

Entertainment always comes first.

Story, story, story.

But our vision of half truth, half fiction held fast.

We wrote books as we wanted to write them. Nevertheless, I occasionally felt something was missing: a tool that would let us tell stories about worlds our detective superintendent couldn't reach in any natural or credible way (though of course still fictitiously – no matter how alive he felt to us). Around that time, I was contacted by a very good friend who tracked down the first fragments of that strange piece of information, the Swedish police seemed to be using criminal infiltrators, despite this being forbidden. He suggested that Roslund

& Hellström might want to research and write about it. That very afternoon I sketched out the beginnings of a character, working name Hoffmann, who was able to inhabit the widened scope of action that Ewert Grens never could. Hoffmann became Piet Hoffmann, and soon after he brought along Zofia and Hugo and Rasmus, our fictional family grew by four new members.

These slightly adjusted conditions enabled us to write *Three Seconds*, a novel about modern crime and the two authorities – the police and the criminal world – responsible for it. About how the police used criminals as infiltrators and informers – a cooperation that was denied for years. But only a criminal can play a criminal, so they were recruited by the Swedish police while serving time in prison. In order to provide them with cover and credible backgrounds, the police's own official records were manipulated. Lies and truth in the same police corridor. Falsifying information essential to the rule of law became their method of working, and the criminal infiltrators turned into the outlaws of our time: when an infiltrator was exposed, law enforcement abandoned him. Police commissioners protected their own jobs, but not their employees, and by looking the other way they allowed the infiltrated organisations to solve the problem for themselves (read: kill the infiltrator). During the writing of that book, we collaborated with criminal infiltrators and police officers, with prisoners serving long sentences, and prison staff, brave people who gave us the legitimacy to allow Piet Hoffmann to face Ewert Grens in novel form. And to describe how the work of infiltrators and informers calls into question the very concept of justice in a democracy where we take it for granted. That's how it worked for a very long time. And – despite the denials of the Swedish police – that's how it still works (as recently as this morning, I spoke with one of them). Because the Swedish police, like their colleagues all over the world, are completely dependent on the results they get from their cooperation with criminals. And is that good or bad? You, the reader, will have to decide that for yourself.

After our sixth book together, we decided to dissolve our partnership. We liked each other very much, Börge and I. We had become something beyond friends (Börge could sit opposite me, stare deeply into my eyes, then stand up and shout: I hate when you look straight through me, Anders). We knew each other inside and out. So we knew we were heading in different directions. I, Anders, had the life I'd always wanted, writing full-time, and I had so many more stories to tell, especially now that Piet Hoffmann was part of the cast of characters – the world's leading infiltrator, able to take us to places and people we never would have met otherwise. And Börge had things he'd like to do. We said goodbye, without drama or nostalgia, we'd spent many wonderful years working together.

Then everything changed again. I had published another book and outlined the structure for two more, and Börge had continued with what lay closest to his heart. Then a contact whose confidence we'd worked long and hard to gain, several years without success, suddenly decided to trust us. Got hold of us. Was ready. A door to the world of the drug cartels opened – and we reconsidered our decision. We decided to write another book together. *Three Minutes*, on a subject we'd talked about exploring from the very first day, but had abandoned – how would we ever get there? Because: in our six previous books, though dressed-up like thrillers, we had sought to describe the consequences of many different kinds of crime, human trafficking and sex crimes and young people in gangs and . . . and when your mission is to explore contemporary crime, sooner or later you have to get to the source of so much of it. To what drives it. To the umbrella of crime. Or as our very own Detective Superintendent Ewert Grens puts it to his boss, almost everything we investigate in this damn building goes back to drugs. Drugs don't just drive crime, they drive our whole society! When you think about it, Wilson, do people even want it to end? When there are so many who make their living from the consequences?

We had Ewert Grens. We had Piet Hoffmann. And we had a real source. Together, they were our novelistic ticket as well as our real ticket into the heart of crime, where everything begins – they took me, then Roslund & Hellström, then our readers, on a harrowing journey, and in the process hopefully expanded everyone's knowledge.

I travelled with our contact to the centre of the drug cartels, a journey I never could have imagined. Even though I had lived through a death threat, both as a journalist and writer – I was the anonymous television reporter in the headlines, threatened with a summary execution, and I had to move into hotels and live under fake addresses, had an armed bodyguard in my living room for a long time – I'd never been as afraid as I was when I entered the bizarre world where life means nothing if it's standing in the way of profit. And when I returned from South America, Roslund & Hellström were able to complete the crime novel that would connect Sweden to the outside world, the police station at Kungsholmen to a shed in a jungle where cocaine is extracted.

The book we'd pursued from the start was finished. And we could go our separate ways again. For real this time. This was long before Börge got sick, and now that he's with us no longer, I'm glad we said goodbye to our partnership on our own terms – not because goddamn death forced us apart.

After we decided together to disband our partnership, I began writing a next book based on the characters I'd lived with for so long, and who had more stories to tell. *Three Hours*, I called it. The book you're holding. The third in a series within a series I planned for an infiltrator that could take us to worlds a Swedish detective superintendent never could. The third book in which Piet Hoffmann meets Ewert Grens. Their paths would cross again for a new reason. In the first book – *Three Seconds* – they never had a confrontation. Just an absurd dialogue over the phone in the middle of a hostage crisis in a high-security prison. The second time they met in Bogotá – *Three Minutes* – under equally extraordinary circumstances, but no longer two express trains headed straight for each other. Hoffmann needed Grens's help, and they didn't fight each other, they fought side by side. In *Three Hours* it's the opposite. This time Grens, despite agreeing to never meet again, is the one who seeks out Hoffmann. Grens needs the answers. And it's Ewert Grens who, if the answer is right, needs Piet Hoffmann's help. And – of course, they'll meet again a fourth time. For another reason. For another shared adventure. The title? Well, it's two words. The first one you've probably already guessed.

Stockholm, Spring 2018
Anders Roslund

The author would sincerely like to thank

S and *M* and *L* and *R* – so brave and strong.

and

Lasse Lagergren for your expertise on how incredibly small an amount of blood an awl would leave behind and other noteworthy medical questions. *Calle Thunberg* for your knowledge on how best to blow up a warehouse and open a safe door and other things only you would know. *Märta Kleveman* because you speak Arabic and French so much better than I do. *Michael Ermenc* for your knowledge of fluorine in groundwater and everything tooth-related whenever Ewert Grens needs your help. *Stefan Thunberg* for your generosity, creativity – and quite simply a brain unlike anyone else's.